Also by MESHA MAREN

Sugar Run

PERPETUAL WEST

PERPETUAL WEST

a novel by

Mesha Maren

ALGONQUIN BOOKS
OF CHAPEL HILL 2022

Published by
Algonquin Books of Chapel Hill
Post Office Box 2225
Chapel Hill, North Carolina 27515-2225

a division of
Workman Publishing
225 Varick Street
New York, New York 10014

Printed in the United States of America.
Published simultaneously in Canada by Thomas Allen & Son Limited.
Design by Steve Godwin.

LIBRARY OF CONGRESS CATALOGING-IN-PUBLICATION DATA

Names: Maren, Mesha, author.
Title: Perpetual West : a novel / by Mesha Maren.
Description: First Edition. | Chapel Hill, North Carolina :
Algonquin Books of Chapel Hill, 2022. | Summary: "As Alex and Elana
try to make their home among the academics and young leftists in El Paso and Juárez,
they are pulled from each other by an affair with a lucha libre fighter,
their struggles to define themselves, and the loud cry of home"—Provided by publisher.
Identifiers: LCCN 2021021981 | ISBN 9781643750941 (hardcover) |
ISBN 9781643752211 (ebook)
Classification: LCC PS3613.A7396 P47 2022 | DDC 813/.6—dc23
LC record available at https://lccn.loc.gov/2021021981

10 9 8 7 6 5 4 3 2 1
First Edition

Tubi

Call a truce, call a war
Everyone is a bastard, everyone is a whore
Everyone is a saint, everyone is redeemed
Everyone is at the mercy of another one's dream

—SAM BAKER

PERPETUAL WEST

ONE

August 2005

They came by way of the Blue Ridge. Crossed the first state line at Kingsport and tracked the whole of Tennessee. Memphis at night in the rain. The Mississippi charging angry under them. Past the bluffs were floodplains, Arkansas, and then nothing but Texas. They came by way of the Stay-Inn Motel, Krystal, Taco John's, and Dixie Cafe. Burger wrappers shifting under their feet. Receipts on the floorboard like a poem of their journey: Aquafina, Butterfinger, medium coffee. They came by way of brown grass and thirsty names. Sulphur Springs, Mineral Wells, Sweetwater, Big Spring. They came for their schooling, for his past, her getaway.

When they reached the border it was late August, evening, and still hot outside, but the sunlight was thinning. It fell through their car windows in long slashes that illuminated the dust on the dashboard, the cracked windshield, and expired inspection sticker—details that the police would eventually note in their report after finding the Honda abandoned in the Candy Club parking lot, but that was still four months away. On this August day the evidence suggested only that Elana and Alex were too poor to fix the windshield and too distracted to keep the inspection up to date.

Behind them, a slope of treeless mountains hunched in shadow and before them, past the squat concrete bunker of the Paso del Norte border station and the brown gulch of the Río Grande, Juárez rippled with headlights and neon signs.

Alex drove or, rather, he sat in the driver's seat and stared at the line of Jeep-Toyota-Chevy-Mitsubishis behind them and the equally jammed vehicles in front. After days of whip-by miles, they'd arrived in a funnel. US stagnancy and, to the south, the flash of Juárez. Elana sat in the passenger's seat with *Wuthering Heights* open in her lap.

"Maybe we should stop and eat before we get to Jorge's," Alex said.

Elana's eyes traced the same page, the same few lines, over and over again, but the point was not really reading. She'd read *Wuthering Heights* at least four times before.

"Just grab some tacos and a beer," Alex said. "There won't be any beer at the mission."

Elana found it funny that he should worry about beer. He hadn't drunk alcohol at all until he turned twenty-one, just two months ago, but now he'd incorporated it into his vision of how to be an adult. Adults drank beer at the end of a long day.

"We should find our way to the mission before it gets dark," Elana said, without looking up.

Alex fished a cassette out of the shoebox that sat between them and pushed it into the tape deck. The staccato drums and frenetic screams of Orchid reeled out and formed a screen between them. They'd kept the Honda more for its tape deck than anything else. The air conditioner was long gone, the gas mileage was not great, the heater worked only half the time. Alex turned up the volume. The line of cars inched toward the border, but the maroon van directly in front of them did not move. Alex edged closer to it.

"You don't want to stop for one beer?"

Elana looked at him, holding her finger on the sentence she'd been reading.

"After eight hours of driving."

She blinked.

"You're afraid," he said.

The cars beside them jerked ahead. Alex lifted his foot off the brake. He looked at Elana again. The Honda rolled forward and: smack. Elana's arms slammed against the glove box as the windshield darkened above her, tumbling with movement. A series of dull thuds. The back doors of the maroon van swung on their hinges and box after box of Froot Loops, Cheez-Its, Hamburger Helper, Chips Ahoy!, Honey Nut Cheerios, and finally, a case of Pepsi wheeled out and landed on their windshield in an explosion of dark sugar.

Alex pulled up the emergency brake and leapt out. Elana opened her door slowly, watching as a blonde woman emerged from the passenger's side of the van.

Alex pushed the boxes out of the way, inspecting the point of impact. No one in the border station up ahead seemed to have noticed, though there was a growing cyclone of noise, horns honking and voices barking, as cars swerved around them. Elana watched the blonde woman light a cigarette.

A man came around from the driver's side of the van, paunchy and sunburnt.

"Damnit," Alex said, glancing over at him. "I'm sorry, I should've been paying better attention, shouldn't have been so close to your bumper." Alex touched the place where the Honda had dented the metal and suddenly the sunburnt man was moving fast. The look in his blue eyes, wet and vulnerable, like physical pain.

"Don't touch my van, boy," he said, and as he drew close to Alex, his expression changed from pain to disgust. It was the look of rusted wheels beginning to turn inside his brain and he did not seem to have any control over it.

"Chester?" the blonde said quietly, stepping forward. There was fear in her voice and she was looking at the man with a strange focus.

Alex stepped back, hands out at his sides.

"I never wanted to come down here in the first place," the man said, his eyes still locked on Alex. "But Lindy says it's a good idea. Start over fresh, she says, south of the border!"

The woman looked away before he even turned to her. The cigarette in her hand was shaking.

"A white horse. Isn't that right, Lindy? Something about dreams of white horses you had."

He had not touched her, but her body shrank as if she'd been slapped. She dropped her cigarette and looked down at it. "And you're the idiot who thought we could use our EBT down in Mexico," she said, barely loud enough for Elana to hear.

"What'd you say?" The man lunged.

"Nothing." She hugged her skinny arms across her chest.

For a moment Elana thought the man might hit her, but he just watched, his eyes focused on her ass as she bent over and picked up a bag of dill pickle potato chips.

Elana looked over at Alex. His face was tight and his hand gripped the door of the Honda, but none of them moved except for the woman tossing the boxes and bags into the open van.

Up ahead, against the pinkening skyline, a white and red and green billboard announced: ¡HOLA AMIGOS! WELCOME TO JUÁREZ! And behind, the final rays of sunlight struck the glass buildings of the El Paso business district, burnishing them in liquid opalescence.

TWO

December 2005

The counters at Susie's Tex-Mex Cafe were long and yellowed, with menus laminated right into them, covered over with bubbly plastic. Elana sat at the far end beside the jukebox, holding empty ketchup bottles while Rubi refilled them from a large plastic bladder.

"No, you know, I'm just like asking because I've never seen a white boy's junk in real life before," Rubi said, wiping the edge of a ketchup lid with her thumb. She glanced at Elana's face. "You've never like fucked a Mexican, huh?"

"Yeah." Elana pushed her hair behind one ear. "My husband."

"Oh, right, I forget. He's so pocho, sorry," Rubi said. As she moved, her bra slid up. It was exactly the same color as the ketchup. Elana looked back down at the bottle. The thick corn syrup and tin tomato smell and the wet fart sound of the squeezed bladder pushed her hunger away. A little bile in the back of the throat and she was glad again to be empty. Waitressing was beautiful in that way. The more food that passed through her hands, the more ugly it became. The same plate of chilaquiles that she carried steaming to the table would, momentarily, chill and congeal into a yellow-brown mass that slurped as she scraped it into the dumpster. Most of the other waitresses didn't eat during their shifts either. They complained of hunger but opted for cigarettes first. Here, she was not so unusual. Here, no one noticed she consumed only coffee, coffee, coffee, cigarettes, a bag of jalapeño-flavored sunflower seeds, and a house salad—the cucumbers thin and cool on her tongue, the iceberg like half-frozen water.

"What about a black guy?" Rubi set the bladder down on the counter where it wobbled like a fat sea creature. "You ever fuck a black guy?"

Elana shook her head. She was no good at lying, though she didn't like to come right out and say she'd never fucked anyone besides her husband. It felt too weird. A virgin wedding was not something she'd ever imagined for herself.

"Where's your family from?" Rubi sat down on the stool beside Elana, the rhinestones that studded the sides of her jeans catching in the light.

"Uh, West Virginia and New Jersey," Elana said.

"But where are they really from, before that?"

Elana shook her head. "Poland, I think, on my dad's side, he's Jewish."

"Is that where you got your black eyes and black hair?"

Elana shrugged. She liked Rubi maybe best out of all the other waitresses at Susie's. Sometimes she tried too hard to get Elana to share an order of huevos a la mexicana, but at least she talked to Elana. The other waitresses went silent whenever she entered the kitchen or spoke to one another in a hushed Spanish that she was slowly beginning to understand. And then of course there was Lisa, the only other white girl, who was perhaps the reason the other waitresses were so distant. If Lisa was what they thought all white girls were like, no wonder they wanted nothing to do with Elana. Lisa was a single mother from Alabama with a body like a giraffe who had moved to El Paso for Cormac McCarthy. She estimated, out loud to anyone who was within earshot, that she had written him one thousand pieces of fan mail. She liked his earlier works best, she said, but all of it was *untouchable*. When he didn't respond to her letters, Lisa had moved to El Paso and over the course of several months had somehow located McCarthy's residence, or at least what she claimed to be his residence. At night she prowled around the house, collecting trash from his bins and spying with binoculars.

"I'm gonna go have a cigarette," Rubi said. "You coming?"

Elana shook her head. She was trying not to smoke during the day so she wandered instead into the hallway where her coat hung and slid her hand into the pocket, searching for a cinnamon toothpick. There was a crumpled bit of paper there. A note from Alex. She did not even need to read the words to know he *loved* her, hoped she *had a good day.* He'd left her notes for as long as she had known him—four years' worth of big, looping cursive script—but lately the note leaving seemed more frantic: every morning, on the mirror, in her purse and her pockets. For a while he had left them on the fridge, but now he'd noticed that she didn't touch the fridge in the morning. Sometimes when she looked at his paper scraps crumpled in the folds of her purse, she thought of the Alex-origin: tiny dark-eyed baby nestled inside the clothing donation box outside the Heart Cry Holiness Mission House of Juárez, yellow blanket, no note.

Their first night in Juárez, back in August, Elana had asked Jorge at the Heart Cry Mission House about the donation box—the basket in the reeds, the beginning. She wanted to see it. Alex got embarrassed and then Jorge said they couldn't leave donation boxes out anymore, the whole place was fortressed now. The street-facing wall of the mission was embedded on top with shards of bottles in jeweled greens and browns and blues. The outside was a blank face, no sign, no number, just a high wall and a big metal sliding gate with a smaller human-sized door cut into it. Outside was all deflection, but inside was the heart. Elana had called it the walled-in yard, which Jorge thought was funny. Alex told her it was Spanish-style, porches were American—put it all on display—but in the Old World they guarded their privacy. The street was no place for home and family. The rooms at the mission faced the courtyard. High ceilings and rounded doorways. Elana thought of paper wasp nests, all channels and corridors.

When she pictured those first few days, Elana remembered chalk drawings and the ricochet of basketballs. She remembered diesel fumes. At night her loneliness had beaten loudly while Alex talked with Jorge in the green-lit kitchen on the far side of the courtyard. Between them: a small saguaro in a painted pot, an empty basketball hoop, their Honda, and the mission van. Between them: words she could not understand. Alex's Spanish was both sharper and slower than Jorge's, each word enunciated carefully, book learned. The drip of the faucet in the courtyard made forever-ever sounds. Elana lay on an army cot beside Alex's empty army cot. When she tried to sleep, all the Spanish words she did not understand had filled her ears and mouth, pushed down on her tongue. *Agua prieta. Agua turbia.*

They'd lasted in Juárez for only a few weeks before Elana begged to move over to El Paso. Now, in December, it was hard to recall the oppression of the heat, but it had ruled her then. She remembered sitting in the patio at Heart Cry and the heat coming on from across the open plain—the sun feeble at first, slanting and thin, causing long shadows, her coffee cup stretching across the whole table, while Jorge shuffled out in plastic sandals to pour water over his plants. Then the sun rose above the skyline and the city woke as if to a bad hangover, the sky brightening from gauze white to blue, horns honking and the birds silencing, all pressed into total submission.

A record heat wave had struck their first month on the border, highs of 115, 120. Elana could not move, the sun a constant enemy. Out here the sky felt so different from Virginia—the very quantity of it, a pulsing wash, huge and terrifying. And at night, when the sun was gone and slip-song cricket breezes slid down into the city, Jorge warned her not to go out alone, not even to the tienda around the corner, send your husband instead. Juárez was a feeling of watching and being watched. All day there was the sun above with its withering, godlike view and something else, unnamed but always coming, like a hawk circling on high, its shadow darkening the ground and whooshing on. Every morning Jorge had driven Elana and Alex in the mission van to the border, where they waited in sun-struck lines to take the bus to UTEP for class—master's-level sociology for Alex, undergrad English for Elana—and in the evening he drove them back, rattled down and latched the mission door. Cloistered. She might have lost her mind.

El Paso was maybe only a bigger cloister or, worse, a mausoleum, but it worked for her. She could breathe. The streets were wide and empty, just the coo of a mate-searching pigeon and the riss of wind through the sabal palms. They had found a basement apartment tucked up under the tail of the Franklin Mountains in a neighborhood spiked with cypress and huge turn-of-the-century brick houses. There, it felt as if everything, including any real danger, had already passed. The neighborhood businesses—cafe, taqueria, convenience store—were all closed, either permanently or for today, right now, this afternoon. The tienda across the street from Elana's usual bus stop was called La Solita. When she had pointed this out to Alex, he told her it meant "the usual," but Elana preferred her mistranslation. Solita: alone; La Solita: The Alone Girl.

Rubi was still outside smoking, so she gathered the ketchup dispensers from the counter and loaded them into a plastic bin. The clock on the wall above the register read 2:47 p.m. Her Twentieth-Century British Lit class had ended an hour ago. She felt a little dip in her stomach at that thought, but she'd known that she was going to skip class from the moment she'd woken up. She'd decided weeks ago that she wasn't going to school at all next semester. There was no reason to keep attending class now except that she hadn't quite figured out how to tell Alex that she was dropping out.

She carried the bin of ketchups across the room, setting a bottle on each table. The restaurant had plate-glass windows across the front wall, booths along the back, and strings of faded tinsel garlanded across the ceiling in reds and whites and greens. It was almost always empty this time of day, after the business lunch hour but before family-dinner time. Through the front windows she could see the sleet-gray street and people passing with their collars turned up against the wind, while inside Susie's the heaters ticked rhythmically, mixing with the ranchera songs and the voices of the kitchen guys who'd left their prep work to stand in the hallway and flirt with Rubi.

When the front door opened, Elana was at the counter, stacking up her tips. She turned to see Alex in the doorway, hands in the pockets of his jean jacket. Even after four years together, there were times when his beauty still shocked her, moments when he appeared like this, unexpected, and she was slapped by the loose confidence of his slim but not too skinny limbs, beautiful mouth, dark eyes.

"What are you doing here?" he said.

He needed a coat, a real winter coat, instead of that same old black jean jacket with a hoodie zipped up underneath. Elana didn't nag him about it, though. She didn't want to be the kind of girl who mothered her lover.

"I waited outside your lit class," he said. "Then I went back to the apartment. I called your phone like twenty times."

"I ran out of battery." Elana untied her apron and laid it on the counter.

"You ran out of battery?"

"My phone."

"Why do we even have the fucking things? You never answer and I think something happened and then—"

"Your mother—"

"I know, I know." Alex stepped in and let the door close behind him.

Elana had never wanted a cell phone, never liked the idea that she should be accessible at any moment no matter where she was. But Alex's mother had insisted on buying them and paying for the lines when they moved out west.

"So you couldn't bring yourself to go to one more class before leaving town for a week?" Alex sat on a stool and rested his elbows on the counter. His lips were smiling, but his eyes were too concerned. She looked away.

"We'd already discussed *The Quiet American* in the last class. I don't like it when they cram more and more of their theories down your throat. It kills anything I'd been thinking about on my own."

"That's the idea of discussion, though, right? You raise your hand and add in what you've been thinking about on your own."

Elana folded her apron in half and half again and then rolled the ties around it in a tight bundle.

"Fine, whatever," Alex said. "Your dad called and asked if I thought he should arrange a party for your brother, decorate the house or something."

Elana looked up. "I don't think they make 'Welcome Home from Rehab' decorations."

"Yeah, I told him Simon probably wouldn't care, but you'll be landing in Roanoke at three tomorrow if he needs help."

"Why's he calling *you*?"

Alex laughed, reached over the counter, and plucked a twenty from her stack of tips. "He's all worked up. He canceled his classes for the rest of the week. Says he wants to be there for Simon. I'm sure Simon will really love that." He held the twenty-dollar bill up under his nose. "Money smells so weird."

Elana took it from his fingers and folded it with the rest of her tips, tucking them into a black leather billfold. "He canceled all his classes?"

"Tenure, baby. Hell, they love him so much he could probably cancel the rest of the semester and no one would complain."

"I know. I'm just saying, he's gonna be there, in the house all day long, the whole week? We're all gonna be there with nothing to do. I wish you could come. He loves you." She exhaled. "What do you want for dinner?"

Dinner was the pivot point of their days lately, a tension that built up and then ebbed in the hours afterward. When Alex had started noticing Elana's weight, he'd insisted they eat dinner together every night, but then he tried embarrassingly hard not to make a big deal out of watching her eat.

"I knew you'd forget." He stood and flicked at his barstool until it spun with a loud rattling sound. "I left you a message, but of course no battery, right?" He looked over at her with his eyebrows raised. "The art opening at Voces Unidas and then dinner at Kasa de Kultura."

"Oh right, shit." She tossed her apron into a large canvas bag alongside her billfold. "We have to go?"

Alex rattled the barstool again. "Before we moved here, you were so worried that we weren't going to make any friends, there wouldn't be any people our age who liked the same things, and then we find a collective of punk kids and every time it's 'Do we really have to go to dinner?'"

"I smell like I've been dipped in ketchup." Elana slipped on her parka and waved goodbye through the kitchen window to Rubi and the cooks. "I'm tired and my flight leaves early tomorrow and I've been working all day."

The Kasa dinner was a monthly obligation that felt worse each time for the fact that it was supposed to be fun. She and Alex had found the Kasa de Kultura kids back in August before they'd moved across to El Paso. Actually, the youngest Kasa kid, Chucho, had found Alex in the market one morning. Alex was out buying avocados when Chucho had called to him from three stalls over, pointing to his Los Crudos T-shirt and hollering to him, "Hey, güero, that's a good band." Alex had walked with Chucho back to the collective house in Colonia Monterrey where he and four other juarenses had a little library—*Pedagogy of the Oppressed*, *The Uncomfortable Dead*, vegan cookbooks—and a space for groups to have meetings or bands to play shows and a zine shop with their own photocopied publication, *Gritos de fronterlandia*. Alex came home that afternoon, grinning and talking too fast, avocados forgotten somewhere along the way, and Elana had never seen him so happy. It was almost enough to make her forgive him for those hours in which she'd been positive he was dead.

"You've been working all day?" Alex pushed the door open and ushered her outside.

She glanced back at him.

"Oh, that's right, I forgot," he said. "You've been slaving in this shit-hole cafe instead of sitting comfortably in a classroom and furthering your undergraduate degree so that maybe you won't have to smell like ketchup for the rest of your life."

"Fuck off."

The wind out in the street was picking up, blowing newspapers and snack wrappers around their feet and needling its way in under Elana's coat. She tucked her head down and Alex grabbed her arm.

"Hey, hey, slow down." He linked his arm through hers. "I just wish you could have been there for Viviana's talk. I tried to find you before your class so you could go with me. I sat in on most of it. I think you really would have loved it, she's fucking fierce."

"Viviana?"

He laughed and the sound rang out like a bark in the cold air. "The opening we're going to."

"Oh, she does paintings?"

"Mixed media, a lot of photographs of the land art she's done in the desert. You'll see, I think those pieces are mostly what she has up at the show."

They crossed Campbell Street and headed east on Magoffin. A few downtown businesses were warmly lit from within, windows decorated for Christmas and blinking signs advertising hot coffee or half-off department store sales, though most of the neon came from the jail bond offices along San Antonio Avenue. The darkening streets were almost empty. Farther east they cut through the back lot of Texas Foam & Fabrics where two teenage boys shared a single cigarette. Most of the buildings around them were boarded up, whole blocks gone dormant.

Though she'd been there for four months, Elana still could not get used to how starkly dead El Paso was in the evening. In the pearly-cold mornings and sun-bleached afternoons the downtown bustled, vendors crowding the sidewalks with tables of bright plastic wares and the clipped strut of young bankers revolving in and out of their chrome-glass doors, but after 5:00 p.m. the place froze while just across the river Juárez amped up and up and up. Sometimes Elana imagined the two cities from above—hip to hip, spine to belly—the one going dark and curling quietly in on itself while the other unfurled in lights and night movement. It occurred to her that the officials on the US side—the ones who touted statistics about El Paso's low crime rates (Top 5 Safest Cities in the USA!)—liked the wild west of Juárez being so close. It served as a great contrast. So much pain so close to home only bolstered that feeling of being chosen: the promised land, the magic line. They wouldn't really want the violence to go away, Elana thought, because then what would make the US so special?

"If you don't like listening to other people's theories about dead writers, switch your degree." Alex pulled her in closer, slipped his hand inside her coat pocket.

"No, I—"

"As long as it's something else in humanities, your credits could—"

"No, it's not that, it's the whole academic—"

"Believe me, I understand. That's why I chose sociology over history for my master's, to your dad's horror. I needed it to feel relevant, applicable. That's why I'm reorienting my whole thesis now. I can't write about something that feels done and already talked about to death."

"Dead writers are not the problem." She picked up her pace, fairly dragging him along beside her now. Her pet project, the thing she worked on when she should have been preparing for class, her deliciously pointless ongoing project, was all dead writers: strings of quotes from Rebecca West, D. H. Lawrence, and Graham Greene—a collection of their colonialist impressions of Mexico. "It's the institution itself I think, the noise, I can't—"

"You'll find it, though—that feeling when you finally stumble on the thing you can't *not* write about—I know you will. You've just gotta be patient."

Elana looked over at him, but he was watching his feet. She let go of his arm. "You're embarrassed by me."

Alex stopped walking. The muscles around his mouth twitched. "Fuck you. How could you be hearing that in what I'm saying?"

Elana itched for a cigarette. They were there at the bottom of her bag, but she didn't like to smoke around Alex. When he smelled it on her, she told him she'd bummed one at work.

"You're putting your dad all over me. That's not me."

"His most promising protégé."

"Not anymore. Not since I swapped history for sociology."

"Okay, enough about my dad, let's not get all *Who's Afraid of Virginia Woolf*?" Elana turned to keep walking, but he grabbed her shoulder and spun her toward him. His eyes were a little wet, from the cold? from emotion?

"Lana, please, I just want you to be happy."

He reached over and pushed her hair behind her ear and she shivered at the gaudiness of it, that claiming action.

"No," she said, rearranging her hair so that it fell back over her ears. "I don't think so. There are so many moments of happiness in my days—my first cup of coffee in the morning, the perfect blue of the church door on Ochoa Street—but they don't count in your system."

Alex's mouth was twisted with annoyance again. "I'm not talking about sensory perceptions of happiness, Lana. Bigger picture. I don't care if waitressing in a Tex-Mex cafe is what makes you happy, I just—"

"Working in a Tex-Mex cafe does not make me fucking happy. I'm trying to hear myself think. Okay?" She shook his hand off her shoulder.

They were walking again, not holding hands but walking at a matched pace.

"I think you're scared of what would actually make you happy."

Elana laughed. "Is getting a master's degree actually making *you* happy?"

"Yes."

"Happy? Oh, so that's why you complain about how stupid your program is, how everyone wants to fit everything into their formulas, how they don't actually see anything around them. That's your happiness?" She turned to face him and he was smiling. He grabbed the front of her parka and pulled her in until their lips met, jarringly at first with a bump of teeth and chins, their escaped breath fogging up between them in the darkening air.

ON THE CORNER of Myrtle and Palm they passed the bronze plaque that told the much-abbreviated story of the women of Voces Unidas. Elana paused, though she already knew about the dramatic last stand of the female factory workers. The women at the Levi's jeans plant had seen the end coming. They could not know exactly which day, but they had seen the factories all heading south after NAFTA, they had seen the wage theft and had seen their sisters turned away until only the bare minimum remained on the ghostly factory floor. They had talked at the bus stop, in the break room, and in the barrio after work. They had talked and in the pockets of their aprons they all carried chains and locks. But still the day began, like every day, before the sun came up, with a baby's cries and a husband's deep snores, with coffee, fresh tortillas and reheated beans, the call of roosters in the backyards, and on the tin roof, the tic-tic of pecans falling from the trees. It was only after they'd arrived at the factory and been called, all of them, immediately, in for a "meeting," that the day wrenched itself into the unusual. Ignoring the announcement, they sat down at their sewing machines—those whirring, stitching, clicking companions of twenty-five years. The women moved in a beautiful unison, as timed and organized as if they themselves were the joints of some greater machine. Each helped the other to twine the chain about her hands and then up around her sewing machine until only one was left, who secured her lock with her own silver teeth.

The security guards called in reinforcements and initiated the media frenzy that the women had hoped for. The factory, they knew, was already gone, but they themselves would not disappear so quietly. They had been through the Farah strike in the seventies and they knew their own power. They wrested their back pay from the owners and with it they joined together to buy the empty factory building, which they divided into three cooperatively owned businesses: a cafe, a day care, and an art gallery / arts-and-crafts store.

It was impressive and inspiring, what they had done with the businesses, but the building still retained the utilitarian chill of a factory floor. It was, Elana thought, as if every event there occurred not for its own sake but within a diorama, as if, at any moment, someone would peel back the huge metal roof to see the table set with glasses of champagne going flat, women in high heels and too much turquoise jewelry cocking their heads pensively as they walked past photographs of sand fields and blood, and in the corner, a young man with blond curls and dark eyes talking excitedly to a young woman, dressed all in black, undoubtedly the artiste.

Despite the tug of the argument with Alex—there at the back of her brain, a stranglehold that settled in each time they fought—despite the fact that as soon as they'd arrived he had gone off to speak to the disarmingly beautiful Viviana Vicente Reyes, Elana found that, looking at the photographs, she felt more awake than she had in days. They were strangely, unsettlingly beautiful: images that seemed at first to be empty landscapes, sweeping deserts and dry grass plains with a dark scar of mountains in the background, or tall rocky cliffs, the stones bleached and crumbling. After a moment, though, after your eye had taken in the grandeur of the landscape, you noticed there, half-hidden beside the ocotillo bush, a glistening, bloody knot of heart muscle; and there, in the tawny shrub grass, a pale circular collarbone; and at the base of the cliff, a set of slick pink lungs. The pieces were named *Adriana Torres Márquez, Argelia Irene Salazar Crispín, Elizabeth Castro García, Eréndira Ivonne Ponce Hernández, Olga Alicia Carrillo Pérez, María Sagrario González Flores, Silvia Elena Rivera Morales.*

Elana filed past the photographs three times, noticing, on her last lap around, how loud and yet silent they felt, the stillness of the huge blue sky, the grass bending and reaching, and that small but devastating tremor of horror pulsing there, in and out of focus. She hated it, really, how beautiful that raw human anatomy looked.

Alex was still in the corner with Viviana, and as Elana joined them, he introduced her as "my wife, who was kind enough to move here with me."

Viviana smiled. "You can call me Vivi," she said. She was sleek, angular, and pale, with her dark hair pulled back into a glossy ponytail.

Elana took a glass of champagne from the table and stood a few feet away from Alex and Vivi. She could smell herself sweating, but she didn't want to unzip her parka, her white button-up underneath was stained with ketchup.

"I loved what you said, at your talk this morning, about influence," Alex said. He was beaming at Vivi. Elana was struck by a memory of the Alex she first met: the scrawny, awkward boy her father brought home from his university class. A boy who knew almost nothing beyond his parents' Pentecostal universe and who would, six months later, beg Elana to go to the courthouse and marry him before they had sex.

"It's like everyone goes around thinking that admitting the legacy their work came from would tarnish it somehow." Alex reached for another glass of champagne and offered it to Vivi, but she shook her head and he sipped it himself.

"It *should* be obvious, though, that Boris Viskin's work has influenced me. So has Ana Mendieta's," she said. "That doesn't make *my* work derivative."

"Exactly!" Alex said. "I can't tell you how many mornings I've woken up thinking, what can I possibly say that Roland Barthes hasn't already said a million times better? But then I remind myself that while his influence speaks to my work, I am trying to explore something different, in conversation, but different."

"You're trying to explore?"

"A knowing silence." Alex gesticulated with his champagne glass. "Within wrestling, lucha libre, the intelligibility of every moment within a match, as Barthes points out, but more specifically, here on the border, the way that lucha extrema forms an outlet for an unspoken conversation about violence and government corruption."

"Lucha libre?" Vivi cocked her head.

The room was thinning out a little, half a dozen couples bunched up in groups and a cluster of men at the end of the hors d'oeuvre table watching their women look at the art, a few of them glancing over at Vivi but not approaching.

"As a diacritical societal text," Alex went on, "'the intelligible figuration of moral situations ordinarily secret.'"

"Lucha libre does all that?"

"Are you a fan?" Alex said. "You know El Vengador del Norte? That's who I've been studying mostly."

Vivi shook her head. "My dad—when I was little, we came to the US for some business trip and he was so embarrassed when the wife of one of the men asked my mom if next time she could bring 'one of those cute little Mexican masks.'" Vivi laughed and turned to Elana. "Do you like wrestling?"

It took Elana a long moment to realize she was being included in the conversation. "I, uh, I'd never been before we came here. I don't think I really understand it."

"But that's the beauty." Alex set his empty glass on the table. "In one way, you don't have to know anything to understand, it's good guy versus bad guy for three rounds, right? But it's signifying on multiple levels. The corrupt authority of the referee, the unspoken knowledge of the fixed ending—don't tell me you can't see the parallels to the presidential elections."

"Ha!" Vivi reached up and tightened her ponytail, her silver bracelets clacking down her arm. "So it's all really a setup to critique the PRI?"

"To call attention to the artifice of the dominant system."

"Oh, wow, I see. Did you tell El Vengador del Norte that's what he's actually doing?" She laughed. "Of course, we need an American to explain to us what it is that we're doing, right?"

"No, no." Alex looked up, his eyes wide. "I, that's not—I'm not—"

"Not what?" Vivi was smiling. "American?"

"No, I mean yes, yeah, I'm American. I mean, I was born in Juárez, adopted and raised in West Virginia, whatever, that's not important. I'm not trying to tell anyone what they are doing. Hell, maybe I'm just reading all that into—"

"Now I want to go watch a fight and see what I think. You know, my dad got rich working for the PRI." Vivi looked down at her feet. "These heels are killing me. I'm gonna go outside and have a cigarette."

THEY CROSSED THE border an hour later, Vivi and Alex in front and Elana two steps behind. Alex had explained to Vivi that he and Elana had to head to dinner at a collective house in Juárez, and it had turned out that Vivi knew one of the Kasa members from art school back in Mexico City and she had planned on stopping by too. They crossed together at Puente Santa Fe and Elana watched the Mexican soldier in the doorway of the guard hut. He tracked them with his eyes but did not move. It always unnerved Elana how easy it was to cross the border here—going into

Mexico, no one asked for any documents or even recorded the passage at all, as if the border only mattered when you were headed north.

Avenida Juárez was lit up with the neon of tourist bars and off-track racing facilities, the sidewalks crowded with money changers and candy vendors with tables covered in plastic-wrapped sugar jewels, and the voices of newspaper boys rising and blending with food peddlers, *Burritos de chile relleno, diario, burros, diario*, El Diario.

Alex turned to the right. "La linea nueve bus goes up near the Kasa," he said, nodding toward an old American school bus painted purple and red and parked in the narrow side street beside half a dozen other buses, each blaring a slightly different bass rhythm.

"Oh, let's just take a taxi." Vivi turned back toward the avenida and nodded at the taxista who quickly herded them into his Ford Taurus.

As Elana squeezed in, she wondered why she hadn't ever questioned Alex's insistence on taking buses instead of taxis, although truthfully she already knew the reason, even if he wouldn't come right out and say it, something about the gringo-ness or class elitism of taking the dollar taxi ride instead of the ten-cent workingman's bus.

In the taxi their conversation turned from lucha libre to Paolo Freire and something that Vivi was calling Theater of the Oppressed. Elana was listening only a little. She was thinking, and trying not to think, about her trip back to Virginia in the morning, her brother's release from rehab, her father's mix of incompetence and worry, and the fact that at the Kasa dinner they were now speeding so rapidly toward, she would be the only one not fluent in Spanish.

The bustle and glow of Avenida Juárez gave way to muted cinder-block colonias, the streets nearly empty now, single-story homes with gated patios and rebar reaching tentatively into the cold sky above. And every few blocks, the spill of yellow light from a tienda or comedor, cigarette and soda ads stenciled above the door, dogs and drunks and children huddled just outside that halo. In the hills above there were trash fires, taillights, and at the top of the bony sierra, radio towers, blinking their red signals out across the border.

The Kasa was tucked into a row of low concrete houses in a colonia that was not so far out as to be in the tarp-roof territory but in an area rough enough to have unpaved streets. For the people, of the people. Except that Elana had noticed that not many neighbors attended the dinners and talks and screenings. Children came sometimes, lured by their stomachs and curiosity, which was good, Elana guessed, to reach them while they were young and impressionable, before the dead-drum rhythm of the factory pulverized their ability to give a shit. Alex said that the Kasa kids did more than just the dinners and shows. They organized protests but also safety brigades—stationing themselves all night at secluded bus stops so that the women working at the maquiladoras didn't have to wait alone in the dark.

"Hey, Alex, Elana," Ana called from the doorway as they piled out of the taxi. She was the matriarch of the group, with round cheeks and warm eyes, her long hair braided.

Elana wondered if Alex was embarrassed to have arrived in a taxi and the thought made her smile a little. He was busy now introducing Vivi, who looked so out of place in her high heels and silver bangles, standing in the dirt street, talking to Ana, who wore a faded band T-shirt and torn khaki pants. It was Damian that Vivi knew from art school, but it seemed he wasn't here right now.

"Come in, come in." Ana ushered them into a big low-ceilinged room with a patchwork of carpet squares on the walls to muffle the noise of the bands that played and practiced there. There was a partial drum kit set up in the corner, a makeshift plywood table in the middle, and a cinder-block bookshelf along one wall.

Chucho jumped up from a beanbag as they entered and raised his beer can high.

"Enough," Ana said to him, walking quickly to the kitchen. "Put it away, now." There was no alcohol allowed at the communal dinners.

Lalo was sitting at the table, outlining letters on a large sheet of paper. He nodded at Alex, Elana, and Vivi, then turned to Chucho. "Come on."

Chucho grinned, tipped the beer back, and emptied it into his mouth.

Luis came out of the kitchen, licking his fingers. "Hey, Alex." He clapped Alex on the back and dipped his head at Elana and Vivi. "You planning on going to San Cristóbal for the beginning of the Other Campaign?"

If she concentrated enough, Elana could understand almost everything that was said in Spanish, but joining the conversation was a whole other story. She was slow to conjugate properly and mostly she felt sure that she'd missed the context of what was being said. It was worse if Alex tried to explain to her; then the conversation stopped entirely and everyone watched while she sweated and nodded. As long as no one acted like it was weird that she wasn't saying anything, Elana was fine with interpreting what she could and putting the pieces of the evening together in her head.

"I hadn't thought much about it," Alex was saying.

"We should all go." Luis waved his hand at the room. "I keep telling Ana that—"

Ana's head appeared in the kitchen doorway. "We should spend our resources traveling to Chiapas instead of continuing our work here?"

If Elana remembered correctly, the Other Campaign thing had something to do with the Zapatista rebels down in the southern jungles—a movement to critique the upcoming presidential election and to unite the Left. She would ask Alex more about it later.

"And who was at La Garrucha in September? Huh? You? Oh, no, that was me," Luis said to Ana.

"Lalo," Ana called, "Alex, help me out, am I not right? Spending money and time on traveling to San Cristóbal, to what? Celebrate the twelve years? I don't see that as a good use of our resources."

"So when Marcos calls for us to boost the numbers so that capitalist media can't ignore us anymore, that means nothing?" Luis said, his voice rising. He was nearly shaking, his shoulder-length hair tucked behind his ears, his eyes concentrated on Ana.

"What about"—Vivi stepped forward suddenly until she was almost standing between Luis and Ana—"when Marcos called for 'women and homosexuals' and other 'people of differences' to organize only on the sidelines? In a 'special place for differences'?"

"Oh." Luis turned to her. "You're a feminist? Or a lesbian? Or both, naturally."

Vivi smiled. "Naturally, of course, our concerns are so peripheral that they need a special place outside of the Other Campaign."

"You weren't there, at the encuentro. I'm just guessing, but I'm right, no? Where did you read that divisive capitalist bullshit?"

Luis and Vivi were facing each other now, and in her heels, Vivi was taller than Luis and he had to look up to address her face.

"Marcos's words from Marcos's mouth," she said.

"Why are lesbians always so focused on division?"

"Equating feminism with lesbianism is pretty low, even for you, Luis." The voice came from behind and they all turned as Damian walked in, carrying a bag of rice and a liter of Squirt soda.

"She's the one who said homosexuals."

"Vivi." Damian ignored Luis and walked to Vivi, kissing her on the cheek. "I see you've met my comrades."

Vivi nodded and Luis turned away, pretending to be interested in something on the bookcase. Damian looked over at Alex and Elana.

"Why is everyone standing like this?" he said. "Take off your coats, sit down, you want some soda? Coffee? Relax, the revolution doesn't start until after we eat."

He disappeared into the kitchen and came back with a stack of plastic cups and they all sat at the long table, leaving Lalo at the far end, still scribbling. Elana shrugged her coat off. Here, her ketchup-stained work shirt did not feel so embarrassing.

"When I saw the article about your show, I wondered if you would stop by," Damian said to Vivi.

"There was an article about it here?"

"*El Paso Times.*"

"Ah," Vivi said.

"Sorry to have missed it, you know, the international border can be a real bitch when you're brown. I've applied for a Border Crossing Card three times. This last time they wouldn't even give my passport back after they refused the application. Now I'm totally screwed."

"Shit, Damian."

"Did you ever think about having a show over here? I could have helped you set it up, in our space or this other collective closer to downtown. They do mostly theater stuff, but they might have been interested. Or is it more important for Americans to see?"

A muscle in Vivi's cheek twitched. "No, of course not. I've shown the pieces in México. It was just that I was invited to El Paso, the university and—"

"Right, right, of course, the university and the chamber of commerce, and they were the ones offering the money, so—"

"You know how much money they gave me? Like three thousand pesos, it's not about the money."

Damian leaned forward, arms on the table. "Oh, of course not, forgive me. It's about feeding the American appetite for brown violence then, right?"

"What?" Vivi gripped her soda cup.

"You traveled up there to show the Americans more images of México as beautiful but violent." His eyes darted from Vivi to the rest of the table and then back to Vivi. "Seventy percent of the guns in México come directly from the US. We wouldn't have this level of violence without the help of the USA."

"Okay," Vivi said, "but I'm not trying to make polemic art."

"Oh, no? Then why did you name the pieces after dead women from the news?"

Elana looked down at her cup of Squirt, fizzing and seething with sugary chemical calories. The nice thing about dinners at the Kasa was that so much was going on no one noticed what she did not consume.

"Elana."

She jerked her head up and saw Ana's face in the kitchen doorway. "Bring me that rice," she said, nodding toward the bag on the table.

THE KITCHEN WAS long and narrow, cinder-block walls painted purple, and a stove giving off gusts of spicy steam down at the end of the room past the counter where María stood chopping cilantro. María was the only other female besides Ana who lived at the Kasa and she reminded Elana of the character in *For Whom the Bell Tolls*, not only because of her name and short-cropped hair but also her shy but beckoning demeanor. Elana thought maybe she slept with Chucho, but she wasn't sure. Mostly María stayed in the kitchen, under Ana's wing. None of the boys ever seemed to cook, even though they talked of building new forms of community. When she had mentioned this to Alex, he had said he'd never noticed that, but maybe Ana liked to cook and didn't want them messing up everything.

"How's it going?" Ana took the rice from Elana and handed her an onion. "You can cut this?"

Elana nodded. She'd been in the midst of forming an answer to the "How's it going?" but stopped now and said to María instead, "A knife?"

María nodded toward a wooden-handled paring knife. She moved her pile of cilantro to make room on the cutting board and leaned her head closer to Elana. "Ana likes it cut thin," she said.

Ana put the pot of rice on the stove and stirred the pozole. Neither she nor María spoke as they cooked, and the voices came in clearly from the main room.

"How much do you pay for, say, a replica heart?" Damian asked.

"I have a friend," Vivi said. "He casts them at a really reasonable rate."

"So it is affordable for you to pay for your replicated violence that you then set out in a beautiful field and photograph so that you can shock your patrons. But wouldn't it be even cheaper if you didn't have to replicate? Right? Three houses down from here, their daughter, Valeria, she disappears on her way home from school, and when they find the body, her left tit is cut off and her panties used to strangle her neck."

"I'm not a documentary photographer, I—"

"Of course not, that—what happened to Valeria—that's not pretty enough, right?"

"The purpose of my photographs is not to be pretty."

"Better to have only her lungs, shiny pink in the sand."

"You haven't even seen my work, Damian, you saw a newspaper image of one piece."

A hand tapped Elana's shoulder. "Enough." María reached over to still the knife and Elana realized she'd been so intent on listening and understanding, she had chopped the onion to thin, glassy smithereens.

"Okay, girls, come here for a taste," Ana called.

Elana felt she had already tasted it, the scent greasy and hot on her tongue, but she followed María who reached for the ladle. "No, not that." Ana brushed her hand aside. "Here." She held up a small bottle of mezcal, the pale worm bumping along the bottom of the glass.

"But—" María said.

"The no-drinking rule is for the boys," Ana explained, beckoning Elana closer. "They're the ones who can't handle it, but I think we've earned a taste."

THEY CARRIED THE huge pot of pork and hominy stew out to the table, Ana gripping one handle and María the other. Elana followed with a bowl of rice and then one of beans, a tortillero filled with the hot tortillas and the platter of onion and cilantro. Despite the overwhelming richness of the food smells that stirred a simultaneous hunger and nausea, and the fact that she'd already been waiting tables all day, Elana liked the festive, frenetic atmosphere. The room was filling up and there were not nearly enough chairs so they filled their bowls and sat on the floor or leaned up against the bookcase. Chucho perched on the stool behind the drum kit until Luis yelled at him that he was dripping soup on the cymbals. The dinners made Elana think of the industrious orphans from *The Boxcar Children*. Although almost everyone was in their twenties, there was still the feeling of playing at adulthood and family. Sleeping bags and blankets rolled up in the corner and the band practice space converted now into a dining room, later into a plenary meeting hall.

Each time Elana and María hurried into the kitchen for salt, or limes or more tortillas, Ana would wink at them and whisper, "A little taste," so that by the time she had finally settled on the floor with a small bowl of rice and salsa, Elana was drunk. And happy. She was happy to have helped produce all this food and at the same time to have not eaten it. Her appetite felt to her like an unclean room—sloppy, messy—and resisting it was like tidying up, checking things off a to-do list. It gave her a zip of pleasure that pulsed through her body, a clean feeling that was mirrored by the sharpness of her hip bones, the way they rose now, would soon rise more. After Alex left for school in the mornings, she would lie in bed and run her hands rhythmically over her hips, hoping to feel the bones a little more each day. Clean, sharp angles that focused her mind.

She set her bowl on the floor and watched the room buzz around her, Vivi and Damian still arguing, Alex deep in conversation now with Lalo, talking about that wrestler El Vengador again. They were just far enough away to be mostly out of earshot and she was glad not to be pulled into the conversation, not to have to struggle to interpret the words. A blonde gringa had shown up after a while, a girl with flushed cheeks and the limp, pitiful beginnings of dreadlocks. She spoke much worse Spanish than Elana. Also, she was apparently Luis's new girlfriend, which nearly made Elana laugh out loud. Luis with his high principles and fuck yous to the United States, and here he was nuzzling this exchange student who could not look more Caucasian if she tried, her thick tongue blundering confidently, conjugations be damned. Luis was no less susceptible to love or lust than anyone else and Elana liked to see it.

At night in Colonia Monterrey, there were no passing taxis to hail and so Alex, Elana, and Vivi walked to the Linea 9 bus stop. Damian said he'd see them off and they headed out together into the dark. There were no streetlights this far out and the road was empty except for the skittering shadows of stray dogs, but bundled up in her coat and warmed by the mezcal, Elana felt almost giddy. She pulled her cigarettes out of her bag and lit one. Alex turned to look at her.

"Hey," he said. "You started smoking again?"

Elana shrugged.

"Can I have one?" He bent toward her and then pulled back. "You're drunk?"

Elana laughed.

"Wait, how'd you get drunk?"

She stopped walking, handed him a cigarette and then lit it. "The secret side of helping in the kitchen."

"Ana?"

"She said the no drinking is for the boys. We were cooking and sweating while you all fought your little art and capitalism fights and we deserved a drink."

"Ha! I like Ana."

Alex linked arms with Elana and she snuggled in close and everything felt smooth and nice for once, the warmth of Alex's body beside her, the patter of Vivi and Damian's voices rattling on about legislative theater and invisible theater and someone named Augusto Boal, the bark of dogs in the alley up ahead, and the fact that the stars, with no streetlights to obscure them, shone down wild and cold over Juárez.

THREE

Mateo could feel something coming up behind him, but he could not see what it was and so he kept moving. The hallway was dim and led into a concrete room. Water on the floor, in his shoes, up around his ankles. The room had a short metal door. He tried the handle, felt it turn, and a rush of relief filled him. He opened it, bent, and stepped through to another room now, identical but the water was higher here. When he looked back, there was no door behind him, just another one in front, and when he passed through that one into the next room, the water rose even more. He sloshed across the floor, water up to his waist. He could not open the next door. The water weight was too heavy against it, rising quickly now, surging up past his waist to his chest, his neck. The cold, metallic taste of it was what shocked him awake. He woke up struggling, muscles tensed and his body snarled in the sheets.

He was panting and he did not know where he was. A dark hush surrounded him and he could see a stripe of gray light between heavy curtains and the orange feet of a pigeon stalking the windowsill outside. Then he remembered: Hotel Puebla, the same room he had stayed in for the past six months every time he came to the capital to fight as El Vengador del Norte.

It was a huge improvement over the bunk room he'd slept in before that. This one was paid for by Neto, the man who was now his sponsor, and it was spacious, carpeted, with a red-tiled Jacuzzi, mirrors and draping dark red blankets that were cinched about his feet now. He started to push himself up and a wave of pain flashed across his back. He wrapped his arm around and reached to knead the tight muscles along his spine. His legs felt swollen and useless. He lay still in the swirl of night-sweat blankets and listened to the pattern of feet in the hall, the rattle of the housekeeper's cart. The room felt too hot, too dark, and as his eyes adjusted, he could see the mounted TV like a single watchful eye over him.

Last night in the club, Neto had asked him again and again how he liked the room, was it nice enough? The TV, the Jacuzzi? They were in the back of the club, beyond the dance floor, in a quiet little mirrored cube. Just him and Neto and Neto's bodyguards. Of course, the hotel room was great, he'd said, although it had seemed like there was supposed to be a different answer, something more. He never understood what he was supposed to say or do with Neto. The big-name wrestlers got sponsored all the time by beer companies and music labels, but Mateo had been shocked when six months ago his manager came to him and said a private sponsor, Neto, wanted a meeting. And Neto did not seem to want anything in return—not his name on promotional materials (he had not even shared his full name with Mateo)—nothing except to spend time with El Vengador del Norte. It did not entirely make sense, until last night, when things had started to click. Sure, he'd heard the rumors before that, the guys at CMLL whispering about Neto's family's connection to the cartel, but he hadn't wanted to believe it. People were always talking shit like that.

He stood up from the bed, legs shaky and heart still beating too fast. Bits and pieces of conversations from the club drifted into his mind and mixed with the dream. He'd been doing too much coke lately and it left him feeling unsure of the edges of reality. More than the metallic taste, it was the feeling of someone at his back. He walked to the window and parted the drapes. The world was busy, traffic streaming down Avenida

Puebla past the 7-Eleven and Pemex station, where a man hosed the concrete in dark looping arcs while another swept the wet leaves into a grated gutter. Calle Morelia was crowded with auto parts stores, tire shops, narrow warehouses of steering wheels, hoses, fan belts. And above, the staggered skyline of Roma Norte: crumbling concrete residences and flat red roofs, skinny ash trees. Mateo turned from the window and walked to the sink. He splashed his face, ran his finger over his fuzzed teeth, and glanced in the mirror. The stitched cut above his left eye was oozing a little. He turned to dry his hands. On the edge of the Jacuzzi was a towel folded into the shape of a swan. It stared at him. He wiped his fingers on the bedspread instead.

"The Consejo is just using you," Neto had said last night. "You know that, right? They're letting you rise so it will be more impressive when El Hijo del Diablo Satanico takes your mask." He had leaned back in the leather booth, smiling a little and pushing the coke mirror toward Mateo again. "You can't really think they're going to let you keep winning?" he said.

And that's when the conversation had flipped. When Mateo tried to piece it together now, it sounded like a part of the dream.

"When you join me, though, that's a whole other story," Neto had said. "I'll build my whole company around you. Consejo Mundial doesn't care about you. They'll chew you up and spit you out in a year or two. Me, I'm starting a brand-new promotion company, and I'll build you up unbelievably."

It hadn't seemed possible that Neto was asking Mateo to leave the oldest and biggest promotion company in the country, right when his career was rising meteorically.

"I don't know," Mateo had said. "I don't know if it's a good idea for me to leave the Consejo right now." He'd wanted to scream, Who in their right mind would leave the most prestigious company to join some no-name organization funded by shady money? But Neto's men were right there, the reflections of their holstered guns glinting in the mirrored walls, and so he stayed quiet and let Neto talk on and on.

"Of course, we would have to give your fans some kind of transition narrative," Neto had said. "Your next fight is in Acapulco, next week, right?"

Mateo had nodded.

"Well, I'd say you'll be hurt pretty bad in Acapulco," Neto said. "They'll have to take you out of the circuit for a little while to recuperate from your injuries. And when you come back, it'll be with me. No one will care about El Hijo del Diablo anymore, they'll be watching us and our new company."

Our new company. Mateo had not managed to tell Neto that there would be no "our." He would do it soon, though, he promised himself, at the next meeting he would say no, he was not going to leave CMLL.

He got up off the bed and walked past the Jacuzzi. He'd never used it before in all the times he'd stayed in this hotel and he thought now that he should at least have taken advantage of the perks that Neto had set him up with. He should have enjoyed it all more. His younger self would not have been able to believe this situation: a room with a private Jacuzzi, paid for by a sponsor. He felt the rising swirl of the dream-water against his legs, his hips, his chest. He dropped to the floor and started in on a round of push-ups. Pain rippled through him and he focused on it, breathed into it. By the time he reached fifty, he was panting, his heart knocking hard again, but this time it felt good. He stood up and grabbed the towel swan by its neck and wiped the sweat from his face. He pulled on track pants and gathered his stuff from the floor—sunglasses, wallet, dress shirt, and jeans—and shoved them into his duffel.

The hallway was empty. In the elevator a housekeeping girl with a feather duster in her hand looked at his face, looked away, and then back again and he remembered burst blood vessels in his eye, swollen cheek and stitched-up brow. He smiled. Glad she was there because it made the elevator feel less like an extension of the box-rooms of his dream. This whole hotel was too dark, too quiet. He got out on the ground floor, and there were two men in the lobby, both in black jackets, waiting for someone. Mateo's blood spiked. Neto's men? He couldn't be sure. Neither man met his eye. He walked quickly past the almost empty dining hall, where bored waiters in long black aprons paced the tiled floor, and on past the front desk, through the double-glass doors. A jackhammer in the street, swerving traffic, ding of a bicycle bell. He looked back. Neither man had come outside. He turned onto Puebla Avenue and broke into a run. They probably had nothing to do with him. He slowed his pace. They *had* looked like Neto's men, though. He glanced back again, saw nothing, and turned east. He was moving instinctively toward Arena México where he had fought the night before, but when he hit the crossroads at Cuauhtémoc, he took a left. There was a gym for all the Consejo Mundial fighters at the Arena México, but he did not want to go there as he always did. He headed instead to a gym he had not been to in years, Gimnasio Victoria, where he had trained when he arrived in DF. That was back when his Juárez trainer had sent him to the capital to live and work with El Águila, who owned the Victoria and knew people in the Consejo Mundial.

And it had all worked out, all his biggest hopes; he'd gotten his license and been contracted by the Consejo. But it never felt as good anymore as it used to, up north, in the beginning. His first big fight had been in a shitty gym on the outskirts of downtown Juárez, a concrete room with a leaking roof, puddles of water, and an audience so alive, their hate and love so palpable, you could see it, snaking up and out of them, tentacles of rage and pride rising and twining. This was in the NAFTA years when the North was filling with maquiladoras and factory workers blowing here and there for work. The North, so far from the capital that the heart pumped almost no blood up to it, had been tossed like a scrap to the capitalists. It had been nearly lost in the 1840s, cracked in half and abandoned, and then nearly lost again to the free trade agreements. But as the Avenger of the North, Mateo was fierce fronterizo pride, puro norteño to the core, a shining golden son.

He had not thought of wrestling as a career in the beginning. He'd thought he wanted to be a musician. From his school janitor job he'd go straight to band practice with his friend Lalo after work. Lalo had introduced him to some local hardcore groups, Hij@s de Maquiler@s and Arena Roja, and he'd played him LPs from Masacre 68, Los Crudos, Limp Wrist.

They'd started their own three-piece, La Plaga, with Mateo on bass, but he'd always known he had no real talent. He did it not for the music even but for the deep belonging he felt listening to David from Hij@s sing about growing up poor and proud and the electric goosebumps he got when Martin Crudo screamed about being queer. Then one day, after band practice, Lalo invited Mateo along to a lucha training session and he'd felt it in his body, even on that first night, that this was what he was good at.

He threw himself into it, hour after hour with his trainer, Babe Sharon, watching, pushing, correcting. Babe Sharon saw how important it was to him and let him pay next to nothing for the classes. He focused on it for whole days in that tiny, muffled gym with the old-timers sitting on the edge of the ring nursing warm Carta Blancas and calling out to him, *No, asi, asi, mi'jo,* their hands fluting up like startled birds to show the rolls and pins and flips their own bodies were too crippled to hold.

As the months went by, Mateo had moved up the card, from tiny luchas in the dusty plazas of jagged frontier towns to bigger and bigger arenas. One night in Ciudad Chihuahua, a middle-aged woman rushed the ring, chanting "Mi'jo, mi'jo, mi'jo!" My son! My son! She was scrambling through the sweating, shouting crowd. "Mi'jo," she screamed. "You make us so proud, you fight for the North and you fight clean and good and fill us with pride!" Her eyes wet and frantic. She had clawed at the ropes until she could pull herself up high enough to kiss his mask.

His own mother had never been to one of his fights until he moved to the capital and paid for her to visit him there. But now he was everyone's son and he had moved to the capital for them, that woman in Chihuahua City and all the rest of them with their spangling norteño pride, to show the capital what a clean-fighting borderland tecnico looked like. When he signed with the Consejo Mundial, though, he'd had to start over again at the bottom of the card and his northern pride felt diluted too, more like a character role than an identity. He did not come from a wrestling family and he'd feared he might never truly belong. No one in the audiences here spoke to him like that woman in Chihuahua had, the cheers were thin with no pulse, at least until Neto had taken notice of him and pumped up his career. But Neto, Mateo feared, had taken notice for the wrong reasons. The pull there was a thing both hazy and heavy.

Now he ran, steady, passing the taqueros and torta vendors under the shaggy palms of Tolsa Park and on up Calle de Balderas, where the shiny red city buses lined nose to ass. He crossed Emilio Donde, dodged a bicycle cart carrying five-gallon water bottles, and hurried on. He could feel the city all about him, moving like some great geared clock, ugly and glorious and ancient, and when he looked up again, he saw his own masked face plastered over and over down the length of a concrete wall: EL VENGADOR DEL NORTE VS. EL HIJO DEL DIABLO SATANICO on a series of wheatpasted posters; his own arms raised in challenge; his black-and-silver mask. A shiver passed over him each time he saw an image of himself writ large like that. Something so impossible it cracked reason. And what's more, no one around him knew it. Almost no one outside the empresa had ever seen him put on his mask. He could stop anyone on the street and point and shout, *Look, that's me*, and no one would believe him. Outside of the empresa, only his parents and his wife, Alicia, knew, and a few old friends from a collective, Kasa de Kultura, that he'd joined years ago in Juárez, but those friends knew only his first name. A masked wrestler's most important possession was his identity. No one outside of the business could know his real name. And so, as El Vengador del Norte was becoming famous, Mateo slipped through his days unnoticed. Only Neto had seen him with and without the mask and it would not be in Neto's interest to reveal the face and therefore ruin the career of his favorite fighter, one he had invested so much money in.

Gimnasio Victoria was in the basement of a sweets and cigarettes store, tucked into a row of electronics and refrigeration distributors near the National Police Museum, which was at the moment advertising a traveling exhibit on serial killers. Mateo took the steps two at a time, down into the dim vestibule where half a dozen middle-aged men sat playing cards on moldering couches. One of the men looked up.

"Member?"

"Friend," Mateo said, "of El Águila."

The man nodded. "Locker key?"

Mateo took the key and passed through into a long concrete room with roped-off areas for free weights and a few machines, some punching bags, and down at the far end, a raised ring. The clatter of voices and stutter of the speed bag echoed up and down the walls. The place looked no different than it had five years before. A subterranean smell of sweat and damp cloth and mildew. The guy at the squat rack rested his bar and stared at Mateo, and Mateo nodded and moved on past. He ditched his bag under a bench and walked back to the ring where El Águila was lining up a group of students. El Águila's hair was streaked with gray now, but his stocky body looked almost unchanged. Mateo waited silently until he turned and saw him there and then Mateo raised his hand in a sort of salute-wave. El Águila's broad face opened into a smile and his gold teeth gleamed. He had not seen Mateo since El Vengador won El Campeonato del Norte del Pais. El Águila leaned over the ropes and gripped Mateo's hand.

"Órale, son of a bitch, what brings you here?"

Mateo smiled back. "I need a good workout."

"Pues, get your ass up here."

Mateo slipped through the ropes and joined the line, and as they moved forward one by one, he felt his body take over, breath in-out-in and feet planted, and the rest of it—the coke and Neto and the dream—was drowned out by the hypnotic rhythm of the roll and break fall.

THE MATCHES AT the Arena Coliseo Acapulco began at seven-thirty, but Mateo's fight wasn't until nine. His was the next-to-last event; after Neto had started sponsoring him, he'd been moved from the first slot up to almost headliner. It meant a lot of waiting, pacing, losing energy. As the crowd warmed up, he cooled down. From the concrete locker room he could hear their voices out there rising and falling as he laced up his boots, loosened them a little, then tightened them again. He stretched, paced, tried not to think about Neto. *In Acapulco.* He felt outside his body tonight, disconnected. He was anxious to be in the ring already with the music and cameras and shouting.

Ángel Dorado came back into the locker room breathing heavily and dripping sweat. Mateo nodded at him. Only one more fight before his own. Mateo pulled his El Vengador mask on and checked it in the mirror: black Lycra with silver slashes across the cheeks and a sparkly *V* in the middle of his forehead. He pulled out his shimmery black cape with silver sequins and tied it on. Beneath it, he wore his silver briefs, silver wristbands, and black boots with shiny laces.

When El Hijo del Diablo Satanico's entrance music came on, El Vengador was ready in the tecnico wing. There was a roll of drums and then the frantic high-pitched sawing of violins and screaming vocals. It was a song from this stupid Spanish folk metal band called Mago de Oz that Diablo loved. El Vengador rolled from his heels to his toes and back again, waiting for the song to fade and his own music to replace it. A scampering accordion rhythm and Juan Gabriel's infectious voice, *Ciudad Juárez es número uno . . . La frontera más fabulosa y bella del mundo!* El Vengador felt better immediately.

He moved out into the aisle, his cape flapping and arms raised. Voices rose beautifully around him and he could feel himself being lifted on their adoration, balmy and loved as he bounded toward the ring. He smiled, though no one could see it through the mask. He picked up momentum and dove over the top rope, landing in a cartwheel. The voices gushed louder. He lifted his cape and spun. He could see himself sparkling, but as the voices quieted and the referee checked his boots for weapons, he realized that the dizzy disconnectedness from backstage was still with him. Usually, a fight was one long moment of total focus. But now, suddenly he was separated. He was Mateo watching El Vengador move this body.

He tried to shake it off, but the bell had already rung and immediately Diablo had him down in a leg lock. El Vengador rolled out and reversed into an arm bar, but Diablo escaped and hooked El Vengador's elbow and pinned it against his back. This was what Diablo loved to do, keep the fight down on the mat as long as he could to prevent El Vengador from the high-flying acrobatics the crowd loved. They rolled together across the canvas until El Vengador slipped away and leapt up, taunting Diablo as he climbed to the third rope. Once up there, though, he froze. You couldn't stop in a moment like that or you'd lose all nerve, but there he was, stunned and swaying in the corner while Diablo grabbed at his legs. He leapt over Diablo's head and landed clumsily.

By the third round he managed a decent dropkick that sent Diablo over the ropes, but a moment later Diablo came roaring back into the ring holding a metal folding chair over his head, and as Mateo backed away, he realized this was the moment, this was what he had been waiting for all night. He focused on Diablo's red leather mask until it was blocked by the chair that rose and then crashed down onto El Vengador's legs. There was the smack of contact and then something burst and his left leg was all wet and a burning pain rose through him, blocking out the lights, the voices. He collapsed and he let go of everything, finally fully in the moment now, under the wall of pain.

FOUR

Alex stayed in the departure zone long after Elana had gone inside the airport. The morning light came sharply toward him across the winter plain. The car engine was churning and the radio was turned so low the Spanish words could be mistaken for the voices of birds. For a few moments she had been visible inside, hair big and body small under the hump of her backpack, face tipped up as she looked left and right and left again. Then she was lost in the glare of the glass, and vehicles merged and honked around him. A weaving stream of goodbyes. To the north was the Biggs Army Airfield Base and behind him, the sun-struck flank of the Franklin Mountains. Somehow even the sunlight looked cold. The Honda's heater was out again. His breath clouded like smoke.

She was gone, he could smoke now. The thought came and a half a second later the internal laughter. She'd been the one who gave him cigarettes last night. It would be good to have a little break from her. It was sad to acknowledge it, but he and Elana were never quite enjoying the same moments anymore. The things that excited him—exploring Juárez, hanging with the Kasa kids—stressed out Elana and the moments that interested her, well, he wasn't quite sure what those were anymore; she kept them close to her chest.

He took Montana Avenue down toward the 10, passed a Wendy's, Starbucks, El Taco Tote, then car dealerships, frost crystals sparkling on the hoods. He wondered what kind of security, what kind of crazy insurance they had to have in order to play at the American dream like that—a sea of shining vehicles in a place where ten-year-olds were trained to sneak across the border and slide a metal rod beneath the window glass. At Paisano and Gateway he joined the I-10 and the sun was at his back now, the city waking around him. He passed the chubby white cheeks and gluttonous smile of the Sunbeam girl, the sweet starchy smell of baking bread spilling out from the factory and across the lanes of traffic. He wanted coffee, a cigarette, a sweet roll.

Almost two months now and he and Elana hadn't done anything more than cuddle. It had seemed mutual to Alex, neither one of them initiating. She was going through something, that much was obvious. At first, he'd wondered if she was cheating. He never said the word *anorexia*. It seemed scarier to say it out loud. He'd watched her, trying hard not to seem like he was watching. He did research and read up on it. She was still getting her period, he'd counted the Tampax under the bathroom sink.

Then last night, as soon as they got back to the apartment, she shucked off her coat and unbuttoned her shirt.

"Fuck me."

He'd laughed, walking to the bathroom to brush his teeth.

"That's funny?"

"You're not joking?" He'd turned to face her.

"Sex with me is a joke?"

"Lana." He'd squinted at her where she stood, just inside the front door, shirt open to reveal her jutting collarbone and a beige bra. "Your flight leaves really early in the morning. And you're drunk."

HE TOOK A right on Mesa Avenue and drove up the hill into the no-man's-land of box stores and college dorms. A left on University Drive and the Sierra de Juárez swung into view, pale brown and lunar, with the huge white words painted down her flank—LA BIBLIA ES LA VERDAD,

LEELA—each letter looming thirteen stories tall over the great dusty bowl of the city: *The Bible Is the Truth, Read It.* He'd come so far from his Bible-reading days only to move to a place where those words shouted out at him every morning. Had been shouting at him always, maybe. He wondered when they had been painted, if they'd been there, staring down at him from the very beginning, even before he'd been adopted.

The university campus resembled a prison compound. Bhutanese architecture, Alex had been told, to complement the desert landscape, but to him the high, nearly windowless walls looked more like a penitentiary. He pulled into a brown gravel parking lot and stared through the windshield at the spiked arms of an ocotillo, shaking as a pigeon lifted and took flight.

He still had an hour before his meeting with Dr. Nelson. He knew he should be nervous, but lately his brain had been whirring too much to care about their discussions of ethnographic approaches. Two weeks away from his thesis proposal deadline and his whole idea had flipped, what was once a focus on the psychogeography of accountability—the way the physical separation of the border let American entities shift blame—had given way to the slam of shoulders against the wrestling mat. Ever since meeting Mateo, he didn't care to write about anything but lucha libre.

It was not advisable to change topics at this point in the semester and he could already see Dr. Nelson's crimped lip, but he knew too that they loved you more when you failed a little first and then overachieved. He'd learned this early. Redemption was much more moving for the audience than no sin to begin with. This knowledge had twinned with an awareness of the slippery limits of his parents' love. All the adults around him, the entire church community: so conditional. He'd been brought to West Virginia from that strange, parched place where Jim and Noreen Walker had gone as missionaries—a small brown trophy to show for their time in Mexico. But he was suspect as soon as he was not a baby anymore. He slept too much, ate too much, sweated too much. His body letting loose loud alarms all in and around him. And then, when he'd taken up the call and started preaching at age thirteen, their love surged again, overboard. Doubled and tripled for the fact that he had been suspect. A throwaway babe from a throwaway place, reborn.

He got out of the car and followed the road around past the big fortress of a library. A kid shuffled in front of him down the sidewalk, slumped inside an oversized Miner's sweatshirt.

"Hey," Alex called. "You got a cigarette I can bum?"

Across from the library and down a flight of concrete steps there was a pedestrian bridge to a parking deck that overlooked the blurring stripes of the border highway. Alex ashed his cigarette on the railing and turned west where, two miles away but clearly visible in the thin winter air, the smokestacks of the ASARCO smelter, the starting point for his original thesis, sat like some dystopian Soviet relic. The old Guggenheim copper and iron extracting plant had been closed for five years now, but Alex had found a newspaper interview with a former worker who admitted that the higher-ups had instructed them, whenever the wind turned south toward Mexico, to crank production up, gushing dirty yellow smoke directly into Juárez. That was where Alex's thesis idea had begun, an attempt to show how the border can serve as a moral stopping point: my compassion does not go beyond this invisible line. The same with the maquiladora owners who'd relocated their factories from El Paso to Juárez, only a few miles away geographically but beyond the moral boundary. And even the US Attorney's Office had allowed a cartel informant, paid by the US Immigration and Customs Enforcement, to commit murder. They'd allowed him to do it, record it, get paid, and do it again less than ten miles from the ICE office, but notably not in the United States.

It was so similar to what had happened in West Virginia, and maybe that was why he had been drawn to it at first. Both places had been stretched thin, cadavered for their resources and labor and then abandoned, their people rendered subhuman in the national dialogue. In West Virginia it had been mining, and here too that was still happening: just a few weeks ago, one of Alex's professors had mentioned that a colleague, an archaeology professor, had been down in the Samalayuca dunes reserve and had run into a group of Americans test-boring for copper.

In his first few months in El Paso, Alex had followed the stories of the yellow ASARCO smoke across the line into Colonia Ladrillera, where the streets were named like twisted jokes: Calle Nadadores—Street of the Swimmers—running beside the arsenic-ridden dribble of the Río Bravo-Grande. And he could see Ladrillera now, from this side, the concrete block, curling sheet metal and wooden pallets punctuated by the flapping of a blue tarp roof, but ASARCO's effects no longer drew him in. His whole idea, those words, *psychogeography of accountability and morality*, sounded like just that—words—something to say in class or at a dinner party, but what was he really trying to talk about? How we other-ize people, separate ourselves from them, and how this allows us to stop feeling compassion. There was nothing new in that idea.

What was going on over there—right there, where the smoke of trash fires rose now in a cloud so close that he could almost taste it—was something else, something bigger than borders and governments and corporations, something ancient and enormous, a rising insistence on the valuelessness of human lives. Aided and abetted by the United States—this was a new kind of dirty war, one where the deaths could be blamed on the cartels instead of government killing squads. But where did those lines bleed? Who, in the end, benefited from the dead women, dead campesinos, dead cops, dead journalists? And what happened to someone who grew up in this? What he wanted to write about was the way a young man could slide a mask over his face, step into the wrestling ring, and blur out his class, his background, his name. In the trust-pain struggle with another man, he could pantomime the death that dogged him daily and rise through it. *See these boys, here in the ring they could be anything*, Mateo had said in his first interview with Alex, his arm sweeping out to encompass the ring, the arena, the city. *This is a factory of dreams.*

THE SUN SET at 5:00 p.m. and the cold crept in as Alex waited for the downtown bus, feeling the tug of Juárez and the empty space where guilt should have been. Elana had called while he was napping, after his meeting with Dr. Nelson, and now her voice was trapped inside his cell phone and he could replay it, poke and prod himself with it, as often as he wanted. *Hey, Ali, I made it. And I remembered to call you. Bet you thought I wouldn't. Okay, love you. Dad should be here in a few minutes to pick me up.* She expected him to call her back and ask how the flight was and tell her about his meeting with Dr. Nelson, if she even remembered his meeting. He left his phone in the apartment and headed to the bus stop instead. Even if she did remember to ask, she wouldn't really be listening. She was never really listening to him these days. And he didn't see the point in talking about it. The meeting had gone fine, as fine as a complete-changing-of-the-thesis-at-the-last-minute meeting could go. Dr. Nelson had asked the questions that Anglos always asked about lucha libre. Is it just like American wrestling? Which of course it wasn't exactly, but the roots of it did come from the US, brought down by Salvador Lutteroth, who had experienced his first wrestling matches right here in El Paso in the 1930s. Right, but is it *really* like American wrestling? everyone asked. No one wanted a history lesson. What they wanted to know was if it was "totally fake." Which was missing the point entirely. The prefight knowledge of who would win an individual match didn't matter to the wrestler. What mattered was the long arc of his story line. Who rose and who fell across the stretch of many months. They were athletes absolutely, but what they were participating in was theater.

Alex boarded the bus and it whooshed out of the barrenness of the north neighborhoods, scrubby juniper yards and chain-link fences, and into the slow-motion decay of downtown. The San Jacinto plaza was empty except for a paper Subway cup skidding in the wind. Above it, the flat glass eyes of WestStar, Chase, Wells Fargo, and Bank of America stared lidless over the quiet failure of the Plaza Hotel, Rican Furniture, Bassett Tower. The Art Deco buildings—huge old fossils with buttercream frosting–dripped doorways covered in plywood—looking out of place like someone's grandmother, refusing to dress down no matter what.

South of Paisano Drive, the city shifted and came awake. Sidewalks busy with families, bicycles, young couples, girls in puffy winter coats and red lipstick. Warehouses with their metal gates rolled back and goods spilling out into the street. A bustle that Alex could only associate with the flea markets he'd known in West Virginia. EVERYTHING $1, PERFUMERIA, HOUSE OF BEAUTY, SEXY JEANS, TODA BODA, BEST BRANDS NOW, ANNY'S CASA DE FASHION, TRAJES DE SEÑORA, VESTIDOS DE FIESTA, UNITALLA PLUS, BLUSAS, PANTALONES, BOTAS. And the warm yellow interiors of cafes with handwritten signs: GORDITAS, BURRITOS, FRENCH FRY, CONSOMÉ DE POLLO, BISTEC, TACOS DE CABEZA, LENGUA, CHICHARRÓN.

The bus took a right on Fourth and wove its way to the Central Transit Station at Santa Fe, where it emptied, everyone shuffling off, their grocery bags in hand, cowboy boots stepping into the blue-black cold. Months after moving here, it still thrilled Alex how he visually fit in. He could feel eyes on his skin and how they glanced off, slid, and kept right on moving. He walked toward the border with no second looks. Of course, when he opened his mouth, everything changed. His accent was not right and the interaction would shift, but that discomfort felt deserved, or maybe not deserved but useful, like this experience could burnish him into something new, not like the discomfort of being brown-skinned and foreign-born in West Virginia. Elana didn't understand why he wanted to spend so much time in Juárez when El Paso was full of people like him who looked Mexican but didn't speak perfect Spanish. It was the friction that he liked, though. He couldn't pick up where he had left off as an infant, no, of course not, he would never be Mexican like that, but here in Juárez he felt like he was being etched into a more precise version of himself. Instead of carrying around with him the face of a country and people he did not know, he was joining himself here—not *finding* himself, that was stupid and cheesy, no, he was joining himself.

Back at Hall College, he'd had to answer over and over again the question "Where are you from?" and each time, even before he could finish saying Render, West Virginia, his teachers, classmates, acquaintances would interrupt with "No, really, where are you *really* from?" As if he were tricking them, lying, playing some sort of joke. If he said I don't remember Mexico, not even a little bit, he was met with a snort, a laugh, a shrug.

At the Puente Santa Fe, he dropped his quarter in the turnstile. Twenty-five cents to leave the USA, ten cents to return. The vendors on the bridge were selling knit hats—toboggans, they were called back in West Virginia, but no one ever understood what he meant when he said that here—gloves, newspapers, sodas, and one enterprising woman, propped up under a NO VENDEDORES sign, had a huge thermos of coffee and stack of Styrofoam cups.

At the end of the bridge a soldier was posted in a tiny glass and cinder-block room, and past that, the walkway fanned out into a wide ramp and everyone who was snugged together in the crossing spread free and Alex stopped. He eyed the elote vendor across the street with his brazier of coals and bottles of condiments, the *Diaro* boy in the median, the taxista waving a hand. He'd waited here like this more than a dozen times over the past three months. Sometimes Mateo was there already, leaned up against the railing at the bottom of the ramp, but more often Alex waited for him. Once for an hour and forty minutes. He gripped the handrail and released. People spilled out from behind him—a baby stroller, shopping cart, quick passing feet going home, going right where they wanted to, full of direction. He leaned against the rail, tried to see without looking, to not appear desperate or seeking. Across the street, darkened windows of a dental office gleamed, and beyond: the streaming neon of money-changing stations, revving engines and constant horns, the steady crawl of city buses, a police pickup thrashing by with lights and sirens, and then, through a break in the traffic, he saw Mateo's face. Mateo's dark eyes focused on him.

And Alex was moving now, a feeling like a drawstring being pulled through his guts—down the ramp, around a bicycle, squeezing between bumpers. He did not take his eyes off Mateo, as if to look away, even for his own safety, might make him disappear.

"You're just watching me?" Alex said before he'd even finished crossing the street. "How long were you gonna let me stand there?" Everything—the traffic, the horns, the buses—was small now, fuzzy, inconsequential, and out of focus.

A smile spread full across Mateo's face.

"You're more beautiful when you don't know I'm watching."

He stopped, felt Mateo's words land, then lift, felt his cheeks flush. *More beautiful when you don't know.* He must be mistranslating a little. He looked at Mateo and a dizziness zipped up from his stomach.

Mateo reached out, pulled him onto the sidewalk. A horn honked. Engines behind them. "You thought I forgot?"

This, more than anything, was their language, their greeting. *Did you forget? Could you? I'm here, am I not? Again? When can I see you?*

The sidewalk crushed with movement, a woman with a wheeled basket, butting, insistent. *Permiso, permiso.* Mateo put a hand on Alex's shoulder and guided him over against the building. "You're hungry?" he said, his eyes searching Alex's face, and then, before Alex could respond, "Let's get a drink."

He took his hand off Alex's shoulder and Alex felt the lack of weight where the warm pressure had been. Before he could agree to anything, Mateo had turned and headed down Gardenias. They walked single file, away from the neon of Avenida Juárez and into the streaming headlights of city buses and taxis. The silhouettes of passing people temporarily blocked the beams of light, and when Alex glanced up at Mateo again, it looked like Mateo was limping.

"Hey." Alex darted around a man in a broad-brimmed cowboy hat, and under the light of the PHARMACIA 24/7 sign, he saw that yes, Mateo was practically dragging his left leg. "You're . . ." He realized that he could not immediately think of the verb "to limp," and then when it did flash into his mind, he paused: *cojear*, he felt sure that was the verb, but it sounded suddenly so much like *cojer*, to fuck. *Estas cojeando . . . cojiendo.* "Your leg," he said instead, "what happened to your leg?"

Mateo halted and turned toward the wall to light a cigarette, hand cupped, smoke leaking out between his fingers. "In Acapulco," he said. "Stupid fucking Hijo del Diablo hits me with the metal chair, blam, down on my legs and my fucking knee is motherfucked." He started walking again but slower now, keeping his eyes on Alex's face, their arms brushing against each other. "There's a balloon in your knee, you know, like under the kneecap. It exploded. The doctor had a needle *this* fucking long, he put some kind of solution in there. Here, feel how swollen." He paused and rolled his jeans up. People swerved around them on the sidewalk where they both bent in a sudden, intimate focus. The knee was wrapped with a snarl of yellowed rags and Alex couldn't tell if the mound around it was the swelling or just the immense amount of bandages; the bandages did not look particularly clean. Mateo grabbed his hand. "Here, feel," he said, and then, looking up, still holding Alex's hand, "Damn, your fingers are cold." He shifted and his jeans rolled down, catching on the bandages. "You need a better coat, some gloves or something." He lifted his own jacket and pressed Alex's hand up under it, against the heat of his stomach.

EL FRONTERIZO WAS a dark box of a bar, a few sconced lights along the walls and a gleaming wooden counter crosshatched with a hundred nicks and signatures. At the back of the room a group of old men in leather vests and guayaberas played lotería, the gritón standing before them on a small wooden box and calling out the dichos in a reedy voice like a soapbox preacher. Alex took a table near the back and Mateo walked to the bar. If Alex ordered, the bartender would hear his accent and the whole feeling in the room would change. It was unavoidable sometimes, but also exhausting, how it tilted like that. He was working hard on improving his accent, though, and he sounded now a little less like he was parroting classroom phrases. He'd studied Spanish intensively in college and his sentences and conjugations were nearly always correct. But that was the problem, if you studied something too much you ended up sounding like a textbook.

He watched Mateo chat with the bartender and listened to the rattle of the pinto beans in the old men's hands as they tipped their faces to their bingo boards, waiting for the right phrase so they could cover up their images: rooster, devil, lady, umbrella, skull, bell, scorpion.

Mateo lurched toward the table, dragging his leg, drinks in hand, and Alex rose to meet him. He handed Alex the tequilas and turned back for the sangrita, "little blood," they called it, the spicy citrus-juice chaser. At the table they sat face-to-face but did not look at one another. Alex liked the crisp contrast of the tequila and sangrita beside each other in their little cups, the clear liquor and red, red juice. He sipped from each and focused on the lotería game.

"Why do you run, coward?" the gritón chanted, holding up a blue card with a man brandishing a long hooked knife. "You who has such a good blade." His voice threaded out over the rhythm of the jukebox. "Here we have the one and only lamp of the lovers."

Alex watched Mateo shift in his chair, take a drink, and lean back, eyes fixed on the gritón. The air was dark around him and full of the yeast-sweet smell of seventy-five years of spilled beer.

"It is he who waits who most despairs."

The decorative red lights strung from the rafters reflected in Mateo's black eyes, his lashes so long they nearly brushed his cheek. His dark hair was shaved short on one side and grown out long on the other, combed across his forehead and tucked behind his ear. He was not a large man, but something about the athleticism of his body made him seem bigger than his actual frame.

"The world is a ball and we a great mob."

"¡Lotería!" one of the old men called, and the gritón bent over to inspect his board, then snapped his head and the men all swept their cards clean with a clattering of dry beans and the gritón began again. "Here we have no one less, no one more, than the one who ate the sugar." He held high an orange card with a sharply dressed black man with a cane.

"What's that one supposed to mean?" Alex said, leaning into Mateo who looked up at him as if he'd woken from some deep reverie.

"The little black man who ate sugar?" Alex went on.

"I am black, but lovely, O ye daughters of Jerusalem?"

"I didn't know you knew your Bible verses."

Mateo shrugged. He drank from his tequila glass and then looked up at Alex. "What does it mean, black but lovely, Pastor?"

Alex shook his head. "No, don't call me that."

"No? Pastorcito?"

Alex shook his head again, but he was smiling. He drank down the last of his tequila and reached for his sangrita. "The 'but' is translated from a Hebrew word that can mean 'but' or 'and.' So she could be apologizing for her blackness or proud of it."

"That line is from the Songs part, right?"

"Song of Songs."

"Yeah, that was always my favorite. It reads almost like a dirty book. Or a soap opera," Mateo said. "'Love is strong as death; jealousy is cruel as the grave; many waters cannot quench love, neither can the floods drown it.'"

His face, as he spoke, turned soft and distant, his eyes half closed, his lips feeling the syllables, speaking them low but sure over the voice of the gritón and the flittering jukebox accordion. Behind him the bartender wiped the counter mechanically and the fan spun overhead with its garlands of dust.

"I opened to my beloved, but my beloved had turned and gone. My soul failed me when he spoke. I sought him, but found him not; I called him, but he gave me no answer."

Mateo's words stayed there in the thick air. Words from the most familiar book in the whole world, bent into something private, secret somehow. Alex was pinned to his chair with a pure, bold longing to touch him, run his fingers along Mateo's cheek, pull him in.

"You know the whole thing?" he said.

"No." Mateo shook his head and looked away.

"You remember more than I do."

"I just liked it, as a kid." He pushed himself up from the table, wincing as he moved his left leg. "Come on, let's go."

CALLEJON CAMOMILA DEAD-ENDED against a cinder-block wall spray painted with election slogans and decked out with a basketball hoop made from a plastic crate. Mateo's rented room was on the corner of Camomila and Ignacio Mariscal. One set of windows overlooked the pickup basketball games on Camomila, dogs snuffling through trash, an old woman sweeping her steps as she waited for the water truck; the other ones looked out onto Mariscal, the running pink lights of Tito's Sex Shop and Playboy Disco across the way.

Mateo fumbled and dropped the key in the dark of the stairwell.

"Fucking shit, motherfuck, it's so fucking dark in here. One day I'll step on a dead body and not even know it."

Alex waited, two steps behind him, fingers stuffed in the pockets of his jacket.

The door was a metal panel with a tiny window. It squeaked as it swung in and clapped closed behind them. The air shifted, stood still. Mateo did not turn on the light and Alex was glad, for almost immediately tears came to his eyes, his throat locking up unbreathably tight as Mateo's fingers unbuttoned his jacket, found his belt—stopped—moved up to his mouth, pulled him in. Their lips together, incredibly, profoundly warm in that cold room.

The mattress was in the far corner and they stagger-danced there, Alex's eyes adjusting as he peeled off Mateo's coat, lifted his T-shirt, and bent to kiss him, there where Mateo had pressed his hand an hour ago. The soft hair tasted of salt and smelled faintly of laundry soap. When they reached the mattress, everything sped up, their breath, their movements. They wrangled off all their clothes, Alex jerking at Mateo's jeans, then remembering the knee, pausing, Mateo finishing it for him. Their dicks hard in the thin light, nipples stiff. Alex thought—stopped thinking. Wanted—nothing more. An ocean wave ripping, rising, rising. They crashed. Hearts like hummingbirds. He fell across the mattress, sinking slowly back into the room, the night, the cold, shocked that the world seemed to have gone on and not felt this enormous axial shift.

Mateo's hand pressed against Alex's heart as if to hold it in place. The ceiling above them brightened and dimmed with passing headlights. The plaster was cracked and the paint peeling down in strips, forming a particular constellation that Alex knew instinctively he would never forget, no matter how long he lived. There was a cluster of three pockmarks whose origin they had argued about. Bullet holes, Alex said when he saw them on a wind-bright morning after Mateo first moved in and Alex skipped class to come see this place where they could be alone together, a place that was not an hourly motel or movie theater. No, not bullets, Mateo had said, insisting that a woman had tried to install hanging lanterns there, or someone had opened three bottles of champagne and the corks bit into the ceiling in fierce celebration.

"Where did you go?" Mateo leaned up on one elbow, his face over Alex's, eyes searching. "My little pastor is gone down into his garden, to the beds of spices, to feed in the gardens, and to gather lilies?"

Alex laughed. Hand on the back of Mateo's neck, he pulled him in, kissing his mouth, his cheek, the stubble above his lip. Mateo lay back again, smiling. His hair fell from his forehead and Alex could see the shiny skein of scar tissue there, a muddled pattern of razor bites on top of razor bites. It was a mark that any extreme luchador carried and sometimes he seemed crassly proud of it; when he was lost in thought, forgetting that Alex was in the room, his fingers went to the scars, tracing them over and over again. But also, he seemed a little horrified by it. *It's really ugly, isn't it?* he asked often.

Mateo pulled a yellow rayon blanket up from the foot of the mattress and lay down again facing Alex. "How was your school meeting?"

"You remembered?" Alex turned, reaching for him under the blanket so that their arms tangled together.

"You never think I will remember anything about your life." The pale light from the high windows hit his hair but left his face in shadow.

"No, that's not true." Alex propped his head up on his hand. "Dr. Nelson wanted to believe that I was an idiot for changing my thesis and for wanting to write about lucha libre. Like how is lucha libre not just a joke with a fixed ending? But now she thinks I'm a genius." He couldn't help but smile widely. "'So original,' she kept saying."

"And what did you tell her about lucha?" There was an edge to Mateo's voice, a tone that came in sometimes when they spoke of other people's ideas of lucha. He was always eager to talk about wrestling, but if the conversation shifted to jokes or questions about fixing the matches, he snapped like a cat petted one too many times.

"How it's a staging ground for contradictory sociological domains: tradition and modernity, violence and security, machismo and feminism."

"A contradictory what?"

"Nothing. The academics want you to say it in the most garbled way, otherwise—"

"You don't think I'm smart enough? To understand?"

"No, no, that's not what I'm saying at all, *they* want us to talk about it in this stupid—"

"I have to pee." Mateo stood. The blanket fell from him and the smooth muscles of his shoulders and arms were silhouetted against the light of the window, his butt so perfect that Alex stiffened again immediately.

Mateo moved slowly toward the kitchen sink, favoring his left leg. The bathroom was down the hall, one shared toilet for the whole floor.

Alex swallowed, his throat thick with desire. "What did the doctor say about your knee?"

Mateo's piss hit the porcelain sink with a loud syncopation. "Antibiotics, anti-inflammatory, pain meds."

"It has stitches?"

Mateo nodded and turned to Alex. "You have to go back to El Paso now?"

"No, Elana's gone." Alex lifted the blanket and patted the mattress and then felt suddenly strange, as if he were calling a pet to him, and those words, *Elana's gone*, sounded awful and too final out loud.

"Gone?" Mateo came back to the bed.

"For a week, back to Virginia. She left today." He wanted to reach out and pull Mateo to him, but it seemed suddenly inappropriate. He almost never spoke of Elana here unless he absolutely had to. He looked away. "I can stay," he said. "All week."

Mateo bent over, took hold of Alex's chin, and turned his face, pressed his thumb into Alex's lower lip. "You stupid asshole, why didn't you say so?"

"I told you, I know I told you, I said I'd have this whole week in December."

"A whole week, you never told me." Mateo let go of his face and straightened up.

"Why does it matter? I'm here now and—"

"I have to go get my son."

"Now?"

"Alicia's friend is getting married and she has some bridesmaid party."

Two months ago, when Mateo had broken things off with a girl in Mexico City and had stopped calling a Juárez girl he'd been fucking, both women had figured out how to get in touch with Mateo's wife, Alicia, and had told her all about their affairs. Mateo had sworn to her those relationships were over, but she was dizzy with rage and had kicked him out. Now she lived alone with their five-year-old son, Martín, in Mateo's condo in a gated neighborhood near the airport, while Mateo stayed in this concrete room on the edge of the red-light district. With the expenses for Martín and Alicia, and money for his parents, he couldn't afford anything more than this. It didn't matter, though, he told Alex, he was traveling all the time anyway, sometimes six fights a week, each one in a different city.

"She won't let you see him for almost a month and now suddenly she needs a babysitter?"

Mateo shrugged and bent over a pile of clothes on the floor, rummaging through them in the dark, separating his own from Alex's. "I'll be back after a while."

"I'm not staying here alone." Alex was surprised by the nervous sound of his own voice.

Mateo looked over at him. "You want to come hang out with Martín?"

Alex had never met him before, had seen only one outdated photo. He nodded.

"Well, okay, I guess." Mateo flipped on the overhead light and they both closed their eyes.

THE DOS AMIGOS NIGHTCLUB was on the corner of Avenida Juárez and Acequia Madre, one of the swankier clubs, with pink and blue strobe lights around the front door and an armed guard in the parking lot. Seven p.m. and the night was barely beginning as Mateo and Alex walked up Mariscal past the table dancers with duffel bags over one shoulder, anonymous for now in their jeans and sweatshirts, heading to work at Eduardo's, Irma's, the Bunny Club, and the valets in pleather jackets, pacing and smoking in puddles of neon. Mateo paid a steep weekly price to park his Lexus in the Dos Amigos lot, but it was his only option in this neighborhood, he said, you couldn't leave it on the street or it would be gone in half an hour. When he first rented his room here, he and Alex had known each other for a month, and though they never talked about it, Alex knew he could have rented a cheap room in a hundred other neighborhoods, but this one was a ten-minute walk from the international bridge where they always met.

"Hey, what's up?" Mateo raised his hand to the guard in the entrance of the Dos Amigos parking lot and the young man turned, AR-15 slung across his chest. His face changed from a mask of bored don't-fuck-with-me attitude to a toothy grin.

"Hey, dude, what's up?" The guard shifted his enormous gun and pounded fists with Mateo.

"How's my baby?" Mateo nodded toward his Lexus, glowing creamy opal in the back of the lot.

"Ah, well, she's lonely, you know, she misses her papi." The guard laughed, glanced at Alex, and bobbed his head. Without his professional anger face on he looked about seventeen.

"You've been taking good care of her, though?"

"Well, clearly, yes, she's the most important."

Mateo grinned. "Yeah, that's the way." He reached into his pocket and pulled out a wad of bills, peeled three off the top, and held them out to the guard. "This is just for you, don't tell the guys inside, but I know you work hard."

He click-clicked the Lexus open from halfway across the lot and turned to Alex, slapping him on the shoulder. "You hungry? We'll take Martín to eat. Alicia won't let me hang with him at the condo, but I'm not taking him back to that fucking room."

Mateo ran his hand across the top of the Lexus, opened the door, and slid inside while Alex made his way around to the passenger's door. He always felt like a child in this car, daunted by the clean luxury of it, completely out of place in his dirty jeans and worn jacket. It also planted a small nauseous anxiety in his stomach, an itching question of what he was doing with a man like Mateo. How could he even be attracted to someone who placed so much importance on something so stupid and consumeristic?

"I know." Mateo turned the engine over and reached for the glove box. "I like this car too much, right? You're just jealous, though. You think I love her more than you."

Alex blushed and hated himself for blushing, the heat in his cheeks matched by a cold weight in his stomach.

Mateo pulled a tiny glass vial from the glove box and unscrewed the top.

"You're gonna get high *now*?" Alex said as Mateo lifted the miniature spoon to his nose and snorted.

"It's the medicines they gave me for my knee, they make me tired all the time."

"Right, of course, your opiates make you tired so you need to balance it out with coke."

Mateo shrugged and tossed the vial back into the glove box. "It's only a tiny bit," he said, grabbing Alex's chin and pulling his face to him. He kissed him hard and pulled away quick.

THEY DROVE SOUTH on Francisco Villa past the red cupolas of the old customs house and the Guadalupe Cathedral beyond, her bell towers glittering in the night. Three blocks down, at the statue of the slave liberator, the avenues spilled into one another and wound around the unbending lines of the railway. The sidewalks were colored with little tables and scraps of plastic fashioned into flags to draw the eye to sneakers, jackets, pocket mirrors, household cleaners, and wheeled carts of gorditas, elotes, churros dripping with caramel. The vendors turned their backs to the wind and Mateo drove on past the carnival of buses that churned in toward the center from the maquiladoras. Old school buses, deemed too unsafe for US children, had been painted with bird plumage, outfitted with spinning hubcaps, and stenciled with Playboy bunnies. They roved the city day and night, purple lights and techno spilling forth, while inside the maquila workers draped themselves across the worn seats, exhausted into a state beyond dreams.

Mateo gave the Lexus more gas and they streamed south, where everything widened into one long flight of road, the moon rising behind scattered clouds, the car thrumming, headlights burrowing on into the night, and in these stretches, with nothing but the hush-hush of tires against road, Alex could understand the desire for a new car. Mateo had taken him up on the periférico once so he could see the whole jittering bowl of Juárez down below and then south to Samalayuca, where everything dropped away. Here in the desert, there was so much space, everything scattered under the sun, even the buildings themselves seeming to hunker, then disappear. Concrete and cinder block in various states of hope and decay, rebar poking out the top for a future that might include a second floor, while the concrete eroded in the sand. Alex came from a landscape of ridges and switchback curves, everything up on top of everything else, tin and wood, and coal smoke snaking up the mountainside. Back home, the sky was a shiver up there between sharp green shoulders. Land that cut deep. Sandstone, shale, limestone, clay. He had thought vertically all his life, but out here it flipped. The land rushed out away from you, both endless and dissipating.

Juárez had been and would always be a weigh station. Even for those born and raised and dying here, the city had a feeling of not quite being there yet. You saw the promise of it wavering in the desert-mirage distance, always coming, always going. Nothing really was very old, but everything was ancient. It had gone back to the earth—built with mud, adobe, whitewash—built for now for the moment, a small part of the long time. It was a map of the future of everywhere, how everything became nothing eventually.

At the Municipio Libre roundabout Mateo slowed and lit a cigarette. Sparse snowflakes gusted in the headlights and factory buildings rose up on both sides of the road. Great windowless whales, they stretched long and silent behind bales of concertina wire and floodlights. ADC, Electrolux, Bosch, Foxconn, Flextronics, Lexmark, Delphi, Visteon, Johnson Controls, Lear, Boeing, Cardinal Health, Yazaki, Sumitomo, Siemens. Farther south the maquiladoras gave way to enormous luxury shopping malls that looked almost identical to the factories from the outside; you could mistake one for the other except that the shopping plazas were tightly encircled not by barbed wire but by the deathless neon of Little Caesars, McDonald's, KFC.

South of the roundabout, Alicia lived in a gated community on Milky Way Avenue. From a distance the rows of identical windows peering out over the razor-wire fence looked like army barracks, but closer up they reminded Alex of images of Martian colonies he'd conjured as a child. Endless rows of identical buildings set against the cosmic stillness of a gigantic empty parking lot. Cineplex and Walmart outlined under the Sierra de Juárez.

Mateo rolled down his window and chatted with the guard at the gatehouse and the iron bars retracted and they drove in. Many of the condos were still under construction and even the completed ones had mounds of red dirt piled outside the front doors and pipes jutting up out of raw earth yards. They were narrow two-story gingerbread houses with tiny barred windows and concrete cornices sculpted along the roofs, painted beige or sand or baby-shit yellow to hide the constant dust.

"You gotta stay here," Mateo said, and parked the car.

Alex watched him walk past a row of lime trees, their leaves splotched and curling under the orange glow of the streetlamp, and up the path to the single lit house in a row of darkness and quiet. He looked back once, just before entering, and smiled his sweet smile that never failed to strike Alex so that suddenly his body felt too small and everything he was experiencing in it spilled out around him and refused to fit.

He'd first met Mateo on a sweltering evening in the second week of September. Elana had been busy arranging things in their new apartment in El Paso and Alex had crossed the border by himself to meet up with the Kasa kids for a lucha libre event where Lalo was going to be wrestling. They were all there at the end of the bridge, in the dust and churning traffic, and seeing the gang of them there, waiting for him (Ana, her braids swirling as she pushed Luis nearly out into the traffic, and María grabbing him back, the rest of them on the sidewalk behind), Alex felt a bell strike inside his chest and ripple out with the deepest sense of yearning and belonging he'd ever experienced. Those were *his* people, waiting for *him*.

As he crossed the street, he noticed that there was one among them whom he did not know, a man with his hair half-shaved, half-long, and his clothes neater and cleaner, his shoes much newer than the rest.

"Lalo thinks he can wrestle," Chucho said. "But Mateo here is professional."

"Shut up, you idiot." Luis punched Chucho in the arm.

"What?" Chucho jumped back.

"It doesn't matter," Mateo said. "This guy's American, right? He doesn't know anything." And he turned to Alex and smiled.

It would be a while before Alex understood this exchange and knew enough about lucha libre to see that Mateo had to guard his anonymity, that no one but his family could know who El Vengador del Norte was. That evening all Alex knew was that he was part of something bigger than himself, part of a group that was part of a ritual through which he finally, physically understood Aristotle's catharsis.

They'd taken their seats in metal folding chairs, the muraled walls sweating as the space filled with families, grandmothers, babies, and teenagers and the temperature rose until he almost didn't feel the heat anymore, it was all a part of a great liquid emotion that washed everything else away. The referee checked the ropes of the ring while the concession vendors made their way up the aisles and then suddenly the lights dimmed and the announcer's voice boomed out of the speakers, "Goooood evening, ladies and gentlemen!" followed by the twangy guitar and lilting voice of Juan Gabriel. The crowd rose to their feet and erupted into a raucous sing-along with "El Noa Noa." And then it was on: a man in a red Lycra bodysuit and black mask bounded out of a back room, swung between the ropes, and rolled into the ring, rising up to cheers from one half of the arena while a man in a sparkling green bikini bottom and silver mask strutted around the other side of the ring and leapt up to a scattered applause. The two circled each other, closing in tighter and tighter until they locked, grappled, and fell to the mat. They separated, and the black-masked fighter stood and swung in again with a backspring and grab to the neck that sent the silver-masked fighter flying against the ropes, and the night rushed on like this. Estrella Diabolika vs. Guerrera followed by Arkero vs. Super Comando, El Libertador (Lalo) vs. Black Fish. Some with masks, others without, all with flash and sequins and sweat. The crowd roaring and surging around them, cursing and laughing and booing and praying and railing. Akantus vs. El Dragon, Crazy Fly vs. Meteoro, and finally Romano the Roman, sweeping to victory over Conan the Barbarian.

Alex walked out of the arena dripping with sweat and glowing with a rush he had not felt in years, a feeling he thought he had left behind forever in the tent revivals of his youth. He took the bus back to the Kasa, grinning the whole way and pestering Lalo with questions, How did he train? When was his next fight? Lalo shrugged it off, said he didn't fight much, didn't have time now that he was in university, and besides there were other more politically important things to do. He looked straight at Mateo when he said this last bit and then turned to Alex, "If you want to know about lucha, ask Mateo, he'll show you." And Mateo had laughed, but he'd given Alex his number and two days later they met up.

Mateo had seemed shy and serious without the gang of Kasa kids around him. They met in the park by the monument to Benito Juárez and greeted each other awkwardly. Mateo went for a handshake, nodding and squinting against the blazing sun. He insisted on driving Alex in his car.

"You didn't expect this, huh?" He flashed a smile at Alex as he click-clicked the Lexus open from half a block away. "I love Lalo and them," he said, "and I agree it's good to put your community ahead of your individual success, but I'm proud of this car."

He cranked the air-conditioning and scanned the radio dial, explaining all the while how he was from a town in southern Chihuahua but had come to Juárez after high school. His father had lived here in his twenties and Mateo had always wanted to know it. He'd met Lalo and Damian in a street market where he had sold burritos, and Lalo and Damian had a booth with paintings and jewelry. They had invited him to a punk show at the Kasa—Elektroduendes on their Mexican tour. After that he had lived in the Kasa with them for a few years and Lalo introduced him to lucha. They trained together, but Lalo was never as serious about lucha as Mateo was. Now Mateo worked professionally for a big promotion company and they sent him all over the country, different fights in different states each day. But it all felt more real here, he said, Juárez was the place he learned to love lucha, and he wanted to show its raw heart to Alex.

They drove west into the setting sun, dust shimmering in pinkish-brown halos around the cinder-block buildings while Mateo talked about the old-time border wrestlers, Indio Medina, Tigre Romano, Rosy Solis, Chino Chow, Gorila Ramos, and Babe Sharon, Mateo's own instructor who had wrestled in drag and coached young fighters until the day he died.

"He dropped, in the ring, had a heart attack on my birthday, three years ago," Mateo said.

There was a special subset of wrestlers, he said, who dressed like women. Exoticos. "It's kind of a joke, but not really," Mateo said. "Babe Sharon, he was proud, it wasn't a silly thing for him, he was an amazing wrestler and everyone respected him. The outfits and mannerisms, maybe you could sort of see it as homophobic, but I don't think so." He glanced at Alex. "That's not how Babe Sharon saw it anyway. He was out and proud."

They were winding their way out of the center of the city, off into the colonias toward the Arena Anahuac where Mateo had trained. He drove slow and Alex watched him from the corner of his eye as he lit a cigarette and scanned the road. He was muscled but not grotesquely, just clean and smooth, at ease with the power of his body.

"It bothers you if I smoke in the car?" he said, and Alex shook his head. "You want to know something embarrassing?" He took a long drag on the cigarette. "I don't think I can remember how to get to the arena." He laughed a sort of cough-laugh and looked away out the window. "This is my town." He waved his cigarette to encompass the tienda on the corner, the little single-story homes and beyond, the endless streets of Juárez. "Everywhere I wrestle I'm 'the wrestler from Juárez,' but they keep me on the road all the time." He shook his head, slowed the car and pulled off to the side, rolled the window down, and called to a boy dribbling a basketball on the broken sidewalk. "Hey, compa, you know the Arena Anahuac?"

For all the lore it seemed to hold, Anahuac was small, nothing but a little concrete pen, four walls decked with plank bleachers and no roof. Mateo said that when he first started training the room had had a ceiling, but it was caving in and the wrestlers hit it each time they did a flip and so they had torn off the roof and now juniper trees sprouted from behind the rows of seats. None of that mattered, though, he said, for this place was magical. You could come from nothing, piss-poor nothing, and put on a mask and transform everything. "Here in the ring, you can dream," he had said, his arm sweeping out as he turned, face tilted up into the last rays of sun. And Alex, watching, had realized with a sudden terror that he wanted more than anything to kiss this man.

"WAIT, WAIT, WAIT," a voice called now, and Alex looked up to see a little boy stumbling down the steps of the condo, silhouetted against the light of the doorway where Mateo stood, holding a child's backpack and talking to a woman. Alex had imagined that Alicia would look like one of the actresses from a telenovela: long brown hair streaked blonde, frosted nails like talons, and mounds of cleavage pushed up out of a tiny V-neck shirt, but she was actually small and nondescript: ponytail, sneakers, and royal-blue tracksuit.

"Slow down, don't go into the road." Mateo turned and followed the boy. He click-clicked the Lexus, though it was already open. Alex was pretty sure that click and flash of lights was the main reason Mateo loved the car so much, the rush he got every time he pressed that button.

"Alex," he called as he opened the back door and lifted the kid inside. "I present to you Don Martín!"

Martín laughed. "Gimme my bag, Papá."

"Martín, this is my friend Alex."

Martín unzipped his backpack and pulled out a bottle of strawberry soda. He was small for a five-year-old, with hair the same burnt-straw color as Alex's and a round face with hazel-green eyes.

Mateo settled himself in behind the wheel and turned to Alex. "How about the Ribs House? I know you hate it, I know it's not 'real México,' but it's got a playroom for kids."

Alex shrugged.

"You judge me."

"No," Alex said. "I get it."

Mateo put the car in Reverse. "I just gotta stop by a pharmacy first. You want some ribs, mi'jo?" He glanced in the rearview mirror.

"Chicken nuggets," Martín said.

The pharmacy was in a strip mall, wedged between a barber shop and a nail salon. Mateo left Martín in the car with Alex, and they watched the barber pole spinning into infinity, the silence growing around them until Martín cried, "My papá?"

"He's coming." Alex leaned forward to try and look inside the pharmacy. He could see nothing but the banks of fluorescent lights hanging from the ceiling.

A woman locked the nail salon door and walked across the parking lot with a tap, tap, tap of her black heels. The barber pole spun.

"My papá?"

When he finally came, Mateo was furious, ripping the door open and revving the engine. "They wouldn't give me my fucking meds."

"You have a prescription?"

"I had one, I used it before, but now I'm out and I need more."

He swerved around the parking lot and back onto the main road. "One more stop before your nuggets, okay, mi'jo? Then nuggets, ice cream, whatever you want." To Alex he said, "I've got a friend who works at this other pharmacy, we'll just go by real quick."

They flashed north again, Mateo's cigarette smoke disappearing out the window. This other pharmacy was in a row of rundown pawnshops.

"Real quick," Mateo said, and locked the door behind him.

In the windows of the pawnshop, behind iron grates, watchbands and switchblades gleamed dully. Alex turned around to watch Martín, in the dark of the backseat, running his tongue around and around the top of his pop bottle. "Do you like kindergarten?"

Martín looked up at him. "You know my papá could smash your face in with just one fist."

"Uh, yeah, that's probably true." Alex looked away toward the pharmacy.

"I gotta pee."

When Mateo returned this time, it was with a grin and a white paper bag in hand. Alex opened his door and got out before Mateo had reached the car. "He's gotta pee."

"Who? What?"

"Your son. He's had to pee for a while."

"Well, we're going to the restaurant now, get back in the car."

Mateo opened the driver's door and sat down.

"Papá, I have to pee!" Martín cried.

"We're going to the Ribs House now."

"No, no, I have to pee *now.*"

"Hold it a minute."

"Noooo."

"Don't whine."

"Buuut . . ." Martín's voice broke in the middle of the word and he began sobbing, his little shoulders shaking with each breath.

"God, fine, okay, don't cry." Mateo got out and opened the back door, pulling his son roughly across the seat. "Just pee here, okay? Don't cry like a little baby."

Alex's stomach tightened as he watched and remembered the long pleather seat of his father's car and his father's voice in the front, practicing his sermon, his words dipping and rising and Alex's own voice, small at first but growing, "Dad . . . Dad . . . hey, Dad."

MARTÍN FELL ASLEEP before they reached the Ribs House. Mateo was fiddling with the radio dial when Alex saw blue lights in the rear windshield. He willed the cop to move on, pull around, and chase after the car ahead of them, but it stayed there at the back bumper, the lights shimmering over sleeping Martín.

"Mateo," Alex said, "police."

Mateo looked up at the mirror and his face dropped. A cold unease entered the car. He pulled to the side of the road. "Can you see? I can't see. Are they municipal?" His voice was strained and he had opened the console and was digging, shuffling. "Fuck, where's my license?" he said. "They're not Federales, no?"

Alex could not make out the markings on the car. He could not stop thinking about the reports he'd read of all the missing and dead in northern Mexico who were last seen with police. He thought of the vial of coke, the bag of opiates, Martín sleeping in a puddle of strawberry soda in the backseat.

A flashlight beam crawled along the windows until it reached Mateo's face. He blinked, rolled the window halfway down.

"Good evening, sir."

"Your papers." The cop was young with small hands and a pencil-thin mustache, but his face held the same still seriousness that Alex had seen on hunters back when he had gone with his father into the woods. A focused patience that presumed complete power.

"Yes, sir, of course, that's what I was looking for. It seems, I must have left them at the house, see I was just taking my kid out for dinner and—"

"And who is that?" The white beam of the flashlight played over Alex's face and he closed his eyes.

"A friend. An American friend."

"American?"

Alex opened his eyes and watched the young cop calculating this information.

"Yes. Was I driving too fast back there?"

"Taillight." The cop was still looking at Alex.

"Oh, okay, I hadn't noticed. You won't mind if I make a quick phone call?"

The cop snapped his attention back to Mateo. "Who do you know?"

"Rosales."

"Rosales?"

Mateo held up his cell phone. "I'll just call really quick and explain my mistake so we can arrange to fix it later, when I'm not taking my son to dinner."

The cop's face tightened. He turned his flashlight off and looked away, then back to Mateo. "What's your name?"

"I work with Neto."

The cop nodded. "Wait here," he said, and walked back to his car.

The blue lights flashed rhythmically over the seats, and when Alex looked out his window, he saw that they had come to a stop almost directly in front of the mansion of Juan Gabriel. There was a tall filigreed white iron gate and beyond that the Moorish balconies and rounded towers of the melancholic megastar's Juárez home. Snow was falling harder now, great wet flakes tumbling, hitting the windshield with audible splats, the windshield wipers thwack-thwacking and out of the backseat a little voice calling, "Papá?"

"Look at the snow, mi'jo!" Mateo said.

"Where are we?"

"Visiting Juanga."

"What?"

"Look, there's his house. He wanted us to come by and see how beautiful his house is in the snow."

Martín sat up and scooted across the seat to the window, his small face pale in the shimmer of the snow and police lights. "That house?"

"Yes, mi'jo, he wanted you to see it."

The cop pulled up beside the Lexus and rolled down his passenger's window. "Okay," he called out. "Rosales says don't worry about it." And he drove away into the wet black streets.

"Who's Rosales?" Alex said.

"Police chief."

"You know the chief of police?"

"Not really."

"Well enough to call in favors."

Mateo shrugged.

"And who's Neto?"

"That guy I told you about." Mateo put the car in drive. "The one who's sponsoring me."

The Ribs House was closed by the time they made it there, and Martín was starving. There was a McDonald's across the street, the neon-yellow *M* glowing in the falling snow. Mateo looked at Alex. His hair had fallen down over his right eye and he was almost smiling. "You won't like me at all anymore," he said. "I eat at McDonald's and I'm friends with cops."

"Oh, come on, shut up." Alex punched him in the arm. "Let's go, Martín's hungry."

Violations of the punk moral code had become an ongoing joke between them. They both held a nostalgia for punk, although neither of them was really committed to it anymore. Mateo definitely was not and Alex could feel his allegiance slipping. Back in Virginia, in college, punk gave him the feeling that he was on the outside of the mainstream because that was where he wanted to be—not because he would never be accepted. It was a fuck-you community and it had felt good there, but here, in Mexico, he wasn't so sure he wanted to be always in defiance.

At McDonald's, only the drive-through was open. A young woman extended her bare arms from the warm window, snow gusting up as she handed them huge steaming bags smelling of salt and grease. They parked and turned off the windshield wipers and the snow piled onto the glass until they were entirely enclosed. The light from the parking lot lampposts barely filtered through and a heavy quiet settled over them, nothing but the churning of the heater and the hiss of wet tires on the street, invisible beyond the white-blind curtain.

Martín fell asleep again before he'd even finished his chicken nuggets. Mateo called Alicia's phone, but she did not answer and so they headed back to the Mariscal. It was too snowy to keep driving around all night and too late for anything other than bars to be open.

"He can rest in my room until Alicia gets home," Mateo said. "You can carry him up? I'll park and be right there." He pressed the key into Alex's palm.

The street was sloppy with half-frozen snow. Martín stirred and moaned as Alex lifted him. In the dark stairwell their fogging breath was the only thing visible. The sounds of car horns and garbled shouts echoed up from below and each door that he passed added its own rhythm of TV, music, conversation. Alex concentrated on not falling, concentrated on the warm weight of Mateo's son in his arms and the cold metal key in his palm. He felt the tip-shift of the moment, the strangeness of being here in this place where no one else in the world except Mateo knew that he was, holding this child, and entering this room.

As Alex laid him on the mattress, Martín began mumbling. Alex turned the light on.

"It's cold," Martín cried, curling over and covering his eyes.

Alex cast about for a lighter or matches. The room was nearly empty. The mattress in the far corner, a sink and two-burner hot plate on a laminate countertop, a card table littered with Carta Blanca bottles and cigarette butts, two folding chairs, a mop bucket, and a small gas heater. The wall beside the bed was decorated with a collage of posters featuring El Vengador del Norte in his black-and-silver mask and hooded cape, posing with his arms raised in victory.

"I'm cold," Martín said again.

Alex found a box of matches and struck them, one after the other, over the pilot hole of the heater, anticipating the ripple of blue flame, but nothing came, not even the scent of gas.

"Where am I?"

Alex looked over at Martín. He was sitting up now, hugging his arms around himself, his face scrunched and serious.

"Lie down and rest, okay?"

"Papá?"

"He went to park the car."

Alex joined him on the mattress and pulled the yellow blanket up over Martín's lap, his stomach roiling at the image that came to mind: the blanket, just hours earlier, falling from Mateo's waist as he stood and walked naked to the sink.

"My papá?"

"Soon."

He tried to get Martín to lie down under the covers, but the child refused. He wanted his backpack that had been left in the car, his soda, his nuggets, his papá. It seemed that a great deal of time had passed, but Alex had no way of knowing; he'd left his cell phone back in El Paso—his departure from there feeling now like a completely different day or week—and the room had no clock. Light flashed across the ceiling, then disappeared, snowflakes skimming up and then drifting back down past the windowpanes. The TV in the room next door shut off. Laughter from the street rose and fell away again. Martín chirped, "Where's my papá? My papá? My papá?" and with each repetition, Alex felt a panic rising in them both. They sat side by side, the yellow blanket across their knees, and stared at the door. Mateo was hurt? Someone had carjacked him and he'd fought back. Mateo was an ass? He'd stopped into a bar for a few beers before returning to the room. No, Mateo was hurt. No, Mateo was just an ass. With each "my papá?" Alex's mind skipped back and forth. Here he was, in a cold little room in the red-light district of Juárez with a five-year-old boy who belonged to a man whose full name he did not even know. This did not feel like reality; it felt like a channel you flip to late at night and you know you should not be watching, but you pause to see what it feels like. Reality was a wife named Elana Orenstein who was visiting her family and the two more weeks of classes and presentations he had to stumble through before Christmas break.

"Where is *my papá*?" Martín's voice screeched and Alex stood up.

"Wait," he said, "wait a second, he's coming, but first he has a gift that he wanted me to show you. Have you seen these?" In searching for the matches, Alex had found a bag of plastic El Vengador del Norte action figures from Mateo's promotion company. Four identical little dolls with snap-off capes and adjustable arms.

He held the bag out to Martín.

"For me?"

"Yeah."

Martín gathered them all in his small hands at once, El Vengador times four. He smiled. "Papá dolls!"

The four Vengadores tumbled across the mattress, backflipping from the pillows and pinning one another expertly. Alex sat in a metal chair and watched, smoking butts from Mateo's ashtray. After a long while Martín drooped in exhaustion and Alex covered him with the blanket where he lay, gripping two Vengador dolls. He was fretful in his sleep, though, and the room was so cold and quiet. Alex began to sing to him. The first hymn that came up from memory was perhaps not an appropriate lullaby, but Martín couldn't understand English anyway and so Alex sang, eyes closed, remembering his mother's tremulous voice on Sunday mornings and the wildfire images the words had conjured in him when he was Martín's age.

There's a call that rings from the throne it springs
To those now gone astray
You have blushed with sin as He knocked within
But still you hide your face
Leave the downward path kindle not His wrath
Or He'll set your fields on fire

FIVE

Mateo was pulling the Lexus into its spot in the Dos Amigos lot when his cell phone rang. He expected Alicia, but the numbers that scrolled across the screen were unfamiliar. He wanted to ignore it. He wanted to get back to his room as quickly as possible, not that he didn't trust Alex, he did, but Martín had never spent time with anyone outside of family. The ringing stopped and then started again. He put the car in Park and picked it up.

"Yes?"

"Mateo, how are you? How's the knee?"

"Who is this?"

"You don't recognize me?"

It was Neto, he was sure of it, but he did not want to let it be true. Neto had never called him directly before, their meetings always arranged through Mateo's manager.

"We need to talk," Neto said. "You can join me?"

"Join you?"

"I'm in town for the evening. You know the club Los Padrillos?"

"No," Mateo said. *In town for the evening.* He had never met with Neto anywhere besides DF. Of course, he knew Neto traveled a lot and he'd heard that Neto was originally from Chihuahua, but this did not feel like a coincidence. This felt like a closing in. He had not seen or heard from him since the night in DF, a week and a half ago, when Neto had proposed that Mateo leave Consejo Mundial. Mateo had not said yes to leaving, but he had still not managed to actually say no either.

"It's in the Plaza Bosques del Sol off of Teófilo Borunda, down by the US consulate," Neto said. "Okay?"

"Okay," Mateo said, and the line went dead. His throat felt incredibly dry. He swallowed and put the car in Reverse.

The guard walked over as he nosed out the entrance of the parking lot. "Is everything okay?"

Mateo nodded. "Yeah, I'll be right back, forgot something."

The Dos Amigos was rocking now, strobes of green light and bass rhythms bursting out each time the door opened. Mateo pulled out onto Avenida Juárez and drove south. He'd turned the situation with Neto over in his mind so many times in the past week. He should have gone straight to his manager, Arturo, and told him that Neto was trying to poach him, but it didn't seem possible that Arturo would believe him. Or perhaps Arturo was in on it too; he had been the one who set Mateo up with Neto in the first place. And if you snitched on someone like Neto and he found out, at the very least your career would be dropped. More likely, you'd end up dead. He had to figure out how to say no without offending Neto. He had to do it tonight, put an end to this.

At a stoplight on Reforma he took his pill bottle out of the glove box, swallowed another Oxy, and drove on into the maze of streetlights and palm trees of the nouveau riche. Los Padrillos was in a plaza beside a steakhouse, marooned in a neighborhood of half-built mansions with snow falling softly over the construction sites. The club was obviously new but was built to look as if it were from the Revolution, replete with decorative balconies and a stone facade.

Mateo left the Lexus with the valet and walked up the marble stairs toward the security guard.

"Are you a member, sir?" the guard asked, dipping his head deferentially.

"No, I'm supposed to—"

"ID, please," he said, stepping toward Mateo.

"Shit." Mateo patted his pocket, though he knew he did not have his license there. "See, the thing is—"

"You're Mateo?"

He looked up at the guard's face. The man tipped his head toward the open door. "Go on in," he said.

Mateo looked at him for a long moment and then walked past slowly. The hallway was dark, antlers on the walls and a coat-check boy who looked up hopefully, but Mateo had no coat to check. Another young man with white gloves opened a heavy oak door into the main room, which was darker still and filled with men. A crush of pearl-snap shirts and starched button-ups, voices bobbing and weaving over the music, the air close and heavy with the scent of smoke and hair oil. A conjunto norteño was playing in the back of the room, the accordion pleading and bajo sexto running heavy underneath.

As his eyes adjusted, Mateo began to see faces on the walls. Mouths twisted and frozen in simulated fury. Shiny teeth. Ragged hair. A marbled tiger, jaws pitched in an endless scream. A lynx. A rhino. An enormous mottled bear. And at the far end of the room, a full-body taxidermy of an ice-white lion.

A hand squeezed his shoulder.

He jumped and turned and Neto was there, so close he almost knocked into him. Hair slicked back, pale blue oxford shirt unbuttoned to show a thin, tasteful gold chain. Each time he saw Neto, Mateo was taken again by how small he was. Even in his Lucchese crocodile cowboy boots, he was barely as tall as Mateo, and slim too, but commanding, chin always up, shoulders back, teeth flashing. He was beautiful in a sharp, clean way, markedly middle aged but with delicate beauty in his face.

He kept his hand on Mateo's shoulder. "Let's go upstairs."

Among the crowd his bodyguards, dressed all in black, had nearly disappeared, but as Neto turned, they turned too, a semicircle hovering around him. Neto led Mateo through the bodies, the music and voices engulfing them like a wave, and up a steep staircase to a balcony with leather chairs that overlooked the main floor. Mateo settled himself across from Neto and the bodyguards took up the corners.

Neto slid a slim black case of Insignia cigarettes out of his pocket and offered it to Mateo. "This place is interesting," he said. "You never know who you'll see here." He waved his hand off toward the bar. "There's your mayor. I was just catching up with him before you came. He lives in El Paso now, but apparently the nightlife isn't so great there."

A young waiter in a bright white button-up with a black bow tie came up the stairs carrying a tray with a bottle of Gran Patron. He looked no older than eighteen.

"Thank you." Neto took the bottle and glasses and pressed a bill into the waiter's hand, and then as he was straightening up and lifting the tray, Neto spoke to him again. "Come here," he said. The waiter froze, staring at him. "Just a little bit closer. Come here." The waiter leaned in and Neto turned to look at Mateo. He kept his eyes on Mateo while his hand reached for the waiter's bow tie. He loosened it a little and then his fingers moved to the white shirt and he unbuttoned it slowly—one, two, three—exposing the dark skin below. The waiter stayed there, obediently bent at the waist as Neto traced a finger across his chest. Mateo looked away, his face hot.

"There," Neto exclaimed. "That's much better."

Mateo kept his eyes on the wall and the creamy sconce that covered the lightbulb.

"Mateo, don't you agree?"

He flicked his eyes over to Neto. The waiter brought his hand up to his open shirt and then turned and ducked down the stairs. Mateo watched him disappear into the crowd below and he felt something settle in him, a confirmation of a feeling that he'd tried hard not to know, a feeling he'd had for a while now, the hazy undertow of why Neto had chosen him. He'd feared this. Not that Neto desired him, no, sex would be simple, straightforward. It was not even about being straight or gay. This was something else, a question of power. Cabrón or puto. The one who fucks or the one who gets fucked. Neto had been sniffing at him all along, the way that animals circle each other, smelling for weakness.

Neto poured two snifters of añejo and held one out to Mateo. "I'm sorry about your knee," he said. "You understand the necessity, though, no? The press, the fans, they need a reason for your absence, like an intermission before we announce that you have moved over to the Empresa Estelar." He swirled his tequila and took a sip. "I told you the slogan? 'Star Promotions: The Best Wrestlers in the Galaxy!'"

"You want an outer-space theme?"

"No, no, no, you keep your character, your character is perfect, although we did talk about you transitioning to rudo, right?"

Mateo set his drink down and lit a Delicados. They had not spoken of this, but he had felt it coming all the same. It was not entirely unheard of to switch from good guy to bad guy, but almost always, if a wrestler's career was going well, the transition went the other way around, as El Santo had done. The audience loved a tecnico and loved to hate a rudo. El Vengador was too wrapped up in pride to make a smooth transition to rudo; he was puro orgullo norteño, a clean fighter who took no shortcuts and had no secrets to hide. The one you brought home to mama. He was hometown pride personified.

"I think it will be important." Neto lit his own cigarette and gesticulated with it. "An important part of your story. It needs to be more than just a switch to a new promotion, it needs to be a whole transition that will grab everyone's attention."

"A turning toward evil," Mateo said. He felt like screaming, but instead he smiled. It would be truthful at least, more truthful than his supposed avenging. Might as well come out with a sign around his neck that said I'M OWNED BY THE NARCOS NOW. He looked down at the drink in his hand. Fucking two-thousand-peso bottle of añejo that Neto would probably abandon here when they left. How had he gotten himself into this? How fucking stupid he had been to be impressed by the Hotel Puebla. A room in the

Puebla was nothing to Neto, the Puebla was old and rotting in on itself. Neto should have put Mateo up in a penthouse if he was going to ask him to leave CMLL like this. But he had looked at Mateo and seen that he didn't need to go that far, he'd seen that the Puebla would impress him and he had judged correctly. He had chosen him for this reason, Mateo saw now. A young wrestler who came from nothing, easily impressed and not very well connected, and with a penchant for fucking men. How many different ways can you leave yourself vulnerable? If he were going to tell Neto to go fuck himself, it should have been when Neto first approached him about sponsoring. Now? Now he was in too deep.

"I know I say this a lot, but it's always been a dream of mine, ever since I was small," Neto was saying. "Build up a promotion with the best wrestlers, a state-of-the-art gym, events that will raise the bar beyond anything anyone has ever seen. The problem for promotions is always money. Money is not a problem for me. I want a wrestling school for the youth, get them off the streets."

This was another part of Neto's plan, to build wrestling-focused schools and orphanages for the street kids, just as Juan Gabriel had done with music. It enraged Mateo, the comparisons to El Divo, but as he watched Neto talk, he saw a flicker of vulnerability in his face, a childish eagerness barely contained.

"Neto." A voice came from the stairs.

Mateo looked over and Neto's men were moving. One stepped in. "Don Neto," he said, "your brothers."

Neto rose and Mateo saw behind him, two men coming up the stairs. Neto turned quickly and met them halfway.

They were both larger than Neto, not taller but more solid in their bodies, with round bellies and round heads. Neto greeted them, but there was something awkward in his movements, the way he held his neck stiff and shoulders up. All his men were watching them. Mateo pushed his own chair closer. The rhythm of their voices rose up, but he could make out only half their words over the accordion tune and the noise from the room below.

". . . meeting in Chihuahua," one brother said. ". . . up here in Juárez chasing ass?" He was smiling as he grabbed Neto's shoulder.

Neto shifted, ducked out from under his hand and pointed to Mateo. When he turned, Mateo could see the muscles pulled tight around his mouth.

". . . wrestling?" the other brother said, leaning in.

Neto was standing one step above them and he looked precarious there.

". . . supposed to be in Chihuahua . . ." the first brother said.

"Tomorrow," Neto responded.

The second brother leaned in again and said something Mateo could not catch.

"Well, tonight then," Neto said, turning from them, eyes down.

He came back up the stairs and reached for his drink. The brothers moved down toward the bar and Neto's men filled the empty space.

"Sorry for the interruption," Neto said. His voice was steady, but his shoulders were still raised and it took a moment for his confidence to settle back. Mateo could see the edges of it now, the places where it peeled away.

"Family." Neto shook his head and smiled and the smile seemed to bring a true ease to his face. "My brothers think it's an ignorant idea, a waste of money to start a promotion company. That's why I need stars like you. CMLL would squander your talents. I'll build you up, though, whatever you need, it'll be great for both of us. Give us five years and we'll blow them away."

Of course, Mateo thought, watching Neto's eyes light up, of course wrestling was Neto's dream, the dream of a fey boy with raw hope painted all across his face, maneuvering his body through a world built for men like his brothers. Men who knew how to take up space. Men who never doubted the needs of their bodies. Neto had fumbled and faked and then he'd found lucha libre, where every type of manhood was some wild stunt, an inside joke, a parade.

"Mateo," Neto said.

He looked up.

"Monday then?"

"Monday?" Mateo blinked. He had taken too many Oxys and he could feel his brain slurring.

"We'll meet with Arturo and the rest of them at CMLL to terminate your contract. Arturo already knows the plan and I'll offer to pay whatever they need for the remainder of your contract. You were going to sign a new contract in January anyway, right?

Mateo nodded. Every time he wanted to open his mouth and say, No, stop, I can't do this, Neto's men would shift, their guns catching in the light.

"We'll take care of it, whatever's necessary, no need for legal action. You can fly down to DF in my plane for the meeting. I'll have my men come by your place and pick you up."

Mateo could feel the word forming on his tongue—*no*—like a bright bubble about to lift off, but it did not come out. He swallowed the last of his añejo and set the glass on the table. "I need to go check on my son," he said instead.

"Of course." Neto stood up and grasped Mateo's hand. "Good night."

Outside, the snow had stopped falling. The cold reached up and surrounded him and the plaza was silent, the lights of the city bright against the white carpeting. The valet brought the Lexus around and it was only after he was inside it that his shoulders released and he could breathe normally. He drove up Teófilo Borunda Boulevard, glancing in the rearview mirror. When he was sure that no one was following, the dizziness left him and he felt his hands grip the wheel and he wanted to drive and drive and never stop driving.

SIX

It was the sound of rattling metal that woke Alex. He jerked and opened his eyes. Someone was coming at him through the dark. He stood, chair tumbling under him, backed up, and hit the table.

"You didn't lock the door."

The air left Alex all at once. He sat down on the edge of the table. Heart still ratcheting in his chest. It was too dark to see much of Mateo's face, just a streak of hair across his forehead and his left eye catching the light from the window.

"Where have you been?" Alex said.

"You didn't lock the door. My son is sleeping in here and you didn't lock the motherfucking door." Mateo's voice bashed back and forth between the walls. "Give me the key."

Alex found the key in his jeans and handed it over. Mateo had never raised his voice at him before and Alex almost felt he should point this error out to him, as if he were violating some universal rule—*you don't yell at me*—but something about the way Mateo was moving stopped him.

Mateo walked to the mattress and scooped Martín up. "I'll be back." He walked toward the door, Martín cooing in his arms.

"No." Alex's voice struggled out. "I'll come."

Mateo did not turn around. "Just wait," he said. "I'll be right back."

The door closed and there was a rasping click. Alex did not understand at first. He crossed the floor and pulled on the handle. The metal panel would not move. He pounded his fist on the door and the sound echoed out horrifically loud. He turned and set the overturned chair upright and dragged it to the counter and climbed up to look out the high window. From there he could see down onto Avenida Mariscal, snow and pink neon. A woman in a minidress, slick black hair in a high ponytail, talking to a man in a huge cowboy hat. A car slowing down in front of her, then speeding past, spraying snow-slush. Alex had always imagined that his mother—his birth mother—had worked the street, though he had no real evidence of it. Before he knew of the Mariscal, he'd pictured a Hollywood-movie red-light district. He saw her with neon rainbows in her eyes, lipstick marks on cigarettes, patent-leather heels. His parents must have said something to him, or around him, about her being a prostitute because when, at age ten, he saw *True Romance* on the TV in his neighbor's trailer, he'd felt immediately that his mother was a Mexican Alabama Worley. Hot-pink leopard print, bubblegum, and lots of grit. He knew his mother could not possibly be so milk white and corn-silk blonde, but he needed some sort of image for her. Breathy laughter, hair in her eyes. Tits so big and warm they said *how can I not love you*? He'd ripped a picture of Patricia Arquette from a *Star* magazine in the checkout line of the IGA grocery while his mother, Noreen, chatted with the cashier. He'd stuffed it down his jeans and felt it crinkling there, almost cutting his thigh the whole ride home. He hauled the groceries in and then he ran up the hill behind the woodshed, leaned his back against a red oak, braced his feet on the leafy incline, and stared at Patricia's toothy smile.

From that day on she lived in a shag tobacco tin buried in the leaf mold among the roots of the oak tree. Two years later she was joined by

Billy Allender, his face torn from the sixth-grade yearbook after he followed Alex to the church basement during choir practice and kissed him behind the baptismal robes. Neither of them could look at the other directly, but their lips and hands had been quick and hot. The choir singing on above like a plodding herd. Billy's breath sweet-rotten and dizzy making. *A mighty fortress is our God, a bulwark never failing.* Billy's nipples were the same pink as his lips, his cock perfect and beautiful, growing in Alex's hand, until breathless, they wiped their pearly cum on a robe and sneaked a peek at each other's faces. Smiling now as the organ thundered above them.

Four months later, Billy's father had caught him masturbating over a photo of Ethan Hawke and Billy told his father it was all Alex's fault. Billy's father told Alex's father and the world cracked. The only way to get back to reality was upstream through His words. Alex emptied himself. Vessel. Vassal. Servant to His will.

The only other boy he kissed was years later, in college, at a punk rock show in Richmond. The band was playing a cover of Leatherface's "Dead Industrial Atmosphere" when the shockingly beautiful boy beside him—long limbs and a sad smile—had twined fingers with him, and when Alex had looked up, surprised, the boy pressed his lips against Alex's in a long, thirsty kiss. Three days later Alex married Elana in a whirlwind courthouse ceremony that could have come straight out of *True Romance*, minus the leopard print coat and red dress.

WARM LIPS AGAINST Alex's ear.

"I'm sorry, hey, okay? You forgive me?"

Alex turned and curled deeper into sleep. Breath on his stomach, tongue tracing his belly button. Ombligo, he thought, pleased to have remembered the Spanish word even in his dream. Kisses along the waist of his pants, fingers tugging, the scrape of the zipper. Alex jerked up and gulped in air as if just released from under water. Dark room. Cold air. Mateo crawling toward him, pushing him onto the pillows. It was not a dream. He resisted for a moment, remembering Mateo yelling at him, and then he fell back, blinking away images of Elana's face as Mateo peeled his jeans down and cradled his balls with warm fingers and ran his tongue up the side of his cock. He thrust into Mateo's mouth and felt his breath lift, everything gone as he climbed to a shattering climax. He opened his eyes.

Mateo sat up and smiled. "Just a minute," he said, and got up and walked to the table. He was still fully dressed. He filled a coffee mug from a jug of water, drank long, filled it again and carried it to the mattress. Alex propped himself up on one elbow while Mateo unlaced his shoes and climbed under the blanket.

"I have something important to ask you," Mateo said.

Alex looked at him over the rim of the mug.

"You can take a few days for me?"

Alex did not understand at first, trying to translate fast and pull meaning from the words. "How do you mean?"

"Take a few days away from your schoolwork to make a trip to the town where I grew up."

When Alex did not answer, turning instead to set the mug on the floor, Mateo said, "Even Alicia has never been to my hometown." He tucked his hair behind his ear and looked straight at Alex.

"Please," he said. "I need you."

And it sounded more like *Please, I'm scared*, but Alex could not imagine what Mateo could possibly be scared of.

In the morning they had an early breakfast at La Nueva Central, tall, milky glasses of coffee and plates of eggs and rajas and beans, but when Mateo's cell phone rang in the midst of the meal, his face furrowed and he stepped outside. Alex watched him pace in front of the plate-glass windows of the restaurant, and when he came back in, he would not sit down. He said that Alicia's car would not start and the repair shop said it would be at least a day before they could look at it. He could not leave town if Alicia did not have a working car.

"So we'll leave tomorrow or the next day," Alex suggested, but Mateo's face tightened. There was some desperate frenetic energy about him that seemed outsized to the situation. Alex couldn't understand it, but he felt the balance tipping and if he questioned too much, he thought, the trip would be called off and so he'd offered his own car. "Alicia won't like it," he said. "I mean, it's not fancy, but it works."

After breakfast Alex crossed back to El Paso and took the bus to their apartment, where his cell phone still sat on the kitchen table. He never brought it to Mexico with him for fear of extra international charges. There were no new messages from Elana. He held it for a long moment in the dim kitchen with the refrigerator humming beside him and the bathroom fan buzzing. She would not be awake this early and he did not want to explain why he was calling at 7:00 a.m. and did not want to lie either. He would be back in a few days and she almost never looked at her phone anyway.

He drove back to Juárez and followed Mateo to Alicia's condo, where Mateo told him to wait in the Lexus while he took the Honda's keys in to her. Alex turned up the heat, cupped his hands around the vent, and stared at the Honda, looking so small and rust bitten among the shiny Suburbans and F-150 pickup trucks. When Mateo came back, he was fierce and silent and turned the Lexus around quickly.

"Everything's okay?" Alex said.

Mateo kept his eyes on the road. "Yes," he said finally. "Everything's okay."

They took the Panamericana down past the airport out to where the buildings dropped back and then disappeared completely, and by 9:00 a.m. they were driving down Carretera 45 into the great empty trough of saltbush and creosote, the mountains like rumpled bedsheets along the far horizon.

South of Villa Ahumada, the highway was flanked by groves of pistachio trees with blinkering frost crystals on their bare branches and the dizzying rows gave way after a while to abandoned roadside restaurants with rusted COCA-COLA signs, empty chile fields, and crumbling adobe huts. At

Vado the road drew near to the purple folded mountains, and the fields were tawny all around and gilded with sunlight, the scarf of snow melting quickly now and the long grass lifting in the wind. There was such little traffic that Alex was surprised each time the dark dot of a truck came up over the horizon. There was space here like nothing else, like the inverse of everything he'd ever known and loved in West Virginia, so much space here it seemed troubling.

They crossed a dead river, left it behind, and then crossed it again. Or it crossed them. Under the scrubby basalt of the Cerro de la Campana, tiny ranch houses nestled among the silvery grasses and clumps of pinyon pines. And in the distance, slow-moving bison grazed, their woolly backs humped dark against the yellow hills.

"You see them?" Mateo asked, pointing. "Like the real Old West, huh?"

Alex nodded. Mateo had said almost nothing so far during the drive and Alex could not tell if the silence was shaped by some tension between them or just between Mateo and himself.

"What's your hometown called again?"

"Creel, well, near Creel, it's called Vinihuévachi."

"Creel? Like a fishing creel?"

"How's that?"

"In English, 'creel' is for catching fish."

"Oh, it's named for some American, I don't know, from before the Revolution."

"How long since you've been home?"

"Ah, well, almost a year, I guess."

The road went on straight forever toward a vanishing point where the striated clouds rushed up, feathery with light. The only thing that changed was what they flew by: corrugated cattle sheds, concrete desponchadora shops with stacks of ruined tires outside, and every once in a while, a man with a crumpled hat held tightly against the wind. Traffic picked up as they entered Chihuahua, the long white factory buildings rising up out of the stunted hills, decked in razor wire. They turned onto Technological

Avenue and took it over to the Avenue of Youth, which ran along the western edge of the city past half-built mansions, banks, and box stores, the ritz of the San Francisco Country Club, and then, less than two miles later, the Industrial Park of the Americas, where buses unloaded lines of workers, mostly women, arms clutched against the December wind.

They stopped for lunch at a tiny diner called El Papigochi, squeezed in between a tire shop and a toilet wholesaler. The only other customers were two truckers drinking Tecate in a booth by the window and keeping one eye on their rigs outside and the other on the waitress's ass. The consomé de res came in enormous crockery bowls with whole hunks of beef, potato and carrot, and rounds of corn on the cob. Mateo ordered a tequila blanco, but the waitress said they didn't have liquor.

"Fine, Victorias then, two," he said.

The beers came, and Alex picked his up tentatively. He'd never drunk before sundown, had never even drunk at all before the previous June when, after college graduation, something had shifted in him and he'd felt interested and not so afraid.

"Salud." Mateo tapped his can against Alex's.

"What are we celebrating?" Alex said. He wanted to ask more about the sudden franticness that enveloped Mateo last night and this morning, but he sipped the icy beer instead.

"Pues, life," Mateo said. "The road!"

AT CAMPESTRE DEL Bosque they took the 16 west and a train ran along the highway, the slats of sunlight between the freight cars striping the road for miles, and then the train curved off and they kept on into the small hills, the highway cutting deep through the layers of red-orange rock and then opening suddenly into a great plain of tobosa grass with a single enormous and pure white obelisk in the center of the field.

"What is it?" Alex asked as they passed under the shadow. There were no buildings in sight, no cars or signs of human life.

"To mark two brothers, from the Revolution."

They climbed again, north, into the scrabbly hills and then out into Ciudad Cuauhtémoc, passing low brick and concrete buildings, trucks loaded with hay, dormant apple orchards.

Alex could feel the beer in his head, a weightlessness behind his eyes, and an inkling of a question of what he was doing here. He listened to the Lexus's engine and the whoosh of passing trucks. At least out here there was no academic talk of functionalist vs. interactionist, no counting his wife's Tampax under the bathroom sink.

"You don't have any fights for the next few days?" He looked at Mateo whose dark sunglasses reflected the road ahead.

"My knee," he said. "Doctor's orders to rest my knee for a week."

"Oh, I see, so then the visit."

"The visit?"

"It's a good time for a visit."

Mateo nodded, but Alex felt that he was working to layer logic onto something that was not that rational. It didn't matter anyway, the truth was that from the moment that Mateo asked him to come, Alex had felt the tug of something like fate. Or not fate, he didn't believe in fate, but something bigger than himself, something to do with the self that he was joining here. Since August, he had been going to class, working toward his degree, practicing his accent, and all the while hoping something bigger would take over. Not like something you could plan, nothing tangible like looking for his birth mother—an idea he had toyed with briefly before throwing it away—nothing as straightforward and obvious as that, more of a deeper sense of what he was doing here. He wasn't naive enough to think he could ever become Mexican, but he had hoped he could somehow become more himself, whatever the hell that meant.

At La Junta the road dropped south and then they were driving directly into the mountains, the embankments crowding now with oak and pinyon. There were no other cars, just the occasional overloaded logging truck crashing past in a squeal of stripped brakes. No houses or buildings or fences at all, and as they climbed, water appeared, first a trickle down the rock face and then a stream wide enough to warrant a bridge and finally cascades, churning white froth through the pines. SLOW, the road signs warned, DANGEROUS CURVE, and on particularly snake-backed turns, little shrines were erected for the dead, the cliffside whitewashed and la Virgen painted in cheery yellows and reds.

Alex felt a weight building against his temples, a grip he thought at first was the midday beer and the lack of sleep, but soon his ears were popping too.

"It's high, no?"

"I thought you were from the mountains." Mateo turned to face him but did not slow the Lexus as they roiled around a curve. Alex gripped the door, and Mateo smiled for the first time all day.

"Yeah, like three thousand feet, this has got to be more like—"

"We don't use feet."

"I know, I don't know why the US even got started with feet. To meters it's like . . . I think three thousand feet is less than one thousand meters, this here has to be more than twice that?"

Mateo shrugged and Alex felt desperate to make him smile again. "You told me we were both from the mountains, but I didn't know you were from the big, big mountains."

Mateo shook his head. "The big, big ones are the volcanoes down south," he said.

THE SUN HAD dropped below the tree line by the time they reached the altiplano and passed through Bocoyna and on to Creel. Little shops appeared, painted pastel pink and sea-foam green, advertising internet, artesanias, pizza, cabañas, and horseback tours, but most of them were shuttered for the season and the road was almost empty save for a pack of splotched dogs. A dusting of snow covered the roofs and the pines. Mateo turned off onto a side street and parked in front of a log-walled lodge with a crude balcony along the second floor and a stuffed wildcat on the porch.

"Your parents' place?" Alex said.

"No, we'll see them later." Mateo opened his door and Alex reached for his, but Mateo told him to stay, and when he returned he was holding a key attached to a varnished chip of pinyon wood.

The room was cold and smelled of old smoke and Mateo disappeared into the bathroom immediately. Alex stood at the window and watched a couple fighting in the parking lot below, their voices barely audible but their mouths stretched wide with hurling words, and emotions rose off them in nearly visible waves. After a while Mateo called from the shower and Alex joined him, shivering as he stripped on the stone floor and pulled the plastic curtain back. The steam formed a wall he had to pass through and his blood jumped loud in his heart and his head. He was hard before he even stepped in. Mateo appeared slowly through the wet air, his muscled shoulders shining, his long neck and sharp jaw. He handed Alex a bar of soap and pulled him under the flow, and when the hot water hit Alex, he cried out loud.

Before dinner, they walked down to the Plaza de Armas with its two Catholic churches, one a studiously humble stone chapel with a little wooden belfry and the other a loud yellow monument to Nuestra Señora de Lourdes with a bright red roof. Their bells were a few seconds off so that they overlapped in a not quite harmony. Mateo led Alex down the right side of the plaza, their fingers brushing as they strolled. A man in a white cowboy hat passed on horseback, bent against the wind. It had begun to snow, and the flakes clung to the electrically floral skirts of two women who stepped out from under the portico of the Artesanias Misioneras building. There was a rustle of movement and a girl of maybe five appeared between the women and raced toward Alex and Mateo.

"I've got spoons, dolls, baskets." She stuttered to a stop in front of them and peeled back her neon-green shawl to reveal a handful of intricately carved figures.

Mateo stepped around her as if she were a fallen branch temporarily blocking his way. Alex watched her bobbing up and down, her nose red with cold.

"Come on," Mateo called to him, and he turned away.

"For Christmas," the girl pleaded. "A gift for your mother?"

"My mother makes those." Mateo looked back over his shoulder.

The girl stopped and cocked her head. "What's that?"

"We're not tourists, mi'ja."

In the center of the flagstone plaza was a small bandstand and a statue of a hugely mustachioed Enrique Creel, son of an American ambassador and great friend of Porfirio Díaz, the pre-Revolution autocrat of seven terms.

BACK AT THE LODGE, Mateo ushered Alex into the entryway of the dining room.

"We're not going to eat with your parents?"

"Tomorrow," Mateo said. "What's your hurry?"

"Oh." Alex stepped inside, smelling woodsmoke and chiles and stewing meat. "I just thought that's why we came."

"Take a seat," a woman called from the end of the room, where she stood, turning flour tortillas on a wood-fired cookstove.

"If you don't want me to meet them," Alex said, "then why beg me to come here? You're embarrassed of them, or me?"

"We're going tomorrow."

Mateo chose a spot by the window at a table made of heavily lacquered pine. The chairs were made in the same style and the low ceiling was planked in pine also, the log walls hung with goatskins and mounted wildcat and deer busts. When the woman came, wiping her hands on her apron, Mateo ordered for them both, cabrito al pastor, caldillo, steak, and a pitcher of tesguino.

The fermented corn beer was milky brown and sour.

"You like it?"

Alex nodded.

"It's sacred, they say. So you can get drunk and pray at the same time." Mateo called for another pitcher and, after their first course, two glasses of mezcal. He stepped outside to smoke before the steak came and Alex watched him through the leaded glass, trying to make sense of his pleading need from the night before, *I have something important to ask you, please*, his frantic insistence that they not wait another day, and his reticence to visit now that they were here. Aimless walks in the Plaza de Armas, long celebratory meals. He did not want to ask again, You're okay? Everything's okay? But there was a skin of something bitter hanging there over the spontaneous festivities.

"Hey."

He looked up. Mateo stood in the open doorway, watching. "What are you thinking about?"

Behind him night had fallen snug over the little town, snow spitting against the tin roofs and, in the distance, the echo of street dogs and strike of horse hooves.

SEVEN

Mateo woke early and lay listening to the hiss of the gas heater and Alex's steady breath in the bed beside him. This was only the second full night they had ever spent together, all the times before Alex had needed to go back to El Paso. Mateo turned to face him where he lay, warm breath spilling onto the pillow, hair curled across his forehead and eyelids fluttering. What were they doing here? It was like they were already on the run, although Mateo reminded himself that he had not yet broken any promises. He had technically never made any promises. Neto had just assumed he would follow his plan. It would not be until tomorrow morning when—if—he did not show up to fly to DF with Neto that anything would shift. *I'll have my men come by your place and pick you up*. It wasn't until after he had left the club that night that it had occurred to Mateo that Neto never asked his address. That's what spooked him more than anything really. But Mateo still wasn't sure that he wouldn't show up. They could drive back to Juárez today, after breakfast. He pictured Neto as he had seen him last, in Los Padrillos, the way his body had changed around his brothers, shoulders up and eyes downcast. There was something slippery about the way he presented himself, all smooth talk and confidence, and then that moment when just the presence of his brothers, before they even spoke, had shifted it.

Mateo got out of bed and dressed beside the heater, holding his clothes over the blue flame before slipping them on. He could feel the presence of the snow outside before he even saw it, a kind of blanketed silence. The sun was not yet fully up and in the parking lot the only tracks were those of a single dog. Smoke rose from a few of the houses, but there were almost no lights on yet and at this hour the town seemed half-formed, like a thing he was dreaming or vaguely remembering. He'd told Alex it had been a year since he'd been home, but truly it had been almost two. He couldn't figure what tunnel in his brain, what tripped synapse, had convinced him this is where he needed to come now. After his meeting with Neto it had been the only thing that made sense—take Alex and go home—it had seemed like the only safe place to be. Though now that he was here, the thought of visiting his parents deadened his blood. His father, listless in his chair. If he didn't go to see them soon, though, the news of his arrival would travel to his mother and she would be crushed he hadn't come to them immediately.

After breakfast, he thought. For now, he would let Alex sleep. He left the lodge and walked out on the far side of town toward the Valle de las Ranas, glancing back and half expecting to see Neto's men trailing him, but nothing moved. The snow had stopped falling and gobs of it were caught on the branches and cupped inside the spiny nopales. It stuck only to the windward side of the trees, marking there where it had touched and where it hadn't. Through the white layers, the dark trunks shone with an almost unnatural blackness, like hollow spaces in the landscape. His eye went back to them over and again, those flat black strips, a darkness there that the eye could sink into and never return from. He shivered and turned back toward town.

AFTER BREAKFAST THEY drove up into the hills behind Creel until the town was nothing more than a scattering of red roofs and ponderosas descending away into the valley. The sun had come out and illuminated the snow in bright washes. Mateo drove slowly, navigating carefully around the rutted curves. Alex had hardly said anything since waking, but he had looked happy when Mateo told him they were going to visit his parents. He seemed content now, watching out the window.

Vinihuévachi was just a dozen log and adobe buildings straddling the road to Pitorreal. One dry goods store, a few tethered goats and horned cattle snuffling the snow out of feeding troughs. Smoke piped up above the roofs into the clearing sky. At the sound of the Lexus's motor, doors cracked open, small faces peeking out. By the time they had reached the end of the settlement, they were trailed by a posse of children. Mateo pulled off onto the side of the road below a cinder-block house, the single lasting result of the money his father had once managed to bring home from his years in Juárez.

The children rushed the Lexus as soon as it stopped, boosting one another up onto the bumper and the roof, their faces flushed in the cold morning air, noses dripping and eyes wide.

"Hey, hey, be careful, get down, come on." Mateo stepped out of the car and turned to lift the children from the roof.

"You're Señor Jaime's son?" one of them called, leaping off the far side of the car. "You brought presents? What did you bring us?"

"Give us a ride!" another one yelled.

Alex had opened the passenger's-side door and the children were swarming him now.

"Let us see inside? Give us a ride!"

"Hey, listen," Mateo called. "Be good, watch my car and make sure no one messes with it and I'll give you a ride when we're done, okay?"

"Yessss!" they chorused, and then, as Mateo and Alex made their way up the path toward the house, one boy yelled, "Ariché is messing with your car, she touched it, she made it all dirty, señor!"

The front door opened and a woman's face appeared, her eyes darting over Mateo, Alex, the car, and then coming back to rest on Mateo's face. "Mi'jo," she said quietly, and then more loudly, "What are you doing here?"

"Mamá," he said, and suddenly he felt the cold around him, the emptiness of his hands holding only the keys to his own car. Why had he not brought any gifts? Fabric and foodstuffs she would try to refuse but would have coveted nonetheless, presents to inspire envy in the neighbors, things you could get only if you were lucky enough to have a son who came to visit from the city. And if the son came but brought no presents? That was a situation far more embarrassing than not having a son in the city at all.

She reached out for his hand, drawing him inside. The windows were hung with thick blankets, and the room was dark and smoky but not much warmer than outside.

"Mamá, this is my friend Alex," Mateo said.

"And your wife? Your son?" María said. "You didn't bring me my grandbaby?"

Mateo could hear his father breathing in the far corner even before his eyes adjusted completely. Jaime was tied into a wheelchair with two soft cloth belts, one across his chest and the other about his waist. His head listed to the left. His eyes locked on Mateo's face.

"Papá."

All around his father, hanging from the walls and stacked up on the floor, were velvet paintings: snowcapped mountain scenes with waterfalls and pine trees, dogs playing poker, unicorns, clowns, panthers, and two on either side of chair that looked like Marilyn Monroe in a sombrero and Elvis robed and haloed like the Virgin Mary. The fabric had gathered dust so that the images on some were hardly visible and his father sat propped up among them, gathering dust himself.

Mateo could feel Alex behind him, taking it all in. He had warned him of nothing, not the paintings nor his father's paralysis.

He knelt before his father and made the sign of the cross, reflexively, without thinking. The room was silent apart from children's voices filtering up from the road below. He took the handkerchief that lay in his father's lap and wiped the saliva from his shoulder, folded it, and laid it back. He avoided his eyes, darker than the black velvet and breathlessly sharp.

Mateo crossed himself again and then stood and turned away.

"You're hungry," his mother said.

He knew better than to contradict. "I'll bring in more wood."

Alex followed him out the back door and across the snowy yard to the shed. A goat poked her head out of her stall. Mateo picked up the hatchet, his breath blowing out in white clouds.

"Your father," Alex said. "Those paintings?"

Mateo looked back at him. Before Juárez was the mother of all maquiladoras, he said, before car part and appliance plants, there were velvet-painting factories. Assembly lines of fabric stapled to frames and passed from boy to boy, one layering in the ridges of mountain peaks and handing it along to the next who painted the sun and so on. His father's specialty had been waterfalls, but he'd had more talent and drive than some of the others. He practiced in his off hours, mixing latex paint with wax and linseed oil and perfecting the strokes until he could complete Marilyn Monroes and Elvises of his own design. The factory paid only ten dollars a day, but wholesalers gave him four dollars for each complete canvas. At his peak he could do twenty canvases a day. Nights he spent drinking and running wild. He returned home to Vinihuévachi to throw money around, married María when she was fifteen, and put her up in a concrete-block house with real glass windows. He saw her only often enough to get her pregnant and then leave again. She lost the first three babies and then, finally, Mateo was born. By this time, though, it was the beginning of a new decade and the eighties did not love blacklight art the way the seventies had. Jaime sent money sporadically, then not at all. María was prepared to leave him, there was an older farmer outside town who had offered to care for her and her infant son, and then the news came: a car accident, Jaime's spinal cord snapped. A good Catholic woman could not abandon a disabled husband and so she enshrined him instead. Until death, he would never leave her again.

Mateo filled Alex's arms with wood and then his own and they carried it inside where his mother was stirring the stew and talking to his father.

"He drives a silver Lexus now," she was saying, and she glanced over as they came in.

Mateo stacked the kindling beside the comal where his mother flipped flour tortillas, the flames licking up around the clay griddle, her fingers staining with soot.

They ate the potato stew in the half-light, scooping it up with the tortillas until it was gone, and then they wiped the bowls and drank down the café de olla in silence. Mateo could feel his mother's disappointment bloating the room. No wife, no grandson, no gifts. He still couldn't even explain to himself what he was doing here. Running or hiding or saying goodbye.

When he first started making money in the ring, he had tried to get his mother to move. He'd told her he could pay for them to come to DF or Juárez, where there would be better medical care and things would be easier for her. She had looked at him like he'd slapped her. *This is my home*, she'd said, *why would I want to leave?* And he'd realized then that she loved this place, for all its hardships: not just the house but maybe more so the forest, the sky, the brilliant snow. It had been arrogant of him to assume she would want to leave, to assume that she could not find joy here.

"I'm going to show Alex around." Mateo looked at his mother. "Take him to Valle de las Ranas."

"And the lake," she said, nodding encouragement.

"We'll be back after a little while." He wanted to say, Tell the busybodies I'm coming back, I'll bring you gifts when we come back, I'll bring you things to light their envy, but he could not bring himself to pronounce the words out loud and so he went to kneel again before his father and tucked two thousand pesos beneath his damp handkerchief.

At the door his mother clutched Mateo's hand and pulled him to her. Her head rested under his chin. She smelled of smoke and piloncillo. "Be careful," she said.

"We'll be right back." He drew away from her and she looked up.

"Wait," she said, and thrust her hand down the front of her sweater, pulling up a metal pendant on a red cord. She loosened it from around her neck and held it out, then looking past Mateo to Alex, she called, "Take care of him."

"We'll be back," Mateo said, and turned away.

OUTSIDE, THE CHILDREN were still waiting. They gave them rides in the Lexus, up and down the road from one end of Vinihuévachi and back until all of them had gotten a chance. The temperature had risen and the snow dripped from the trees in wet splats. The road turned to mud as they wound back down toward Creel. At the roundabout with the Monumento al Tarahumara, Mateo paused, glancing about for the black SUVs of Neto's men, but there were no vehicles at all to be seen. The roads spoked in three directions: Vinihuévachi behind him, to the south Guachochi, and to the north Chihuahua and Juárez beyond. Above the plumed statue, the sky flooded with light, stratus clouds striding across the piercing blue. Alex sat as still as a votary and Mateo felt himself suspended between the left turn, the long drive to Juárez and Neto, and the right, the road that spilled down into the towns of the copper canyon. The way back to Vinihuévachi felt already closed to him. He turned right.

The asphalt ran out away from town and into the pines and past crooked rock formations, house-sized boulders balancing on slender stone necks and stalagmite-like pillars bursting up out of the meadows. They raced past Lake Arareco and Alex turned to Mateo then.

"I thought you were going to show me the lake," he said.

"There it is. Lake Arareco." He pointed out the window.

Alex did not move his eyes from Mateo's face.

"What? You want to stop? We can stop."

But in truth, they could not, even if Alex asked to. Now that the decision had been made, Mateo needed to drive and drive and keep on driving, as far in the opposite direction from Juárez as possible. Even the Lexus herself seemed to run more confidently now that he knew he was fleeing.

"We're not going back to your mother's," Alex said. His eyes hadn't left Mateo's face.

"Not right now, no."

On they went, past little Rarámuri cabins and remnants of ancient graves, crumbling crosses in the half-melted snow, out to where the road began to cut and curve and the high white cliff of El Cinturón rose over the Río Cusarare valley. They reeled down and crossed the sandy flats of the river, then climbed again only to dive once more to the Río Urique, then wind back up where the stone face of the mountain was swept clean by years of intermittent water that cut away tree and rock alike. In between the gashed boulders were stretches of incongruently soft meadows with cattle grazing and stacked pine barns and houses. They crossed a dry river and then, at Samachique, Mateo slowed and took a sharp right away from the main road that wound on to Guachochi.

"Where are we going?" Alex asked.

"Batopilas."

"You didn't think to ask me first?"

"Ask you?"

"I've got class tomorrow and a presentation on Tuesday."

"Class, really?"

"Yeah, when, can I ask, do you plan on going back?"

"You didn't come out here to go to class."

"Out here?"

"To the border, Juárez, you didn't really come here for your classes." Mateo looked at Alex and saw the force of his frustration draining away from his face. He was shaking his head now and Mateo went on. "The theories, the jargon, the silly required classes. You're always complaining about them. You came here for México, so here you go." He took his hand off the wheel and waved it out at the jagged mountains.

Not much past Quírare the road gave out to dirt and began to resemble more and more the old mule train trail it had once been, zigzagging violently down toward the Batopilas River, which glinted like a silver thread between rumpled folds. Mateo braked and the Lexus skidded. A shower of umber gravel hissed and ricocheted down the cliffside. Between the car and the abyss, nothing but a staggering of stunted acebo trees. That would be one way to avoid Neto.

"Jesus, fuck," Alex said. "Is this road even supposed to have cars driving on it?"

Mateo jutted his chin at the river below. "You can see it now, that's Batopilas down there."

"Why are you driving us off the ends of the earth?" There was an edge of terror in Alex's voice.

"I'm taking you somewhere special." Mateo looked away, out to the mountains that rivered on, canyon after canyon, past the Verde to the Fuerte and on. Something so big you couldn't help but feel the single wing-beat nothingness of your own existence. "You trust me?"

Alex nodded and swallowed audibly.

Two hours later, they descended into a shimmering green heat. At La Bufa Mateo rolled down the windows, the sun gauzy and tropical on their skin, the valley choked with vegetation, that morning's snow like some mis-remembered dream. They crossed the plank bridge over the Río Batopilas and wound up the far side of the canyon and along the ridge until the road turned to asphalt again as they drove into the old silver mining town.

EIGHT

When he thought back and tried to trace the order of events, Alex could not pinpoint the moment he started to feel sick, and he wondered if he hadn't been feverish the entire time. It was all tangled, Mateo's sudden urgency followed by endless brooding, the defiantly short visit to his family, and the violent dash down the canyon road. What he did know, or thought he knew, was that they had entered Batopilas in the early evening on a Sunday, the late-day heat lay over the town like a syrup, and as they drove along the narrow cobblestones, church bells were ringing and the streets stirred with a movement toward mass. The town had appeared suddenly, out of the bristling rocks and overflowing forest. There came a glimpse of whitewash and then the full-on anachronism of hotels, restaurants, and the ayuntamiento in haughty colonial style, cupolas, crenellated arches, latticed benches. And above and around it, all the jungle was seething.

They parked at the Hacienda del Río and took a room on the second floor with a balcony, stained-glass windows, a heavily carved chifforobe, a hideously uncomfortable settee, and two wrought-iron beds.

"It's like staying in a museum," Alex said, turning the heavy metal handle to open the balcony door. Mateo came up behind him and slid one hand down his arm to still his hand. "Our museum," he whispered, his lips against Alex's neck. "The museum of love." He laughed and pulled him backward to the bed and Alex felt glutted with it: the heat, those words, his own desire.

They stripped naked in the shadows of the lace curtains and pushed the two single beds together. The metal frames were squeaky and at first Alex worried, expecting a knock at the door any moment, but quickly he was carried far away from anything outside himself, swept into an utter exhaustion that permitted no thoughts at all. They lay trembling, slick and weak, their breath the only thing left.

Later they ate in the patio of the Restaurante Carolina. White-shirted meseras, napkins fanned inside tall glasses, trout served with the head still on, Carta Blanca, and snifters of reposado. The plaza at night was lit with blue lights, the clock tower like a hologram above the fecund trees. Alex could barely keep his eyes open, and when they returned to the room, he fell into a dark sleep, only to wake with an immense thirst. He thrashed in the sheets. White cotton tangling all his limbs. As soon as he sat up, his head split and his stomach raced up his throat. He spilled out of the bed, trailing blankets on the way to the toilet. He felt he was heaving up his own shame, his inability to control his body; there it was on the floor all around him, but he could not stop it.

Mateo's voice came from somewhere behind him.

He did not leave the bathroom for a long time. The distance between the bed and the toilet was too far. The tile floor felt good against his face.

When he was finally empty, he let Mateo carry him back to the bed and he felt weightless, exhausted but beautifully empty. He thought he understood Elana now. To put something inside your body was a heavy decision; to break the boundary and let something in, it could wreck you. Emptiness was safety. Mateo brought him water, but he would not take it. He wanted nothing but to lie naked and feel empty.

Empty, he could rest. He wanted nothing more than sleep. He concentrated on sinking into it, felt himself rise to the surface and fought his way back down deeper. A baptism he wished would never end. As the sky grew light, he saw the fringe of the jacaranda tree and it looked like the locusts back home, branches tapping the window of his childhood bedroom, their purfled leaves speaking of tropical winds he'd never known, his mother entering. *Sit up now, you'll feel better if you sit up. You can't give in to it.* As if getting well were simply a matter of Protestant resolve, sickness a decadent indulgence.

The vomiting was such an embarrassing display of his Americanness. He'd never gotten sick this bad before, but in Juárez too he had to be careful of the water and the carefulness always read like a rejection: *I can't handle too much of you, Mexico. Is the water filtered? I'll have a Coca-Cola, no ice please!* And he couldn't help but think how he had fallen ill the night after eating Mateo's mother's cooking. Of course, there had been dinner at the Carolina too.

Mateo's face appeared above his, haloed in sunlight. He wiped Alex's forehead. "You were calling for Elana," he said.

Alex did not know how to respond. More than anyone else, ever, Elana was comfort. More than his parents, who too often seemed to be reconsidering the choice they had made in taking him in, more than Mateo, who always seemed about to slip from his grasp. Elana needed him as much as he needed her. That was their pact.

He dozed again, floating in and out of sleep. He couldn't tell how long they'd been in Batopilas. Time felt elastic and untrustworthy, but his body at least seemed to be done punishing him.

In the morning he woke with an appetite. He ate bread and fruit and by the afternoon he and Mateo went for a walk. The outside world was hot and bright and green. They walked to the plaza and sat in the shade of the filigreed bandstand and watched a crowd of boys chase a cat up a tree. After a while the boys grew tired of throwing stones at the cat and turned to throw stones in the river instead. Slowly, arm in arm like an old married couple,

Alex and Mateo made their way back to the Hacienda del Río, passing little street-side Christmas shrines to the Virgen, glass boxes with running lights and plastic palm fronds. That night Alex slept a sleep with no dreams.

The next morning he woke with a bolt. All that day he was rabid, for food, for sex, for air and sunlight. The night after tomorrow Elana would be home. But when he thought of El Paso, he felt a rush of dread. Mateo had said, *You didn't come here for the classes,* and it was true, Alex had been using school as a way to get close to Mexico without looking directly at it. Now that he was here, he felt simultaneously desperate to flee and desperate to stay. If any place could, this town would hide him, outside of time, outside of decisions. But once he left, nothing would ever be this sweet again. He felt sure of it. No food would ever taste so good, no body would ever feel so necessary. He pulled Mateo to him. He put his hands about his waist and felt the strong shape of him, burnished into his fingers. The salt of his skin. The morning sun through the lace curtain. Birdsong. Tapping of the jacaranda tree against the glass.

In the afternoon they took a picnic basket from the hotel, stuffed with fruit and sweet bread and tamales, across the river to the ruins of the old mine owner's house. Three floors of stone and red-orange clay, arched windows and arched doorways and pillars like bell towers at both ends. The whole place was ripped open to the sky with fig trees bracing themselves against the inside walls. The Revolution had wrecked this place, sent the Americans running, forced finally to weigh the value of their own lives against the silver lode. They'd be back, they assured themselves over scotch and sodas up in Washington. But time pressed on, the miners left, the land was divided into goat grazing pastures, and when a flood took out the hydroelectric plant, the town fell backward through the ages, all vehicular roads cut off and no electricity again for another fifty years.

Alex and Mateo ducked under the stone arch and into the old Shepherd mansion. The interior was gone completely, all three floors rotted away, leaving nothing but the shell of the outside walls, and in what must have once been the cellar, rows of hip-high corn were growing, their electric green leaves shushing in the breeze. Hoes leaned up against the wall. They crossed the room and settled their picnic basket in the shade of a fig tree whose forked trunk spread across the interior wall. Alex rested his head in Mateo's lap and Mateo pressed the back of his hand against Alex's forehead.

"You're feeling much better?"

Alex nodded.

"You had me scared." He pushed Alex's hair away from his forehead and Alex closed his eyes. "Maybe you should have just rested in bed again today, I shouldn't have brought you over here."

"I'm fine."

"You were really sick, you have to build your strength back."

Alex opened his eyes. "You liked it when I was sick, huh? Helpless, feeble, needing you?"

"Shut up, no, that's not what I meant."

Alex was smiling. "Let's eat," he said.

The apricots were palm sized and delicately ripe, splitting at the touch of their teeth, and the tamales were still warm in their corn-husk jackets, filled with shredded pork and chiles. There were little pots of bright red raspberry jam and fresh yellow butter that melted as Mateo spread it inside the mantecada muffins. They fell asleep after eating, curled together among the roots of the fig tree, and woke to voices of the village boys on the far bank, screaming in glee over the trout they had caught.

That night Alex tried to say something about going back to Juárez, but the words would hardly form. "I have to pick up Elana at the airport Thursday night," he managed finally, and Mateo nodded. Since they'd arrived in Batopilas, the tension that had haunted him seemed to have evaporated, so much so that Alex half thought he had imagined it. But the next morning it was back.

He was stepping from the shower when Mateo came into the room. He'd left to go buy bread at the bakery around the block, but his hands were empty.

"We have to go," he said.

"What's wrong?" Alex came out of the bathroom. "Will you hand me that towel?"

"Get your clothes on now." Mateo moved to the chifforobe and began stuffing things into his bag.

"Mateo, what the fuck? I thought we were leaving this afternoon. What's going on?"

Mateo had his back to Alex, every movement jerky and outsized. He grabbed the towel from the chair and tossed it at Alex. "I'll tell you, but first we have to get in the car. Now."

"You're joking?"

"Get your fucking clothes on, we're leaving now."

Alex had seen the same look when Mateo first asked him to come on this trip. Terror, Alex could see that now, though it hadn't been so clear then. He watched Mateo's face and he knew that he would follow Mateo's orders. He was good at it—doing what he was told—he always had been.

WHEN THEY REACHED the lobby, they were both out of breath and Alex's shoes were still untied. There was no one behind the desk and Mateo dropped the key along with a handful of bills and headed for the door, but a voice called from the hallway behind them.

"Señor Mateo!"

Alex looked back. It was the receptionist.

"Señor Mateo, a man was just here, asking for you. I told him I couldn't give him the room number but he could leave a message, but he—"

"Thank you." Mateo stood, one foot out the front door, silhouetted in the morning light, his body fairly vibrating with tension. "That's fine, thank you," he said, and then, to Alex's horror, he stepped out the door, looked both ways, and flattened himself against the wall, creeping along to the edge of the building where the alley ran back to the parking lot, moving like some caricature movie villain.

"Mateo, what the fuck?" Alex felt his stomach drop out as he watched him peering around into the alley.

"Go get the car." Mateo turned back and held the keys out to him.

"What?"

"Go get my car and pull it around front here. When you get here, scoot over and I'll get in the driver's seat."

"What's going on? You have to tell me what is happening," Alex.

"Go get the fucking car." Mateo threw the keys.

Alex caught them.

"And act normal, don't run, just go get the car."

"I—"

"You have to help me."

Alex could barely take a full breath, but he walked down the alley and out into the sun-drenched lot, bordered on all sides by a ten-foot wall topped with wire. His eyes found the Lexus and he felt himself moving toward it as if down a long tunnel. He refused to look around, but his body was braced—he realized in a rush of terror—braced for bullets. *This is a dream, this is a movie.* The car opened. The motor turned. He backed out and nothing happened. His hands were sweating so much he could barely grip the wheel. He was heading into the alley now, turning the corner, and Mateo rushed toward the car and ripped the door open. Alex did not have time to get out of the way and they jumbled together in a snarl of legs while the car was still rolling.

"Move, move, get the fuck out of the way," Mateo screamed, and Alex gripped the passenger's door handle and hauled himself across the seat. He tipped his head back and felt the vertigo of the moment, the trees streaming by, the high white face of the ayuntamiento, Carolina's restaurant, and the river wandering along below. He kept looking into the side mirror, but there was no one behind them. The mountains fenced them in on all sides, but Mateo took a right onto a small dirt road that wound up and along the ridge. He looked at the rearview mirror and then slowed the car a bit, eased it through a pothole.

"Talk to me," Alex said. "What did you do?"

"I didn't do anything."

"What do you mean you didn't—"

"That's the problem, I didn't do what Neto wanted me to do." Mateo glanced over at Alex and his face looked thin and exhausted. "You remember me talking about that guy who started sponsoring me?"

By the time he had finished explaining to Alex, they were well up into the mountains, nothing out either side but thick stands of yellow pine and the Fuerte River far down below.

"So," Alex said, "you didn't tell him no, you don't want to join his new empresa, you just decided instead to run away for a while. That was the plan?"

"You can't just say no to the nephew of the head of the Juárez Cartel."

Alex turned to Mateo. He felt his blood moving too fast through his veins. "You did not tell me that's who Neto is."

"That's the rumor at least. He's connected, I know that much, and he travels with about ten bodyguards. I wasn't about to say no to them and their rifles either."

"Okay, so explain to me then, after that you come back to the apartment and fuck me and then beg me to come to Creel with you, so that . . . I think this is where I don't understand." Alex felt the words slow in his mouth. He couldn't go further. He had always been good at showing people what they wanted to see, not only in him but in themselves also, reflecting back to them their own best selves. He knew it was what made people like him. The way he made people feel about themselves endeared him to them, but it meant he couldn't confront anyone either. He found it physically painful.

"I don't know . . ." Mateo gripped the steering wheel more tightly. He did not look at Alex. "I . . . I wasn't thinking."

"Did Neto call you after you didn't show up?"

"I turned off my phone. I haven't turned it on since Sunday."

"So then . . ." Alex looked out the window at the brown wash of mountainside. "Then this morning his men show up in Batopilas looking for you?"

Mateo smashed his fist against the steering wheel. "Fuck, yes, fuck."

Alex watched him and felt himself conforming already to this new reality, reaching out to feel for the expectations and meet them. He was always so good at meeting expectations. It was the curse of the overachiever.

"Where are we going now?" he asked. Everything would be okay as long as Mateo remained the one with the plan. As long as he didn't ask Alex what to do, Alex could keep his cool.

"The beach," Mateo said. "You want to go to the beach for a little while?"

"Fuck you." Alex turned so that his whole body was facing Mateo. This was too ridiculous, even for this new reality. "What do you mean, the beach? You have to call him."

Mateo slowed the car but did not stop. He glanced in the rearview mirror. "I can't. I'm not calling him."

"You just have to explain you can't do what he's asking of you. Tell him you want to stay with CMLL. He should find someone new to sponsor."

Mateo made a sound like a laugh strangled by a cry. "If it were that easy, I would have already said that to him. My manager at CMLL, Arturo, he's in on the deal with Neto. I can't go back there."

"Where's your phone?"

"In the hotel."

"Fuck! Of course." Alex buried his face in his fists. "What am I doing here? Mateo, what am I doing here?"

"I . . ."

"Why did you bring me here?" He lifted his face.

Mateo looked over at Alex and his eyes were wet and huge. "I love you?"

Alex laughed a fierce bark of a laugh. He could feel the hysteria unleashed, ringing all through him now. "Revelation 3:15," he said.

"What?"

"God is laughing at me." He'd been waiting for this. He knew it now. He'd been so pathetically indecisive about everything, his sexuality, his identity, his marriage. "I know from thy works," he quoted aloud in English, "that thou art neither cold nor hot. I would thou wert cold or hot. So then because thou art lukewarm, and neither cold nor hot, I will spew thee from my mouth."

They drove in silence for the next two hours until they crossed the river into the town of Tubares. The river was wide there and the bridge elevated for floods. There was a single crumbling church in the center of town, the yellowed bell tower streaked with rust from the massive campaña. Out beyond lay a cemetery that seemed too large for such a small settlement and in the plaza a lone white dog stood, surveying their passage.

"You want to stop and eat?" Mateo asked.

"I thought we were running for our lives." Alex watched the bony dog disappearing out the window.

"I don't think they saw us leave."

"I can't eat."

The road followed the river and then split away south and they crossed into Sinaloa, though neither of them knew it until later. There were no towns there, no signs, nothing until they dropped down into El Cajón and then on to Tasajeras. It was cattle country, big white humpbacked Brahmas moving slowly through the terrifically green fields and disappearing into mist and palm trees. If Alex could forget for a moment that this was a nightmare movie, it might feel like a honeymoon dream.

Outside Choix it began to rain and little streams sprang from the mountainside, threatening to wash the dirt road away. They wound on slowly with nothing but the sound of the windshield wipers, and by the time they reached the paved road into town, Mateo was shaking.

"I'm too hungry, we have to stop," he said. He'd been driving for more than five hours.

They ate pozole in a tiny brick comedor and each moment seemed to Alex to stretch out longer than the last. It all seemed so saturated, each second slow and full with the steam that rose from their bowls of red soup, the drip of rain on the awning outside, the snap of radish between his teeth, and the fierce beauty of Mateo's face, dark and lean with rosebud lips, sharp cheekbones, and those huge black eyes that could still, even now, make him blush with heat.

In the pueblito of Barotén on the banks of the Fuerte River, where there was nothing much but a few granaries and a donkey with a leather saddle tied to a blue bicycle, Neto's men found them. By then, all the anger had washed out of Alex and in a strange way it seemed that his sickness had been preparing him for this—the fever altering reality until his life in El Paso with Elana seemed distant and inexplicable and everything outside these dreamy travel days was unreal or at least unreachable. And here in this bubble, they were running, sure, but really it felt more like endless waiting so that when the black SUVs surrounded Mateo's car—two pulling out in front from side roads, two closing in behind, and one butting up, pushing the Lexus to the side of the road—there was something that flooded through Alex, alongside the terror and adrenaline, something a little like relief.

NINE

Elana's father's house was all wood and dust, paper and smoke, cat hair, damp furniture, deep rugs. There were no curtains or blinds, but still the light struggled to get in under the wide planks of the porch roof and through untrimmed boxwoods bushed up against the windows. A three-story brick plantation-style house with massive chimneys on both sides and chipped white columns across the front. It was a place that had always been Elana's *father's house*, always and forever. She thought she could even remember her mother referring to it that way, *in your father's house*, though Adair had died when Elana was three so the memories were fragile at best. It could make sense, though. Meyer had owned the house already and had been living there for two years before Adair met him and she might have always thought of it as his, even after she had married, moved in, and given birth there.

"You're hungry?" Meyer asked, dropping his keys in a bowl by the door.

"No," Elana said, and she felt a little prick of anticipation as she waited for him to insist so that she could refuse again. At the airport and in the car, he had said nothing about her weight loss. He was the first person to see her since she'd moved west, since she'd cut down to one small meal or meal and a half a day. If her project was not visible, then it could not be as important as it felt. She regretted the pretzels she had eaten on the plane. Five of them she had eaten whole and the remaining few she had just licked off the salt.

Meyer walked through the living room and into the kitchen. It was the brightest room in the house, the light coming in all smudgy through the dirty glass. He picked up the kettle and went to the sink, kicking aside the half a dozen empty cat food cans scattered across the floor. Standing in the entry hall, Elana wondered how many calories you gave a cat when you opened one of those cans. It was a leap her brain made often. The neat rectangle of Nutrition Facts, the way it was always laid out the same way in perfect little stanzas: Serving Size, Servings, Amount per Serving, Calories, % Daily Value, Total Fat, Sodium, Total Carbohydrates, Sugars, Protein, *Percent Daily Values are based on a 2,000-calorie diet. Last week she had found herself sitting at her desk and unthinkingly turning a box of paper clips over and over in her hand, eyes absentmindedly searching for the Nutrition Facts.

"I'm going upstairs," she called out, her hand trailing along the dark wood banister.

"Hey," Meyer said.

She turned to look back at him where he stood in the doorway wiping his glasses on the corner of his shirt and squinting up at her.

"Thanks for coming," he said. "I really appreciate it."

She nodded. She had never considered not coming, but she'd always thought of it as something she was doing for Simon, not Meyer. Her whole life he had always seemed so preoccupied, so cerebral, that she didn't consider his emotions much. There was something in his voice now, though, a shaky tone in his thank-you, that made Elana wonder for the first time if he might be scared about Simon's return.

The incident that led up to rehab had happened a month after Elana left for Texas. Meyer told her later how he'd come home from teaching and found Simon in the kitchen, hopped-up and frantic, eyes all screwy. He told Meyer that he needed money, a few thousand dollars. Meyer said no and at first Simon had begged—*Just give me my inheritance now, don't make me wait until you die, you selfish prick.* When that didn't work, he'd turned threatening. Picked up a knife off the counter. *I could fucking kill you, you know I hate you so much I could fucking kill you right now.* Meyer had acquiesced then. He said they should go to the bank, but when they got to his car, he slipped in before Simon, locked the doors, and called the cops.

This kitchen. Elana looked back again. It happened right here in this kitchen. It seemed so unbelievable that her baby brother could do something like that. She'd muted it, labeled it in her brain as "Simon's drug problem," and pushed it away like a bad dream. The cops had taken him to a mental hospital, and later, when they realized how much meth he was on, he was transferred to rehab. He and Elana had written letters, but neither of them brought up the knife incident. It was here, though, Elana could feel it now, alive in the house. And Meyer had been living with the ghost of that violence all fall, alone in a place that was once so full. Before they'd moved to El Paso, Elana and Alex had lived in the attic. And before they were married, they'd lived on the second floor in bedrooms side by side, down the hall from Simon and Meyer. Alex had moved in late fall of his freshman year after Meyer found out that while Alex's scholarship to Hall College covered his room and board, it did not afford him enough money for his books. Meyer had spoken to admissions and arranged for the room and board money to be refunded and turned into books and supplies money if he moved out of the dorm. Elana and Alex had both been just seventeen, but he was already a college freshman and she still a junior in high school. When they married six months later, they had moved to the attic. It had been her father's idea. The only other thing he said about their marriage was, *Wow, huh, seems almost a little incestuous, doesn't it?* Simon, who was three years younger than Elana, had moved his extensive collection of bows and arrows into Alex and Elana's old second-floor bedrooms.

The attic had four deep dormers and custom-built bookshelves on the two long walls, a wedding gift from Meyer. Alex's books on one side and hers on the other. His side was only a little more than half-full while hers had overflowed with paperbacks stacked up at the far end awaiting more space. Her father had never fully respected the books she loved—Genet, Keats, Lorca, Plath, Flaubert. He thought fiction and poetry were mostly a waste of time, no matter who wrote them, but he did respect her quantity. Alex liked to point out that he had had far less time and resources to build his collection. Before coming to Hall College, the only acceptable books for him to own were Bibles and Westerns.

Their bed was an old iron frame with a queen mattress and a quilt from Alex's mother. She lay down and clouds of dust puffed and spun above her face. It was always cold up here, but then again, she was forever cold no matter where she was these days. She could warm up when she was waitressing, but when she stopped moving the chill set in again. Wrapping the quilt around her shoulders, she reached for her backpack. Late afternoon was always the hardest. She could not pretend that the hunger was anything else and the dizzy-faintness rose steeply. With a cigarette and a seltzer, though, she felt almost royal in her weakness. She knew it was a stupid thought, but still there it was. She opened the window above the bed and lit a Slim, of course, what other cigarette could she possibly choose. She smiled. The Nutrition Facts rectangle on the seltzer can was goddamn beautiful: 0 g 0% 0 mg 0% 0 g 0% 0 g 0 g. Not a significant source of other nutrients. That glorious crack and fizz.

The great thing about the dizzy-faintness was what it excised: all complicated thoughts. Her mind flitted and could not stay for very long on any one thing, even the big, important things: Simon pulling that knife, or her future if/when she dropped out of school, or how Alex almost never touched her anymore, his affection so solid and stable it crippled even the whisper-thought of sex. In her afternoons of hunger she was blinkered from all this. There was the cigarette between her lips, seltzer bubbles rough on her tongue, the cool of the water going down her throat and making her neck feel beautifully long. There were the boards in the ceiling above her head, varied honey hues darkened in places by water stains, and the book spines along the wall, alphabetical within genre and time period with separate sections for each decade or century. She'd experimented with different organizational methods, but this one she'd found most satisfying. She had thought she would miss her books terribly, only a small portion had fit in the Honda when they drove out west, but while she did miss being in their presence, she only referenced and reread a select few of them. What she loved most was consuming them. At the far end of the bookcase was a stenographer's pad with a series of lists she'd developed last year, her second year at Hall College: an average of 115 books in a year, approximately 10 per month, 2.5 per week, 40 pages an hour, 250 words per minute.

AT THE TRAIN STATION her father stayed in the car, listening to NPR. Elana got out and walked across the old bricks, veined with moss, to the taut tracks running east–west. On the far side sat a row of drooping Victorian houses and a half-collapsed hotel from the time when the train line was the artery of Hartsville, and beyond, the river, loud and greedy in its passage. She found two pennies and a dime in her front pocket and bent to feel the track, cool and still as a rippleless lake. She placed the pennies side by side on it.

Farther down, by the station house, a mother and child sat, the girl in leopard-print coat and huge red bow, waiting . . . for a favorite aunt, Elana decided. And up above, the sky was breaking apart, shafts of light escaping and leaking onto the gun-colored hills.

She could feel the train before she could hear it or see it. A tremor, increasing. A sensation becoming audible and then the silver nose rocketing out from among the bare trees. The Amtrak was so sleek and self-contained compared to the raucous graffitied boxcars of the Texas–Mexico trains. It sang to a stop, the fourth car aligning with the station house. And then there he was. Simon. Tall and slim in a gray hoodie with his blond hair buzzed short. Long legs in faded blue jeans. Nothing with him but an empty-looking backpack. His face a fletched arrowhead.

"I didn't know you'd be here."

His voice was flat. The distance between them decreased and the air was silvery now with the sunken sunlight. He held his body like an afterthought, present but unimportant, and the way he moved was more familiar than anything she had ever known.

"Dad didn't tell you?"

She could feel their father, in the car behind her, and she wanted to keep him there, outside this moment. He brought with him the fear—the incident—but if she could separate for a moment, then this was a pure reunion. Here was her sweet, smart, funny baby brother whom she hadn't seen in four months.

Simon shrugged. "I don't know," he said. "Maybe I forgot."

He pulled her in and her head fit perfectly against the middle of his chest. The train was leaving and it mixed with the rip of sadness and joy. Emotions her hunger could not cover up. He looked like he had been to war and her brain toggled with the blame for it: Meyer—herself—Meyer. First she had abandoned him and then Meyer had called the cops.

Simon moved past her before she was ready for the hug to end, and as he approached the car, Meyer stepped out.

The car. Elana watched the door swing, the shadows swirl around their feet. Aside from the rehab visiting room, this was the last way they had seen each other—one inside, one outside. Simon's fists on the windshield, his voice keening high at his father's trick. And Meyer inside, doing what? Elana pictured him curled, hands over his head, awaiting the cops or the crack of glass, whichever came first.

They embraced. Elana's heart beat loud as she watched. Simon pulled away and headed for the front passenger's side.

"Ready?" Meyer called to Elana.

She nodded.

It wasn't until they were backing out of the parking lot that she remembered the pennies.

"Stop, wait," she said.

The temperature had dropped and her bare fingers throbbed as she searched, eyes straining against the dim light. Her boot hit the track and the copper chirped where it fell against a spike. She grabbed it and ran back to press that pooled-out-smooth friction-warmth into Simon's palm. He glanced at her and then down at his hand and then pocketed it.

"I thought we'd go to Kathy's," Meyer said, turning the car around.

Kathy's Kountry Kitchen had sustained the three of them through Elana and Simon's entire childhoods. After school they'd walked there and sat in a booth doing homework until Meyer joined them for an early dinner five nights a week. In 2000 Kathy had died and the restaurant was bought by a couple of Hall graduates who added hummus and sprouts to the menu, jacked up the prices, and renamed it Blue Moon Café.

"I'd like to go home so I can shower before my meeting," Simon said.

"Tonight?" Meyer glanced at him.

"NA."

"I know, but tonight? You just got here."

"It'll probably be the most important meeting of my life."

Elana watched them silhouetted and reflected in the windshield: her father, sixty-eight years old, plump in his Hall College sweatshirt, owl-eye glasses and a rim of white hair, and her brother, eighteen, tall and sharp and zippered in.

"I won't know anything—*we* won't know anything—for at least three months," Simon said. "You should stop feeling proud of me right now."

The brakes squealed as they pulled up to a stoplight.

"Jesus can bring me through this if he wants to, but it's not a given and it will be harder than anything yet. Much, much harder than rehab."

"I see."

"The meeting's in Roanoke. I'll need you to drive me."

"I thought the NA-AA thing was nonreligious."

"My Higher Power is Jesus Christ."

"So are Jews welcome?"

"You won't be coming in. It's a closed meeting, you can only attend if you're working the steps."

Meyer found a few cans of chicken noodle soup in the cupboard. He heated them while Simon was showering, and when Elana looked up and saw Simon standing in the kitchen doorway, she felt the shiver of fear again. This kitchen. That countertop.

"Dinner's ready," Meyer said.

Could you ever really forgive your own child for threatening your life? Could you feel sure it was just the meth?

"What?" Simon said.

Elana realized she'd been staring at him. "Oh, you look nice."

He was gleaming from his shower, dressed in a blue-striped button-up. Maybe Meyer had exaggerated the incident. Maybe Simon hadn't really meant to point the knife that way.

"Here you go." Meyer handed her a bowl.

The soup did not smell good to Elana, but it engulfed her all the same, the steam clammy against her neck and face and everything else fuzzing away as she set herself to conquering it, pushing all the noodles and chicken and most of the carrot and celery to the side and slowly lifting one clear spoonful.

"Jesus," Simon said, "we thank you for granting us this day. We thank you for blessing us with nourishment and safety, though we do not deserve it."

Meyer looked at Elana, raised his eyebrows. She looked away, spoon held in midair.

"Even as we sin against you in our very hearts and minds and bodies, you forgive us. I know I do not please you, Lord. I am weak and low and dark and yet you lift me from the flames."

His eyes were closed and his face pinched with sincerity. As Elana listened to him, a sadness entered her and settled, dull and solid inside her.

"Jesus, for this I thank you, now and forever. Amen."

Elana looked down at her soup again. There was no sound in the kitchen except for the tink of spoons against bowls and Meyer's five cats lined up below the stove, slurping noisily from their tins.

"You're only gonna eat the broth?" her father said.

Elana glanced up and shrugged.

"Why?"

His eyes were impossibly round.

"Because I want to," she said, almost smiling. With Alex, she felt she had to protect him, pretend she wasn't doing what she was doing, make excuses about not liking the texture or having already eaten at work, but now it felt rushingly good just to say it straight.

IN THE CAR on the way to Roanoke, Elana pushed away the fear and let herself time-travel back to being part of a small one-day-at-a-time family cupped around a wound. Now the wound was no longer her mother, but it all felt perfectly familiar—this talking around the most obvious thing—this desperation to stay in the present moment, moving forward. In the backseat Elana could have been five, ten, fifteen. She'd sat alone in the backseat ever since Simon was old enough to move to the front. He had begged for the privilege until Elana realized she liked the back better anyway and gave in. In the backseat she breathed easily, her physical presence was enough to satisfy everyone; meanwhile she could go off in her mind—leap, skip, jump: the tracer lights of passing cars illuminating the lacy ruff of brush along the roadside, the stars through bone branches. In the front seat Simon was talking. Simon had always been in the front seat talking, her father interjecting and Simon explaining. Now he was talking about Jesus, lamb, blood, God. He'd never talked about this before—they'd been raised atheist with a menorah gathering dust on the mantelpiece, lapsed Baptists on their mother's side and, in Meyer's family tree, a grandmother who was a converted Christian Scientist and a bunch of ancient Jewish family members up in New York whom they'd never met. But Simon throwing himself 200 percent into his passion was nothing new, he always attacked whatever he was studying with a cyclonic hurl of interest. Woodworking, archery, hide tanning, violin, tai chi. In the seventh grade he begged Meyer to let him switch to a mail-order homeschool program. Public school was moving too slowly for him. He supplemented the packets by sitting in on classes at Hall College. Meyer's colleagues couldn't believe he was only thirteen. He apprenticed with a baker and learned to make French pastries, got a woodworker to teach him to build guitars, and then got his maternal uncle to show him how to make methamphetamine.

Elana watched him get out of the car and walk down the stone steps into the basement of the Calvary Methodist Church of Roanoke. He had always been bigger than her. Even when she was three and he was a preemie, snarled in tubes and cords and monitors, his presence had been huge. And then he'd grown blond and confident and tall enough that Elana could tuck her head into his armpit.

At the door of the church a man was ushering people in. Simon paused and talked to him, and though she could not hear his words, he smiled widely and she realized then that he had not yet smiled for her.

They waited at a Waffle House. Chocolate pie for Meyer and coffee for Elana. Fluorescent lights and the small talk of waitresses. She could not watch the pie go steadily in her father's mouth and so she watched the lights on the jukebox instead.

"How's Alex doing?" he asked with his mouth full.

She shrugged.

"What's that supposed to mean?"

"I think he's a little disappointed with the program."

Meyer made a sound like a scoff-laugh. "I told him no one there was at his level. They would have loved him at Princeton."

Before Meyer became an undergraduate history professor at an unknown liberal arts college in bumfuck Virginia, he had gone to Princeton. He finished his BA there, but then something had happened that Elana never fully understood, some sort of crackup that involved years in and out of hospitals, trips to Europe, and periods spent living in his parents' house. Eventually he had completed a PhD in American history, writing a thesis titled "The Appalling Appeal of the Octoroon: The Shifting Status of

Mixed-Race Prostitutes in Early Twentieth-Century New Orleans." Then there had been talk of a book contract, but that never panned out, and at age forty-five he had taken a job at Hall College and two years later married one of his most promising students.

"I knew he would regret it. He could have gone to Mexico to explore his heritage after he finished his graduate studies."

All through Alex's time at Hall, Meyer had groomed and preened and polished him, promising that he had connections enough to get him into Princeton for his PhD.

"I think," Elana said, "he was also considering me, programs for me too. You never offered to get me into Princeton."

"Oh, Elana." Meyer ran his spoon along the edge of his plate, then brought it to his mouth and licked it clean. "You didn't have that kind of GPA."

She looked away. Now that she'd claimed that they were at UTEP for her, it would make Meyer even more angry when he found out she was dropping out. Oh well. It was better than the truth, that she'd had no real part in the decision to go west. The day before she and Alex left, Meyer had said she could always come back and get free tuition at Hall College. For months after that she'd hung suspended above her selves: the self her husband assumed would live with him in Texas and the self her father assumed would ricochet back.

UP IN THE attic bedroom, Elana found her cell phone in the pocket of her bag. Alex had not called. It did not worry her, though. Checking the phone was like asking herself before a long drive if she needed to pee one more time, something she tried to remember to do so as not to inconvenience others. Outside, the wind had picked up and it rushed over the house in waves, scraping the oak branches against the roof. She changed into sweatpants and a worn T-shirt with HOLLER RATTLERS across the chest, the band that Alex had played bass in when she first met him. She got out her notebook and stack of books, a seltzer, and her pack of Slims and set herself up at the long table at the opposite end of the room from the bed.

When they'd lived here, she hadn't smoked inside, but now it seemed almost silly not to. Her father would never notice unless he came up to the attic, which he almost never did, and what would the consequences even be? She wanted nothing more right now than to smoke and read and take notes and feel her brain moving. Her mind worked differently when she was alone and knew that she could continue to be alone for hours without interruption. The apartment in El Paso was so small that there was no room to be alone. Even when Alex was not there, the whole place felt like his space. Maybe it wouldn't be a terrible idea to come back here for a little bit. She was shocked to even be thinking it, but really, without classes to attend, what was she going to do in Texas? Here, in this room at least, she could feel her brain breathing, narrowing and expanding at the same time, a sharpened tip that could build out endlessly.

Her project was a gathering and assembling of reflections. Like Anne Carson's "The Gender of Sound" essay, the way she synthesized perspectives on the female voice from Aristotle and Aristophanes to Margaret Thatcher, Aiskhylos, Hemingway, Alexander Graham Bell, Freud, Pythagoras, and *Playboy*. What Carson said her critics called "ethnographic naiveté." Elana wanted to commit ethnographic naiveté but with quotes from Americans and Europeans on their views of Mexicans and Mexico. It had started with Graham Greene when she learned that he'd written two "Mexico books," *The Lawless Roads* and *The Power and the Glory*. She'd begun to read *The Lawless Roads* and was both sickened and mesmerized by Greene's description of Mexicans as "mangy animals" with "aged, painful, ignorant [. . .] untrustworthy mestizo face[s]." The Texans Greene met before crossing over had "sensitive face[s]," and an expat German was "aristocratic," and "the young American girls looked pale and weak and self-conscious before the dark sensual confident faces of the half-castes—who knew instinctively, you felt, all the beauty and the horror of the flesh." All food in Mexico was "repellent," the tequila was "a rather inferior schnapps," the landscape had no beauty, and the markets were "grim, squalid" with "hideous toys and trinkets" and "ugly" Native craftwork. Only the maids were sometimes "pretty and nubile and faintly insolent" or "fine young instruments of pleasure" who stared with "sexual impertinence" and "dim, suggestive smile[s]." This was Graham fucking Greene, writing in the late 1930s, not the ancient Middle Ages. And no one blinked. The copy she had, which had been re-pressed this year, was covered in praise for his "foreign ear and eye" and "spiritual hunger."

She read D. H. Lawrence's *Mornings in Mexico* next. There, the Mexicans were "dumbbells" with "black eyes of incomprehension." They lounged around "bare-bosomed and black-browed" with a "sort of richness of the flesh" that goes "the complete absence of what we call 'spirit.'" The Mexicans were "beasts of burden" with an "Indian stupor," a "pure reptilian hate." Lawrence found even the water in Mexico to be "rather lifeless" and the Native myths had "no grace or charm, no poetry." Yet for Lawrence, like Greene, at least the shyness of the Mexican women "really gets one's pecker up."

Female writers did not do a much better job. Some thirty-odd years later, in her *Survivors in Mexico*, Rebecca West described the people she met as "delectable" as "coffee or chocolate," though "especially subject to rage." And when speaking of "Mexican brown majority" (created by the rape of Natives by Spanish conquistadores), she said, "to use a Shakespearian phrase, there was good sport at its making." Just over ten years later, Maryse Holder wrote of "that dark stone Indian mask" and Mexican boys like "coconuts macheted open for their plentiful sweet juice."

All of it was sickening, but what struck Elana most were the repeated allusions to darkness and masks and incomprehension. As if the pigmentation of a person's skin and eyes made it probable that they lacked a spirit or any "burning ambition" at all. "Rosalino, the Indian mozo, looks up at me with his eyes veiled by their own blackness," wrote Lawrence. "Between us is the gulf of the other dimension, and he wants to bridge it with the foot-rule of the three-dimensional space. He knows it can't be done. So do I. Each of us knows the other knows. But he can imitate me, even more than life-like. As the parrot can him."

"Hey, Lana."

She jerked up. Simon stood in the doorway, leaned against the frame. He looked comfortable, long legs crossed. "How long have you been there?" she said.

He shrugged.

She looked down at her cigarette, the ash quivering over her notebook. She looked up at him.

"I don't care," he said. "I won't say anything."

She ashed into the empty seltzer can.

"So you're anorexic now."

She put the cigarette between her lips and closed her eyes. No one had said that word to her yet: not her classics teacher who asked if she was ill, not her coworker Rubi who always tried to get her to share food, not her father, not Alex. She was simultaneously sickened and gladdened. He'd noticed. But an anorexic was a stupid girl who looked in the mirror and thought she was fat. Elana knew she was smarter than that. This was not about her body, it was about choices, making her own individual decisions without influence. Her own voice ringing clear. She didn't want the label *anorexia* because with a label came other people's interpretations—anorexia is a desire for control, anorexia is an externalization of internal emotions, anorexia is a result of abuse—like the shamelessly shouted interpretations her lit professors spewed out every day.

"No." Elana opened her eyes and looked at Simon. "I don't think so, not yet."

Simon laughed. "Not yet?"

She dropped her cigarette into the seltzer and shook the can. "How's it feel to be done with rehab? What'd you do there, besides learning Jesus-love and self-hate."

Simon tilted his head. "Self-hate?"

"Whatever it was you said, I can't remember exactly, about being dark and low and deserving nothing."

"Dead," Simon said. "Dead in trespasses and sins. Brought forth in iniquity and conceived in sin. The Lord saw that the wickedness of man was great in the earth, and that every intent of the thoughts of his heart was only evil continually."

"But I like your heart." She felt the sadness that had begun at dinner settling in her again. "You have a good heart," she said, but even as she pronounced the words, she felt that maybe she'd meant them to be a question.

Simon flinched. "Evil," he said slowly, looking at her, as if it were most important that she clearly understand, "is woven into all our hearts and to make a false diagnosis of our condition would lead to flawed remedies. And to do so would be fatal, especially for me."

Elana focused on her pack of Slims, opening it with great care. She wanted to ask him, Are those just standard religious words they taught you to say or do you know it to be true now, does the darkness stay with you when the drugs are gone? But what she said instead was, "Did you tell your new Jesus friends that you are a miracle? Almost as good as a virgin birth?"

Simon's eyes snapped. "I told them that she'd chosen Life, even though everyone around her tried to convince her that murder was not evil."

Elana froze, cigarette halfway to her lips.

When their mother was eleven weeks pregnant with Simon, she had been diagnosed with acute myeloid leukemia. The doctor told her they needed to terminate her pregnancy and begin chemotherapy immediately. She refused. By twenty weeks she was so breathless she could barely walk to the bathroom and Elana lay in bed with her through those sickbed days, bringing her cups of water and rubbing her forehead. Meyer was angry, and when the anger was gone, he was empty. Simon was delivered by C-section at twenty-nine weeks and Adair died five days later.

"All so you could grow up to hate yourself," Elana said.

Simon shook his head. "Mom's choice was a holy, blessed one."

"But she was dirty and wicked and evil in her heart, just like the rest of us?"

"What are you working on?" Simon jutted his chin toward her notebook.

"Nothing. An essay." She closed the notebook.

"On?"

"A collage of quotes from Europeans and Americans on Mexico and Mexicans."

"Oh, like an essay on how Anglo-European literature instructs Alex to view himself?"

"It's not about Alex."

"Oh, I see." Simon pushed off the doorframe so he was standing up full and tall. "So an Anglo woman's perspective on other Anglo perspectives on Mexicans, no Mexican perspective necessary at all."

"Shut up," Elana said, but she was smiling a little. "I don't know what it is, really, it's nothing." She looked up at Simon. "I'm glad Jesus didn't take your sense of humor."

He shook his head and turned away. "G'night. See you in the morning," he said.

Sunlight hung between the sycamore trees in long shafts and Elana focused on reaching and then passing each new shaft, like climbing a flat ladder. Her lungs were burning and Simon was far ahead. She looked down at her pink sneakers slipping through the dry leaves, an old pair she'd unearthed in the basement after Simon woke her at six-thirty in the morning and insisted they go running.

When she looked up, he had stopped in the path and turned to face her, jogging in place.

"Too many cigarettes?" he yelled.

She did not respond.

"You gotta burn those calories, though, right, fatty?"

She squinted at him. He was smiling and still jogging in place, waiting for her.

The path was an old railroad bed that followed the Lark River through town and out into the cattle country beyond, punctuated every so often by abandoned skiffs and empty beer coolers. It was totally flat and easy to run, but beyond the miles she walked while waitressing, Elana hadn't exercised in months. Her stomach was tight with cramps by the time she reached Simon, her breath coming in and out raggedly.

"Rest," she said, panting. She bent over and spat, hands on her hips. She could feel her hip bones through the fabric of her shorts and it made her smile. Her metabolism would be high after the run. She could eat a whole banana and half a dozen almonds.

"We can turn back when you're ready." Simon had stopped jogging and was stretching now.

There was a mist that clung to the river, lit as if from within by bands of light, and in the shallow edge-water, little cups of sycamore bark rocked listlessly. As children, Elana and Simon had fashioned the brown flakes into miniature canoes and released them into the rapids to see how far away they could be carried.

"I'm going up to Frazier this afternoon," Elana said when she'd finally caught her breath. "You want to come?"

Simon straightened up and stared at her. "Why?"

"Oh, come on, visit your grandmother? your mom's grave?"

Simon turned and started jogging again, back toward the house but more slowly now. "That's not her grave."

"Oh, so you prefer the one Dad made for us?"

"She doesn't have a grave."

After Adair died her mother, Dulcie, had wanted her body buried in the family plot on Bethlehem Mountain over in West Virginia, but Meyer claimed that Adair had wanted to be cremated. Adair hadn't written anything down and so it was word against word. After the cremation Meyer sent Dulcie a bit of the ashes and she'd interred them under a headstone in the family cemetery. The rest Meyer kept on a shelf in his library. At some point a child psychologist had told him that his kids might benefit from some sort of stone or marker, a place that they could physically visit, and so he had set up a piece of limestone in the backyard. But there was nothing at all buried under it and nothing on it but a crude carving of her name. Meyer had encouraged them to place small stones on top with their left hands, but Elana had always felt sickened by the monument. It looked like a pet animal's grave.

"I forgive you, but I can't forgive them." Simon glanced back at Elana.

"Forgive *me*?"

"Yes."

"For not visiting you in rehab? Simon, I was in Texas, I'd just moved and had no money and—"

"No, Lana, for giving me weed when I was *twelve years old*." He slowed his pace until they were side by side.

"I didn't—"

"Didn't what? Give me weed?"

"No, I mean, I just offered to share. I didn't mean—"

"Yeah, you just offered and I liked it, a lot, more than you ever did, and then you told me that Coe was growing and then Coe realized I was good at selling and then Coe started making crystal. I can forgive you, but I can't forgive Coe and I can't forgive Dulcie or any of the rest of them."

After he'd switched to homeschooling at thirteen, Simon started spending a lot of time up in West Virginia with Adair's family. He'd show back up at Meyer's house randomly and stay a while and then disappear again. Elana would hear the screen door snap and call for him. Sometimes he was gone an hour, sometimes three weeks. Eventually she realized he was taking the weed their uncle Coe was growing and selling it to college kids at Hall and then going back and living with their grandma Dulcie. Elana had felt the space in her father's house widen without him there, the tall-ceilinged rooms all quiet with their limp curtains and dusty furniture, but Simon seemed happier up in West Virginia. He told Meyer and Elana that school was awful for him, too slow and penal, designed to make you move with the herd. In West Virginia he was learning to hunt and garden. When Elana married Alex, the empty spaces in her life had been filled with sex, punk rock, and Marxist theories and she'd stopped really paying attention to what Simon was doing. Meyer couldn't control him, and so instead he pretended he was okay with Simon's choices. Most of the time Simon seemed like an adult, though he was fourteen, fifteen, sixteen. And then somewhere in those years, he and Coe had started cooking meth.

"What did Dulcie do, really?"

Simon stopped. His face was drawn in, eyes still and mouth set. "I was a child," he said. "I was a child and Coe used me and Dulcie did nothing, *nothing*, to stop him or help me."

Elana looked down at the dry leaves under her feet. She had lived with Dulcie for almost three years after Adair died and Dulcie's name brought with it woodsmoke and apple butter and the green smell of ripening tomatoes. "Dad didn't do anything to stop him either."

"Nope, he didn't, but he also didn't see it in front of his eyes every day, like Dulcie. And then he did put me in rehab eventually, saved my fucking life."

FRAZIER WAS LESS than two hours from Hartsville, but the landscape was sharply different. Driving her father's car up I-77, Elana watched the mountains, heaved up there at the state line like a great wall around some sacred kingdom, the water gaps at the splits in the ridges like crenels for gun barrels. The only way in was under, first the Big Walker Mountain Tunnel and then, twenty miles later, the gray bulwark of the East River Mountain and the narrow passageway beneath.

Despite the empty trees, the mountains looked almost soft this time of year, the stands of oak and hickory etched in a fuzzy purple-gray. The sun that had been shining in Hartsville was blanketed behind a cloud-ripe sky. It had taken Elana a while to convince her father to lend her his car. He'd tried to cloak his reasoning, but Elana knew that even just the mention of his in-laws made him sweat. Adair had been the first to go to college. It was a point of intense pride for the Burns family, her scholarship and straight A's. Then she'd met Meyer, gotten pregnant with Elana, and dropped out. Before her sickness, Meyer had managed to duck them. Then suddenly they were there in the hospital room every day with mud-caked boots and deep suspicions. Cousins and uncles he'd never even heard Adair speak of. They vehemently supported her choice to refuse treatment. After her death Meyer hadn't wanted Elana to live with Dulcie, but Simon was in the NICU in Roanoke and Meyer was traveling back and forth for work and so she'd stayed in West Virginia until she was old enough for kindergarten.

The Burns family land was a cleft that ran down the back side of Bethlehem Mountain toward the Milk River and Route 63. A fold where some ancient runnel had split the limestone and carved a hollow, wide at the base and narrowing up to the ridge. It was terraced now with mobile homes and campers, the older abandoned ones up at the top, swallowed by greenbrier and blackberry vines, and newer ones set in front so that they stuttered down the hill in stages of disrepair. In the midst of them, halfway up the hill, was the old farmhouse, too proud to crumble, though now it sheltered only barn owls, cats, and squirrels; still it sat, hollow eyed and beautifully severe among the clotheslines and cannibalized cars.

Elana drove up the ravine past a dump truck with a FOR SALE sign and a board with faded letters advertising night crawlers. The winter colors of the land stood out against the gray day: pale mint lichen, ocher shocks of poverty grass and the nearly neon purple of wild raspberry vines. Her father's car struggled over the dirt ruts and so she parked and got out. The curtains shifted in the windows of the trailers on both sides of the road. The blue one was her cousin Sheila's, she thought—the maroon-and-white one, she couldn't remember. The air smelled of river mud, woodsmoke, and kerosene. In Dulcie's yard a brown-and-white pit bull was chained with a BEWARE OF DOG sign hanging from his neck. As she climbed the clay embankment, he rose, his chain slinking along behind him. She tried to read his face. His ears were pricked forward and eyes wide.

"Hey, buddy, hey, good dog."

She put her hands out for him to smell and stepped closer. He barked.

"Hey, it's okay."

She stepped closer again and he lunged, snapping. She jumped back, heart punching against her chest. "Shit," she mumbled, and looked past him to the porch, crowded with boxes and garbage bags and a mixture of Halloween and Christmas ornaments. "Grandma," she called. "Hey, Grandma Dulcie."

The dog growled, lowered himself to the ground, and then leapt up, his head snapping to the side when the chain caught.

"Fuck." She glanced behind her, but no one had come out of any of the other trailers. She kicked at the dirt with the toe of her sneaker and thought of her father's satisfaction if she were to come home without getting to visit.

"Jake."

She looked up. A man in a camouflage jacket had come out on Dulcie's porch.

"Hey, boy, quit." He walked down the front steps, his graying blond hair falling into his face as he grabbed the dog by its collar. "Sorry about that." He looked up at Elana and tucked his hair behind one ear. "Mom's got the TV up so loud we couldn't hardly hear you."

It was Coe. Elana flushed with recognition. She hadn't thought there was any chance he'd be here. After the cops had taken Simon away, Meyer had gone down to the station and told them all the information he could cobble together about Coe's operation.

"Thanks." She walked in a wide ring around the dog and up the steps and Coe followed.

"How long you back for?" he asked.

"Just a few days."

"You like it out there in California?"

"Texas."

The trailer was dim to the point of blindness when she first stepped in, and so overheated her hand reached for the zipper of her coat automatically. The TV was blasting a home shopping channel and the air smelled of soup beans and cigarettes.

"E*lawn*a."

She could feel the familiarity wash over her before her eyes even adjusted enough to see Dulcie. No one else said her name quite that way.

"That dog was fussing at you? I told Coe to keep him out back, but he don't listen." She was sitting in an easy chair, wrapped in an orange afghan with a half-eaten bowl of oatmeal and the TV remote balanced on her knees. "Coe, chain him up out back, you hear me?"

"Yes, Mama," he said, and disappeared into the bedroom.

Elana could feel the rhythm of their days in this exchange, a rocking repetition that stretched across whole lives.

"I've got some things for you." Dulcie set the oatmeal on a stack of *Reader's Digests* and pushed herself to her feet. "In the kitchen."

A lick of panic surged up in Elana. She'd known coming here that food was the axis for all Dulcie's social interactions, there was no way not to be rude. "I'm not hungry right now, I just ate," she lied.

"You ate before coming to *my* house?" She turned and gave Elana a snakebite stare.

"I couldn't help it. Simon made a nice lunch."

"Simon's home?" She settled into a kitchen chair with a little huff. Movement seemed to be harder for her than it had when Elana left in August, or maybe Elana had just forgotten how slow she walked.

"Got home yesterday."

"How's he doing?" She wouldn't meet Elana's eyes, concentrating instead on smoothing out the little folds in the tablecloth.

"He's going to his sober meetings and exercising. He found Jesus."

"Well, that's good." Dulcie inspected the lace edge of a place mat. "The way your daddy done him, I'll never forget."

"How's that?"

"I don't know how they do things up where he comes from, but it ain't right to call the police on your own child and have him locked away in a hospital of mentally insane." She looked up then, her watery blue eyes steady on Elana. "He set the police on Coe too, you know."

"Simon pulled a knife on him."

"We don't do like that around here. Call the police on your own family." Dulcie shook her head. "Police tore all through my house, turning up everything. If it hadn't been for Judge Eskins, they'd have locked Coe up for a long while, left me here all alone."

"I thought you hated Coe living here. You always told me you wished he'd get his own place."

She shrugged. "Well, he got out, what is it, two, must be three, weeks back now. Brought that dog with him. I told him to chain that dog up out back, but he don't listen. Never did."

She pushed herself up and shuffled to the counter that was crowded with Nilla wafers, a tin of Crisco, strawberry crisps, and bags of flour. "I don't know why I expected anything less. You know your daddy wanted to throw away little Simon's life before he was even born."

Elana felt a tingling in her throat. She brought her hand to her hip, pressed her thumb into the bone for comfort, and looked out the back window. She focused on the dried stalks of sunflowers and corn husks yellowing among the dead grass. They'd had this conversation many times before. If she took the next prescribed step and said, What about your daughter's, my mother's, life, what about that life thrown away, then they spiraled into a black hole of bruised-sick emotions.

"Can I help you put those groceries away?"

Dulcie turned to look at her. "Oh, I can't reach the top shelves no more. I've got to get a stepladder in here and rearrange these things."

"And Coe can't help, huh? Too busy?"

"Coe's got his parole meetings now."

Elana laughed and opened the cupboard door. "We could take out some of these things that you don't use so much and make room here where you can reach."

Dulcie grabbed her arm and slid her fingers down to Elana's wrist. "They're not feeding you out there at that Texas college?"

"No, I eat."

"It ain't setting right with you, though, being out there, is it?" Dulcie stared at her intently.

Elana looked down. "I do all right," she said, but her mind looped back to her thoughts from the night before, her thoughts of returning, of staying.

"You know your daddy'd love to have you back," Dulcie said. "Or you could come here."

Elana freed her arm from Dulcie's grasp. "You know what your name means in Spanish?" she said.

"What's that?"

"*Dulce* means 'sweet.'"

"Is that right?" Dulcie smiled and her eyes brightened.

THE BURNS FAMILY cemetery was up on the top ridge of Bethlehem Mountain, not as far as the crow flies from Dulcie's trailer, but you had to drive through Render and up the main road to get there. Once, mule and oxen roads crisscrossed the mountain and there were footpaths the men used generations back, walking the hills and crossing the river together in a rowboat to work all day in the quarry, then carrying supplies from the company store back up the cliff on their shoulders. But those paths were grown over now and the drive took a good twenty-five minutes.

As they headed out through the east end of Render, they passed the Blue Sulphur Pike that led, two hollers later, to Alex's parents, Noreen and Jim Walker's house. Elana knew she ought to go out there after she dropped Dulcie back at her place, but a panic-grip tightened and dug in at her temples. She had been to Jim and Noreen's only four times over the past four years, for Christmases that managed to be both picture perfect and as stilted as an awkward dress rehearsal where everyone was trying very hard but had only half memorized their badly written lines.

"Been since July that I ain't been up here," Dulcie said. She looked like a little child, perched on the passenger's seat of Meyer's Subaru, watching out the window.

"Nobody's brought you up here since the last time you and I came?"

Dulcie shook her head.

"We used to play baseball in that field," she said, pointing off to the right. "But then come the year when there was all those foxes. Rabid foxes. All us kids had to carry sticks 'cause they'd come right up on you. We were renting at that time up at the Fields' place and it was a half-mile walk to the school bus stop and there were foxes in the woods all along that stretch. Mama said she used to stand up on the hill there with the milking cow and watch us kids until we was out of sight and then she'd start crying for fear.

"I was the littlest and Peggy and Bill and the others were s'posed to keep me in the middle of them, but one time I had to pee real bad and I stopped there in the ditch and they all got on ahead. I was pulling up my jeans, we wore jeans underneath of our dresses in the cold weather back then, and a fox comes down the pine hill toward me. I run so fast I didn't have a breath left in me when I made it to that bus. You know the bus driver drank too, there'd be beer bottles rolling all up and down the aisles. Daddy complained to the school board and they replaced him with a new driver and that one didn't drink beer, he drank whiskey. You could smell it all over him in the mornings."

Elana steered the car up over the top of the mountain. The view opened into fields of dry yellow grass straining under the wind and wild holly bushes with their last few red berries still clinging. They turned off toward the cliff and followed a dirt road that forked three times before reaching the cemetery. At the last fork a red pickup was idling. Dulcie rolled down her window and waved. Elana squinted but could not make out the figure in the truck. Dulcie waved again and the truck window came down.

"Mrs. Burns?" A man's bearded face appeared. "Is that you?"

"Charlie, how you doing?"

Dulcie's voice sounded almost giddy and Elana realized then just how trapped and lonesome she must feel in the trailer with only Coe and the TV for company.

"You remember Elana, my granddaughter," she was saying. "Adair's girl. Can you believe she's mine? Dark as she is?" Dulcie was laughing and gesticulating.

By the time they reached the cemetery, the wind had picked up and was scuttling the clouds, their shadows passing across the valley below like water moving over the ocean floor. The gusts were so strong they sounded like the pounding of waves and it was easy on days like this to picture how this land was formed by a great sea.

"I can't hardly get my knees to do anything anymore." Dulcie clung to the doorframe as Elana helped her out, her face stiff with pain.

"I thought the doctor gave you something for that."

"It's gone." Dulcie took a deep breath and grabbed onto Elana's arm and stepped down.

Elana knew her mother's grave by sight even from this far. It was the rosy-colored stone, five stones down and four deep. There was a pin oak over top of it that still held leaves, and when the wind blew they lifted a little, a tiny upward breath before the fall.

"Sheila brings me to my appointments and so I give her a few, I know how her back's been hurting since the accident and I don't mind giving her a few, but I got to keep some for me and time before last, the morning after my appointment, they was all gone. Next time I locked 'em in the lockbox your granddaddy used for the paperwork and whatnot, but now the whole lockbox is missing and I got three more weeks before my next appointment."

"Sheila stole all your pain pills?"

"Well, now, I don't believe it was Sheila. I think if she was needing 'em that bad she'd a asked."

"Coe?"

"I don't like to—" She stopped midsentence, gripped Elana's arm fiercely, and pointed out at the field. "Oh, I nearly forgot how pretty it is up here. Ain't it pretty? I almost can't wait until I'm resting here. I can't think of a prettier place. This wind today, though, this wind feels like February." She looked up at Elana and her face was beaming. "You know what you said to me once? That first winter you come to live with me, you must have been about three and we were up on the ridge hunting a Christmas tree and you looked at me and said, 'Granny, the wind feels like a briar in my hat.'"

On the staircase Simon and Elana sat side by side, their faces pressed to the banister, watching guests file into their father's living room. They were couples mostly, all from the college. Their voices rose up above the string concerto that filtered from the speakers. *Thank you, oh, yes, thank you, Meyer, so nice of you to invite us.* The coatrack was full and Meyer had pulled his desk chair out of his office and begun to pile garments on it.

"My, my," Simon whispered. "Quite well attended, I'd say, especially on such short notice."

"What do you mean?" Elana asked.

"You know he didn't plan this thing until after I got home."

"Why?"

"To bother me, to rub it in my face, his supposed Jewishness."

"You don't really think that."

"Seriously, when was the last time he organized a Hanukkah party? Do you ever remember him celebrating?"

She had a few smudgy memories of Meyer lighting the menorah but not a regular yearly pattern and definitely no parties.

"Besides, Hanukkah doesn't begin for another two weeks."

"Wait, what?" Elana pulled her face away from the banister and looked at Simon. It was fun sitting here on the stairs with him, like they were kids again, watching the adults down below, but when he talked about Meyer, he sounded too mean.

"Yeah."

"Really? How do you know that?"

"I looked it up," Simon said. "Of course, the timing wouldn't be convenient for a Hanukkah party. Too close to Christmas and all his Hall College buddies will be out of town."

Elana glanced down at her father's yarmulke-clad head as he ushered the last few guests into the living room. "Maybe he's just trying to be social," she said. "Like maybe it's not supposed to really be a Hanukkah party but more like a holiday-season party."

"He's got that lamp lit and his little hat on." Simon wasn't bothering to whisper anymore. "I didn't even know he owned a yarmulke. He's trying to bug me, or one-up me. He's so wishy-washy he can't stand to see his son become principled."

Elana felt a sudden urge to protect Meyer. "He's trying to relate to you," she said, looking at Simon. The firm conviction in his face was almost frightening in its intensity. "Give him a break."

The doorbell rang and Meyer bobbed out of the living room into the foyer again.

"It's disrespectful to real Jews," Simon said loudly. "Not that these phony intellectuals would care. They're just delighted to think they have a Jewish friend."

"Yes," Meyer was saying down below as he took more hats and coats, "both of my children are around here somewhere."

Elana ducked out of sight behind the big corner baluster.

Simon shook his head. "What are you reading?" He picked up the book that had slipped from her lap. *A Miraculous Lack: Fasting Girls, Mirabilis Nuns, and the Intersection of Female Intellect and Appetite.*

"I'm just borrowing it."

"You gonna write about anorexia now?"

Elana shrugged and took the book back from Simon, turned it over, and set it under her leg. She'd found it when she went into her father's office to use his computer. He frequently received books from university presses that hoped that he might assign them to his students. Elana had opened this one while waiting for her email to load and been jolted by the first chapter. A story about an eighteen-year-old girl named Mollie Fancher who in the spring of 1866 stopped eating and gave herself over entirely to her studies instead: "Her books were her delight."

"You're going back to Texas tomorrow?" Simon said.

Her flight was due into El Paso at eight the following evening. All week she'd played with the idea of not going back. What was the point of finishing her classes? But as the tensions between Meyer and Simon rose, she felt more and more convinced that she should return to Alex. She'd gotten an email from him last Sunday morning, apologizing for not calling her. He'd misplaced his cell phone somewhere and hadn't been able to find it, but he promised he'd be there at the airport to pick her up on Thursday night. She hadn't heard from him again all week, over email or phone, and it seemed odd, but she tried not to worry. She was the one who always complained about being expected to answer her phone at any given moment.

"You like it out there?"

She looked up at Simon. She wanted to say, I don't think I know what I like. But she just shrugged instead.

"Well," Simon said, "I'm hungry. I'm assuming you're *not*, but I'm gonna go eat."

He stood and walked past her. She pressed her thumb into her hip bone and listened to his feet, loud on the stairs, and then, as he crossed into the living room, she could hear his voice above the banter and music, announcing that the Festival of Lights did not officially fall for another eight days, on the twenty-fifth day of Kislev according to the Hebrew calendar, and so what, might he ask, was Meyer doing tonight with the menorah lit?

IN THE MORNING Elana found Meyer in the kitchen, nudging his five calico cats this way and that as he moved between the stove and sink, his slippered feet making a softly familiar sound. He did not hear her enter and she watched him fill the kettle and then pause to stare out the back window, at what? The patches of sunlight under the apple tree? The wren's nest in the porch eaves? He was not wearing his glasses, and as he squinted and stood there, teakettle shaking a little in his hands, he looked, Elana realized, like an old man. She felt the dredge of time sucking steadily under them. She thought of him alone here in this huge house, waiting for Simon's rehab to end. And now it was over and what? Could they really live together again? Her pulse fluttered from her belly to her neck and she thought of Dulcie too, just three mountains over, complaining about Coe and then welcoming him back, fearing him most likely.

"Is there coffee?" Simon's voice boomed behind her and she turned to see him unlacing his sneakers in the hallway, dripping with sweat from his run. He smiled at her, then lunged and grabbed the top of the kitchen doorframe, pulling himself into a chin-up. His body moved all elastic, so young and confident, the proportions of that doorframe and the movement of that exercise so familiar. He'd been stretching himself in that exact place since the day he realized he was tall enough to reach the top and the inside wood was scarred with dates and heights and ages.

"I'm making a second pot," Meyer said. He had lit the flame below the kettle and was back at the sink, washing plates from the night before.

Elana watched Simon walk past him to the fridge, open the door, and stick his whole upper body inside, pawing at the Tupperware. Something about the proprietary ease of his actions bothered her, though why shouldn't he get food out of his own father's fridge? But it reminded her too of Coe, moving his dog and all his problems back into Dulcie's trailer, spreading out and taking up space with no second thoughts.

"I'm worried about Dulcie," she said.

Meyer looked at her over his shoulder, water still splashing between his hands, and Simon pulled his head out of the fridge.

"Someone's been stealing her pain meds," Elana said, "and Coe's staying at her place, but nobody's really taking care of her."

"*Someone's* been stealing them?" Simon laughed, closing the fridge and leaning against it. "She should never have let Coe move back in."

"Oh, come on," Elana said. "Dad's let you move back in."

"It's a classic 'you reap what you sow' situation," Meyer said, drying his hands on his pants and turning to face Elana.

"And what did she sow?" Elana asked.

"Not just her, it's all of them, they practically eat their young, keep them so close it smothers any possibility—"

"Them, who's *them*?"

"Working-class Appalachians."

"Oh, because all working-class Appalachians are exactly the same."

"It's a cultural thing, moving up in the world, especially through education, it's perhaps the worst sin. Do you know how much your mother hated them?"

"I don't believe you."

"The ways they shamed her—"

"Dulcie is proud of Mom."

"Now, yes, now that she's a dead angel saint who died bringing a precious boy child into the world."

Elana glanced at Simon, who was staring at the back of Meyer's head, then she looked back to Meyer's eyes again. "You had no problem letting Dulcie raise me for three years while you were grieving and no problem letting her raise your teenage son when you couldn't handle him."

Meyer blinked. One of the cats made a mewling sound from the end of the counter.

"And now," Elana went on, "she's an old woman who—"

"Is surrounded by family," Meyer said, "quite literally surrounded."

"Yeah, but—"

"I would give her money," Meyer said, "but you know she wouldn't take it, and even if she did, it would go straight to Coe's habits."

Elana couldn't quite believe that they were talking casually about money, about Meyer's money, here in this kitchen. She watched Meyer, waiting for it to hit him, but he seemed unfazed.

"She doesn't want money," Elana said, "she wants someone to take her to visit the cemetery, someone to sit and talk with her." Elana looked over at Simon, leaned up against the fridge, silently watching. "What would Jesus do?" she said, making eye contact with him.

"Jesus?" He unfolded his arms and stepped closer to her. "Jesus? I don't know what Jesus would do, Lana, but I'm only two months sober, I can't go up there into—"

"Shit, I'm sorry. I know." She squeezed her eyes shut. She had a physical urge to stuff her own words back inside her mouth, to fill herself up with the selfishness of them. It was her own guilt speaking and she felt the full force of it hit her then: the deep-down sadness she was drenched with every time she left Dulcie, every time she left West Virginia, over and over again since she was six and had gone back to Hartsville for kindergarten, not that it had even been her own choice, but still she'd felt she was abandoning them, she was prioritizing everything else over Dulcie and the mountains.

Her flight left at 1:00 p.m. and she still had not heard from Alex, but she'd emailed him her itinerary again. Roanoke to Charlotte, Charlotte to Dallas, Dallas to El Paso. In the Dallas airport her body finally relaxed a little. She chewed on sunflower seeds, spat them back into a napkin, and drank a twenty-ounce Red Bull. She was incredibly glad to be away from Simon and Meyer and their huge tensions and voices and appetites. She pictured Alex waiting for her in El Paso and a warm gratitude filled her. She loved him and they would be fine. She would come right out and tell him that she was quitting school and it would be fine. She didn't know why she had made it into such a big deal in her head. Of course, he would understand, he had his own frustrations with the university.

It was dark by the time the plane left Dallas and the streetlamps of El Paso / Juárez were glittering as they landed. The plane circled, dipping south, and out the window Elana watched as they crossed over the border highway, the lights like a choker pulled tight across a woman's neck, and then swooped back north again toward the airport. Watching the runway rush up, Elana realized that she was happy to be back. She had not expected that one week could change the way she felt about this place, but suddenly she was relieved to be here, or at least not to be in Virginia anymore, and all the wide, open space felt freeing. A clean slate. This time, saying goodbye to Virginia was her choice. She had wanted to leave.

Alex was not at Arrivals, not by Baggage Claim or parked out front. She set her backpack down to look for her phone, expecting any minute to hear his voice calling out her name as she fumbled through her belongings. She switched the phone on and waited for it to light up, glancing through the glass windows at the Arrivals drive. No Honda. No new messages on the phone. She pressed his speed-dial number and it clicked immediately to the voice message.

"Hi, this is Alex. Leave me a message and I'll call you back."

That was new. Earlier when she'd called, it had at least rung before going to the message. The battery must be dead. He had never found his phone. It seemed strangely out of character, his losing the phone in the first place and especially his not being able to find it, not replacing it, and not being here to pick her up. She was the one in their relationship who lost things, forgot dates and appointments. He was the one who worried too much.

She glanced at her phone, though why? Obviously, his phone was not working. He could call her from another phone, though. Why had he not called her from another phone? He would have her number memorized, right? Did she know his without the speed-dial button? Five four oh, three three oh, eight two . . . shit . . . shit. Another reason that cell phones were stupid. Before, you always memorized important numbers, now you just expected the machine to do it. She flipped open her phone again. Funny how much she disliked this little thing and how now it felt like such a lifeline.

She picked up her backpack and walked outside. It was cold and windy. Most of the traffic had left and there were only a few idling taxis. There was so much freedom in being the forgetful one. Was this what Alex felt like all the time when she didn't answer her phone or didn't show up where she was supposed to? This ugly pit-of-the-stomach weight? She'd have to try to be more conscientious. She'd tell him she could relate now. He'd say that's why he did it, to show her. Though of course that would be a joke, he couldn't do something like this on purpose even if he wanted to. They'd have a good laugh, though. And her commitment to being more aware would last maybe a week.

She zipped her coat up to her neck, stuck her hands in her pockets. The big electric star was glowing up on the side of the Franklin Mountains, the radio-tower lights creating a red haze around the peak, and as she watched, the clouds above blinked white against the dark sky. There was a rolling clap like a metal drum and the clouds lit up again. A bolt of lightning stretched down the mountainside. She couldn't remember ever seeing lightning in December.

"Miss?"

One of the taxis had crept closer and rolled the passenger's window down.

"Miss, you need a ride?"

"No," she fairly shouted, and picked up her bag and went back inside.

By ten o'clock all the airport restaurants had shut down and she was alone with a single janitor mopping the long corridor.

"You're closing?" she called to him.

He looked up and took his headphones off. "Sorry?"

"The airport's closing now?"

"It's twenty-four hours," he said. "I don't think there are any more flights till the morning, though."

"Oh," she said. Her hand was on her hip and her fingers were wriggling, pressing her waistband against the bone. She couldn't feel it sharply enough. She pressed harder and then noticed the man was watching. His eyes were focused on her waist. She jerked her hand away. It made it feel dirty, having anyone else watch that desperate movement.

She picked up her bag and walked out to the bus stop, where the sign told her the last bus had passed at 8:13 p.m. There were no taxis waiting at arrivals anymore and she had to walk all the way down to Montana Avenue before she could flag one down, twenty minutes in the cold, past empty parking lots and sleeping construction vehicles, the wind shaking the chain-link fence and lightning brightening the bare ridges.

The ride cost twenty-eight dollars—nearly half of what she would make in a shift at Susie's—and it angered her to have to pay it, angered her so much that as she unhooked the gate to walk around back of the building to their apartment she wondered if it would be totally unreasonable to ask Alex to pay her back. She had been the responsible one this time, she had emailed him the itinerary twice!

There was no light shining through the living room window. The door was locked.

"Alex!" she called, and pounded on it. "Alex, what the fuck?"

She dropped her backpack and scrambled in the front pocket for her keys. As she was fitting them into the lock, she glanced over at the driveway. The Honda was gone. She let go of the keys and turned toward the back alley. Maybe someone had taken their usual spot and he'd had to park in the alley? But the alley was empty.

She turned back to the door and jerked it open. Darkness, full and complete.

"Alex!" she screamed.

She flipped on the light and ran to the bedroom. The room was empty, the bed messy. He was not in the bathroom either. She turned and walked slowly back to the kitchen and that's when she saw it, there in plain sight on the edge of the table: his cell phone.

TEN

With the hood over Alex's head, everything had become at once focused and amorphous. The past, the moments leading up to this, were crystalline, but the present was formless: pain, deep in his gut, his legs, his head, his hands. He could not see anything and so he did not know if he was bleeding. Without sight, the pain seemed to spin out around him, drifting and then yanking him back into his body when the vehicle jolted and he was flung across the floorboard. The voices were muffled and he seemed to have lost his ability to translate them. *Átalo allí . . . ¿Y con que mamón?*

The hood was scratchy and smelled of damp earth and fried chicharrón. From within that thick darkness he saw again and again the brilliance of those last few moments in the Lexus: crossing the river on an old iron bridge, the willow trees bent there toward the current, the donkey on the far bank, tethered to a blue bicycle, and then Mateo's face, shifting as he looked from the mirror, back over his shoulder and then at Alex. In the rearview mirror black SUVs appeared; in the side mirror, more of them. The Lexus stopped moving and the men, five or six of them, spilled from the vehicles in slow motion and then fast. The way you might see flood waters swell slowly and then burst up over the lip of the dam.

They rode for hours. How long exactly, Alex had no idea. Long enough for him to teach himself to breathe with the hood on, how not to panic and suck the dirty cloth into his mouth, how to inhale slow and shallow. Long enough for the initial pain to drift away and come back less and less with each bump in the road. Long enough for his need to piss to rise up inside him, paralleled by his fear of asking to use the bathroom and his fear of angering them by pissing himself. It consumed him, this need, and it went like this: hold it, just hold it, okay, no, no, no I can't forever, okay, just motion, show them what you need, fuck no, pee just a little bit, slowly.

After a while one of them smelled it. Alex's mind had come back enough to be able to translate most of what they were saying. *What the fuck is that fucking smell, dude? It smells like fucking piss in here, doesn't it? Oh, fuck, I think he fucking pissed himself. You motherfucking son of a whore.* There was a pounding of fists and more yelling and the vehicle stopped. The back doors opened and even with his hood on Alex could feel the waft of fresh air and then boots against his legs, his back. He was flying. He was in the mud, legs under his stomach.

Get up, you buttfucking cunt.

Alex mentally located his hands. He felt sand between his fingers and wet soil.

Get the fuck up. A white leap of pain swept from his ass all the way up his spine. He gagged. He stood up.

Take your fucking pants off.

He unbuttoned, unzipped. He imagined what must be around him. A dirt road with the caravan of vehicles, the armed men, he himself standing in his pissed pants and underwear and all around them fields of hip-high grass, dripping shock-tops of royal palms, looming mountains, and ghost-white cattle, watching.

The fuck off.

Someone pushed him down again. He managed to catch himself with his hands, but something in the road cut his palm.

Your fucking shoes.

He fumbled with his laces and he knew he was bleeding now, he could feel it transferring from one hand to the other and onto his shoes, his pants and bare legs.

They lifted him back up into the SUV with only his hood and T-shirt on. His bare ass against the metal floor, his butt cheeks and tailbone aching from the kicks, his dick so incredibly and profoundly vulnerable. He curled over on himself, arms around his shins. He knew that Mateo was somewhere in the same darkness in one of the other SUVs and he hoped he was not naked like this.

After a while everything became very simple. If he dug his fingers into the grooves of the floorboard in one particular way, his body would not tumble with each bump in the road and the men would not kick him back into place. He could almost disappear. Their voices hung above him, far away. Fingers in the floorboard was all that mattered. He felt a small flare of pride at figuring it out. He held with the fingers of one hand until they went numb and then he switched to the other. In holding tight, something else let loose and his mind coasted into sight, sound, tributary into river, backward through the days, water down the side of the mountains, night wind in the jacaranda, branches against glass, flash of Mateo's skin, dip of waist into hip, the shape of the back of his neck, snow in the road, the muffled dream of it falling over dogs and church bells and the ticking corner heater. Steam and miles and log trucks groaning home. Winter orchards. Bowls of fat soup. Angry clouds.

At this point they were just memories, familiar but still slippery, like the words to a newly learned song. At this point they had not yet become a prayer.

Pine sap and diesel exhaust. Roads like a racerback snake.

The SUV stopped. Went quiet. Then feet, doors, voices all around him. Cold air against his legs. He loosened his fingers a little. He tightened them again. There were hands against his back. Hands up under his hood. He bucked. In all those hours of riding, no one had touched the hood, his private space. Another hand gripped his arm and held him still. Fingers on his face, his eyes. Fuck, fuck, fuck. Would they gouge his eyes out? His muscles went taut. Someone lifted the hood. A rush of air and a voice shouted. *¡Dejalo!* A blindfold. Yes, yes, a blindfold across his eyes and the rest of his face exposed. His heart slowed, his breath came in, out. But he was shaking now, cold all through. Without the hood, he felt more exposed than without his pants. Now he was with these men here. Present and terrified.

". . . his fucking pants."

"He pissed them. It smelled like a goddamn urinal in there so we made him take them off."

"Find some others then, I'm not bringing him to Neto without any pants on."

"Whatever, we just tell him that he—"

"I'm not bringing the fucking mark to Neto without any pants. We don't even know who the fuck this guy is yet. Put some fucking pants on him even if it means you go around with your own little bird hanging out."

Alex moved his fingers along the grooves to the end of the tailgate. He was sitting near the edge. The men must be standing just beyond. *We don't even know who the fuck this guy is yet.* That could mean they would freak out when they learned he was American and release him. He had seen none of them. He could not point them out in a lineup. He would repeat it as many times as they needed to know.

"So then you decide you're gonna run for it." A voice came now from farther away, pointed in another direction. "And you decide you'll run west into Sinaloa. Now was that planned or just a really stupid oversight? Looked like you were running straight into the arms of El Chapo, but I kinda think that's giving you too much credit. Either way, Neto thinks it's interesting that we found you in enemy territory."

"I . . . I . . ."

Mateo! It was Mateo's voice from the darkness out there.

"Not to me," the other voice said. "You don't answer to me. It was up to me, I'd fucking shoot you right here."

Mateo went silent.

"Fucking disrespectful little faggot. You don't mind taking his money, huh? Spends real good, right? And when you get pulled over by the cops, you don't mind using his connections to get you out of it. No, I'd fucking shoot you right here. And your little boyfriend too. Him first, then you."

Alex gripped the grooves of the tailgate. He wanted to lie back down again, it was too exhausting sitting up, exposed like this. "But see, the thing is, Neto doesn't want that yet. So here we go."

ELEVEN

It made her feel nauseous, the sight of the cell phone. Nauseous and faint. She had to sit down hard on the floor before she could even reach the table. She sat there, staring at the phone, its presence like an ugly wound suddenly uncovered. She couldn't look away, but it made her sick to look straight at it. *Sorry, I haven't called, I seem to have lost my phone somewhere and can't find it. I've looked everywhere. Anyhow, I'm sure it'll turn up and I'll call you as soon as it does. See you Thursday!*

She was aware of the cold air coming in the open door, aware of the sound of something rustling outside.

"Alex!"

A cat walked across the bar of light from the open front door. Elana stood up unsteadily. She shooed the cat, dragged her bag inside, and closed the door. She turned to the phone again. It was dead. They had the exact same model, twins gifted to them by Alex's mom before they left. She found her charger in her bag and plugged it into the outlet beside the couch. It occurred to her that she should do something while it was charging, but she couldn't think of what. She sat and listened to the cat snarl and hiss in the alley outside.

There were seven messages. The first, from 3:00 p.m. on Friday, December 2, had already been listened to and marked as saved. Her own voice: *Hey, Ali, I made it . . .* The remaining six messages had not yet been listened to. Saturday, December 3; Sunday, December 4; Wednesday, December 7; Thursday, December 8; Thursday, December 8; Thursday, December 8. They were all from her, except for the Wednesday one which said: *Hey there, honey, it's your mama. You got some mail that come here to the house and I was wondering if I should send it along to you out there. One of 'ems from the Southern Baptist Convention, I think they've got a retreat coming up, I'm not sure where it is this year, but*—Elana pressed Delete and closed the phone.

He had emailed her on Sunday, meaning that he was still . . . what? *Alive* on Sunday. She couldn't believe she was even thinking in those terms. She flipped the phone open again and pressed 9, then snapped it shut and reached for her own phone instead. Holding them both in her hands brought on a fresh panic. There it was, absolute proof that she could not reach him. She dialed 911 from her phone.

"Nine one one, what's your emergency?"

"My husband's missing."

"Missing?"

"Yes."

"Uh, okay, hang on, I've gotta transfer you."

The line went blank and then a man's voice said, "Central Regional Command."

"Hello?" Elana said.

"Yeah, Central Regional Command, Officer Lopez."

"Umm, I think they transferred me to you."

"What you got going on?"

"My husband is missing?" Each time she said those words they felt stranger and stranger.

"Is that a question?"

"What?"

"Your husband is missing? Look, you're gonna have to come down to the regional command office and—"

"No, I, I was wondering if you . . . I don't know what to do."

"So when's the last time you saw him?"

"I don't know, I mean, I just got home and—"

"Whoa, whoa, take a deep breath, okay. He probably forgot to tell you he was staying late at the office, I'll bet."

"No!" Elana shouted.

There was silence on the other end of the line.

"I haven't heard from him in a week."

"Okay, ma'am, you're gonna have to come down in the morning and file a report."

She stared at the phone after he had hung up. She wanted to throw it against the wall, but she set it down carefully on the cushion beside her instead. She lined both phones up, side by side. His was considerably more smudged and chipped than hers. Maybe he'd been driving to the airport to pick her up and he got in an accident. He could be in the hospital. She jumped up from the couch. The hospital, yes. But they had no phone book in the house. How did they have no phone book in the house? She could hear the upstairs neighbor, Tommy or Timmy or whatever his name was, his music seeping down through the ceiling.

He was stoned when he came to the door, reeking of weed, eyes glassy and red.

"Hey, what's up? Lana, right? You live downstairs?"

"*E*lana," she said. "I was wondering, have you seen Alex, my husband, have you seen him recently?"

Tommy-Timmy leaned against the doorframe and ran his hand across his face. "Wait, what? Like seen him around?"

"I just got home from a trip. He was supposed to pick me up from the airport, but he's not here."

"Ooh, shit. Hubby's in the doghouse now!"

"But have you seen him this week?"

"Like this last week?"

"Yeah, the week that just passed, not the one that's coming."

"Oh, right, right. Uh, I'm not really sure. I mean—"

"Has his car been gone from out back all week?"

"Out back? I don't really go around back."

"Do you have a phonebook?"

Tommy-Timmy licked his lips. "A phone book?"

"Yes, a phone book."

"You gonna call him?"

"Fuck you."

He blinked again and backed away from the door. "Whoa."

"Sorry," Elana said. "I'm kind of panicked, I just need . . . I want to call and see if he's in the hospital or something."

"Oh, yeah," Tommy-Timmy said. "Yeah, oh shit, here, lemme look."

He turned away and walked slowly through the crowded living room and disappeared behind an enormous fish tank. Tool's "Prison Sex" was blasting from the stereo. *Won't you come on a bit closer, close enough so I can smell you.* There was one big gray fish in the bottom of the tank. It was not moving.

He reappeared empty handed. "I don't think I've got one," he said. "You wanted a phone book, right?"

Elana made a tiny nod and turned away. She was afraid if she opened her mouth to say anything, she might start screaming.

"Hey, why don't you call 411?" Tommy-Timmy said. "They'll give you like all the numbers. That's what I do when I like forget a number."

There was no Alex Walker registered at the University Medical Center of El Paso, Las Palmas Medical Center, Providence Memorial Hospital, or the Sierra Medical Center.

Elana lay down on her couch and closed her eyes. She started counting backward from one hundred. When she reached one, Alex would walk in the door. She got to negative five before she sat up and called her father. She knew it was a bad idea before he even picked up.

"Hello?"

"Dad! Dad, I can't find Alex."

"What's that? Elana?"

"Yeah, it's me, I—"

"What's going on, Elana? It's one-thirty in the morning. Your flight get delayed?"

"No, I'm here, but Alex didn't come to pick me up and I'm home now and he's not here."

"He's not there?"

All anyone could do was repeat, she thought, repeat, repeat, repeat.

"Yeah, he's not here."

"Oh."

She took a deep breath in. "I don't know what to do. I called the hospitals."

"He's probably . . . uh, did you remind him that you were getting home today? He's probably out with some friends."

"I told him."

"Your mom once, she . . . well, I forgot to tell her I was going to grab a few drinks after a night lecture I had and she went bananas, the cops came into the Grand looking for me. They escorted me home." Meyer was laughing. "It's a guy thing, I guess, you know we don't realize how much it might worry a woman."

"Oh."

"Hey, try to go to sleep. Call me in the morning."

SOMEHOW GETTING INTO bed felt like giving up, like admitting that he wasn't going to walk in the door right now, this second, like maybe if she just waited on the couch, then he would come home. Maybe he was with friends. He could be out with friends, right? Over in Juárez. But he never ever took the car to Juárez. She tried to picture his days all week while she was gone: classes, research and writing time in his study carrel in the library, long baths, possibly a meal with the Kasa kids, although that was usually a monthly thing and it had already happened last week. Research trips to Juárez for his thesis? Yes, but he never took the car. An image of that painter Viviana's face flashed across her mind. She felt her heart snag. She pictured Alex smiling and talking with Vivi at her opening. Stop it, she told herself. You're not a jealous person. He's not a cheater. Besides, she doesn't even live here.

Something imploded inside her chest, a bomb of breathless debilitating sadness. Not even panic now, just gutting sadness.

"Alex," she said out loud. "Alex, where are you?"

Tool's bass rhythm rattled on in the ceiling above.

She took the *Miraculous Lack* book out of her backpack. She took her cigarettes out too. Certainly there had been something in the lease about not smoking in the apartment. Fuck that. She lit up and stared at the door, hoping the action would summon him to walk in and scold her. She exhaled. Nothing. She ashed into a crusted coffee cup and picked up the book about Mollie Fancher ("Her books were her delight. [. . .] She neglected all for them") and Sarah Jacobs (she "lived on air" and "read earnestly with a musical voice, and composed poetry with marvelous taste"). Elana looked at the door again, focused on the handle, willed it to turn. She looked back at the book and despite herself was drawn in by the parallels between Mollie and Sarah, their ability to leave their bodies entirely by not eating. They did not talk about feeling fat, they talked about reaching for something else, something beyond, and a feeling settled over Elana as she read their testimonies. It was like realizing how much you had in common with a new acquaintance, something Elana had never been very good at—making friends, especially female friends, she had never really needed to, though, because she'd had Simon, and then when he grew distant, she'd replaced him with Alex.

It came for her in the morning. The panic. There was a moment before she knew where she was—a sliver of time in which nothing existed but the bars of sunlight falling through the blinds and the coo of a mourning dove—and then it came, rising up from her feet and washing over her: Alex.

She sat up. She'd slept scrunched on the couch and her neck was tight with pain. She felt dizzy, her vision narrowing and blurring. She hugged her arms across her chest. It was cold or, rather, she was cold, the cold seemed to be emanating from inside her, a deep knitted-into-the-bones chill. She grabbed the afghan from the couch and gathered it around herself.

She hadn't eaten in more than twenty-four hours. This realization rose inside her with simultaneous shock and pride. She reached for her hip, anticipating the thrust of bone against skin. She hadn't eaten since Wednesday evening and it was now Friday morning. This was by far the longest she had ever gone and she toyed with that fact like a smooth pebble, turning it over in her mind. But Alex was gone, and if she did not eat, she would not have the energy to look for him.

The fridge smelled awful. She closed it quickly and stepped away. In the cupboard there were crackers. She set them on the table and forced herself back to the fridge, where she found carrots and a can of V8 juice.

By ten o'clock she was on the downtown bus. After a cup of coffee she had decided that he had to be at the Kasa de Kultura, nothing else made any sense. They must have needed the car for something and Alex had taken it over there and forgotten that she was flying home Thursday night. The cell phone . . . the cell phone she tried to forget about.

She disembarked at Santa Fe and paid her twenty-five cents to leave the country. It had always bothered her a little that no one noted her departure, no one wrote down her name or asked to see any ID upon leaving, but now it seemed horribly, disastrously wrong.

She fumbled with the turnstile, made it through, and kept moving, faster, faster, past the old women with their pull-along carts and the vendors with their newspapers, chicle, dulces. Past the American side and on to the Mexican stretch, where the wire grew patchy and the water disappeared. Past the guard hut and into the sprawl of money changers, dental offices, pharmacies, and off-track betting bars.

She had thought she would take a taxi for speed, but now she realized she had no destination address. She had been to the Kasa more than half a dozen times but always with Alex. She would recognize it on sight from the window of a bus, but she could not remember the colonia or the name of the street. Taxi, taxi, señorita, taxi? they hollered, and she stood stock still in the squirming crowd and felt tears forming in her throat. She swallowed them and got on the Linea 9 bus.

The Honda was not parked outside the Kasa. Sunlight fell across the crumbling pastel faces of the little houses and a scabby cat washed itself in the road. María answered the Kasa door. Elana asked for Ana, and María left the door open and walked to the kitchen. It was silent and dark inside, music playing quietly from somewhere in the back of the room, but no voices. Elana pushed the door open more and stepped in. There were books and papers spread out across the long table, and as her eyes adjusted, she could make out Chucho hunched in a beanbag chair at the end of the bookcase.

Ana came out of the kitchen with her arms wide for a hug. "Elana!" she called. "What a nice surprise."

Elana hugged her, kissed her cheek, and stepped back. She looked down at her feet. Words swarmed her and then fell away. She took a deep breath. "I'm looking for Alex," she said.

Ana tilted her head. "Alex?"

"Yes, my husband."

Ana laughed a little. "Yes, of course," she said.

"I'm looking for him."

"I haven't seen him," Ana said. "What happened, you fought? Here, wait a minute, come here, sit down." She grabbed Elana's shoulder and steered her to a chair. "María," she called. "Bring me a coffee."

Elana shook her head. She pictured Alex the last time she had seen him, dropping her off at the airport, the sun like a halo behind his head; they had kissed, lightly, and he had hugged her from the driver's seat. *See you in a week!* The night before that they had, well, not fought exactly, but . . . she'd been drunk, Ana had gotten her drunk. She looked up at Ana. How to say it? This was all way beyond her language capacity. She needed to concentrate, but María came to the table with a cup of hot water and a jar of Nescafé. Elana wondered if the water was filtered. She did not want to ask. It didn't matter anyway, it was freezing cold in here, she needed the hot cup in her hands.

"I . . . I go home," she struggled to say. "To Virginia for one week and yesterday come back and Alex is not in the house."

It sounded so stupid this way, crassly translated, but Ana seemed to understand. Her face changed. "I haven't seen him since you both were here for dinner last week."

Elana nodded.

"Chucho," Ana called. "Have you seen Alex? Has he come by here this week?"

Chucho lifted his head and leaned back to look at them. "No," he said. He set the zine he'd been reading on the floor and stood up, lifted his shirt, and scratched his belly. "No, man, I haven't seen him since the dinner."

Ana turned back to Elana. "You want some coffee with your water?"

Elana looked down at her mug, she hadn't realized she'd forgotten to add the coffee.

"We should ask Lalo," María said from the kitchen doorway.

Ana and Elana looked over at her.

"He's still doing his research on lucha, no?"

Elana nodded.

"Maybe Lalo has seen him at the arena."

"That's a good idea," Ana said. "We'll ask him as soon as he gets back. You have a phone? We'll call you from the tienda as soon as we hear anything."

"It's an American number," Elana said as she scribbled it down.

Ana shrugged. "We'll buy a calling card."

"Here, let me." Elana reached into her pocket for cash, but Ana stopped her.

"Don't worry about it."

Elana smiled weakly. "Thank you," she said, and swallowed the last of her hot water and set the cup down. "You have seen Vivi?"

Ana's eyebrows arched. "Damian's friend? The artist?"

Elana nodded.

"She lives in DF. You think Alex . . ."

Elana shook her head and stood up. "No," she said. "No."

THE BUS BACK to the Puente Santa Fe was more crowded than the one she had taken up and everyone seemed to be staring at her. She felt acutely aware of being alone. She carried so much space around her, la solita. Everyone else had someone to cushion them from the strangeness of the world. The privacy and comfort of home carried with them in someone else. They relaxed into each other's bodies, heads on shoulders, hands in laps, even the driver was laughing companionably into his cell phone. Elana hugged her arms tighter across her waist, thumbs pressed into opposite hips.

At the bridge she had planned to ask the border guards about the Honda. They did at least seem to record vehicles entering the country, but as she walked down the bus steps into the swirl of *taxi*, *taxi*, *taxi*, El Diario, *diario*, *chicle*, *refresco*, *elote*, she realized that she did not have the language skills to ask and the guards' guns filled her with dread. She slipped her peso into the turnstile and headed back across.

On the American side they told her they could not give out information on the passage of vehicles, even to a spouse. She needed to go to the police station and file a missing person report.

She walked up from the border on a diagonal, across Father Rahm Avenue and up Mesa, past storefronts selling handbags that said I ♥ BOTOX and skin-tight jeans on mannequins that had been cut off at the waist, their bubble butts lined up facing the street. There were perfumes in retail and wholesale, cosmetology, aesthetician, and bridal supplies. And then on the far side of Stanton, there were suddenly no more shops or restaurants, nothing but huge sand-colored parking garages and concrete government buildings. The Central Regional Command office was a three-story pinkish-red square on the corner of Campbell and Overland. On the sidewalk out front, huddles of men stood awkwardly in stiff button-ups and chinos. When Elana crossed the street, one of them approached her for a lighter, his hands shaking. No, she said.

Inside, an officer behind a glass window asked her reason for being there and she started in on an explanation about what the border patrol had told her, but he cut her off.

"Missing person report? Wait here."

She sat down in a plastic bucket seat next to a woman who was cleaning her fingernails with her teeth. Every few minutes the woman pulled a crumpled tissue from her pocket and spat delicately into it, wiped her mouth, and started in again on her nails.

Elana looked at her own nails, cracked and yellowing. She felt hunger lick in her stomach. Her fingers reached for her hip, but the woman looked up, so Elana rubbed her neck instead and pressed the skin, counting vertebrae. She closed her eyes.

"Your neck hurt?" the woman said.

Elana opened her eyes and jerked her hand away.

"Yeah," she said.

The officer who finally came looked as if he had just graduated high school.

"Elana Orenstein? I'm Officer Hernandez."

She followed him through the door and into the chaos of cubicles, phones ringing, copy machines heaving, laughter from somewhere in the back. Hernandez pulled a seat out for her and sat down behind his desk.

"So your husband is missing?"

"Yes."

"For how long has he been missing?"

"I'm not sure, actually, I've been out of town, back home with my family, and, well, I heard from him last Sunday."

Hernandez wrote something down. "Is that normal?"

"What?"

He looked up. "To not have any communication with your husband for a week?"

"No, no, I mean, he's my husband, we live together, I see him every day except that I went back home for a week."

"I see, so you talked to him last Sunday?"

"It was an email."

"When was the last time you spoke to your husband?"

"When he dropped me off at the airport."

"This was also the last time you *saw* him?"

She nodded. "Friday, December 2. Then he emailed me on Sunday and said he'd lost his phone and that's why he hadn't called. But when I got back to the house last night his cell phone was on the table."

Hernandez looked up, his pen stopped moving, and his eyes widened. "I see." He put his pen down. "Do you have some current photos of him?"

"Not here, no, I didn't think—"

"That's okay, we will need those as soon as possible, though. Three current photographs."

They ran through Alex's full legal name, hair color, eye color, height—she froze up, she wasn't sure exactly. They were the same height, right? Five foot seven? But maybe not exactly, maybe he was five eight or five six . . . Weight? She balled her hands into fists.

"I don't know. I mean, he's not fat at all, but he's not like really skinny either." How was there so much that she did not know about Alex. "Uh, maybe a hundred and fifty?"

"Scars?"

"Uh, no."

"Tattoos."

"No, he doesn't have any."

"Medications?"

"No."

It went on like this. What did he have on him when he went missing? She didn't know, obviously not his phone. What clothes was he wearing? No idea. Where was he supposed to be the day he went missing?

"I . . . I don't know what day he went missing."

"Right." Hernandez nodded. "I see."

They could get information from the border patrol, she asked, about whether or not he'd driven into Mexico, right?

Hernandez nodded again. "Yeah, but we'll start this side of the border, check out some the places you say he frequents, the university obviously. We'll need those photos first, though. Bring 'em by as soon as you can."

Elana stood up.

"Oh, one more thing, there weren't any signs of foul play at the apartment, no?"

"Foul play?"

"There's no reason for you to think your husband might have been kidnapped?"

"Oh God, no."

"All right, well, bring those photos by." Hernandez stood and reached out his hand to shake hers. "Oh, and he's not a minor, right?"

"What?"

"I just gotta check. If he's not a minor and there are no signs of foul play, there's a limitation to what we can do, it's technically not illegal for a person to go missing."

"You mean you're not gonna help me."

"That is not what I am saying at all, ma'am." Hernandez came around his desk. "It's just we can't put a lot of resources into looking for a husband who wants a little vacay."

Elana blinked. She felt tears forming and it made her angry to think she would cry. She looked down and stepped away from the desk. "That's not what . . ." But she couldn't finish the sentence.

"I'll walk you out," Hernandez said. "And you bring those photos by just as soon as you can."

On the corner outside, the man with shaking hands walked up to her again. She patted her pockets until she found her lighter and held it out to him. The street was filled with a wavering, watery light, the sun reflecting off the tall glass offices on Overland and sending looped circles of pale green radiance onto the road and the county jail beside it. It reminded Elana of the fish tank in her neighbor's apartment, the slow submerged feeling to everything: the line of handcuffed men waiting silently outside the detention center, each one chained to the next and all of them holding folded white papers, the Texas and American flags snapping on their corner poles and a siren winding up somewhere nearby.

The shaking man was talking, but Elana couldn't focus enough to listen. Time was doing something strange, she felt it all elastic inside her, commanding her in a million directions at once: rush, go, now, find some photos . . . but for what? The police weren't going to do anything. Email! Maybe he'd emailed again. Home! Maybe he was there at the apartment now, at home. Phone! Maybe he'd called her phone. She pulled it out of her pocket and jammed the button on the side. She'd turned it off when she crossed into Juárez. She gripped it and watched the screen come to life slowly. Two new messages. Her heart slammed inside her chest.

"Hey, Elana, just checking in." Fuck, it was Meyer. She pressed Delete. Next message. "Hi, Elana, it's Rubi, I don't know if you're back yet but . . ." The voice kept talking, but Elana had taken the phone away from her ear. Rubi from Susie's wanting to know if Elana could cover her dinner shift. Susie's . . . it was only about seven blocks away, but it felt like it existed in a different universe. When was her next scheduled shift, tomorrow? She could walk there now and see, explain to them that . . . what? She turned right instead and headed to the public library where she could check her email.

"Miss," a voice called from behind as she crossed the street. "Miss, señorita!"

She turned slowly with some strange hope blossoming in her chest, a hope of what she did not know, but somehow, something . . . Hernandez calling her back to tell her they'd found him, don't worry, no need for photos . . . She stared. There was no one there but the shaking man. He was waving, holding something up above his head. "Miss!" Her lighter.

She had to wait for a turn at one of the computer carrels. The librarian asked if she would like to take a seat, but she stood, arms crossed, watching the computer corner. After a little while the librarian went over and spoke to one of the men, who looked in Elana's direction and then slowly got up and moved his backpack and shopping bags over to a table nearby. The librarian smiled at Elana.

"Go right ahead."

There were no new emails in her inbox. She sat at the computer for twelve minutes, refreshing the screen and listening to the man behind her sorting through his plastic grocery sacks. He had pulled twenty or more of them out and laid them on the table and was folding them into tiny perfect squares.

Outside, the sun had gone behind the clouds, and though it was only three in the afternoon, it seemed that night was coming on quickly now. Twenty-four hours ago, she had been in a plane hurtling toward this place, toward Alex, or an image of Alex. Maybe that was it, maybe he wasn't missing but had never been here at all. She'd just imagined it, like some *Twilight Zone* episode.

She took Missouri Street down toward Santa Fe where she could catch a bus home, but when she reached Santa Fe, she kept walking past the bus stop. Each of these things—the phone, the email, the apartment—was a possibility until she looked at it, and then it burst. He could be at the apartment until she proved that he was not.

She turned down El Paso Street and pretended to be interested in ornamental pigs, cheap Chinese shoes, and two-for-one underwear. She bought an elote from a man with a steaming cart and told him no cheese, no cream. She got a coffee, black, and sat in the window at Lola's Comida Casera, watching couples come in and out of the pawnshop across the street. She bought a bottle of whiskey at the duty-free store and got on the bus at the transfer center.

The apartment was dark. She checked his phone: a missed call from Meyer, no message. She poured a glass of whiskey and went into the bedroom to look for photos. Somewhere there was a framed picture of the two of them on the day after their wedding, in the front yard in T-shirts and jeans. Meyer had taken it when they told him they'd gotten hitched and then Alex's mom framed it for them, but they weren't ones to display photos of themselves in their own home. She turned on the overhead light and looked at the bed, rumpled, with her pajamas strewn across the covers. Her pajamas. Untouched where she had left them before heading to the airport. He had not slept even one night here since she'd left.

By the time she found the wedding photo, she was drunk. Four whiskeys in. The photo looked stupidly naive. Arms around each other's waists, awkward smiles. Squinting eyes in the sunlight. She could see even now how she'd been fairly vibrating with anxiety and pride: worry over what her father and brother would say, spit-in-your-eye pride over not having asked anyone's permission. Although, of course, it hadn't been her idea. She flipped the frame over and tried to unclasp the backing, but the cardboard had been glued into place. She tapped it on the corner of the dresser. Nothing loosened. She smacked it again and there was a cracking sound. She turned it over. Glass and blood. Her finger was pulsing.

In the bathroom she ran her hand under the tap and leaned against the counter, suddenly aware of how drunk she was. The fluorescent light was blinking, the fan heavy overhead. Her blood ran bright against the white porcelain, streaming and mixing with the flow of the water. She had some idea she should be holding her hand up above her head, but it was so messy and she liked the feel of the water on her skin. She watched her blood until it thinned and then she wrapped her finger in toilet paper, fetched the whiskey bottle, and sat on the toilet with her hand propped up in the towel rack above. In the mirror she could see the top of her unwashed hair, dark snarling curls, and her hand, the wad of toilet paper turning red.

Stupid, fucking idiot. She started laughing and could not stop. How long had it actually been since she'd paid attention to Alex, to what he was saying, what he was doing, really? She had thought she would be the one to disappear, and she'd been trying, hadn't she? Not so dramatically like this, but little by little, evacuating all the casings around her. She hadn't wanted to be *in* anything anymore, in a marriage, in school, in a body. And when you thought about slipping out of something, you assumed the casing stayed, you were the one choosing to move away. It wasn't that she hadn't wanted to be around Alex; there was a difference, one she thought he might not see, which was why she hadn't said anything. It wasn't about not being with him, it was about having him not be a part of the mold around her, the form to fit her in. But she had married her best friend and so she had no one to talk to about her husband.

If she were honest, she'd been wanting for a long time to see the chaos inside mirrored outside in her life somehow. It was a part of the pain of growing, she thought; when you were young, your personal pains and confusions *were* the whole world, the only thing that mattered. Then as you got a little older, you realized your angst was miniscule in comparison to the world and so you looked for something bigger, politics or music, some kind of movement to refract your identity through, beam it out huge. You went to a certain school or dropped out of school. All the way back to *Robinson Crusoe*, folks had been telling their families, Fuck you and your law school, I'm going on a journey to look for myself. Only no one was really looking for themselves, they were looking for something bigger to externalize their inner selves. Violent colonialism and slavery did the trick for Crusoe. Elana had never been great at joining groups or identifying with anything, but now, she thought, horribly, now she did have something bigger and externally visible, Alex's disappearance, to explain and reflect her unhappiness. Now no one would ask why she was sad anymore.

She focused on picturing Alex's face, his dark eyes, always with a quickness to them and a deep interest, those fucking eyes that said *nothing else exists but you and what you are saying right now.* And still, she couldn't talk to him. Or maybe because of that, she couldn't talk to him.

He was always so engaged, intimidatingly smart, beautiful, and engaged.

TWELVE

They were sitting in the seats of the SUV now instead of the gutted back end and at first Mateo had not known whether Alex was there, until one of the men barked, *You too, up, move along.* Mateo heard a stumble of footsteps and felt a body moving toward him. *Stop, there,* the voice barked. *Yes,* another voice said. Alex, it was Alex there beside him. Mateo could reach out and touch him, but he did not. They were being watched, obviously. Up until now he had taken a sort of refuge behind the blindfold. There was a kind of comfort in not seeing and he did not have to entirely face what was happening. But now, with Alex beside him, he felt his eyes moving desperately behind closed lids.

He did not know where they were precisely, but he knew *where* they were. Neto's compound. Or, more than likely, one of many compounds. They would be dragged before Neto momentarily. It had all played out as predictably as any feud story line he had fought in the ring. The fall after the rise. Why had he thought it would go any other way? Or maybe, if he was honest, he had known all along that he could not outrun Neto, but he had to run anyhow. Same as in any wrestling match, you had to give it your all, even though you were running on a leash, just waiting to feel the snap when you reached the end of it. But at least in the ring you had the audience howling when you lost, you had your own body fighting back, ready for next time. There was no next time here, though. No audience, except for Alex. And, fucking shit, Alex wasn't an audience anymore, Alex was in it.

He heard the men up front talking to someone outside. A guard booth or checkpoint. And then another. And then the vehicle stopped, the engine cut off, and they were unloaded and marched, stumbling. There was gravel underfoot and then smooth stones. A movement all about his knees. Dogs. He could hear them breathing, their nails on the stones. In the blindfold he was constantly drawn downward; lower felt safer and he would have fallen among the dogs if a hand hadn't held his arm vise tight. A shift in temperature. They were indoors now. Tripping upstairs. Footsteps echoing. And a voice, they were approaching Neto's voice.

"Welcome."

Someone pushed him down to his knees. A hand ripped the blindfold from his face. Everything rushed in, separate and symphonic at once. Neto in front of him, seated, bodyguards fanned behind him like a peacock's tail. Domed windows, tiled floors, and tiled walls. Alex beside him, kneeling, still blindfolded and wearing someone else's too-big jeans. Dirt and dried blood on his arms and face and smeared down his long neck. He was three feet away. He was breathing quietly, hands at his sides, fingers tensed.

"Looks like he got it a little worse than you, huh?"

Mateo looked back toward Neto. There was so much light, sunbeams falling through a skylight overhead, through the windows and open door. He realized he had never seen Neto during the day, never seen him outside of a dark club.

"Did you have a good week?" Neto said. "I was disappointed when you didn't show up on Monday. I got over it, but I thought we had a different kind of relationship." He shrugged. "Humans are complicated, though, all of us. Dogs, for example, are much better at reading our intentions. They don't have egos to get in the way." The Doberman pinscher closest to him stood up, ears perked. "Relax," he said, and the dog sat back down. "Anyway, a slight misjudgment on my part, but here we are. I went ahead and met with Arturo without you. It's all arranged now, your contract with CMLL is terminated and your registration with Empresa Estelar is official."

Mateo heard the words as if they were coming from the far end of a long tunnel or from a phone with a bad connection. Their ability to affect him had evaporated. What mattered now was Alex, scraped and bloody on his knees beside him. Tense and trembling. Mateo looked over at him from the corner of his eye.

"Your boyfriend?" Neto shook his head. "Why does he still have a blindfold on?" He looked back at his bodyguards. "Take the blindfold off this man."

"Sir." One of the men stepped forward. "We have not verified his identity fully yet, we haven't finished—"

"Take the fucking blindfold off."

A guard unknotted the black cloth from Alex's face, and Alex inhaled sharply as if he'd been holding his breath. He blinked and swayed, his hands opening and closing as he looked from Neto to the men to the skylight to Mateo. Their eyes met. Blood roared in Mateo's ears. Those eyes, black and wet, and that face, his fat busted lip. He looked away.

"Okay," Neto said. "Enough of the knees. Up, up. This way."

Mateo and Alex rose slowly, unsteady but careful not to reach for one another. Careful not to even look. Mateo followed directly behind Neto, Alex behind him, and the bodyguards behind them with their AR-15s.

Neto led the way down the hall and through another rounded doorway to an outdoor staircase. The house was new, but the architecture was colonial, Moorish arches, adobe, and Saltillo tiles. From the stairs, as they rose floor by floor, the whole compound came into view: the red-tiled rooftops spreading in every direction, a tennis court and huge swimming pool circled by sickly palm trees, a fleet of SUVs and jeeps, an airfield with three prop planes, and beyond, nothing but creosote bush and red earth forever, pocks of boulders, and far off, the curve of the earth itself falling away at the horizon. The sun commanding. A deadly distance. One road out and one road in.

"Quite the view, huh?" Neto turned and walked away from the stairs into a rooftop garden. "But this," he said, "is what I really wanted to show you." He waved his hand out at an intricate maze of red, pink, yellow, blush, and black roses. The front was filled with shorter bushes, but farther back they grew chest and then head high. "You've been to the Chapultepec Castle?" Neto looked over his shoulder at Mateo. "I've always felt they could have done so much more with the second-story gardens."

Mateo could hear Alex walking close behind him. He wanted desperately to look back. He moved ahead instead, the bushes closing in until they were forced into a tight single file, the thorns catching on their clothes and sketching blood lines down their bare arms as they passed. The smell was heavy, sugary.

"I always thought the thornless rose was such a disgusting development," Neto said.

Mateo could see just a flicker of Neto, the shine of his watch through the leaves ahead. It was dim under the highest reaches of the maze and the bodyguards' machine guns ruffled the close foliage. The rose smell was so thick Mateo could taste it.

"I've been breeding a rose just *for* her thorns, actually. It takes time, though, and money. You know David Austin spent five million breeding the Juliet. Five million and fifteen years."

Light filtered in up ahead where Neto stood silhouetted under another arch. He stepped aside and a diamond-shaped opening came into view, the sun fiercely bright again, reflecting off a fountain that leapt in the center. The air was clearer here, less sweet and more breathable. Mateo moved away from the archway and glanced back as Alex emerged, still crusted with blood and dirt, his eyes dull.

"My mother used to make fun of me for loving roses. Women's things," Neto said. "The truth is, though, as with most things, when you get into the serious professional arena, roses are a man's world. None of the best breeders are female."

The bodyguards lined themselves up on each side of the diamond opening, careful not to brush the blossoms.

"Are you ready?" Neto looked from Alex to Mateo and then walked past the fountain to a small stone obelisk at the back. "Don't make the mistake of underestimating her." He knelt beside a simple four-petaled pale pink blossom. The bush was small and thin, clinging to the stones and winding up a few feet off the ground, producing a single delicate bloom. Neto looked up at Mateo.

"A cutting from the Hildesheim Rose. More than a thousand years old. Her mother bush has been growing on the wall of that German cathedral since at least the year 815. She lived through bombings in World War II, devastated down to the ground, burnt, but her roots were strong and she lived. Who knows what other catastrophes. She'll outlive us all. There are rose fossils that date back thirty-five million years."

There was a movement from behind Mateo among the bodyguards, the squawk and static of a radio and hurried footsteps.

"Can I speak to you for a moment?" A guard stepped toward Neto.

Mateo and Alex were left almost alone. The men huddled with Neto at the far end of the diamond garden. Mateo stared at Alex's face, willed him to look his way. This was the moment in a movie where they would break free, vault over the edge of the roof, and somehow make it to safety. The men's voices were a garble, but among the snarled rhythm came the word *American*. Alex blinked and looked at Mateo, his eyes brighter now, almost smiling. Mateo stared back at him. He wanted to mouth something, wanted to say, I'll fix this.

The huddle broke up and the men came back toward them. Mateo bent his knees and crouched instinctively, but the men overwhelmed him, jerked his arms behind his back, and snapped on cuffs. He lost sight of Alex for a moment and then they were all moving toward the mouth of the maze. Alex disappeared into it, the gun butts of the men on each side of him jostling loose a shower of red petals.

"You all go on, take him down below. Leave this one here." Neto pointed at Mateo.

The men disappeared in a rush and rustle, all but two who stepped aside as Neto approached Mateo, grabbed his throat, and forced him down to his knees. Mateo felt the slam of the tiles under his legs, a shock that traveled up his body. His tongue was roiling in his mouth, desperate, choking. The sky was so blue, so bright. The pain in his neck felt tremendous. His blood was raging. He looked at the thin pinstripes of Neto's green-and-white shirt. He could overpower him, kick him in the balls. But then the guns would come out and that would mean death and he wasn't sure he was ready for that. There was something wet on his face. Everything went thin, grainy and out of focus, and then it was gone. He flopped over. The pressure was gone from his neck. He opened his eyes. He was crying.

"You thought an American would save you? Maybe I'd let you go if I knew Americans were looking for you and your boy?" Neto was pacing above him where he lay, sprawled beside the fountain. "And here I thought you loved him, thought you brought him along because you couldn't bear to be away. Or maybe I'm supposed to believe this was another stupid, innocent mistake, like running away into Sinaloa territory?"

Mateo squeezed his eyes closed. Had he brought Alex along for leverage? Had some tiny part of him, even in the very back of his mind, thought about that?

"Get up."

A hand slapped his face.

"Take his cuffs off. He doesn't need to be cuffed."

One of the men hauled Mateo to his feet and uncuffed him. His wrists stung. He looked at Neto and Neto reached over and brushed his hair out of his eyes. Mateo studied his face, trying to find the edges of his confidence, the way it had crumbled that night in Los Padrillos, but he stood strong now.

"Go take a shower." Neto turned to his men. "Show him his room."

They grabbed Mateo's shoulders and spun him toward the maze opening. He looked back. "Where's Alex?"

"James Alexander Walker Junior? He's in the basement."

Mateo jerked around to face Neto again. "I—"

"Shhh." Neto held his finger up to his lips. "You and I need to work on trust. Junior will benefit from trust."

THE SHOWER FELT like falling. Like drowning. The water heavy with guilt and howling sadness. *He's in the basement.* The shower was delicious. Obscenely warm. Mateo stayed under the water until he was too weak to stand. Even then, the smell of roses did not leave his nose.

When he opened the bathroom door, Neto was sitting on the edge of his bed. Mateo took a step back.

"How was it?" Neto stood up and walked toward him. Mateo tightened the towel about his waist and then reached for another to cover his upper body.

Neto stopped. "Really?"

Mateo hugged the towel about his chest.

Neto laughed, but his eyes were hard. "You think I want to see you? Touch you?" He smiled tightly. "You're just like the rest of them, huh? Like any male body I see, I must want to fuck." He turned away, walked toward the purple upholstered chair in the corner, and Mateo felt it like a kick to the chest. He did not want to relate to Neto, but he did. He thought of the locker room in the gym in DF when he had first moved there, after that moment with the other new wrestler who must have said something to the rest of the guys, what exactly Mateo never knew, but after that they were quick to leave whenever he entered the locker room and never undressed around him. He'd felt the rage like a steady boil under his skin and he'd wanted to scream, I don't want to fucking touch you. But he couldn't say anything, couldn't do anything but be more careful, oh so careful, of how his body moved and where his eyes fell.

"Mateo," Neto said. "You are not doing so well on the trust building."

Mateo moved to the end of the bed where he sat, facing Neto. "I'm sorry." He looked down at his bare feet and then up. "Listen, though, you don't need to keep Alex in the basement, really, we won't try to—"

"You miss him already?"

Mateo looked away again. He swallowed and took a deep breath. "Or you can put me down there too. I don't need to be up here in a nice room if he has to stay down there."

"You think I have him in some kind of dungeon of doom?"

Mateo looked back at Neto quickly. "Is he in a bedroom down there, a bedroom like this?"

Neto shook his head. "Not just like this, no."

"I'd like to be down there too, for as long as you feel it's necessary, I can—"

"Shh, now. We can't have our star wrestler down in the basement. You know that. You have to rest up for your big debut, *our* big debut. I need you to focus on that right now. Everything else will fall into place. Your wife wishes you the best of luck. You don't need to worry about her, and Martín either, they have a new car now, they're comfortable."

Mateo snapped his head up. "Martín? You saw Martín?"

"We couldn't have them driving around in that piece-of-crap Japanese car with American plates. They're comfortable now and your wife is so proud of you, the star of a new promotion. Your mother too. My men visited her in Vinihuévachi and she was so proud, and so helpful."

THIRTEEN

From a block away Elana could see the yellow lights of Susie's Tex-Mex Cafe spilling out onto the sidewalk. A warm beacon in the otherwise dark street. The Central Regional Command office did not open until eight, but Susie's opened at six. Elana could not sleep despite, or maybe because of, the whiskey pounding in her brain. The buses didn't run this early and so she walked under the silt of stars, past houses and apartment buildings with tentative morning movements silhouetted against the curtains, the outline of a head with curlers, a cowboy hat, low radio voices leaking out. When she passed the Labor Ready office, the line already snaked around the corner, but there were no lights on inside yet.

Maybe she was still drunk, Elana thought, for there was some distance now between herself and the horror of Alex being missing. A distance that, amazingly, stayed with her as she came into Susie's and greeted Rubi and Lisa, the white girl, who were prepping the coffee urns behind the counter.

"Hey," Rubi said. "You're back! Did you just get back? You look exhausted. Is everything okay?"

"Can I have some coffee?" Elana sat at the counter, but she did not collapse and she did not cry. Instead, she narrated the plot to the movie she'd been living recently.

"Oh my *god*, that's awful, I'm so sorry!" Rubi said. She came around the counter and squeezed Elana. Her skin was warm and her coconut perfume spread over them.

Lisa went to refill her customer's coffee, and when she came back, she leaned in close, her face serious. "You heard from him on Sunday, but it was email?"

Elana nodded.

"So obviously you didn't hear his voice, so it could have not been him."

"What do you mean? Like someone hacked his email?"

Lisa drummed her nails on the countertop. "Potentially. Have you inspected the garbage?"

"The trash at the apartment?"

"In case there is anything unusual, something he doesn't normally eat, tickets to somewhere. Receipts often have dates printed on them."

"You're way better than the cops," Elana said. "They think he's on vacation."

AT EIGHT O'CLOCK she brought the wedding picture to Officer Hernandez. The corner of the photo was smudged with dried blood. He turned it under the light.

"That's mine," she said. "I cut myself trying to get it out of the frame." She held up her toilet-paper-bandaged hand.

"This is it?" He tapped the photograph.

"It?"

"The only photo you've got?"

"Here, yes, I mean I'm sure I have more back in Virginia, but—"

Hernandez stood up and walked to the end of the room where he spoke with an officer. Elana inspected her bandage, picked at the Scotch tape edge until the toilet paper unraveled and she could see the wound. It started bleeding again as soon as it was unwrapped. It did not hurt, but the blood was fiercely red and it ran down into her palm.

"You need to get that seen."

Elana jerked her head up.

Hernandez stood over her. "Looks like it might need a couple of stitches."

She gripped the wad of toilet paper in her sticky palm and stood up. Blood dripped onto the floor. Hernandez looked at it and she looked at him. Although the whiskey had worn off, the sense of distance had stayed and with the distance she could see now that she was not actually standing here talking to a police officer about the disappearance of her Alex, she was inside a neo-noir art film where she played Wife, distraught and potentially insane, looking for Husband, missing and potentially on vacation.

The blood dripped beautifully. She hoped the camera was catching it.

"Ah, shit, we've got a first-aid kit around here somewhere," Hernandez said. Once her hand was bandaged, he told her he needed to contact Alex's parents.

"That's just about the last place he would go on vacation," Elana said.

"We need to speak to all immediate family members."

Her finger was throbbing now, the bandage too tight. "His family isn't really immediate."

Hernandez stared at her.

"He was adopted."

OUT FRONT THE street was filled with watery light and wind. The shaky-hands man asked her for a lighter. She smiled. "Wrong movie," she said. "This is not *Groundhog Day*."

She opened her cell phone and pressed the speed-dial key that Noreen had preset with her own phone number.

"Elana!" Noreen said.

"Noreen," Elana said, and then she told the plot of the movie again, only this time Husband became Son. "I wanted to tell you myself before the police called."

"You were in Virginia?"

"Only for a few days, I—"

"Why didn't you tell me?"

"It was just for Simon, coming home from rehab. Just for a few days."

"Why wasn't he with you?"

"Simon?"

"Alex."

Elana drew in her breath. "We were gonna plan a proper trip home, to visit, over the winter break. This was just so I could welcome Simon."

"Alex told me over a month ago that you two weren't gonna make it home for Christmas this year."

"Well, yeah, he thought we should save our money and stay—"

"I'm coming out there."

"Here? Noreen, no. I wouldn't have bothered you with this at all if the cops hadn't said they'd be calling you."

"My son is *missing*."

"He's probably just on vacation."

"What?"

"Nothing. Don't come right now, okay, let's wait."

SHE TOOK THE bus home and dragged the garbage can out from under the sink. On the cream-colored linoleum she separated granola bar wrappers from Kleenex and ramen noodle containers. She found a receipt from the student union for a coffee and muffin totaling $5.53, sold on Friday, December 2, at 9:03 a.m., an empty packet of Bic pens, a Post-it note that read *Dr. Nelson—Thesis—Friday, 10:15*, some brown banana peels, and a crumpled Slims pack filled with butts that she had hidden under coffee grounds at the bottom of the bin a week and a half ago.

She put the Post-it and receipt on the counter and dumped the rest back into the trash. She washed her hands. Her finger was throbbing. She took off the bandage. It began to bleed again. She wrapped it in toilet paper and looked at her phone. No new calls. It was only 10:02 a.m. Rubi and Lisa had told her they would cover her shifts until this got resolved. *He'll be back soon*, Lisa had said, *I can feel it, it's just gonna be one of those weird things, but it'll be fine.* Now Elana had nothing to do. She glanced at her phone again. She wished Meyer would call, although he would be no help and she wasn't even sure she wanted to talk to him. They hadn't spoken since the night she got back to El Paso and he'd assured her that Alex was just out with friends.

He had called the next morning, but she hadn't called back. Now she wished he would try again, even though she didn't want to talk. On Thursday she'd been so happy to leave him. She thought of their last morning together, his words about Dulcie, *they practically eat their young, keep them so close it smothers any possibility.* But what if you kept your children too far off? Meyer had never been more proud of her than when she'd been accepted into the March of the Living study-abroad trip. It was a Jewish heritage program for middle schoolers—a week visiting the Holocaust memorials in Poland followed by a week of visiting kibbutzim in Israel. He had found a pamphlet about it at the Holocaust museum in DC and had prodded Elana to apply. When she was accepted, he beamed. But she was barely thirteen and had never even been on a plane. In the end, she was too terrified and had begged Simon to convince Meyer that she was sick. The disappointment rang out from him for weeks and months afterward.

By ten-thirty the stillness of the apartment was too much. She made her way back to the bus stop, but before the downtown bus arrived, she realized that she had both her own phone and Alex's with her. If he came home, he would have no way of knowing where she was. She returned and set Alex's phone precisely where he had left it, lining it up with the metal edge of the table. Beside it she left a note: *Gone to Juárez looking for you.*

On the bus she realized that she had left the only picture she had of Alex with Officer Hernandez. He was not in the command office, but when the Wife cried a little, a different officer brought her a copy of the image. Alex's face blown up grainy and indistinct, her own face cut out.

By noon she was crossing the international border, feeling capable and industrious. This time she knew the address of the Kasa. This time she took a cab and watched the city streak by quickly.

The door to the Kasa was open and voices rang out as Elana paid the driver.

"No, see the thing is you're too busy responding to really listen."

"Does really listening mean agreeing with you?"

Elana approached the doorway and squinted into the dim interior. Ana and Luis were arguing, and María and Chucho were seated at the long table, hunched over baskets with four other people Elana did not recognize. She took another step inside and Ana looked over.

"Hey." She waved to Elana. "I was gonna call you."

Elana's heart zipped up to her throat. Her face must have shown it.

"Oh, no, I mean, I don't have any info," Ana said, "but I wanted to see how you're doing."

Elana nodded. She could not speak. Ana pulled her in and hugged her. She smelled of garlic and corn masa and coffee. "Lalo will be back soon," she said, face pressed against Elana's hair. "He said he hasn't seen Alex, but he'll take you around to ask at the arenas and gyms."

Ana released her and Elana saw Luis staring but trying not to stare, his eyes skittering back down to his feet. She'd never seen him unsure before and it almost pleased her. If the Wife had a superpower, it was making everyone ill at ease.

"Elana, this is José and that's Melchor and Rita and Julieta." Ana pointed to the four at the table. "And this is Elana." She pulled out a chair. "Sit down, we're working on beaded key chains and earrings to sell, to raise money to go down for the beginning of the Other Campaign. You don't have to work on them, though, just relax."

"I'll help," Elana said. "Show me."

While Ana went to the kitchen for more coffee, Chucho showed Elana how to string the seed beads and cinch the ends into place. It was meditative work that helped blur her thoughts.

When Ana came back, Luis started up his argument again.

"So you expect the Zapatistas to endorse AMLO because he gave away cash to single mothers when he was mayor?"

"That's not what I said." Ana shook her head. "I said their definition of the 'legitimate' Mexican Left is too narrow."

"That definition being?"

"Outright resistance to neoliberal capitalism. By that definition, then we should all vote for the PRI candidate, right? Put the PRI back in power because Madrazo did criticize the neoliberal model."

"Or we could vote for Patricia Mercado." Melchor laughed and cocked his head. "Abortions for all!"

"You're all missing the fucking point!" Luis bellowed.

"What?" Ana asked. "We're just supposed to not vote at all?"

"No, that's not what Marcos said. But for real change to happen, we need the people to become totally disillusioned with the federal government so that in the crisis others can step in. AMLO won't bring that, he's just more of the same old politics only sugar coated."

"What's AMLO?" Elana asked.

All eyes turned on her and she immediately regretted saying anything.

"Andrés Manuel López Obrador," Ana said finally. "The PRD candidate, he—"

"Is a backstabbing coward," Luis interrupted.

"Will you shut up? I'm trying to explain." Ana looked from Luis to Elana. "This election in June is going to be only the second truly free and open election in more than seventy years. The PRI Party controlled everything from the time of the Revolution on up until our last election when Fox and the PAN Party won. Now we've got a chance for real change and—"

"AMLO is real change?" Luis laughed.

"I know he's from the political class, but he's proven himself." Ana looked to Elana again. "He was mayor of DF for the past five years and his policies are good."

"He makes lots of pretty promises about subsidies, pensions, jobs, and scholarships," Luis said. "But if any of these things ever even do come true, they will be dripping with the blood of neoliberal capitalism. You can't be a friend of the Zapatistas and vote for a PRD candidate. They've stabbed the EZLN in the back, both literally with their peasant goons and legally through their votes that cut away indigenous rights."

"This is what makes me so fucking fed up. This 'you gotta choose the EZLN or nothing' kind of bullshit," Ana said. "You're saying there is only one way and that sounds a lot like what Marcos cautioned against when he said we have to be careful not to only seek and hear the mirror. We need to respect what is different within the common."

"And all you want is to achieve a short-term goal instead of struggling for a real, new México for the good of the earth and humans as a whole and all the other species, not just for the good of us right now selfishly and specifically. We have to think long term."

"AMLO has a real chance of winning, that's all I'm saying."

"AMLO is the selfish short-term choice. In nature, the way the animals do it, sometimes individual creatures sacrifice themselves to ensure the long-term survival of the whole species."

"Are you sure?"

Elana looked up. It was María speaking. It surprised her every time María talked.

"Yes, absolutely," Luis said. "AMLO—"

"No," María said. "I mean are you sure about in nature? I thought that natural selection made us all selfish, like it's genetically programmed into all creatures to act in our own self-interest."

"That's bullshit," Luis said. "It's culture that makes us that way. They try to make you think it's natural, but it's not, it's just a game they've invented to make us turn against each other. The Zapatistas reject the games of the powerful. They reject power itself."

"You really think you can get rid of power?"

Elana glanced up again. She'd never heard María talk this much.

"I don't mean the people who hold power," María went on. "I mean the power, the hierarchy itself. Isn't it natural to humans and to animals? Predator, prey." She looked down the table, her eyes huge in her small face and her cropped hair catching the light from the doorway.

"The Other Campaign avoids all that. They're not about a single candidate," Luis said. "They're about uniting all the Mexican groups who are already doing the good work of struggling against neoliberal capitalism."

"And if we succeed," María said, "if we refound México and write a new political pact, as Marcos says, won't we just be putting ourselves into power?"

"Power in a different way," Luis said, "in the sense of good government."

"Those words always sound strange together," María said quietly, "in my ears at least."

When Lalo returned, Ana told him that Alex was still missing, that no one in El Paso would help Elana.

"Wow," Luis said from the far end of the table, "now American cops won't even listen to white girls? What's the world coming to?"

Ana told him to shut up. She told Lalo that he should take Elana to the lucha gyms and arenas. Elana got up slowly from the table where Chucho was throwing key chains at Rita. She dreaded going off one on one. In the crowd she could hang back and blend in, no one much noticed her lack of perfect Spanish. She was good at keeping quiet and excellent at imitating. Teachers always told you that you had to talk a lot to get better at a language, but she had realized that if she kept quiet and listened hard, perfected her accent, made little mental notations and adjustments and collected a pocket full of colloquialisms, she came across as more knowledgeable than if she blabbered on. But one on one you were expected to talk.

She followed Lalo, out of the darkness of the Kasa and into the sunbright afternoon.

"You spoke to Alex on Sunday?" Lalo glanced at her as they crossed the empty street.

"Email," she said. "You haven't seen him?"

Lalo shook his head. He walked a loose, sexy walk, his dirty jeans tied around his hips with a hemp belt and his black T-shirt ripped along the bottom.

"Not since the dinner," he said. "When you were both here."

Elana wanted desperately to ask how long Vivi had stayed in El Paso and Juárez after her show, but she felt embarrassed both by the idea of a jealous question and by the fact that she couldn't figure out how to grammatically formulate it, which verb to use: *quedar, estar, visitar*. In the end, all she could say was, "Damian's friend, Vivi, how is she?"

Lalo glanced up, looking startled. "Vivi? I don't know. Did something happen?"

Elana felt a fresh wave of embarrassment rise and smother her. "No, no," she said, tangled inside the shame and lack of vocabulary, feeling physically lost inside it, like a sticky web. "I just remember her." What the fuck did that even mean?

At the corner of Rafael Velarde and Maríano Escobedo, a taxi sat idling in the meager shade of a mesquite tree. Elana jumped at the chance. It would take all day to visit the gyms and arenas if they took the bus and she had cash in her pocket, it would cost her next to nothing to pay for the taxi.

She pulled out a wad of bills and caught Lalo's attention. "Let's take a taxi, I'll pay."

They were American dollar bills, a handful of fives with twenties mixed in, and as Lalo spoke to the driver, Elana thought of how outrageously embarrassed Alex would be if he were here, if he knew about this, this flaunting. He tried all the time to pretend like he was not so different, like he also could not afford a taxi, as if the price of a ride converted into dollars was not less than a cup of coffee on the UTEP campus, like he was not more comfortable speaking in English, like if he could just follow the right steps, exactly, precisely, then poof! he would suddenly become Mexican. Having a white wife with bad Spanish was not one of those steps.

Elana, though, if she were perfectly honest with herself, loved taxis, even beat-up, smelly ones. She loved them for the same reasons Alex was shamed by them: class. They connoted ease and excess, someone else driving while you relaxed in the backseat, *here you are, let me help you with that!*

"Do you want to go to the poniente first?" Lalo asked as they settled in.

"Poniente?" She searched briefly for a seatbelt and then gave up.

"Yeah, or to the oriente?"

Poniente, oriente, she'd never heard the words before. Fuck. She felt the weight of the words pulling on her, singular and heavy, with no context.

"I don't understand," she mumbled, looked down at her lap. This was the problem with pretending, passing yourself off as better than you really were by staying silent: when you had to admit defeat it was ten times more embarrassing.

"Oh," Lalo said. "There are a few gyms to the west or we could go first to the arena in the east."

Este, oeste, east, west, those were words Elana knew easily. "*Poniente* means 'west'?"

Lalo nodded.

"Okay, to the west," she said.

The driver was squinting at her in the rearview mirror. "American?" he asked.

She nodded.

"This your boyfriend?" He tilted his head at Lalo.

"No." Elana turned to the window.

"You like Mexican men?"

Elana shrugged.

"She doesn't speak Spanish?" he said to Lalo.

"Yes," Lalo said. "She speaks it and understands it."

It was one of those perfect desert winter days, warm and cloudless. The air pure and clear and every tree and rooftop articulated incredibly against the blue. They crested a small hill and drove down into a dusty colonia, where kids played street soccer and old men watched time pass under bodega awnings.

"Right here on the corner is good," Lalo said. "We'll be right back."

The outside walls of the gym were spray-painted with caricatures of wrestling masks, signatures, and dates—*Arkero 2003, Guerrero, Drako, Jr., 4/05/00, White Princes, Peluchin*—and before they had even opened the door, Elana could hear the rhythmic bounce and slam, slam, slam. She had been to only one match, back in September, and it had felt utterly confusing and overwhelming. Everyone, even the grandmas, had been shouting and throwing beer bottles, and children were running around like crazy, spilling soda and popcorn on the audience and leaping into the ring as soon as the wrestlers had stepped down. She couldn't follow the fight, couldn't figure out who was winning or who she should be cheering for.

"You have a photo of him?" Lalo asked.

Elana fished it out of her pocket as they walked into the dark interior, her eyes going black for a moment so that all she had was sound, a rising, ricocheting echo of voices and pounding bodies, and then the room came into focus. There were two teenage boys in the raised ring, two middle-aged men on the outside, and younger kids racing around the base of it.

"Not like that, you'll break your fucking neck landing like that." One of the men pointed at the boy in the purple T-shirt and then slapped the back of his own neck. "Tuck and roll. You never land on your neck. Again, try it again."

The door slammed closed behind Lalo and Elana, and the men all turned to look. The concrete room was lit only by the light that trickled through a row of small windows up near the ceiling. It smelled of sweat and decay. The men eyed them. For a long moment no one moved and Elana felt something that was nearly fear prickling up her back. What was she doing here? And where was *here*? A room of sweating men. She felt incredibly small, incredibly female. She didn't know Lalo that well really, did she? She felt her muscles tense as if to run, but she wouldn't know how to find her way home from here.

"Akantus!" Lalo called. "What's happening?"

The smaller of the two men raised a hand and walked toward them.

"Liber." He nodded at Lalo. "How are you?" They clasped hands and looked each other up and down.

"Haven't seen you in a while," Akantus said.

"Yeah, I didn't know you were training here."

"Sometimes, yeah, over at the San Pedrito sometimes too."

Lalo nodded.

Elana hung back, watching the teenagers in the ring. In the quiet here, without the confusion of the crowd, she could appreciate the bounce-and-snap acrobatics as the boys flipped off the top ropes.

"Elana?"

She turned to Lalo.

"The photo."

Akantus stepped closer as she held out the grainy photocopy. He took it from her, squinted, and then handed it back, shaking his head. She almost wanted to suggest they take it out into the daylight, it seemed impossible that he could even see it clearly in that darkened room. But then again, he would probably have remembered a sociologist taking notes on the sidelines, even if he did not recognize his photo.

"Leave it here," Akantus was saying. "I'll ask the others."

Lalo reached for it and Elana pulled back, trying quick to explain, feeling the surge of her intentions slam against the dam of her limited vocabulary. "No, only," she said. "I don't have another."

They went to a copy shop before continuing on to the other gyms. It was a grimy little cybercafe crunched full of modems and plastic chairs and an anxious clicking energy. The manager seemed not shocked at all that they were making a missing person flyer. He nodded, pulled a large black marker out of his shirt pocket, and used it to copy out the words from Lalo's scribbled note. SE BUSCA: ALEX WALKER in crisp block letters across the top and then, at the bottom: *ojos oscuros, cabello rubio, mide 1.74. si tiene algún información, llame al 540-731-441.*

A new, sharper sense of sadness leapt up in Elana at the sight of flyer. Alex's name there in this stranger's careful script and that horrible copy of a copy of a photo. Ali, her Ali, reduced to pixels and the deep chemical stink of Sharpie markers. The frantic rocking of the copy machine. A brown bag full of posters.

Back in the taxi, she hugged the bag tight, pressed it until she could feel it against the bones of her hips. Lalo told the taxista to stop at a little outdoor arena with rows of weathered bleachers, then at a gym in the storefront of an old department store, then a gym housed in two third-story apartments with the conjoining wall busted out, and finally the big commercial arena in the center of the city.

No one had seen him. Everyone was sorry. Everyone would post the flyer. Everyone would call if they saw or heard anything. Elana began to wonder if he had really been doing lucha libre research at all. He *had* taken her to that one fight and *had* seemed to know about lucha when he talked about it. Lalo seemed to believe he'd been doing research, but what kind of ghost trail was this? She asked Lalo about that fighter, the one that Alex had talked so much about, Vengador or something like that, but Lalo said he lived in Mexico City now.

"He was up here last fall, but I think he's too busy being famous now. I doubt he has time to give interviews for a social science thesis." Lalo laughed.

Elana could not shake the feeling that it would all be different if she were speaking and listening in English. Lalo did most of the talking, and though she could understand almost everything that he was saying, the translation made it feel like this was all a dream or another dimension, like the pixelated copy of the copy of the photo of Alex. If she could just say to them, in her native tongue, Help me! This is impossible, my husband has vanished, this is totally crazy, then everything would be clear and they would know what to do.

In the taxi, as they crept through the downtown traffic, the driver smoked and listened to love songs and one bled into the next, full of huge-hearted bravado and dripping with saccharine endearments: my love, my life, my heart, my soul, my sweetness, my everything, I would give anything, I would change everything, never, forever, always go on. Elana watched out the window as the sidewalks thickened with couples and families. It was early evening now, the setting sun turning pink, factories and stores letting out workers and everyone rejoining, regrouping, eating, shopping, walking home with hands clutched, recounting their days to one another. The traffic slowed even more and Elana noticed the telephone poles bristling with posters. MISSING, DISAPPEARED, LAST SEEN, INFORMATION PLEASE! When she and Alex first arrived in Juárez, she had been shocked by the quantity of missing person flyers, but over time she had grown used to them. Now the breeze snatched and lifted the corners so she could see the grainy images of women's faces stapled one on top of the other, layers of panic and grief. She gripped her papers and closed her eyes.

"We can get out here," Lalo said. "The border is only a few blocks that way. I can take the bus back home."

Elana opened her eyes and looked over at him, and as she did, she realized she had been crying. She rubbed her hands across her face, feeling flustered and unconnected to her body. She shook her head. She could not go back to the apartment. Evening was the worst. Evening was when it was most obvious there was no one waiting for her. It did not matter to anyone if she went home or stayed out, no one would know, and the knowledge of that fact felt like a widening black hole. In a relationship you lived your life on two tracks: there was you going through your day and then there was the you in your partner's mind, the *you* they pictured going through her day while you were apart, and in the evening you reconnected, the you in their mind morphed into the real you and matched up. If you did not come home on time, there was a schism, a fracture in the two tracks. If no one was waiting for you, though, then there was only one you.

"I can come back to the Kasa?" Elana asked.

Lalo nodded. "Of course," he said. His face read: pity.

Elana swallowed her tears and snot and turned to the window again. A couple walked by, her arm around his waist and his hand tucked into the back pocket of her jeans. Mexico was maybe the worst place to be if you were feeling grudgeful toward lovers. Americans stared at their cell phones and fought openly, but Mexicans were all park bench kisses and hand holding. The kings and queens of public displays of affection. As she watched, Elana dipped down into a slurry of emotions, something familiar but heavier now. Truth be told, she had been lonely for a long time, but with Alex there she had been almost enjoying it. It had felt like a choice, sort of, or a phase, not a sentence. Melancholia, not desperation. The cool black-and-white solitude of whiskey and cigarettes. The comfortable sadness of a long autumn day. But a day that would definitely end, soon. This day, though, this new Alex-less day, was not ending; she could feel it opening before her, a terror there at the door, waiting and growing by the moment.

"Hey," she said, taking a deep breath and leaning forward to the taxi driver. "Change the radio. Please? I give you a big tip."

BACK AT THE KASA, a touring ska band had arrived from Monterrey: four grimy punk dudes in an array of Zapatista T-shirts, hemp and recycled rubber tire jewelry, and dreadlocks in various stages of development. Chucho was practicing break-dancing moves in the corner with one of them; the other three were working with Luis and María to clear a space for the show and merch table. Ana was directing: stack the chairs up over there, move this rug under the drum set, take these beer bottles to the store for the deposit.

Elana followed Damian and Lalo to the tienda, carrying a sack of empty Victoria caguamas. The two of them walked ahead of her and talked among themselves for the most part, for which Elana was grateful. She could not be alone tonight, but she did not want to have to struggle to engage either. She wanted to be a pair of hands to carry bottles.

The smells of cooking laced the air outside the homes as they passed and there were snippets of voices and shadow movements against curtains. Night was coming on quickly, the skyline muting and darkening behind the snarls of electrical wires that threaded house to house across the colonia.

The band was tuning when they returned and the room was filling up. Among the crowd, Elana noticed Luis's blonde girlfriend, downy dreadlocks tied up on top of her head. Damian put the new caguamas in the fridge and then pulled one back out, opened it, and passed it to Elana. His eyes read: more pity. She looked away and drank quickly, the fizz of the beer hitting the back of her throat. She coughed and then forced herself to swallow and swallow and keep on swallowing. She hated drinking from the big brown bottle—the shape and color of it made her feel ugly and bloated, the opposite of the thrill of the clear seltzer bubbles. She might as well keep going, though, now that she was already slathered in pity. Also, getting drunk meant that her hangover tomorrow would change her hunger and make it so much easier to say no. If she could have just said no earlier, her life wouldn't be this way. If she could have been sharper about her decisions, cleaner and clearer with her choices, she might not have lost Alex this way.

The band had a saxophone player who was cute, with silver-rimmed front teeth and nice eyes. Elana focused on him. She focused on the upbeat bounce of the music. She'd never really liked ska but whatever. She focused on the beer in her hand and then the tequila María gave her and then the cigarette she bummed from who knows who. By the time the show was over and the band was packing up their equipment, she was drunk—everything happening through the wrong end of a telescope.

The crowd drifted out slowly and after a while the band boys and a few others sat in a circle on the floor and played hot dice and smoked weed. The silver of the saxophone player's teeth winked at Elana. She was pleased with the distance she had achieved, pleased with the fact that she felt nothing too deep.

"You look really wasted," Luis was saying to his blonde girlfriend. "Are you super drunk?"

Blondie was grinning at him. "What?" she said. "What, my love?"

"He's saying you're wasted," Elana said in English. "He says you look drunk, wasted, sloshed."

Blondie looked up and across the circle at Elana. She tilted her head. "You speak English?" she said.

Elana nodded.

"Oh my gosh. I thought you were Mexican. I mean, you like look like you could belong here kinda. I guess it's just your black hair, but I had no idea."

"I'm from Virginia."

"Oh, wow, I'm from Portland." She bobbed her head. "Oregon, not Maine. I'm an exchange student, are you an exchange student?"

Elana took the dice that Lalo passed her and tossed them. "I live in El Paso," she said.

"God you're lucky, I mean you can like go around incognito! I like walk outside and everybody knows I'm like a gringa immediately." She laughed and picked up her beer bottle, but Luis gripped it before she could take a sip and redirected it to his own mouth. "Hey." She swatted him away. "Stupido."

After a while the band dudes straggled off to their sleeping bags and the Kasa kids split up into their usual corners. Ana made a blanket roll for Elana and set her up on the rug with María and Luis and Blondie.

"It's warmer and softer here," she said. "There's more space for privacy over there, but the concrete floor gets cold at night."

She herself retired to the kitchen and after a few minutes the outline of a body that looked very much like Chucho picked its way across the room and followed her. It was hard to tell in the dark, but Elana was fairly certain that's who it was. Giggles leaked out through the kitchen doorway. Elana propped herself up on her elbows and watched the shadows skate along the wall above the bookcase. The room rustled here and there with readjusting bodies, slight snores, muted voices. María, beside her, seemed to be dead asleep, but Luis and Blondie on the other side were tussling and not even really trying to keep their voices down.

"You look so white," Luis said in Spanish. "So white and plump."

"White?" Blondie laughed and then charged ahead in her broken Spanish. "Luis, Luis, I have a dream, always, and . . . and . . ."

"You're tired, my love?"

"No, a dream, with a snake, eating."

"You're tired."

"No," she fairly shouted. "A *dream*." And then in English: "Why's it gotta be the same word for sleepy and dream? Hey, um, what'd you say your name was?"

Elana had been studiously ignoring them, but she glanced over now. "What?"

They lay tangled together and half-naked in a single sleeping bag three feet away from Elana.

"Hey," Blondie said in English, "can you tell him about this dream I keep having? I like never know if he understands me and then 'sleepy' and 'dream' are the same word, right? So it's confusing. But like every night I keep having this dream about this snake, this huge snake eating like an apple or something."

Luis had tilted his head and was watching Elana, but his arms were still around Blondie.

"Your girlfriend wants me to translate," Elana said in Spanish. "She says she's been having a dream about a snake eating an apple."

Luis smiled and looked at Blondie. In Spanish he said, "Oh, you are my apple, my love." He shifted and looked back at Elana. "Tell her she is my apple. No, no, wait, tell her she's my potato."

"Potato?" Elana said.

Luis started laughing and then hiccupping and then laughing more.

Blondie laughed too. "What's he saying?"

"Yes, potato," Luis managed to get out between hiccups. "Ever since she came back from her Thanksgiving, she's so white and plump, like a mashed potato!"

Elana watched as Blondie bent and kissed Luis on the mouth and then lifted her head and smiled. "What is he saying?"

Elana looked away. "You are beautiful," she whispered. "He says to tell you that you are so beautiful."

FOURTEEN

The basement at Neto's compound was reached by a series of stairs that wound down past a glass mezzanine with a tiled Jacuzzi and then on past the ground floor. The men had marched Alex with his arms cuffed behind him, and as they dropped down, he had expected darkness, but it only got brighter. The basement was huge and white. Tall windows and doorways were cut into the far end of the expanse, rectangles seemingly open to the outdoors, not yet fitted with wood or glass. The men pushed him ahead and turned him to the left and prodded him into a square room with a metal gate across the front and nothing, absolutely nothing, inside. The gate was padlocked. It was the only thing that was not white.

The men left, except for two who stood on each side of the door, only the edges of their shoulders and their holstered guns in view. Alex stood, shaking, in the center of the room and felt the bite of the handcuffs against his wrists. The smell of roses from the roof garden still clung inside his nose. The guards lit cigarettes and grew quiet.

After a long while Alex managed to lower himself to a seated position on the floor. He was afraid of falling, afraid of calling the guards' attention to him. He bent his legs, wobbled, sank to his knees. There was a sandy film on the floor. He sat cross-legged facing the gate. The relief of sitting washed over him. Past the guards he could see out into the rest of the basement, the windows and doors he had spotted before: open cavities facing a dry red embankment. The house must have been built into a small rise so that the southern side was underground and the northern side exposed. The room seemed to be under construction; the white paint stopped three-quarters of the way down and there were bags of concrete mix near the open doorways. Open. Alex stared and still did not believe it could be true, just open, nothing but a metal gate between himself and . . . He remembered the view from the roof. Hundreds of thousands of acres of desert. Not even a single tree to hide behind, and plenty of planes for hunting.

After the relief of sitting ebbed, Alex realized he was cold and still shaking. If he focused on his breath, long and slow, he could almost stop it. Just wait, he told himself, just wait. If he could wait silently enough for long enough, Mateo would come. He would be saved. These men knew now that he was American. Someone would be looking. *Elana*. The room pulsed white around him. Elana must be back now. She must . . . what day? It was Thursday, was it Thursday? No, it must be well beyond Thursday. He focused on the bars of the gate and tried to parse time. It had been Tuesday and he'd been feeling less sick and they had picnicked and then Wednesday they left Batopilas like lunatics in a movie chase scene and then the men had found them . . . He had no idea how much time had passed, but Elana must know by now that he was missing. It was only a matter of waiting.

He had been using Elana as a shield, he could see that now. She was not just a shield for his sexuality, though of course that was part of it, but it was more consuming than that. He felt sometimes that they had both found each other on the road—the way you might meet someone at a bus stop on your way somewhere—and for a time it seemed like they had the same destination. After a while it became obvious that they did not, but they kept on. There was nothing unusual about it, he thought, it must happen to lots of people who got together when they were very young. But the fact that it was commonplace only made it sadder. Still, he thought, she would come for him. She loved him.

Alex lay himself down quietly on his side. The guards paid almost no attention to him. They traded shifts, and the new ones looked in for a moment. They all wore black boots, black pants, black shirts. A few of them had mustaches, one a silver front tooth, one looked no older than eighteen. There were always two of them posted there at the door and they traded between them cigarettes and small words. They mostly ignored Alex.

In the room there was nothing. In the room there was nothing and the nothing became something. Became many things. The waiting shifted too. Changed from waiting to be saved to waiting for pain, terror.

Darkness came in, blue and windy. He could hear it sifting sand across the floor. One of the guards left. It was cold, skin-drawing-in-to-the-bone kind of cold. He shivered until his stomach clenched. When the light came again, he felt worse, because although it stretched long and bright in a path across the floor, it felt no warmer. No sounds came in from outside. Guards' shoulders in the doorway. No conversation.

Alex wormed his way up to sitting. It was the floor that was most cold. His mind swam out from the present moment, pumping up and away before physicality crashed back in.

In the room there was nothing and it was almost beautiful. An art gallery waiting for paintings. No, a painting itself, the way the light stretched across the floor, almost to the bars of his cage. An O'Keeffe. Not the skulls but the church paintings. In a book at Hall College, he had seen a series she did of the Ranchos de Taos Church, pale walls quivering. Light, slow and slim.

At Hall College he had stalked the librarian's reshelving cart. There were so many books in the stacks, he had no idea where to begin. He would study the librarian's cart when she was called away by another student. He looked at the titles and covers and snatched fast before she came back.

His second week there he'd grabbed David Wojnarowicz's *Close to the Knives*. The cover showed a cliff wall and three buffalo tumbling, hooves pawing air, heads down. Back in his dorm room he opened the book: men fucking on a sun-filled bed, drag queens, Puerto Rican boys, queers, ass, shit, dick. It was crazy. It was disgusting. It was exquisitely beautiful. Bodies, docks, coasting wind, a voice that could not be drowned out. Two pages into the second essay, Alex was shaking. He put down the book and gripped the edge of his mattress, snorting in his snot and tears. He prayed his roommate would not walk in. He picked up the book again. He read and reread and reread a single line about a man stroking his palm along the curve of another man's neck, softly, shyly, in a car, with the heat pumping and the clouds growing dark outside.

FIFTEEN

The morning was chilly, but the sun was strong, and they walked all together, the Kasa kids and the band dudes and Elana, down the middle of the street in a big group. Dogs and children looked up as they passed, their voices bouncing off the houses, some of them singing, some of them arguing. They could smell the burrito stand even before they could see it, great pots of bubbling chile colorado and chile verde. There were only enough stools for a few of them and the rest leaned against old oil drums and ate their tortillas filled with hot chile stew and tender pork. An older woman and a boy who looked like her grandson ran the stand. Watching them working there together, Elana thought of Dulcie. She would have loved to have a family-style place like this. A state like West Virginia would be perfect for street-food stands, she thought. It would help the local economy, help with food scarcity, but no, to serve food in the US, you had to pay rent on a building that had been inspected, you had to be in the nonresidential area of town, and you had to have licenses and certificates. Someone like Dulcie could never get enough money together for all that up-front business.

The ska guys ordered breakfast beers and Chucho ordered one too, but Ana took it from him and drank it herself. Luis and Blondie were surprisingly silent, hungover, Elana guessed. She was glad to not be translating. The sun hit the Franklin Mountains and lit up downtown El Paso across the river.

Elana ate and enjoyed it, to her own surprise. The biggest chunks of pork she pushed to the side of her plate, but the stew was delicious with the flour tortilla. It was an extension of this moment, the laughter and inside jokes, this moment that Elana felt, shockingly, as if she were really a part of. It was not foisted on her; she did not have to make a point of saying no.

When they walked back to the Kasa, Elana stopped at the corner to wait for the downtown bus. María and then Lalo turned and waved to her. She smiled. The sun was warm. Her head was clear. When her hand wandered to her hip bone, she stopped and put her fingers in her pocket instead.

As she exited the Paso del Norte bridge on the American side, she turned her cell phone on. It lit up with four new messages. Her heart spiked. She punched in the passcode, her hand shaking as she held it to her ear.

"Mrs. Walker? Uh, hello, this is Officer Hernandez. We found something up at the university that—well, give me a call as soon as you can."

Her whole arm was trembling now. She pushed Save. The next message was from Meyer, the next from Noreen, and the last from Simon. As soon as she heard their voices and knew it was not Alex, she stopped listening. She went back to Hernandez's message and pressed Call Back.

"Mrs. Walker, good morning," he said.

"Orenstein."

"What's that?"

"Elana Orenstein."

"Alex Walker's wife?"

"Yes." She sat down on the concrete retaining wall at the end of the bridge.

"I called you yesterday."

"I was in Juárez, putting up flyers for him."

"Uh-huh. Can you come down to the station?"

SHE WALKED, AND then ran, to the station. He was waiting out front for her when she arrived and he pointed to an El Paso city police car. "Let's take a little drive up to the university," he said. "I want to show you something."

She was out of breath and she could smell her own sweat. "You haven't found him?"

Hernandez shook his head. "You can sit up front with me."

The car smelled strongly of aftershave.

"What'd you find?"

"Have you had any coffee yet?"

"What? Yes."

"You want me to go in and grab you a cup of coffee for the drive?"

"No." Elana stared at him. "What did you find?"

He pulled out into the street and drove through a yellow light. "Mrs. Walker—"

"Orenstein."

"Ms. Warstein. Forgive me for needing to ask, but were you and your husband trying to get pregnant?"

"What?" She turned in her seat to face him. "No."

He was blushing.

"What's going on?" she said.

He did not take his eyes off the road. "What type of protection had you been using?"

Elana felt nausea wash over her. "I'm on the pill," she heard herself saying.

ALEX'S STUDY CARREL was on the second floor of the main university library, a single cell in a row of little cages. Elana had been here only once, to meet him before they headed for lunch. It had a number on the door, 16, a pile of textbooks on the floor and a desk. In the desk was a drawer with notepads, a drawer with pens, and a drawer with a package of Trojan condoms.

Elana gripped the chair back and looked away. From her mouth came a tiny animal sound.

"I'm sorry," Hernandez said. He slid the drawer closed.

Footsteps walked by outside the study room. Elana's legs could not hold her anymore. She used the chair to lower herself to the floor and then she lay flat against the carpet. She felt the mass of chile verde and tortillas, thick and disgusting in her stomach. She wanted to vomit. It was cold in the little room, and claustrophobic, the drop ceiling just inches above Hernandez's head and all these little carrels lined up side by side like a deep freeze for intellectuals.

"You want a ride back downtown?" Hernandez asked.

"What?" Elana did not look up from the carpet. Through the thin wall she could hear someone typing. It was so quiet in here you could almost believe everything else had ceased to exist. She thought of the street songs and rumble of Juárez, incredible that it was still out there, only a few miles away.

"See, at least for now, our investigation's over," Hernandez was saying. "No signs of foul play and, see, well, the thing is, it's not illegal to go missing, not illegal to go away."

Elana pushed herself up. "Is he in Mexico? Did he cross over in the Honda?"

Hernandez cracked his knuckles and swayed his weight back and forth from one leg to the other. He would not meet her eyes. "I don't know ma'am, see, now, that's not illegal either, to cross over, but I don't know, we didn't look into that."

"So you don't know anything?"

Hernandez glanced at her and then back down at his feet. "I spoke to a few of his professors yesterday, no one has seen him since December 2. Then one of them told me he had this corral here." He pronounced it "corral," like an animal pen, and Elana almost laughed. "I got the librarian to open it up for me and then I found . . ." He gestured toward the drawer. "You want your photo back? I'll drive you to the station and give you your photo back."

HER BLOOD WAS still crusted on the corner of the picture. She felt the texture of it there between her fingers as she stood outside the brick building and closed her eyes, listening to the crisp snapping of the flags on their poles and the wailing sirens of every different kind of law enforcement you could hope for: city, county, state, federal. She opened her eyes. Alex's face was there beside hers in the photo. She pressed her thumb over his head, squished the paper until it nearly ripped. It was not supposed to go like this. In the movie version the Wife did not find condoms in the Husband's carrel. In the movie version the Husband was a victim, pure and true, caught up in a world of evil. He shone like a beacon of hope. She lifted her thumb and looked again at Alex's smile. If she let those words become the truth, the ones that Hernandez almost spoke—*affair, he left you*—then she was admitting that she was not worth returning to. If she gave up on Alex, it would be because she agreed that he had given up on her. She could not agree to that, not yet, not now.

DOWN THE STREET from the Regional Command Office, the JCPenney was having a sale. TOTAL CLEARANCE, the store announced, EVERYTHING MUST GO! Elana pushed open the glass doors and the world went soft. Pastel lighting and symphonic film music, quiet chatter of the salesgirls behind the counters, the waxed floors gleaming. She let her fingers trail along the cotton, Lycra, slim fit, tummy-tucker, boat necks.

"Are you looking for anything in particular?"

She turned to the salesgirl: small gold hoops, bobbed hair, pink lips.

"I . . ."

"We're having a sale on silk blouses. Well, everything's on sale, but this is such a good deal. Feel this."

She led Elana to a rack. A pale rainbow: blush to rose to citrus to periwinkle. Shivering thin, breathable threads. Elana took one of every color and walked toward the dressing rooms. The salesgirl followed. Inside the little closet Elana found that she stank, alcohol pushing out through her sweat and the fuzzy rankness of her own breath. She avoided the mirror and slipped her T-shirt off over her head.

"Let me know if you want to try a different size," the salesgirl said.

Elana opened the door.

"Oh!" The girl reached out to touch the blush blouse where it met Elana's wrist. "Beautiful!"

Elana began to cry. Breathing loudly, face crumpled down. She could not locate the noir-film distance she had managed previously.

"Oh, oh," the salesgirl said. "Umm."

Tears wet the front of the blouse.

"I know what you need."

Elana looked up.

"You need a jacket, not a blouse. You need a leather jacket."

Out front of the JCPenney, Elana took her new jacket from its bag and hugged it to her chest, the lambswool collar tucked up under her chin. It had felt great to spend those two hundred dollars that she could never in a million years afford. Rent money. Across the street was a small park and, down the block, the neon sign for the Tap Bar with half the letters gone dark. She pushed open the door and walked in. It was dim, with red laminate countertops and black pleather seats. She sat on a stool at the empty end of the bar, farthest from the door. The customers were all old men, some of whom she recognized from Susie's: a white guy with a long white Fu Manchu and a couple of dudes in worn cowboy hats and boots.

"What can I get you?"

The bartender had a large rhinestone cross nestled in her cleavage and her flat belly was visible between her tank top and hip-hugger jeans.

"Vodka and soda water," Elana said.

The bartender turned and reached for the soda gun. A white rag was tucked into the back of her belt and her hair was piled high with three pens sticking out.

Elana went to the bathroom and when she got back a man in straw hat and guayabera had arrived carrying a Burger King bag. He set it on the counter. "Hey, Jessica," he called to the bartender. "For you. Whopper. Extra cheese."

Jessica left the box of beers she'd been unpacking and walked to the end of the bar with her arms stretched out. "Ay, papi!" She grabbed his hand and squeezed it. "I was just wondering where you were today. I hadn't seen you and here it is nearly noon."

She took the bag and set it behind the bar beside a plastic Virgin Mary shrine.

"You're not gonna eat it? I'm on a fixed income here, sweetheart, I'll eat it myself if—"

"In a minute. I'm working." She went back to unpacking beer boxes.

Elana sipped her drink and watched Jessica and the men. She felt she could practically see the threads of human connections tendriling out between them. That's all we want, she thought, we want someone to notice when we don't show up on time, someone to bring us food. We all just want to hold on. Her mind kept flashing to the condoms in Alex's drawer and it was suddenly so abundantly clear to her how tenuous all her connections were. Hold on, she wanted to scream out loud to the whole room, we have to hold on to one another.

To give up on looking for Alex was to admit that he had chosen to leave her, admit that she was something to be left. There were the Leavers and the Left. All her life she'd been fighting against the passive *left*. On her mother's side it was a family legacy. When Meyer left baby Elana at Dulcie's house, Dulcie had pulled her into that narrative, wrapped her up tight. For Dulcie, being left was as much a part of her identity as anything else. First her husband left her through infidelity, her oldest son left through death, her only daughter left the state and then left life entirely. Dulcie wove it into a tapestry, wore it around her shoulders as a mantle. She pulled in other instances of *left.* State history, family lore. West Virginia itself was in a continuous state of being left. Population numbers dropping. Jobs leaving. Sometimes Dulcie framed it in a fiercely proud fuck-you kind of way. Love us or leave us. We want to be left alone. We want the government to let us be. West Virginia was a state formed from leaving the Confederacy, but soon it became the one who was left.

Elana swallowed the rest of her drink and ordered another. "Like a Virgin" came on the jukebox and a small man in a polo shirt began to sing, waving his hands. Jessica looked up and smiled and the Fu Manchu man sang along too, backlit against the grimy window as he shook to the music.

"What the fuck, Homer?" the guayabera man said. "Esto es pura mierda."

"Órale pues, buddy," the chinos man said. "Pon algo bueno entonces."

"Ay, cabrón." Guayabera pulled a handwritten list from his pocket and made his way to the glowing jukebox.

The men at the bar watched him, nursing their Bud Lights.

"Jessica!" Guayabera called. "I don't understand this new machine." He turned and held out his hands with his quarters and his list of songs.

"Okay, okay," Jessica said. "But if I do this for you, you have to dance."

Guayabera shook his head.

Jessica took his hand and twirled him under her arm. "Sí," she said, "sí."

Guayabera shuffled back toward the bar and stopped just short of Elana.

"Hey," he said, cocking his head. "You're that waitress from Susie's. She's that little waitress works over at Susie's." He turned to the other men for confirmation.

Fu Manchu leaned forward, looked down the bar, and nodded.

"What are you doing here?" Guayabera said.

Elana gripped her nearly empty glass. She looked down at the jacket in her lap. She looked up again. "My husband . . ." She paused. "My husband is missing and the cops think he left me."

"No, no, no," Guayabera said. "You? No, look at you!" He waved his hand. "Who would want to leave you? Crazy, crazy. This man had mental problems?"

Elana almost laughed, almost cried.

"Jessica!" Guayabera called. "You believe this shit?"

Within ten minutes, Elana had arrayed in front of her a shot of tequila, a cigarette, and a plate of tacos.

"No love songs!" Fu Manchu announced, making Jessica go back and change Guayabera's jukebox choices.

"That doesn't leave much," Jessica said.

"Unless you *want* love songs," Fu Manchu said. "Maybe you want love songs?"

Elana knocked her tequila back and shrugged. "He disappeared," she said. "Just poof!, gone, and the cops tell me he's probably on vacation."

"The cops won't help you?"

Elana lit her cigarette and basked in their indignation.

"They can't drop a missing person case like that."

Fu Manchu had come down to the end of the bar and he and Guayabera were having a conversation that Elana did not feel obliged to add anything to. She felt the distance settling in again with a relief.

"They all want the big cases, think they're gonna catch a terrorist now. Their big wet dream."

The front door opened and a man was silhouetted there against the light. The street had felt so far away, but there it was, bright and rushing with noon traffic.

"Aaaay!" Jessica called from behind the bar. "Do you have a reservation? No? Well, take a number at the door, señor, we'll seat you at our convenience."

The man—a black man with gray hair at his temples, dressed in a porkpie hat and white shirt tucked into Levi's and cowboy boots—said nothing as he came toward the bar.

"Toño!" Guayabera called, waving him down to the end of the bar. "I was just thinking about you, hermano. Come here."

Toño ignored Guayabera and took a seat midway down, two stools to the left of Elana.

Jessica brought him a glass of Knob Creek. "Start high and work down, right?"

Toño took his hat off and set it on the bar beside his drink. In his right ear he wore a small crystal stud that shone brilliantly against his black skin.

"What's up?" Jessica said. "I haven't seen you in a while?"

"Yemayá was sick. Bad sick."

"She's okay now?"

Toño played with his hat, turning it in circles on the varnished wood. "I'm gonna have to start trying to picture life without her."

"Nooo!"

"Fact." Toño nodded without looking up.

"Hey, Toño," Fu Manchu sidled up on his left side. "Remember when you had that case back in '92, that trucker that went missing?"

Toño took a long drink of his whiskey.

"Cops tried to say it was a voluntary departure or some bullshit, but you found the body over in Casas Grandes."

Toño set his glass down and Guayabera was on his right side, blocking him from Elana's view. "They're trying to pull that crap again. Like any American who disappears in Mexico is just off at some fiesta."

"I don't even know if he's in Mexico." Elana leaned forward to see around Guayabera.

Toño turned to her. "Who?"

"My husband," Elana said. "I'm Elana, Elana Orenstein." She held out her hand, but Toño ignored it.

He took another drink of whiskey. "Why are you all telling me this?"

"Didn't even have to speak of the devil," Fu Manchu said.

"Swear to God, a few seconds before you walk in," Guayabera said, "I was just about to tell the waitress here that I had a friend she should call, private detective."

Fu Manchu nodded. "Me too. Tip of my tongue."

"I haven't taken a case in years," Toño said loudly.

For a long moment there was nothing but the swaying rhythm of cumbia pouring out of the jukebox and the muffled tumble of cubes inside the industrial ice machine.

"I'm only talking about advice here, Toño." Guayabera stepped back to give him a better view of Elana. "The cops said her husband was on vacation, running around on her."

Toño looked up from his drink and met Elana's eyes. "With most cases," he said, "that's true."

By the time he'd worked his way down through Jack Daniels and Jim Beam to Old Grand-Dad, Toño was willing to talk.

"They didn't check to see if the car crossed over into Mexico?" He took an engraved snuff box out of his hip pocket and dabbed tobacco into his lower lip.

"They said it's not illegal to go to Mexico," Elana said.

"He got anything on him that could be tracked?"

"No, he left his cell phone at the house."

Toño pushed himself up from the stool and stepped back unsteadily. "All right, I gotta call somebody. You got the plate number?"

Elana scribbled it onto a cocktail napkin. She'd come up with a trick to remember it back when they first bought the car—7ZT769—7 zit but without the *i*, 7 sex position.

She watched Toño make his way slowly to the pay phone at the back of the room. There was something about him that she liked, the understated confidence, the way he was not eager to help but at the same time not entirely dismissive. He seemed competent and clear eyed about the Alex situation, like it was a task, like fixing a car, a complicated task but one that you could complete.

Jessica brought Elana a fresh vodka soda and leaned across the bar, her breasts spilling over the top of her shirt. "He's a total sweetie," she whispered. "But people take advantage and he knows it."

The jukebox had stopped and they could all hear most of Toño's words.

"Yeah, I know, I know, I'm just looking into this one as a favor, though, not work. Tell Perez to call me back at the Tap or at home if I'm not here anymore."

An hour passed and Perez still had not called the Tap and Toño was wobbly.

"I gotta go check on Yemayá," he said, pulling his wallet out of his back pocket and nearly falling off his stool in the process.

"Twenty dollars," Jessica called down from the register.

"I owe you a whole hell of a lot more than that."

"Shshsh!" Jessica cut him off, holding a finger to her lips. "Save your money for Yemayá."

"You got some kind of a number I can reach you at when Perez calls?" Toño said to Elana.

"Yeah." Elana reached for a napkin but Jessica caught her eye, and when Toño looked away, she whispered, "Go with him, make sure he gets home okay."

"Uh, how about I come with you," Elana said, standing up and feeling the alcohol rush to her head. She reached out and took his arm and he looked at her like she'd slapped him. She let go and grasped the stool instead. "I'll just come along until Perez calls you back?"

Toño lived in an old hotel building whose first floor had been converted into a wholesale plastics and perfume warehouse. The second, third, and fourth floors were cut into apartments. A Korean woman swept the sidewalk in front of the open warehouse door, her checkered apron gusting in the wind.

"Mr. Toño," she called. "You doing all right?"

The late-afternoon sun was heavy on the street. Elana walked a few paces behind Toño, clutching her jacket in her arms, dizzy from the drink and the bright sun.

"Your niece?" the Korean woman called, but Toño ignored her and walked up a stairwell littered with sales flyers and fast-food bags.

His apartment was on the third floor at the end of the hall, and when he opened the door, a moist heat leaked out. The room was dim but in a deep green, understory-of-the-jungle kind of way. One long, open room, heavy wooden furniture, and plants on every single surface, ferns and potted palms, lilies and philodendrons and orchids.

"Yemayá," Toño called, and something stirred in the middle of the room. A shadow among shadows and a movement that was, Elana realized as she pushed the door closed, a tiny jet-black cat. Two golden eyes. She was the size of a kitten but bony, with hairless legs and a crooked tail.

"She's eighteen," Toño said as he bent to pet her.

They settled at the kitchen table, Yemayá sprawled in the center, her tail keeping time while she stretched one paw out toward Elana and tilted her head back for Toño to scratch. Sitting there with Toño, watching the sunlight trace the shapes of leaves across the kitchen sink, felt to Elana a little like afternoons she'd spent with Dulcie, the same quiet ease, no need to speak, but the silence was not awkward either.

After Yemayá fell asleep, Toño got up and fixed them both whiskeys and Elana entered into a drunk that was as close to relief as anything she had experienced. The plants were breathing and time didn't mean anything. It was all just an envelope, her skin around her bones, her bones around whatever it was we tried to call a soul, all rooms and buildings and marked-off parking lot spaces, everything measured, days, weeks, months. Otherwise it would all be too open, dust and plains and evaporation. Snakes got new skins. Sloughed off the old. Never worrying, not once, about selfhood.

Perez called after the sun was gone. He said the Honda had entered Mexico on December 3 and never crossed back into the US. He said he would put the word through to the Mexican authorities to run a search for it.

"December 3." Elana stood up from her chair. Her head was swimming, but she was pretty sure that was the day after she'd left for Virginia. "December 3," she repeated. "Okay." It would all make more sense when she was not drunk. It would all make more sense soon. "Thank you." She glanced at Toño. His face looked exhausted and she was suddenly aware that she had taken up his whole day. She felt embarrassed. What was she doing in some stranger's house, letting her messy life spill out like this? "Thanks." She turned to walk to the door, but her foot caught on the leg of the chair and suddenly she was falling. She reached for the table, missed it, and hit the linoleum floor.

"Whoa there," Toño said.

Elana closed her eyes. Her stomach was heaving. Don't barf and don't cry, she repeated to herself, pressing her teeth into her lower lip.

"You okay?"

She looked up. He bent over her but did not touch her and she was grateful for that.

"Why don't you go home in the morning?" he said, pointing across the room to a leather chaise lounge.

Elana nodded and made her way slowly over to it, thinking of the tendrils of human connection she'd pictured in the bar. She curled up and dreamt of Maríachi bands and rolls of crepe paper unfurling out of her mouth.

SIXTEEN

The Empresa Estelar debut was scheduled for Chihuahua City and Mateo had assumed it would be in the Bernardo Aguirre Arena or maybe the Coliseo Chihuahua. He had not asked Neto, he had in fact tried over the past few days to see as little of Neto as possible. Neto had shown him his gym, in a building out past the pool. It was a long, gleaming room with weight machines, medicine balls, barbells, and treadmills. Mateo had insisted on training outside instead. Neto laughed and said suit yourself. Mateo had not seen Alex since that first day on the rooftop and he had no way of knowing how he was. Jogging outside, Mateo could at least try to scout an escape route for them, though Neto's men followed him at all times in a jeep forty feet behind him as he ran toward the distant brown mountains.

In Neto's house he was constantly shadowed. All his needs were met, but even that felt like entrapment. He was given food, clothes, even coke. But of course there was no phone. And whom would he even call if he could? Neto's men had already visited Alicia and his mother, *so proud and so helpful.*

In Chihuahua City the chauffeur steered out of the downtown and onto the periférico freeway and Mateo turned to Neto who sat beside him in the backseat. They had eaten at Don Miguel's steakhouse, and afterward, in the dark of the parking garage, Mateo had slipped on his Vengador mask so that no one would see his face when he arrived at the arena. But both the Bernardo Aguirre and the Coliseo were downtown, not off the ring highway.

"Where are we going?"

Neto had a wisp of a smile on his face.

"No, seriously, where are we going?"

Neto bit down on his toothpick. "You're not much on surprises, huh?"

"I've had enough surprises lately."

Neto turned away, out the window. The night was clear and the stars were visible above the lights of the city.

Neither of them spoke again until the chauffeur exited and drove around the looming maquiladoras and into an empty stretch of desert where in the distance sat what looked to be a giant glowing hot-air balloon in a huge parking lot.

Mateo looked at Neto who was already smiling broadly. "What do you think?"

"What is it?"

"Arena Estelar!"

"That's an arena?"

"Temporary," Neto said. "Fabric walls until we can get the brick ones built."

The arena was orange and blue and lit from within, gusting in the wind.

"I see," Mateo said.

The traffic was thick now and the going was slow.

"Pull around." Neto leaned forward to instruct the driver. "Go on the side there, we can't wait behind all these people."

THE DRESSING ROOMS were pull-along trailers, a good-sized one for the tecnicos matched by one for the rudos and two smaller ones behind.

"Yours is private." Neto pointed.

"I don't need a private dressing room."

Neto shrugged. "You're the star now."

The driver swung open the car door and they rushed past the crowd and through the dirt lot toward the trailers. Mateo stopped and turned back for his duffel, but the chauffeur already had it. A voice shouted *El Vengador!* and Mateo glanced as faces turned and arms pointed. A flash of camera light. He trundled up the steps behind Neto and into the trailer. The chauffeur set his bag on the counter and stepped away.

"I'll be back in a bit," Neto said.

Mateo locked the door and took his mask off. He walked to the end of the trailer. There was a minifridge with Gatorades and half a dozen Coronas. He cracked a cherry Gatorade and drank it down, then reached for a Corona. He usually didn't drink before fights. He set it on the counter and walked the length of the trailer and back. He opened it and drank half and sat down at the vanity mirror. From his inside jacket pocket he took out a leather zip purse that contained a vial of coke, a glass straw, and a set of three razor blades.

Mateo cut two lines and snorted them, tilted his head back for a moment, and felt his blood surge. Music radiated from the arena, some high-tone pop song and the boom of the announcer's voice. He wiped his nose and wiped the razor and leaned into the mirror. He brushed his hair back and inspected his forehead. A bulge of mottled scar tissue ran the length between his temples. He brought the razor up and sank it in vertically at the edge of his hairline. When he pulled it out, there was only a little blood on the very tip.

It was after the third cut that he realized it might all be for nothing. The razor was as much a part of preparing for his fights as stretching and push-ups, but whoever he was slated to fight tonight (Neto still had not told him who it would be) might not utilize the cuts. Always before, they had been integral, especially when fighting El Hijo del Diablo, who would slam Mateo's head against the corner post and pull his mask in such a way that the blood would pool and spill out through his eye holes. If the audience wasn't with him before, they always were after that. It was like Christ's bloody face after the crown of thorns, a beautiful long-suffering display of pain. But that was such a tecnico-babyface move, not the sort of pain for a rudo-heel whose suffering needed more buffoonery. And tonight, for the first time, he would fight as a rudo and no self-respecting tecnico would slam a rudo's head like that. He put away the razor.

The cuts never bothered him usually, but now, knowing they were pointless, they stung. He drank the rest of the Corona and put his mask on. From the announcer's voice it sounded like they hadn't even started the first fight yet. He unlocked his door and peeked out. One of Neto's men stood there beside the stairs. The lot was quiet, only a few straggling fans lined up by the side entrance. He walked around the guard without looking at him and crossed over to the larger rudo trailer and stepped inside. The room was loud and bright. A counter along the far wall was spread with cosmetics, cans of hair spray, and rolls of gauze.

"Hey, Vengador!" A man got up from the couch and held out his hand.

Mateo shook it.

"I heard the rumor you'd joined Estelar, but I didn't believe it, dude!"

The man had no mask on and his face was not familiar.

"The Scorpion," he said, pumping Mateo's hand.

At the end of the room Mateo spotted a few older wrestlers, the Archer, and Mr. Thunder painting his face at the mirror, but otherwise he recognized no one: half a dozen cross-dressing exoticos in pleather boots and high-cut bathing suits, a few clown variants, and a bunch of young unknown expectant faces. This rudo room seemed louder and more chaotic than the tecnico dressing areas he was used to, but maybe he was only imagining it because it was what he expected.

The door flew open.

"Mat—Vengador!" Neto stood in the doorway with his hand to his mouth, eyes wide. "What are you doing in here?"

Mateo stared at him. There was another man behind him, in the shadows just outside.

"I gave you your own trailer." Neto dropped his hand and turned to the man behind him. "El Vengador is a man of the people, clearly," he said, "or maybe just vain, can't wait to be the center of attention." He winked at Mateo. "Come on," he said. "This is Raymundo Barrera from *Box y Lucha*, for a prefight interview."

As they crossed back to the smaller trailer, Neto grabbed Mateo's shoulder and pulled him close. "You're fighting Señor Divino tonight," he whispered.

Mateo tried to see Neto's face in the parking lot lights. He'd never heard of Señor Divino before.

"New incarnation," Neto said quietly, "but an experienced fighter. He's a glam ladies' man from Tijuana. You're the real-deal northern fighter, Juárez raw, and you're gonna show him what the North really stands for. Got it?"

Neto pulled open the door of the trailer and ushered them inside.

The reporter sat on the end of the little couch and Mateo pulled out the chair from his dressing table and turned it around. He wanted a cigarette badly. He never smoked before fights, but he also never gave interviews before fights and never didn't know the background of the man he was about to fight.

"Neto," he said. "You got a smoke I can have?"

Neto glanced over his shoulder and raised his eyebrows.

"Rudos can smoke before fights," Mateo said. "That's the thing, right? Rudos are rebels, we can do anything. And we don't really have to wrestle very well anyway, not as good as the tecnicos at least." He glanced at the reporter. "We cheat our way to winning."

The reporter laughed. "Aha," he said. "So you've been wanting to go rudo for a little while?"

Mateo turned and caught the pack of cigarettes Neto tossed him. He opened it and offered one to the reporter who refused.

"No," he said after he'd lit his cigarette. "I hadn't really thought about it."

"Oh, okay," the reporter said, balancing his notepad on his knees. "Well, this is a huge change for you, not only tecnico to rudo but also leaving CMLL. Can you tell me more about your decision?"

"I didn't have a choice."

Neto slammed the fridge door closed and turned around.

"You didn't have a choice?" the reporter said.

Mateo exhaled.

Neto stood behind the reporter, a Corona in each hand. "He means it was his destiny," he said. "When he first approached me about Estelar, he said he was so drawn to the project it was like it was meant to be."

The reporter glanced at Neto and then at Mateo again. "Wait, Estelar was *your* idea?" he said to Mateo.

"Collaboration," Neto said. "Here, have a beer."

"No thank you."

"Come on, don't refuse El Vengador's hospitality."

The Corona opened with a foamy fizz and dripped onto his papers.

"Oh, thank you," he said, but did not take a drink. "So, Vengador, you'll be fighting"—he set his beer on the floor and flipped his pages of notes, scanning—"Señor Divino, from Tijuana, tonight. Can you tell me more about that rivalry?"

"Señor Divino thinks he knows what the North is about," Mateo said, "but he's gonna learn a big lesson." Neto was pacing and drinking behind the couch, but Mateo ignored him. "The North is not what it used to be, a place of opportunity where you work hard and are repaid. Señor Divino with his flying flash might think he can charm his way, but the North is under a shadow of greed now, each for his own, no brother can be trusted."

"That's why you've turned rudo? Gone from protecting and avenging the North to—"

"Each for his own. Bites and bribes. Let's see how high we can each rise!"

The reporter froze, pen hovering over the page. "Okay, great . . . bites and bribes . . . great, what was that you said about a shadow of selfishness?"

Mateo nodded. "A shadow of greed."

"Oh, yes, perfect . . . no brother can be trusted, great." He looked up. "Would you say you've fallen under this shadow?"

BY THE TIME he went into the ring, Mateo had had two more beers and three cigarettes and then, just before entering, another bump of coke. He'd kept his sweats on over his silver briefs and lace-up boots even as he stood in the wings and heard his entrance music beginning. *Ciudad Juárez es número uno.* He could see the corner of the ring, the crowded bleachers, the bright lights and huge ventilators that kept the tent walls inflated. *La frontera más fabulosa y bella del mundo!* He took his shirt off and slipped on his black and silver cape. His entrance music had always felt like pure celebration, but now, after his own words about greed and shadows, Juan Gabriel's lyrics sounded like a terrible joke.

The curtain was pulled back and he walked down the carpet between the high bleachers. Only this time, unlike all his previous fights, the cheers were tainted and garbled, scrambled with boos and hisses and too much uncomfortable silence now that he was a rudo. He tipped his chin up, swished his cape, lifted it so they could see the muscles of his ass. Let it flutter back down about him. He bounded and dove over the top rope into a somersault land in the very center of the ring, realizing too late that it was a total tecnico entrance.

"In his debut as a rudo," the announcer shouted. "Maybe the most technical rudo we've ever seen, El Vengadoooor del Norte!"

El Vengador clambered to the top rope and stood, chest out and arms raised. He did not drop back down until his opponent's music had begun to play. A polka-beat norteña song. Señor Divino was tall and slim in a glittering full-body Lycra suit that connected right into his mask. His arms and legs were accented with fringe and a ring was painted around the top of his head like a halo. El Vengador was momentarily stunned. This man was as flamboyant as an exotico, but exoticos almost never wrestled as tecnicos, and exoticos never wrestled in the headlining fights. As he made his way down the carpet, Señor Divino was also taking great care to show his adoration for his female fans. El Vengador didn't know how to read him.

"And here we have, in the corner of the tecnicos, a Tijuana ladies' man, breaker of the hardest hearts . . . Señor Diiiiiivino!"

He dove into the ring with an entrance that was uncannily similar to El Vengador's own. The crowd went wild.

El Vengador slipped off his cape, tossed it over the ropes, and stepped forward. Divino leapt to his feet and locked in immediately, no circling, no chase. Before El Vengador could think, Divino had grabbed his right arm and crimped it into a hammerlock. He breathed out and bent forward to loosen it a bit, but Divino twisted harder. El Vengador ducked and turned and twisted Divino into an arm bar. Wrestling was like dancing and El Vengador was not used to leading, it had to be painfully obvious to the crowd. He should have thought this out, how different it would feel fighting rudo. He spun Divino and scoop-slammed him onto the mat. He looked up at the crowd. They were booing, but he had their full attention. If Divino weren't so tall, El Vengador could lift him now into a torre, but he wasn't sure he could do it with a man this big. He glanced down and Divino reached up, grabbed his head, and pulled him into a reverse bow and arrow, and as quickly as that, he had El Vengador's head between his thighs and was body-scissoring him and pulling on his mask with both hands. El Vengador struggled and closed his eyes, pushing Divino's legs apart. He'd begun to sweat inside his mask and the sweat stung in his razor cuts.

"One . . ." The referee was counting and slapping the canvas. "Two . . ."

El Vengador turned and pushed against Divino's legs. There was blood in his eyes now and he was struggling to breathe.

"Three . . ."

The crowd rose in a deafening roar and the referee rose too. He grabbed Señor Divino's arm and held it high. Divino released his legs and stood up and El Vengador's head fell to the canvas.

He would have to win the next two rounds.

At the sound of the bell Señor Divino started straight into it again, bringing El Vengador down to the mat with a leg sweep. El Vengador could feel how he hadn't had a fight since Acapulco, more than two weeks before. He hated to go so long between fights, it left him off rhythm and out of sync even if he'd prepped in the gym. Wrestling wasn't about how much weight you could lift or how many sit-ups you could endure; it was push-pull, perfect balance, partner dancing.

Divino loosened and El Vengador escaped and shot up to the ropes. Divino rose also and Vengador charged and they pulled off a pretty good double clothesline. Back on the canvas again, they locked and struggled. He got Divino in a leg bar and kept him there a while. If they stayed low, it was easier for him to play rudo than when they were moving about in the ring; it was hard not to fall back on his somersaults and rope dives that were too quintessentially tecnico.

He finished the second round with a weak rana invertida. His sweaty chest kept slipping against Divino's Lycra-clad legs. He managed it, though, and rose, fist in the air, to a mixture of boos and applause. He could feel his mask sticking to his bloody forehead. The only thing that mattered was to make it to the Gory Guerrero move and into the finale.

In the final round he let Divino wear himself out pinging around the ring aerialist-style. He stepped out of the way of almost every salto until Divino was breathing hard and moving slower and then he circled him and went in for the Gory backbreaker, slipping his arms through Divino's elbows and lifting him, back-to-back. The crowd was shouting, the referee waving. He bent his knees and lifted higher, pushed Divino's legs out, and dropped to the mat, driving his shoulder into Divino's neck. Slam.

The referee held up El Vengador's arm and the tent walls billowed ferociously. The crowd pulsed. Neto came out and held both his and Señor Divino's hands up at once. He said some words into the microphone, but El Vengador was not paying attention to anything but the blood rhythm in his own ears. He walked back up the carpet and someone threw a beer. He ducked. He had no idea how he'd done. Rudos were supposed to be hated, but it felt all wrong.

Neto knocked on the trailer door, and when Mateo said come in, he tossed him a bottle of Chinaco añejo.

"You really earned that!" Neto said, grinning like a kid. "Take a drink and then get back out there for some photographs."

SEÑOR DIVINO'S FAN photo line was twice as long as his and most of the people who approached El Vengador only wanted to ask him why he'd turned rudo, why he'd left CMLL.

"Sign of the times," he said cryptically. "The dark is rising."

The good thing about being a rudo was you got to say whatever the fuck you wanted. The audience expected him to abuse them. Soon he was shouting. "Send anybody you want my way, I'll turn 'em bad like me. Flip 'em over and fuck 'em like a frog. You saw how I did with Divino tonight!"

IN THE CAR Neto was trembling with excitement.

"Did you see how many people came! Let's go to a club, what club do you want to go to? I'll call Divino and see if he wants to come out too." He looked up at Mateo, eyes giddy. "Where do you want to go?"

"I want to see Alex," Mateo said.

Neto's forehead tensed and then released. "Yes, of course," he said, and snapped his phone shut. "Of course, we should celebrate with Junior."

THEY ARRIVED AT the compound an hour later.

"Don Neto." A man stood at the front door, but Neto waved him away. "Follow me," he said to Mateo, and took the stairs two at a time down into a huge unlit room. The walls were white and reflected the moonlight that came in through four big windows and two open doors.

"Lights," Neto called. "Where are the lights in this place?"

A shuffle of footsteps sounded and a guard appeared, AR-15 strapped across his chest and a flashlight in his hand. "Sir," he said. "There are no lights down here, sir."

Mateo saw a look of confusion cross Neto's face, but he tried to play it off with a laugh. "We'll have to do something about that." He stepped around the guard. "Where is he?"

"In there, sir," the guard said, motioning behind a dividing wall.

Mateo felt his throat close. He followed Neto. There was a gate attached to the wall with a padlock. Another guard stood beside it. Mateo stepped closer. There was someone curled up in the far corner.

"Open this," Neto said.

The guard stepped in and released it.

Mateo felt a heat rising within him.

A head unfurled from the shadows. Alex's face.

Mateo ran to him, a sound like a cry coming out of his throat as he moved across the room. And then he smelled it. He slowed, stopped, brought his hand up to his nose. "Alex!" he said, and bent, holding out his hand as he would to a half-wild animal.

Alex turned over to face him. He blinked. Dark eyes, heart-shaped face. He opened his mouth, but no sound came out. His arms were cinched behind his back.

Mateo jerked his head around and found Neto standing close behind him, speaking to the guard. "Where is the bathroom down here?"

"Sir, there is none."

Mateo watched as the shock registered in Neto's eyes. "You've been having him shit and piss and sleep right here?"

Was it really possible, Mateo wondered, that Neto didn't know what was happening in his own basement? It seemed that every little thing was under his seamless control, but then there were cracks. Mateo thought again of the way that Neto's body had moved around his brothers, the front of the house fortressed but the basement only half-complete.

"Sir, I—" The guard shifted his weight from one foot to the other.

"Why did no one tell me that the basement isn't finished yet?"

"Sir, my orders come from Flaco, sir."

"Your orders come from *me*!" Neto was vibrating with rage, shoulders up and neck stiff. "Bring me Flaco!" he shouted.

Mateo could not look at Alex for more than a few seconds or he would start crying. His guilt beat through his body like a second pulse. He looked away. The cell was completely white like the rest of the basement.

Neto had gone to the gate. There were voices from the stairway, footsteps.

"Don Neto," a man's voice said. "What seems to be the problem, sir? I had no idea you were down here. I—"

"Sit," Neto said, and pushed the gate open. A tall, thin man came into view.

"Don Neto, sir, what's the problem?"

"I said sit, goddammit."

The man knelt and then crouched like an obedient dog. Neto pulled his pistol out of his holster and cocked it. The sound of metal on metal rang loud. "I'm the only one who gives orders here." He aimed then and shot the man in his right thigh. The sound of the shot bounced around and around before it faded.

The man let out a strangled moan and collapsed sideways. "Sir," he said quietly, "yes, sir."

The guards stepped in and lifted him by his armpits and dragged him toward the stairs.

Alex was convulsing silently.

Neto turned around. "Someone uncuff this man," he said.

The guards paused. They looked at one another and then one of them let go of Flaco and walked in a big circle around Neto to Alex. He unlocked the handcuffs and held them, dangling from his fingertips, as if the smell were emanating directly from the metal loops. As the guard stepped away, Alex pulled in tighter and draped his arms around his face. Mateo knelt and touched his shoulder. His shirt was wet and he was trembling.

"Alex," Mateo whispered. But he would not look up and he would not speak.

The guards took Flaco away, then returned and carried Alex up to the mezzanine Jacuzzi. Mateo walked behind them and Neto followed. Moonlight fell through the glass walls in long, silvery bands. Mateo stood beside Alex as he stripped off his clothes under the shower. He was still shaking.

"Have you eaten?" Mateo asked. "Have they been feeding you?"

Alex looked at him and shook his head. His eyes were too huge in his face. He hunched over, trying to hide his nakedness.

"Neto!" Mateo called, turning but not letting go of Alex's arm, afraid if he did that he would collapse and fall. "He needs food."

Mateo turned to Alex again. He had to push back tears. That was the last thing Alex needed right now, to know how pathetic he looked. "Let's get in the Jacuzzi," Mateo said, pulling his T-shirt up over his head.

The water was warm. The guards brought trays to the edge, one with fruit, one with meat, one with breads. Alex made a mewling sound. Mateo poured him glass after glass of water and juice.

Neto paced.

When Alex's eating slowed, Mateo reached out and ran a hand along his shoulders and pulled Alex to him so that he leaned against his legs. Alex glanced at Neto and after a moment he began to shake again. He whipped his head side to side frantically and then crawled up out of the Jacuzzi and vomited onto the tiles. Mateo sucked in his breath and looked at Neto.

"Oh dear," Neto said. "Too much too fast." He turned to the guard. "Clean that up," he said.

Mateo exhaled and crawled over to Alex. He bent close to his ear. "I'll get you out of here soon, I promise," he whispered.

Alex coughed.

Mateo helped him to his feet and led him back to the shower.

"Set up some kind of mattress down there," Neto was saying to the man as he mopped the vomit. "And get him some clean clothes. And let him use the bathroom when he needs to, for Christ's sake. He's no use to me if he's dead or crazy."

Mateo helped Alex to a chair.

"I'll get you out of here, I'm sorry," he whispered, tucking Alex's wet hair behind his ear. "Okay?" He turned and walked over to Neto. "You can let him stay up here in a room," he said to Neto, "not down there."

Neto looked up. "Mateo, mi'jo, we're building trust," he said, "*building*, yes, but that interview tonight, that interview was touch and go."

SEVENTEEN

In the still dark of dawn Yemayá stalked a fly across the top of the mahogany dresser and onto a shiny philodendra leaf. The fly arced up and she sprang after it, reached out, and brushed the moth orchid. The pot toppled to the rug. Yemayá looked back at Toño, but he was snoring in bed. On the other side of the Chinese screen Elana lay curled on the chaise lounge, wool blanket gripped tight in her fist. Yemayá walked to the sink to look for water drips.

On the sidewalk below, the Korean wholesaler and his wife were unloading a tractor trailer, dolly load by dolly load, the morning air brightening a little each time they reemerged from the warehouse. The streets were mostly empty, a drunk sleeping on a park bench, a few laborers heading out early. The border traffic was sparse, the floodlights along the fence line still throwing pools of orange incandescence out onto the concrete.

On the Mexican side there was more movement, vendors setting up their tables by the Puente Santa Fe and the maquiladora transport buses making their constant rounds. But in the middle-class colonia of Paseo de las Palmas, the streets were quiet. There were empty sidewalks with trimmed shrubs, fenced yards, and locked garages, modest pastel homes. At the end of a cul-de-sac on Las Lomas, a door opened and a man stepped out, dressed in the navy blue of the Chihuahua state police. His radio barked and he lifted it, looked both ways at the empty street, and answered back, "Yes, yes, I'll move it now."

He disappeared back inside and the garage door rose. There were two shiny bumpers and a rusted one. A Hummer, a BMW, and a Honda with a broken heater and a functioning tape deck. Beyond the vehicles, sacks of lime and stacks of shovels were visible. The Honda backed out into the street and a different estatal pulled the garage door down after and locked it quick.

The Honda crept out of the labyrinth of middle-class colonias, past Domino's Pizza, Hyper-Market, and onto the Ejército Nacional toward downtown and into the heart of the tourist-watering-hole strip. Three blocks from the border, in the back of the nearly empty parking lot at the Candy Club, the estatal parked the Honda, beyond the range of the security cameras, and radioed in to the command office. "Ready."

"Wipe the prints," said the voice on the other end. "Get rid of the keys. Gonzalez will pick you up in fifteen minutes. You write the report then: you and Gonzalez found the gringo's car at Candy at . . . six twenty-eight, and radioed me to contact the Americans immediately."

The estatal got out of the Honda and walked away. His arm lifted, and as the keys left his hand and arced neatly toward the pink roof of the Candy Club, the sun slipped up above the horizon and spewed blinding gold bands all across the eastern sky.

EIGHTEEN

Elana woke to a telephone ringing. She opened her eyes and recognized nothing. The ringing was not coming from her cell phone and around her there was nothing but shadows and plants. She closed her eyes. The ringing stopped. She listened intently, but there were no other sounds, no footsteps or voices. She opened her eyes again, sat up, and a wave of nausea rose to her throat. Her brain felt so swollen it seemed to bump against the inside of her skull. A cat sat beside her, peering up. Toño was snoring at the far end of the room. The air was full of a green heat.

She moved as slowly as possible to protect her bruised brain. The cat hopped to the floor and circled her legs as Elana wobbled away from the couch. Under a kitchen chair she found her sneakers, tote bag, and new leather jacket. TOTAL CLEARANCE, she remembered, but on the collar, there hung a $199 price tag that made her pulse stutter. She scribbled her name and cell phone number onto a piece of paper, tucked it under an empty glass, and left the apartment as quickly and quietly as possible.

Waiting at the northbound bus stop, she flipped open her phone, but the screen was black. Dead battery. She put it back in her pocket. Every few minutes her brain reached out with a *what next, what now* question, but her hangover subsumed any ability to actually think. She just needed to get back to her apartment. That was step one and from there something else would come. She needed to lock the door and be alone. Figure out what the fuck was happening to her life.

The stop-start movement of the bus was excruciating. She got off six blocks before her stop. Better to walk than vomit on a public bus first thing in the morning. She counted the blocks, and then the steps, around the side of the house to the basement entrance.

There was someone standing in front of her door. She stopped. Her breath drew in quick. A female figure with a kerchief tied over her head was pacing and talking into a cell phone. Two suitcases sat side by side at the top of the basement stairs. The woman turned and looked up.

"Well," she said, "here she is, finally. I'll call you back, okay?"

Noreen. It was Alex's mother, Noreen, in a heavy camel-colored coat.

"You didn't have to leave work." Noreen closed her cell phone and slid it into her pocket. "Your landlady's on her way."

"What?" Elana could feel herself trembling. She needed to sit down. "What?"

"To open the apartment for us. She's very nice, actually, said she'd come as soon as she could, though of course it's not really her responsibility to let her tenant's guests in, but—"

"What's going on?"

"Your neighbor couldn't remember the name of the restaurant you work at, but it was his idea to call Mrs. Ramirez. He's a very resourceful young man, really, although I do think we woke him up."

"I have a key," Elana said, patting her pockets and realizing in that moment that she in fact did not have her keys. "I *had* a key." She took out her wallet and phone and then put them back into her jacket and patted down her pants pockets.

"Where's Simon?" Noreen said.

"Simon?" Elana looked up at Noreen's face, her powdered cheeks and pale eyebrows.

"Well, yes. Did he not come back with you?"

"Come back?"

Noreen's faced pinched. "He didn't find you?"

Elana shook her head.

"He said there couldn't be that many breakfast restaurants downtown and he'd poke his head in all of them until he found you, but he's walking and he must be exhausted, I don't think he slept at all on the airplane—"

"Simon came with you?" Elana needed to shake herself awake. She knew she must be dreaming still. What in the world would Simon be doing out here with Noreen?

"Is my dad here too?" she asked.

Noreen fixed her blue eyes on Elana, wide and unblinking. She shook her head slowly. "You didn't listen to any of our messages, did you?"

The wind was blowing her kerchief so that it stood up in a peak above her head.

"My phone's dead."

Noreen's face pinched and she looked away. "I don't know why I bought you two those phones." Her voice dipped and then rose up. "It only proves to me how much you ignore me." She looked back at Elana and her eyes were so bright, almost unbearably blue, and a tiny vein in her left eyelid was twitching visibly. "I think leaving a voice message is like putting a letter in the mailbox, but it's not at all, you speak and it goes where? Out to some satellite somewhere and meanwhile the phone you think you're talking to is *dead*."

Elana drew in a deep breath. "Noreen, I'm—"

"And no one can bother to listen to the messages. No one can *bother* to call me back."

"I'm sorry, Noreen. I'm sorry. You left me messages telling me that you were coming out here?"

Noreen made a sound like a laugh or maybe a cough. "I'll bet Alex has called you too, but your mailbox is full. Were you waitressing in that outfit?"

Elana looked down at her rumpled jeans and sneakers. She looked up. "When did you get here?"

"Six. You can go pick Simon up now. We'll need to rest before we can be of any help."

"I don't have a car." Elana looked Noreen in the eye and her voice did not quiver. "Alex took the Honda, to Mexico."

They waited in silence. With Noreen there, Elana could retreat. It came as both a relief and a defeat. Huddled in the stairwell, waiting for her landlady, she felt about thirteen. Noreen was distracted, not even looking at her. Elana let her fingers wander to her hips and pressed fiercely into the throbbing until she lost all feeling in her fingertips. She didn't even have to look at Noreen to see the pain rippling off her. She should be nicer to her; her son was missing. Elana felt a slash of sadness and guilt. *It only proves how much you ignore me.* It was true. Elana had no room for Noreen's grief or worry, she was too full up with her own.

"Good morning." Mrs. Ramirez's precise eyes took in everything. She nodded when Elana told her she had lost her key. "I'll bring you a replacement," she said, and then, "I hate, in a moment like this, to speak of finances . . . but January is coming."

Behind her, the wind kicked plastic trash across the empty parking spot where the Honda was always parked.

"I'll have it," Elana mumbled, and looked at her feet. It seemed unthinkable that this nightmare could go on that long.

The apartment was dark and cluttered. Noreen set the suitcases beside the couch.

"I'll call Simon," Noreen said, setting the suitcases beside the couch. "Tell him to stop looking."

Elana hurried to the kitchen counter, grabbed an empty cracker sleeve and whiskey bottle and stuffed them into the trash. She stepped back and glanced: the whole kitchen was messy, but there was nothing else terribly incriminating.

"Don't you want to charge your phone?"

She turned to Noreen. *Shit, the bathroom.* She ran and turned the water on. There was dried blood all across the faux marble. She dropped to her knees and rummaged for a sponge.

By the time Simon showed up, she had moved from the sink to the baseboards, then the toilet, the shower, and floor. She worked on through her nausea and headache, because when she thought about leaving the bathroom, she pictured Noreen's face, eye twitching and lips crimped. She could hear her bustling out there in the kitchen, but they had not spoken again.

"Hey," Simon called to her from the bathroom doorway.

"There's something growing in my toilet," she said, without looking up. "A black fungus."

"Elana, hey."

She glanced over her shoulder, her hair sticking to her sweaty forehead. He was leaned against the doorframe, head cocked and eyes big.

"I'm sorry," he said.

WHEN HER PHONE was finally charged, she had twelve messages. She huddled in her bedroom and listened to each one only long enough to know that she could erase it. Noreen, Noreen, Meyer, Noreen, Simon, Noreen, Meyer, Noreen, Noreen, Mrs. Ramirez, Simon, Toño. This last one she listened to in its entirety, twice.

"Hello, hope this is the right number. Miss Elana? Looks like they found your husband's vehicle. Some place called the Candy Club. Don't know if that rings any bells for you. Uh, gimme a call back. I'd like to head over and talk to the club owners, show 'em a photo or two."

NOREEN COULD NOT believe that Elana had only one photo of Alex. Noreen could not believe the terrible quality of the missing person flyer Elana had made in Juárez. Noreen could not believe that the police had stopped investigating the case and that Elana was working with a PI she'd met in a bar whom she knew only by his first name.

"The cops think he's on vacation," Elana said. She could not say the word *condom*, though part of her wanted to see Noreen's face if she were to say it. She should not really say it to anyone, though, she thought. They would think it meant an affair and it could not mean that because that would mean that Elana was disposable.

Simon sat between Noreen and Elana on the couch, his button-up shirt wrinkled from the flight, his lanky body shielding them from each other. He looked like her baby brother, sort of, only too confident, too smooth, liked he'd slipped inside a Bible salesman's body and was coasting along now, full of all-American knowledge.

"Why are you here again?" Elana said to him.

He smiled.

"No, I mean—" She exhaled loudly. "I'm not trying to be rude."

Simon took the wedding photo from Elana and stood up. "We'll go by a copy shop on the way and then bring this to your detective friend."

"Not the photo." Noreen pushed herself quickly to her feet and reached for it. "A *good* copy of the photo."

NINETEEN

The guards had brought a thin mattress down to the basement and Alex lay on it in strange, silky clothes that smelled of Neto. He watched the light move across the walls for hours.

The guards were more at ease now, talking as if Alex were not there. He recognized some of them when they returned by the lilt of their voices, the particular way they stooped in the doorway. Most of them were young and in training, Alex gathered. Cadets in the police academy. They worked here on their days off or perhaps as part of their training, Alex was not sure. They complained of mothers who nagged them to send home more pay and of the terrible food at the academy. Cups of noodle soup for days. No chance to get their dicks wet.

Their boredom was thick in the air. *Goddamn, we need a TV down here. I could go for some* El Chavo del Ocho *right now. That's a fucking kids' show, you fucking idiot, grow up. Shut the fuck up, I'll fucking grow you up.* They were trapped there in the basement too and Alex wondered sometimes what they would do if he proposed they all leave together, sneak off to a bar. There was one very young man with greased-back hair who began to offer Alex a cigarette during his shift. In another world they could all have been college students. Fraternity brothers. Instead, the structure that held them was the cartel. Although Alex had never heard them speak of it. They mentioned Don Neto, but Alex wasn't sure how much they knew. The cartel, he saw now, was like a net that he and they had each walked into without fully knowing. A veil whose entirety was only visible after you were enveloped in it.

The afternoons were long and the guards' conversations dipped into brooding silence. Alex watched the passing light. Stripes of varying whites and yellows, bits of dust and sand floating in them, desert light, dry and endless. He thought of Wojnarowicz's descriptions of deserts. When he'd first read "In the Shadow of the American Dream," he'd never experienced a landscape like the one Wojnarowicz was describing and he had only the vaguest notion that that was the kind of landscape he'd come from. Wojnarowicz described it with the same desire and sensuality as the men he fucked, the dip and roll and curve, so that before Alex had ever seen a desert or loved a man, he'd linked the two in fantasy. The arch of his lover's hip was a sand-covered hill, his thigh was the earth where it met the sky. When it hurt too much to long for a man's body, he let his mind spin out to the landscape instead.

The first time he'd touched Mateo it was September, early evening, a sheen of heat and dirt over everything. They were on Avenida Juárez, going in and out of the off-track racing bars, looking for an older wrestler, Bello Agosto, who Mateo said would let Alex interview him. Bello Agosto was retired now and spent his days at the off-track facilities that lined the Santa Fe end of Juárez Avenue, dark, deeply air-conditioned bars with TVs on every wall, broadcasting the fluid, perpetual motion of greyhounds and thoroughbreds. Tables with little paper cards and pens and men in rolling chairs, squinting, nodding, clinking ice cubes.

But that night they couldn't find Bello Agosto, and they burst out the doors and back onto the avenue. Ripe with summer evening heat.

"Those places freak me out." Mateo looked back over his shoulder. "Like a waiting room for death."

They were walking south, into the pedestrian traffic. They'd driven around all afternoon to the gyms and arenas and then parked Mateo's car and gone on foot looking for Bello. They were walking away from the car now, slow, shoulder to shoulder, letting others spill around them. The sky was pinkening up above and the sidewalk was crammed with taco stalls, the smells of roasting peppers and frying meat. At the corner of Ignacio Mejía a cotton candy vendor scooped crystals into his ancient jerry-rigged machine. Bits and pieces of pink-and-blue fluff stuck to the man's hair and eyebrows and escaped above his head, floating. Alex and Mateo stopped without speaking and watched the little sugar clouds melding in with the sunset. Mateo stood so close Alex could feel the heat from his body, his shoulder an inch away. Their fingers brushed. Alex's stomach dropped and every muscle in his body went taut; his heart beat so loud he thought the whole street could hear it. He kept his head trained on the sky and the clouds of candy. Mateo squeezed his hand.

"Cotton candy, cotton candy?" the vendor called to them.

Mateo let go, stepped forward. "Yes," he said, and grabbed the cone and handed it to Alex. "Come on," he said, "there's one more place we might find Bello."

They walked east across the railroad tracks, Mateo leading and Alex following, holding the cone of cotton candy but not eating it, worried it might stain his face and hands.

"Shit," Mateo said.

"What?"

"It won't be open for a while yet, the place where Bello might be." He turned to face Alex, walking backward up the street. "We've been at this all day. You want to go home?"

"No!" Alex dropped his eyes and blushed at the eagerness in his own voice.

Mateo grinned, reached out and grabbed a handful of cotton candy, stuffed it in his mouth, and turned around.

They ate dinner in the patio of a restaurant a few blocks north of the Monumento a Benito Juárez. There were families scattered among the other tables, mothers fussing at their children and fathers leaning back, blissful, with their bellies on display. The end of another day. Bats swooped in darkened arcs against the blanching sky and in the corner a little boy chased a pigeon, scattering bread crumbs and then rushing after it. The flap of wings echoed against the shuttered buildings.

"I forget how much I love this city," Mateo said. "I'm on tour so much, it's like this becomes just the place where I go to see my wife and kid. I can't remember the last time I spent a day hanging out downtown."

He was sitting on the opposite side of the table from Alex, out of reach, and Alex was pretty sure that he must have imagined that they'd twined fingers, it was an accident, surely.

"I forget that I never feel this good unless I'm here. I don't know what it is, I mean I wasn't even born or raised here, but it's where I belong."

Alex knew what Mateo meant. It was not an easy place to live, but that fact only made it more special. "I was born here," he said. "My adoptive parents raised me in West Virginia, but I was born here."

"Really? So you're like a real juárense!"

"No, I don't think it counts. I'd never even seen this place until a month ago."

"It's not about that, though, it's in you. You're born into it or you're chosen." He raised his beer bottle to cheers. "You were adopted out and came back. Me, I was adopted in."

THE BAR THEY went to was a long and narrow room with a stage at the far end and rainbow lights on the walls. As he followed Mateo up to the counter, Alex realized, with a quickening pulse, that men were dancing together in the corner and kissing. He looked away. Mateo caught his eye.

"You okay?"

Alex nodded. "Uh-huh."

"You sure?" Mateo was smiling.

"Yeah, I said okay."

Mateo laughed. "You want a tequila?"

Alex shrugged and sat down on a stool. "So, Bello might be here?"

"I don't see him right now, but yeah, it's his regular spot."

The tequila hit Alex hard. He could feel it in every inch of his body, but he did not feel relaxed so much as suddenly, intensely aware. Aware of his own body awkwardly propped up against the bar. Aware of where he was and aware of his mother's voice reading from Judges, *No, my brothers, do not do this wicked deed.*

Mateo turned his stool until their legs met, thigh to thigh. Alex tensed his fingers on the edge of the bar. Too much, he wanted to say, stop it, don't move, stop, don't stop. Heat flowed from Mateo's leg into his. He looked away over his shoulder to the end of the room where a tall man in a red dress and blonde wig was climbing up onto the stage.

"You know how to dance cumbia?"

"What?" He turned back to Mateo. His face was so beautiful it made Alex feel queasy.

"You dance cumbia?"

"I can't dance."

"Oh, come on."

"No, it's against my religion."

Mateo grinned. "Even more of a reason."

"No, I don't mean, I mean, I'm not really religious anymore, but I've never—" He shook his head.

Mateo grabbed his hand and pulled. "Come on."

Alex looked away. The heat in his belly felt overwhelming. He glanced back. Smoke hung in rafts over Mateo's head, beams of rotating red mirror ball light draped over him. Alex felt dizzy. He stood up and then he was moving, through the thump of music, the smoke-thick air, he was leaning in and bringing his hand up to Mateo's chin, he was kissing him.

Sound and light wiped away and then rushed back in. Alex steadied himself.

"Let's get out of here," Mateo said.

They went to a by-the-hour motel two blocks away. The bedspread was scratchy so they threw it on the floor, only to find the sheets stained. Alex pulled Mateo to him. He wanted to devour him, to touch every bit of him at once. The strobic beat of club lights and music seemed to have traveled there with them. Everything was fragmented, pieced apart and back together again. Mateo pressed his lips to Alex's eyelids, his nose, his chin. His hands were on Mateo's skin, under his shirt, lifting, pushing him, and he thought he'd die, so much blood pumping so fast in his circuitry. He'd never known a body could feel like this.

They lay curled together for a long time after they were spent. Alex buried his face in Mateo's neck and whispered *don't.*

"Don't what?" Mateo turned to cradle him.

He squeezed his eyes shut and buried his face deeper. "Don't," he said again, but he didn't know what.

THE LIGHT TRACED itself across the basement walls and floor the same way every day so that Alex could tell a sort of time by it. In the evenings it stretched farthest, long bars of gold that almost reached his cell. If the guards were not too close to the door, he would lie flat and worm his arm through the bars. Each day he could almost, but not quite, touch it. That luster on his skin. He would focus on the light until his eyes fuzzed out and painted in new things. Whole worlds inside those beams. Light like water, falling, a glimmery lake bed. Sometimes Elana came into the light, her curly hair haloed around her head. He cried when he saw her because she was smiling.

"Hey," she said. "Why didn't you tell me?"

She walked toward him, head cocked and eyes bright. "You should have just told me, silly," she said. "We were supposed to be best friends."

TWENTY

They walked across the border first thing the next morning, Noreen calling out memories: the spot midway across the international bridge where, in 1983, she had met a young American, the girlfriend of some minor rock star, crossing alone into Mexico for a cheap abortion, and had talked her out of the sin (she still sent a Christmas card every year to the address the girl had given her, telling her Jesus thanked her), the place where a Mexican marijuana dealer had propositioned Noreen and offered her thousands of dollars to carry pot across under her skirt, the corner where she had found a drunk American soldier and dragged him back to the mission to dry out and see the light. Elana, Simon, and Noreen headed to the mission now, dodging tamale vendors and money changers and hopping into a taxi. Noreen sat up front and spoke a mixture of extremely broken Spanish and very loud English. Despite all her anxiety, Elana could barely suppress her laughter as she pictured Alex watching this scene: his mother with her stack of English-only missing person flyers and her earsplitting voice, telling the taxi driver, in English, that he couldn't cheat her because she knew the fastest way.

All morning Elana had wondered how Noreen could act so confident, spouting off stories from her time in Juárez, when her own son was missing and even the police refused to help. But now Elana could see, Noreen was burying her panic under bravado. If she acted like she knew this city and how everything in it ought to be done, then maybe she could bring Alex back through strength of will alone.

JORGE OPENED THE mission door after they rang the bell three times. He was holding a broom. Elana felt the déjà vu of the moment, the way it matched up with the first time she'd come here, with Alex, back in August, and Jorge had greeted them, broom in hand.

"Elana, how are you?" Jorge said. Elana introduced Noreen and readied herself to explain the Alex-missing story, but Noreen interrupted and launched into a speech about the locked mission door and how the hesitant lambs of the world would not persist and ring the bell three times. He could have lost a soul or, more likely, several souls. An open door, that was the right policy. Jorge bobbed his head.

"Our van was stolen," he said. "My first week here, three years ago. The donation box was robbed six times until we gave it up."

"Gave up?" Noreen said.

"The donation box, now we take the donors to the bank to deposit directly."

The mission was empty except for one young woman in an ankle-length jean skirt rolling chalky blue paint over a sign that read JESÚS ES MÁS FUERTE QUE CUALQUIER ADICCIÓN. Morning sunlight spilled into the classroom, where she worked alone.

"What is she doing?" Noreen demanded.

"We can't—"

"I painted that sign," Noreen said. "Myself. Free hand."

"Really?" Jorge seemed genuinely impressed. "When you and your husband were here in the early eighties?"

"We had twenty-three participants in our first substance abuse class. Fifty in the second one."

"We can't have rehab programs here anymore," Jorge said, looking down and tracing a crack in the cement with his sneaker. "Too dangerous. For the addicts. A month ago, a gang hit the rehab center down the street."

"Hit?" Simon asked.

"Killed five addicts."

Simon's face drew in tight. "No one stops them?"

Jorge shook his head. "Rivalries. It could happen again, or maybe not. We help addicts informally now, no signs, no pamphlets, just anonymous beds for detoxing. Even with that I worry, word gets onto the street."

Noreen took over, explaining Alex's disappearance, and Elana was relieved.

"Take these." Noreen handed Jorge a large stack of flyers. "Call if you hear anything at all. My number is right there."

AT NOON THEY met up with Toño in a cafeteria near the Santa Fe bridge. He had gone that morning to the club where the police had found the Honda. He nodded at Noreen and Simon when they arrived and then turned to Elana.

"Either your husband never entered that club, or he entered it with a false ID," he said, pulling out his tin of snuff.

Elana sucked on a peanut. She felt her hunger flare up and her blood sugar dropping, but she would not chew the nut.

"Now, there's a possibility his car was placed there. A possibility he parked there and then went elsewhere. A possibility he went in with a different ID." Toño sipped his coffee. "Security cameras don't reach to the back of the lot where the car was found. Convenient. Coincidental. Your guess is as good as mine. I checked the morgues too. There was no one matching his description. But there is one more place I want to look."

THE ROAD THAT led to the shelter was narrow and sandy. It skirted the city and hugged the bare mountains where a white shape came into view, impressionistic lines that formed slowly into an enormous white horse, more than half a mile long, painted onto the hillside, his legs stretched out, running.

"What in the world is that?" Noreen said.

Toño was seated in the front of the taxi, Noreen in the back with Simon and Elana. Toño turned to look at the hillside. "Epona's horse," he said.

"Epona?"

"Like the one in Britain, only backward. For Epona, the horse goddess."

"Why is it here?"

"She's a giver of life, but her horses will lead you to the underworld. Héctor García Acosta painted her, he said he wanted a problem big enough that it would take him and his son years to solve, so he could show him the beauty."

Simon, Noreen, and Elana tilted their heads to stare. The horse seemed to be moving with them. Elana thought of the biblia sign whitewashed on the mountain in the north of the city. This one was a counterweight.

"It arrived in the years when the cartel came and people whisper that they commissioned it, but we shouldn't give them credit for everything."

The taxi stopped eventually outside a concrete block compound with smoke drifting up from the far side of the wall and the desert stretching out behind. The shelter was run by a radio evangelist, Pastor Morales, Toño said. Sometimes the cops brought people here when they couldn't identify them or had finished beating them and wanted to dump them somewhere. Morales took in anyone and Jesus's love smothered any need for questions or investigations.

They left the taxista waiting and knocked on the metal gate. When a woman opened the door, there seemed to be some sort of project underway, blue tarps spread across the courtyard and plastic bowls of wet earth. Toño spoke to the woman, asking for Morales and describing Alex. He pulled out the copied photograph and showed it to her. She looked at it closely and shook her head.

Behind her, fifteen or twenty people were moving about over the tarps, slopping handfuls of mud from plastic bowls into small rectangular wooden frames, mud bricks, Elana realized. At the back of the patio a tall man emerged. He wove his way through the group of workers, stopping to watch a young man, then pat him on the back.

He looked up and turned to Elana, Noreen, Simon, and Toño. "Welcome. Are you looking for someone?"

Noreen stepped forward and held up a flyer. "My son," she said, replying to his Spanish with her loud English. "He's gone missing and his wife has no idea where—"

Morales held up his hand. "Señora," he said in Spanish, "do you speak only English?"

"What she wants to say," Toño said in Spanish, without looking at Noreen, "is that we are looking for her son, a young American, twenty-one years old, who came to Juárez on December 3 and disappeared. This is a photo of him." He held out the photo and Morales took it from him.

"That's the only photograph his wife had," Noreen said in English. "I know it would help if we could show you a few more, but."

"He's her son?" Morales said. "He doesn't look like it."

"Well," Toño said, "she adopted him."

Morales nodded. "Oh, I see," he said. "A son come home then."

Morales did not recognize Alex's photo. But he was impressed by Noreen's Heart Cry Holiness Mission stories (translated by Toño) and he wanted to show them the shelter before they left. They were expanding, he said. He was not only ministering to addicts and homeless folks now; he'd begun to take in migrants too. Guatemalans, Hondurans, folks from southern México, the least he could do, he said, was give them a place to sleep.

He led Toño, Simon, Noreen, and Elana through an arched doorway and into another smaller patio. A stepladder was set at the base of the wall and he invited first Noreen, and then the others, to climb up. Elana waited behind Simon. She tried to concentrate on what Morales was saying, but her mind kept skipping. She was feeling faint. She did not want to faint here. She wished that she had someone to talk to—someone to tell about the condoms, someone to help her keep believing that Alex would not have left her voluntarily.

"First we're making the bricks," Morales said. "Then the expansion can begin. Instead of these dark little rooms, I want gardens, long desert gardens with rooms looking out onto them."

Elana climbed up the ladder and the desert came into view: sand, mesquite, and brown boulders and, in the distance, the huge white horse running along the rumpled mountainside. Directly below the wall, a maze of bricks was set out across the sand, outlining where the individual gardens would be.

She climbed down from the ladder. Morales had turned his attention to the far side of the patio where, under an overhanging roof, a folding table was covered with various two-way radios. He picked one up and flicked it on, *static*, he switched channels, *static*, he switched again and a faint voice came through: *Veinte las Américas. Al pendiente, bien pilas. Veinte las Américas.* Morales thrust it out toward them.

"Hawks," he said. "The eyes of the cartel. Boys of twelve, thirteen, fourteen, they pay them a pittance to stand on the corners and watch for the army and radio in when there's danger coming."

He tossed the radio to Simon, who caught it and stared down as it spewed static and tiny wavering voices.

"So I'm thinking," Morales went on. "Here I am on the AM radio, spreading Jesus's love, so why not the two-way radios too? These hawk boys, they're on these things all day long. They suddenly hear the words of Jesus Christ coming across their airwaves and who knows? Could change things for a few of them."

Elana watched as Simon turned his face up to Morales.

"We need to find more of their channels," Morales said. "The hawks all use the Kenwood channels. And we need more folks willing to preach. We're working on it, though."

Elana glanced at Noreen. She wondered if Noreen still felt sad that Alex hadn't continued preaching. Sometimes Elana wished she could have seen him—teenage Alex leading the congregation. But then again, it might have scared her.

Simon held the radio up. "So you—" he started in English, speaking directly to Morales, but stopped and turned to Toño. "Ask him, is he saying he can radio back to this kid that we're hearing on this radio right now? He can radio back and start reading the Word to him?"

Toño translated and then nodded.

Morales took the radio from Simon and pushed the button. "My son, listen to me," he said into the radio. "Behold, the Lord will come down and tread upon the high places of the earth. And the mountains shall be molten under him, and the valleys shall be cleft, as wax before the fire, and as the waters that are poured down a steep place."

Elana watched Simon as he listened, fairly trembling, visibly itching to grab hold of the radio himself.

THEY CROSSED BACK into El Paso together and Toño was quiet. Noreen and Simon were so impressed by Pastor Morales that it seemed to have nearly overshadowed the fact that they had come no closer to finding Alex. Noreen insisted on treating Toño to dinner. Elana wanted to sleep. She kept picturing her bedroom, closed blinds, piles of blankets. Toño and Noreen and Simon could handle this strange new reality. She hadn't done one single helpful thing today and she felt like a child's toy, jerked along behind on a dirty string.

"So brilliant," Simon was saying. "To think of using the radios, it's like street preaching on steroids. Those boys are bored and lonely and they *have* to keep their radios on. It's like mainlining the Word of God into them."

Elana stirred her bowl of consomé de pollo. She had only had three spoonfuls of broth, but Noreen and Simon were too deep in conversation to notice or reprimand her. The soup was cooling and forming a nauseating skin on top. She stirred it clockwise five times, then counterclockwise.

When the waitress finally took her bowl away, she realized that there was some kind of commotion happening with Noreen.

"What?" Noreen said.

"I'm sorry." The waitress held out Noreen's debit card. "It was denied. Do you have a different card I could try?"

"No," Noreen said. "I have money in that account. Let me call them." She opened her cell phone and stepped away from the table.

Elana went to the bathroom, and when she got back, Noreen was walking in from the lobby, shaking her head.

"Can you believe that?" Noreen said. "The bank tracked my card, found out I had used it in Mexico and they thought someone had stolen it and put a freeze on my account. She had to ask my entire personal history to verify that it was me."

Elana sat down in the booth. She could hear her blood pounding in her ears and her thoughts swarmed. "Wait," she said. "They tracked your card?"

"Well, yes, apparently."

Elana looked over at Toño and he was already staring at her. "That's why I asked you if he had anything on him that could be traced," he said.

"I thought you meant a cell phone."

"So he's probably got his wallet on him, huh?" Toño said.

Elana nodded. "I haven't found it in the apartment."

"Well." Toño pushed himself up to his feet. "They won't be able to give out that kind of information over the phone. You'll have to prove your relationship. Banks are closed now, but we'll go in the morning."

Elana stood up and felt a lightness in her chest, a hope, small but real.

TWENTY-ONE

Neto kept Mateo on the road every night: DF, Cuernavaca, Querétero. In Cuernavaca he had two fights, one in the early evening, one again at eight, and a press conference in between. Neto said they would slow down after a while, but they had to start out hard, get their name out there. The big arenas were all booked up with CMLL, Promo Azteca, and AAA fights and so their events were held in crumbling gymnasiums, city parks, baseball diamonds, and bull-fighting rings.

The second fight in Cuernavaca was in what Neto had said would be a soccer field. There was no field, though, just a dirt lot out at the edge of the city, circled by graffitied block walls. The streets were full of bloated bags of trash. Families stood on the corners, grilling meat and hawking menudeo wares, Hilfiger socks, sexy jeans, plastic dishes. The man who had rented the soccer field to Neto said there had been a problem with city services, no trash collection, no water, and they'd just gotten electricity back recently. But these folks loved lucha, he promised. Outside the walls a car drove in circles through the neighborhood with a crackling loudspeaker. "El Vengador del Norte versus Fancy Dragon!!! Tonight at eight o'clock, presented by Empresa Estelar. Tonight, ladies and gentlemen, tonight!!!"

It turned out to be a big and boisterous crowd, better than the earlier fight and better than the one in DF. Neto had said he was worried that once the initial curiosity wore off, everyone would go back to patronizing the promotions they were used to. They needed to raise the stakes, he told Mateo, give the audience something they couldn't get just anywhere. He was thinking hard-core fights with barbed wire, glass, tacks.

"I'm not that kind of fighter," Mateo said. "Why did you pick me if you wanted fights like that?"

Neto had reached out and ran his hand along Mateo's jawline. "Well, you know, violence is always better when it comes with a pretty face."

Mateo pulled back. "No one can even see my face."

"Not now, no." Neto stood and turned away. "Not yet."

In DF and Cuernavaca, after the fights and the interviews and photos, Mateo soaked in Epsom salt baths. He lay and watched water droplets roll down the bathroom walls, picturing Alex's face. He wanted to talk to him, to lie in bed in that apartment on Callejon Camomila and watch the headlights pass and talk about anything. He and Alicia had never had a connection like theirs. *Even Alicia has never been to my hometown. You can take a few days for me?* Just like that, he'd dragged Alex squarely into the middle of his mess. *Please, I need you.* He sat up in the bath, the water sloshing loud around him. *Please?* And of course Alex had said yes because that's how he was, open to everything. That's what made him so easy to talk to. He had a way of looking at things that was not quite naive but something close to it—a curiosity that made the world brighten with possibility.

After the fight in Querétero, Neto's pilot flew them back to the compound. As they readied for takeoff, Neto lit a cigarette and fixed himself a drink but did not offer one to Mateo. The lights were low and his cigarette glowed against the dark windows.

"You have no idea who's really pulling the strings?"

"What?" Mateo looked at him.

"That's what you said to the reporter: 'You have no idea who's really pulling the strings.'"

Mateo lit his own cigarette. "That's what I'm supposed to do. Spin a story about El Vengador turning from good to evil, right? Being pulled in to the dark side by the devil and all that shit."

Neto laughed. "Oh, I see, so it was the devil you were talking about?"

"Huh?"

"Pulling the strings?"

BACK AT THE compound, Mateo headed up the stairs to his room, but Neto made a *tsk* sound from behind him. Mateo turned.

"Don't you want to go see Junior?"

Mateo's heart leapt. "I can?"

"*We* can," Neto said.

ALEX WAS STILL locked in the cell, but he was sitting up on a mattress, dressed, hands uncuffed.

"Mateo?" he called out.

"Here I am." Mateo knelt and grabbed his face. He bent in to kiss him, but Alex pulled away.

"You're okay?"

"Me?" Mateo said. "Yes. Are you?"

"Will you leave me?"

"Leave you?"

"How long will I be down here?"

"I—"

"Not too long now." Neto stepped in and stood over them. "Right, Mateo?"

Mateo looked up. He could see Neto's necklace glinting in the dark. He wanted to hurl himself at Neto, but the guard stood right there.

"Let's go upstairs," Neto said.

In the mezzanine Alex went directly to the shower and Mateo followed. Mateo watched Alex strip off his clothes—an unfamiliar blue dress shirt and charcoal slacks that must have been Neto's—and step under the shower. There was a sound of footsteps and Mateo glanced back as four guards entered the room. He felt fear ripple through him. He turned to Alex, who still had his face to the wall, water glistening down over his head.

"Alex," he said. "Hey, Alex, baby, hey."

The guards pushed Mateo aside and he stumbled and fell to the floor as they lifted Alex and carried him to the Jacuzzi and set him in. They pushed him down until he was submerged.

"No. Stop," Mateo shouted, scrambling up from the floor. Alex's body roiled, his feet rising up, but his head still under the water. The guards' rifles were strapped to their backs, black pistols in holsters on both hips. "Stop," Mateo shouted again, but it was as if he did not exist. No one responded to him. A sound came from the Jacuzzi like a terrible, suffocated roar. Mateo felt the cry ring through him and looked across the room to Neto. "Make them stop."

The roar came again.

"Don Neto?" One of the guards looked back over his shoulder.

Neto nodded and walked toward them.

They loosened and Alex's head bobbed up. He rose with a terrific and terrifying inhale, and as soon as he'd pulled in a breath, they pushed him under again.

"Stop," Mateo screamed. He reached out and touched one of the men's shoulders and at almost the same instant a hand grabbed him. He glanced back. Neto pulled him away. Mateo shook him off, stepped out of reach.

"Fuck you. He didn't do anything, Neto, stop."

Neto flicked open his lighter and brought it slowly up to the tip of his cigarette. He looked at Mateo. "You're right," he said. "You're damn right, you know? Around here it is the devil who pulls the strings."

TWENTY-TWO

Alex's card pinged to an ATM in Creel, Chihuahua, a withdrawal of fifty dollars on Sunday December 4. The transaction had been flagged as suspicious, but his account had not been frozen because he hadn't used the card since. Their joint account had not been touched.

Elana and Noreen had met Toño for coffee before the bank opened and he'd shown them a list of everything the cops had found in the Honda: fast-food receipts—Krystal's, Taco John's, Dixie Cafe—cassette tapes, Kit-Kat wrappers. No blood. No signs of foul play except for the cracked windshield that Elana confirmed had been shattered long before Alex disappeared. The inspection sticker was expired, but nothing else was amiss.

They went together to the bank as soon as it opened and a woman in a purple blazer led them to her desk. She looked at Elana's passport and driver's license and checked them against her computer screen.

"A single withdrawal in Creel," she said.

"You must be able to tell us more than that!" Noreen leaned forward.

Elana looked away, across the lobby.

"Sunday, December 4."

The same day he emailed saying he'd lost his phone.

Up at the counter, a young couple were talking to a teller. The man wore a green dress shirt, hair slicked back from his forehead; the woman, a yellow floral dress too thin for winter, her black hair piled high and her lips painted firehouse red. From this distance Elana could not hear what they were saying, but the wife's face was pinched, and when Elana looked more closely she saw that under the counter, out of sight of the teller, the husband was twisting the wife's arm, her small hand hidden inside his and her wrist torquing backward.

"Elana?" Noreen waved her fingers in front of Elana's face. "When did you say that you left?"

"Left?" Elana tried to see the couple again, but Noreen blocked her view.

Noreen sighed. "Went back to Virginia."

"December 2."

Noreen leaned toward the bank woman's computer. Behind her, the husband had let go of the wife's arm and was filling out paperwork. The wife was looking at the ceiling and massaging her wrist.

OUT FRONT, the wind was blowing. Toño took his hat off and held it against his chest.

"Fifty dollars is not enough for extortion," he said.

"What are you talking about?" Noreen's cheeks were pink from the chill.

"They'd have insisted on more than that."

"Extortion?"

"They flash a gun and make you withdraw to the max limit. Fifty dollars is surely not his daily withdrawal limit."

The bank doors opened and the young couple came out, the wife passing so close that Elana could have reached out and touched her wrist. She brought her hand to her own hip instead.

"I hate to say the cops were probably right, but . . ." Toño looked at Elana. "Everything seems to point to this being a voluntary departure. Except maybe the car, which . . . if he's on a bender, maybe he left it there to come back for later."

"My son does not drink," Noreen said.

Elana looked down at her own shoes, faux-leather combat boots worn from black to gray at the toes. She pitied Noreen for her naiveté, but at the same time she had to admit a certain amount of jealousy. Noreen was so sure of her place in the world, so sure of who her son was, so sure of his love for her. She had faith. Not only in God but in herself too. She would never be left, and even if she were, she would never think of it that way. Elana had always lacked that kind of faith. Her whole family, on both sides, lacked unwavering faith. Except for Simon now; he believed. She had never really considered how much self-confidence faith gave, how it moved you into the category of those who would not be left behind; that, in and of itself, made you more self-assured in everything you did. Rapture. That whole idea was to be one of the ones to leave. And if no one was left behind, then there was nothing special about leaving. The Leavers needed the Left to make them special.

Elana looked back up at Toño. "Maybe he did go to Mexico voluntarily at first," she said, "but then something else happened there, something that stopped him from being able to come back." Her voice sounded thin, but she was trying to push more confidence into it.

"Could be." Toño shook his head. "I don't know what to say except that there's probably a pretty good chance he shows back up in a couple of days, calls this whole thing a mistake."

"So you're quitting?" Noreen said.

Toño laughed. "Lady, you can't quit when you're not getting paid. But I'm not going down to Creel, if that's what you mean."

THE APARTMENT FELT crowded, even though it was just Elana and Noreen there. Simon was off making more copies of the flyer at Noreen's request. And as soon as she and Elana were back at the apartment, Noreen began stuffing things in her suitcase.

"*You* want to go to Creel?" Elana said.

Noreen looked up. "You *don't*?"

"I never said that. I thought I'd go and you could stay here in case he comes back."

It was dark inside despite being midday. Noreen was hunched over her suitcase, a pair of white underwear in her hand.

"Oh, so now you want to show some initiative?" she said, straightening up and looking at Elana. "I thought maybe you didn't care."

"About Alex?"

"You sit there like a bump on a log. I can't even imagine how you got that black man interested in helping you in the first place, seeing as how you hardly say two words. And then he quits and you don't seem to care one way or another."

"That *black man*?"

"If suddenly—"

"His name is Toño. I introduced you."

"Yes, well, I'm only saying that if Jim was to go missing, I wouldn't sit there like a bump—"

"You weren't here." Rage coursed up through Elana's body and it felt great—better than hunger, better than anything she'd felt in days. "You didn't see," she said. "By the time you got here, I'd already—"

"And I still don't understand why he didn't come back east with you."

"Would you let me finish?"

Noreen was still gripping her pair of underwear in her fist. "I have one question first."

"Yes?"

"It's normal for you two not to talk for days? You don't hear from him the whole time you're in Virginia and it doesn't worry you?"

"No, it did, I—"

The front door swung open and Simon filled the frame.

"My favorite ladies!" he said. "Anybody hungry?"

ON THEIR WALK to lunch Noreen's phone rang.

"Hello?" she said. "Jim, hey, Jim is that you? I can't hear . . . Jim, are you all right?" She waved Simon and Elana on and then turned her back to them.

They walked half a block up and stood, waiting for her with their hands in their pockets and their hair blowing in the wind. She yelled into the phone for a while and then pocketed it. When she caught up with them, her face was grim. She said Jim's angina was acting up again. There was a silence and then she said, "I shouldn't go down to Creel right now. I think Jim needs me."

"That's okay," Elana said. "Simon can go with me."

AT THE BUS station in Juárez the ticket agent asked for their passports. Elana reached into her bag, but Simon grabbed her arm.

"All I have is my state ID."

"I think it's fine," Elana said. The US customs guys hadn't given him any trouble about it when he crossed back into El Paso the day before. Elana turned to the ticket agent to explain and the woman listened distractedly, clicking the end of her ballpoint pen.

"We can accept a valid driver's license," she said.

Elana handed Simon's ID over the counter. The woman shook her head. "This isn't even a driver's license."

Elana looked at Simon, surprised by the emotion in his eyes.

"I'm sorry," he said. "I haven't gotten it together to take the driver's test."

She turned away from the counter. "It's fine," she said. "I'll be fine. Just watch my bag for a minute."

She bought her ticket and then sat down next to Simon.

"I'm sorry," he said again.

"It's fine." She wanted to hug him, but it didn't quite seem right. "You know what you should do instead? Go help Morales with his radios."

Simon nodded and leaned forward, his gangly arms resting on his knees. "Toño was telling me, the thing Morales has to be careful of is that the cartel can track the radio signal. Like if they use the same radio too much the cartel can triangulate their location. They drive around in this van, so they're not always signaling from the same place. Plus, they have to keep buying new radios."

The room was filled with loudspeaker announcements and TV voices, the shush and hiss of brakes from the bus platform outside. A woman with a mop circled the far side of the room, squirting a pink chemical trail out of a plastic bottle.

"The kids who work for the cartel have to stay on their radio all the time. If they're caught with the radio off or they fall asleep during their shift or whatever, they can be killed, or tableado, you know what that is?"

Elana shook her head.

"Taken out in the desert and beaten with boards."

The cleaning woman wove around two sleeping men huddled on the floor without breaking her stream, encircling them in pink slime.

"I told Morales I'm gonna get *everyone* I know back in Virginia to help raise money for radios. Anyone who calls himself a Christian should be all over this opportunity. This is the kind of project I've been dreaming about!"

Elana liked the spark in his voice, even if it was about preaching Jesus. It had been a long time since she'd heard him sound like this. When he first went into rehab, they had written to each other weekly, but after a little while his letters had turned preachy. *Elana, I know this probably sounds weird and, well, it feels a little weird to write it, but the truth is, I've realized, I'm a sinner, an abomination. But Jesus forgives me. How incredible is that?* She had stopped writing back. She didn't know how to respond and so she waited and waited.

She looked at him now, lounging in the seat beside her, and suddenly she was speaking before she was even aware of what she was saying. "What do you remember about the day before rehab?"

Simon snapped his head up and focused on Elana.

"When you pulled the knife on Dad," she said. Her heart pumped in her throat. She wanted to reach for her hip bone, but she kept her fingers in her lap.

Simon blinked three times and looked down at his feet. "I don't, really," he said.

"What do you mean?"

"If you're amped up on enough of that shit, it's like a fugue state. I don't have like a real memory." He looked up at her again. "But I know I did it. I know that for sure."

Evil, Elana remembered him saying back in Virginia. *I am weak and low and dark.*

Simon shifted in his seat. "When you went up to visit Dulcie, Coe was there, huh?"

Elana nodded. "Yeah. Fresh out of jail."

Simon looked away across the platform. "I loved that man. Loved him . . . well, more than anyone, I guess. More than Dad." He shook his head. "I trusted him."

Elana watched Simon's profile, long eyelashes, his lower lip rolled into his teeth. *More than anyone.* Even though she was older, Simon had been the one to outgrow their I-tell-you-everything-before-anyone-else bond. His was her first betrayal—before she'd known anything about infidelity. Her first experience of being left.

"You want some peanuts?" Simon stood up. "I'll buy you some peanuts for your trip."

Maybe more truthfully, her first betrayal was her mother. But from that loss had come Simon. Simon, who was hurrying back toward her now, smiling, his hands filled with three different flavors of packaged peanuts.

"Lana," he said. "Hey, Lana, don't worry, we'll find him."

IT WAS DUSK by the time the bus pulled out of the station and turned down Juárez Avenue, the headlights sweeping over cowboys and glue sniffers and party-club girls. There was no one in the seat beside Elana and she could stretch her legs across both cushions and press her face up to the window. The lights of the maquiladoras and shopping centers flew by and then on past town, the silhouettes of trees against the gray evening and then nothing. A darkness that climbed up to the stars.

She dozed and woke in Villa Ahumada, then dozed and woke again in Chihuahua City for a layover and transfer. The station was bright and bustling and smelled of urine and floral chemicals. She paid two pesos to the woman in the doorway of the bathroom, collected her squares of toilet paper, and hunkered in the stall until she felt awake enough to face the waiting room.

A man approached her almost as soon as she sat down and she felt a knot of panic rise in her throat. The panic clouded his words and she shook her head in incomprehension, but he kept on.

"You're a student?"

She nodded.

"Where are you going?"

"Creel."

"Oh, you're on vacation!"

She shrugged.

"American?"

She nodded.

"You're traveling so late at night all alone. It's a good thing I saw you over here. You know, not to speak badly of my countrymen"—he looked around as if someone were listening—"but not all men are like me. Some men see a girl like you and they think . . . dark things."

Elana pulled her book out and opened it, concentrating fiercely.

"Some men think a man who lets his wife travel alone at night is no husband at all. And a woman who likes to travel all alone is no wife."

She snapped the book shut and stood up. The man looked at her, his left eye drifting toward the wall. She slung her backpack over her shoulder and walked to the hamburger stand at the end of the room. A middle-aged woman with a hairnet was standing beside the grill. Elana ordered a burger with chiles, tomatoes, and onions, fully expecting not to eat it. But when it was handed to her, it smelled delicious. And to order food and watch it grow cold made no sense here. In fact, it seemed terribly rude. She picked up the burger, soft and warm in her hands; she pressed it into her mouth and her eyes began watering. It tasted incredible, but she chewed slowly, a full minute passing before she could convince herself not to spit it out.

EVERY SEAT ON the bus from Chihuahua City to Creel was full and the second half of the four-hour ride was twistier than anything Elana had ever experienced. On every curve the bus seemed about to tip over, but in the dark there was nothing she could even see, only abysses as deep and jagged as her imagination would allow. The woman beside Elana rattled her rosary round and round, but other than that it was almost completely silent and Elana must have fallen asleep at some point because when they pulled into Creel she was waking from a dream of her mother, the heat of Virginia summers, and the sheet tents she'd made for Elana to play in while she was on her pregnancy bed rest.

The air outside was pearly, just beginning to thin with predawn light, and there was a crust of old snow on the edges of the sidewalks. Elana shouldered her backpack and walked the length of the main road, but nothing was open. She passed the dark-mirrored windows of the trinket shops and "authentic" restaurants and circled back finally to the Nescafé vendor in the bus station. The woman measured two spoons into a cup and then held up a shaker of nondairy creamer.

"Milk?"

"No," Elana said, searching her pockets for change.

The woman opened her thermos of steaming water and ladled it into the Styrofoam cup and passed it to Elana. "Tourist?" she said.

Elana nodded.

"You're traveling alone?"

"Yes, alone," Elana said.

SHE TOOK A room in a hospedaje the Nescafé woman led her to on a side street past the plaza. The building was painted neon orange on the first floor but unpainted from there up. HABITACIONES was spelled out in blue but only half the letters were filled in. The Nescafé woman rang a bell beside the door and after a while a woman came down with sleep still smeared across her face. She nodded wordlessly and gave the Nescafé woman a coin. Thirty-five pesos per night, she told Elana, and led her up the stairs.

The building was colder inside than out and Elana climbed directly into the bed with her shoes and coat still on.

TWENTY-THREE

The light had changed. Those rays that reached across the floor almost all the way to Alex's cell were interrupted now, a shadow cast across them as if something sat parked right outside the door, only nothing was there. Nothing had come. But the light was broken. He didn't know when it had happened. Time was slippery here and that, more than anything, was what would drive him insane. He feared the holes. He surfaced out of the darkness and something had changed. The mattress was gone. Was the mattress here before? The guards at the door were quiet now, and when they did speak, he recognized none of their voices. Before the night in the Jacuzzi, he had nearly convinced himself that they were harmless, pawns caught up in the game. And perhaps they were pawns. But they were not harmless. How much time had passed? He had no idea. Long enough to become attached to the shape of the light on the floor.

The holes. Anything, everything, could disappear into them. Like the holes in the Jesus comics he'd read at Camp Glory, the summer he turned thirteen. The summer of tipping. The following September everything had roared apart, his body gone radioactive and everyone noticing, not just his body but his very eyes, filled with soul-rot; but that summer he'd only been tipping, his child-body still something he could fall back into. He'd gone with his father to Camp Glory as they did each year. The church rented the campgrounds after 4-H was over and the cabins, on that first day, still held the secrets of the sinful campers: crushed cigarette butts, lipstick tubes, and notes with hearts and *X*s and *O*s.

For two weeks the Camp Glory kids memorized Bible verses, sang hymns, and copied messages onto notecards decorated with Popsicle sticks and plastic flowers. *If you declare with your mouth, "Jesus is Lord," and believe in your heart that God raised him from the dead, you will be saved.* Twice a week, the church bus took them to towns around the county. They wandered the streets, lush with a green summer silence, and knocked on doors to press their homemade placards into confused hands. In the evenings they swam in the river, bathed in the warm delight of their good deeds, the water a continual baptism—lifting and embracing their young bodies. And afterward, around the campfire, they reveled, dark hearts banished and faces slick with joy. All those kids yearning, straining, praying, and they looked so achingly beautiful. Bright eyes, upturned faces. Alex knew he was not supposed to love this world, he was to yearn always for the hereafter, but those summer nights he felt so full up he never wanted to leave this place, those faces. He wanted to hold them like a shield against everything that was coming.

"Why can't our hearts stay pure?" he asked his father on the far side of the fire. "Like a cure. Like turn to the light and stay that way forever?"

"Jeremiah 17:9," his father said, staring at him across the flames. "'The heart is deceitful above all things.'"

As the fire died down, one of the older boys brought out a guitar and led them in a praise round. "The Lord is my light and salvation. Whom shall I fear?" they sang. "The Lord is my light and salvation. Of whom shall I be afraid?"

Their child voices wavered up into the night and Alex moved his lips along with them, it was one of his favorite songs, but his throat was too swollen with emotion to let out the words. It was obvious now, the answer to the song. It was yourself. You should be most afraid of your own self.

The Camp Glory children passed out a tiny black-and-white comic book along with their handmade cards. The comic showed a boy going through his day, breakfast with his family, the bus ride to school, his classroom—when suddenly everything began to shake, earthquake cracks appeared, but this was no normal quake. The fault lines fell only between those who were lost and those who were saved. Crumbling fractures snaked their way between the boy and his best friend, his teacher, even his own mother, who apparently did not truly believe, even though she went to church each Sunday. And then, just like that, the lines disappeared. The boy went back to his regular life. He said nothing. He did nothing. And then one morning he woke up and there were holes, frosty white vaporous holes where his mother, his teacher, and his best friend had been. The boy walked through his day weeping and the holes followed him. His loved ones were not just gone but were there with him, haunting him in their goneness. And he could have saved them.

The intent might have been to reach those who said, "I don't need your evangelizing, I'm already saved," but instead the story terrified the Camp Glory children. They clung to one another, clung to their parents, begged, and prayed. Are you *really* saved? Is your heart *truly* pure? Promise me, promise me, please. Will you leave me?

Alex had carried the holes with him through everything. Those frosty vacancies were worse than the idea of his own flesh burning. He had clung to his parents even as they pushed him away. And he'd clung to Elana—*marry me, please*—even after he stopped feeling sure he believed. Let no one I love disappear.

But they were all gone now. Or rather *he* was gone, turned into a vaporous hole. Even Mateo had not come to see him in what . . . days, weeks? Time was like threaded beads, stacked backward, one decision tipped into the next: lucha libre thesis, master's program in Texas, Dr. Orenstein's freshman-year history class, the woman at Youth Ministers United who had handed him a college pamphlet. It lined up like dominoes and marched back to that summer of tipping.

In the midst of the holiness of Camp Glory, he and Billy Allender had swum in the soft green river, hands reaching, fingers twined. How long can we stay? Bubbles rising around them. Billy's hair moving in the current, his skin so impossibly smooth. Underwater they could look at each other openly. Their fingers knotted into each other's, legs crossed on the rocky riverbed. It could last only as long as their breath. Up above, the summer was bursting, cicadas screaming and fucking and roiling on every branch, Bible verses begging to be memorized, hearts turning dark before you could even reach them, roads spoking out in every direction from this place, and the vines and trees and birds and snakes growing and twisting and climbing. But there, underwater, everything was green, everything was still, everything was holy.

TWENTY-FOUR

The preparations had begun in the early morning, a steady traipsing of footsteps and voices that woke Mateo up. He'd stepped out of his room and watched as men carried boxes and crates down the hall and up the stairs to the garden on the roof. He went back to bed, but he could not sleep. His dreams were filled with images of Alex struggling, Alex drowning. Water pouring in. Each time, he remembered how distant he had felt. He had not rushed to Alex but hung back. People say you can never really know what a person is made of until they face a crisis. Mateo kept returning to that moment; everything split into before and after. There was no going back. It was like some twisted baptism. Anything about the situation with Neto that he had once justified or intellectualized was gone. It was much simpler and darker now.

Now that he was in this deep, the path back was almost impossible to see. One decision had led to another and another, but looking back it all became too thick. Lalo had led him to Babe Sharon and with Babe Sharon it had all been community: you help the brother next to you and if you perfected a move, then you gave a hand to the next man. And then Babe Sharon had selected him alone out of the whole group to go to DF and train with El Águila, and there it had been a brotherhood too, though a looser one, not so much hometown pride. Then El Águila had recommended him to CMLL and Mateo had moved up but to the bottom again, the newest, lowest. And then there had come the tap, out of nowhere: this man wants to sponsor you. He'd been moving toward it the whole time without seeing it. And now Babe Sharon was dead and El Águila was nothing more than an aging wrestler giving classes in a basement gym, a man with a few friends left at CMLL, and CMLL was corrupted too apparently, because it was Arturo, his manager, who set him up with Neto. He lay in tangled sheets and sweated.

Neto came to his room in the afternoon and told him no fight tonight, we're having a party. Mateo was still in bed and he did not move. You look awful, Neto told him, get up, clean yourself, and wear your mask tonight, my friends want to meet El Vengador. As he turned to leave, he set a vial of cocaine on the counter by the sink.

AT THE END of the roof garden were tables piled with breads and fruits and raw red meat, marbled slabs and racks of ribs waiting for the flames. In the corner a white-aproned man turned a glistening veal calf on a spit.

Mateo entered and the men all turned, drinks held high. Neto stepped up, grasped his arm.

"El Vengador!" he said, grinning. "The man of the hour!"

The men cheered. It was all men there, heavy with musk and dressed in pearl-snap shirts, picuda boots, and black cowboy hats. Firm bellies, thick mustaches, and fat hands, as soft as calf leather to the touch.

The band started up with a Jesús Malverde ballad. Through the smoke of the cook fires the sun was setting and sending spikes of light up into the gaps of the distant mountains. After the men had all shaken his hand, Mateo took his drink to the edge of the azotea and watched the desert dusk, jackrabbits skittering past the stables and outbuildings and off into the cholla and nopal.

He stayed there, and as the dark fully set in, he saw a group of men moving in the patio down below. A row of lights blinked on and he could make out Neto, leading the group, and beside him a man who looked like Alex. Mateo slipped through the crowd and down the side stairs.

He found the men grouped around the corral. The lights were on in the stables across the way and the beams shone through the rafters and stretched long into the dark yard. Mateo pushed through the crowd and boosted himself up onto the fence. Inside the corral Neto stood with Alex beside him.

"Wait," Neto said to the men, and then he turned and said something to Alex. Mateo leaned in, but Neto's voice was too quiet to hear.

Neto walked into the stable and Alex stayed alone in the corral, so skinny in his billowing silver shirt, eyes dilated and cheeks concave. There was a movement at the stable door and a wave of energy rippled through the men as Neto walked out with a young horse—dark body and pale mane, white tail arched and muscles so tight the tension sliced with every movement. Only his eyes roved wild, the rest of him was held back, just barely, under twitching skin. Neto led the animal straight to Alex, and Mateo felt his blood rush up. He pressed against the fence, breath held in. Neto whispered to Alex and handed him the reins. The moment they passed hands, the horse whipped his head, and seeing who held the lead, he rose, legs articulated against the stable lights. Alex rose with him, arms outstretched, and then the horse broke free, pounding down the paddock and back. Neto leapt out of his way and climbed the fence, but Alex stayed in the center, watching the yearling froth out his fury, step by ringing step.

TWENTY-FIVE

Elana woke to the sound of hammers and footsteps on the roof. The walls of the hospedaje room were unpainted cement; a tea towel covered the window and a hook had been installed on the door. The communal bathroom was down the hall. She arose, ravenous, and gathered her wallet and Alex flyers and stepped from the room to find half a dozen young men moving up and down the corridor with sacks of concrete and boxes of nails. When she peered up the stairwell, she could see them working, fitting the blocks over the rebar on the roof.

She found the proprietor on the ground floor and asked her how many ATMs there were in town.

"One."

Elana nodded. "I'm looking for my husband," she said, unfolding the flyer.

The woman inspected it in the shade of the doorway as the workmen tromped past. She shook her head. "Ask the police."

Elana ordered huevos a la mexicana at the first restaurant she passed. She wrapped each bite of egg in strips of hot flour tortillas and ordered more when they were gone. The burger had ignited a hunger in her that felt bottomless. Still, though, she did not like the feeling of being full, her brain glutted and unclear. The snap-command, *this is what I should do next*, that she had felt before eating was all gone. She walked to the ATM and took out five hundred pesos, though she already had plenty of cash. She turned in circles inside the little glass room trying to make it feel real that Alex, her Alex, had been there. She touched the buttons of the machine, the same ones he had touched. She looked at the light through the glass. She pressed her fingers into the grooves where his fingers had been and breathed deeply.

She'd hoped there would be a hotel close by whose registry she could check, but surrounding the bank there were only postcard shops. She handed out her flyers to the women in the shops and they all shook their heads. The last one mentioned the police again and Elana asked her for directions.

The headquarters was near the bus station. A man in uniform leaned in the doorway, smoking and watching Elana.

"You were robbed?" he said.

"What?" she squinted at him.

"What do you need, little lady?"

"My husband," she said, pulling out her flyer.

"You lost your husband?"

She almost laughed. That was one way to think about it. Maybe she'd just misplaced her husband instead of being left. There was less of a lineage of passivity in it when she thought about it like that.

"Yes," she said, stumbling over her Spanish, "he comes here, to Creel, on December 4."

The man dropped his cigarette and crushed it with the toe of his boot.

"I want to know if anyone sees him," she said, "if he . . ." She'd reached the absolute limits of her language skills.

The man tossed his head toward the building behind him. "Make a missing person report," he said.

Elana felt her bloated stomach twist.

She was directed to a man in a tiny broom closet of a room with a desk and a typewriter and stacks upon stacks of loose papers piled behind him. He took a blank sheet and fitted it into the typewriter.

"Name," he said. "Birth date, nationality, relationship to missing person."

It was the same as before, only more exhausting in Spanish. She could only partially answer most of the questions. Details of missing person, identifying characteristics, circumstances surrounding disappearance, last date of contact. When he finished, he snapped the paper from the machine, tidied the pages, thanked Elana, turned, and set it on the top of the tallest pile.

"You . . . ?" Elana's hand shook as she pointed. She could not think of how to translate any other words.

"What?" The man adjusted his eyeglasses.

"That's it?" she said. "You just . . . That's all?"

"Oh," the man said. "Yes, there's no money in the budget for file cabinets."

In the hallway Elana leaned against the wall to catch her breath. She kept picturing the stacks and stacks of reports. She kept picturing the next person coming in and their pages placed on top of Alex's, and others on top of that, on and on like a snowfall, blanketing.

She walked away through town and out the far side, threading the edge of the road until she came to a lake. Smooth and cold and pine forested. A spill of boulders and children's voices from the far bank. A tiny girl in full blue skirt dodged through the trees, laughing. Elana thought of the piles of missing person reports and she felt nauseous. She felt sorry she'd ever eaten anything in her entire life. She felt a streak of rage at Alex for putting her in this situation, or maybe at herself for marrying him. Without that, he wouldn't have been able to abandon her. But now she had to find him, if only so she could be the one to leave.

THERE WERE FIFTEEN hotels in Creel. It took Elana three hours to parrot out her little speech to the receptionists at every one of them. At the Chihuahua Lodge there was no receptionist at the front desk, but through the windows of the dining room, Elana could see a girl setting tables. At the end of the room was a beautiful blue antique cookstove with pots bubbling on it. The girl moved swiftly among the rough-hewn furniture and looked up when Elana walked in.

"Hello, I'm sorry," Elana said, already holding out her flyer. "I'm looking for my husband."

The girl paused. "You're staying here?"

Elana shook her head. "He stays here, on December 4? Maybe?"

The girl set down a stack of napkins and took the flyer from Elana. She turned it and looked up. "Yes," she said. "He ate here, I remember his face."

"Yes?" Elana reached out to steady herself against a chair. "You see him?"

The girl nodded.

"Oh my god. You see him?"

The girl nodded again and pointed to the desk. "Ask her."

The receptionist was back.

Elana rushed toward her, waving the flyer, but the receptionist did not recognize him. "Maybe I wasn't working," she said, lugging a heavy leather-bound guest book up onto the counter. "Yeah, see, I didn't work that week."

"I can see?" Elana leaned up onto her tiptoes.

The receptionist bit her lower lip. "Okay, quickly," she said.

Elana slid the book toward herself, her fingers trembling.

4 de diciembre de 2005	
Jesús Reynosa Diaz	2 personas
Julio Pacheco Hernández	2 personas
Miguel Fernando Bernal	1 persona
José Perez Rodriguez	2 personas

Alex's name did not appear anywhere. She searched the list twice, tracing her finger slowly over each line. Then she searched for Vivi's name. She turned the pages and searched December 3—*Mateo Soto Macías, David Gómez Gutiérrez*—and then December 5, 6, 7.

"This is it?" she said to the receptionist.

The girl nodded.

"This is all the people who stay here?"

"Yes."

In her room at the hospedaje, she lay in bed and listened to the workmen's footsteps and watched the sun stripe the tea-towel curtain and then disappear. In the blue dusk of early evening, her stomach began to roil. It started as movement but soon became pain. She curled into a fetal position. Outside a car passed, radio blaring. The pain stabbed and she jerked upright, pressing her hands against her belly as if to keep it in place. She was sweating now. There was a trash can in the corner.

The sound of her vomit hitting the bottom of the metal bin was all that she could hear for a while. Even after it was over. And it was only over for a moment before it began again. Her muscles contracted, her stomach, her hands, her arms. She shook, released, shook. The room was dark now. She pushed herself across the floor toward the bed, dragging the trash can with her, but she did not have the strength to climb up onto the mattress.

She wiped her sweaty forehead, tucked her hair behind her ears, and propped herself against the end of the bed. She listened to the rain outside and thought how the workmen would be disappointed with the weather. After a while the door opened and Alex came in. There was a woman with him, but Elana could not see her face. They were dancing now, Alex and the woman, ballroom-style. Waltzing. They did not look at her, and every time Elana moved to get a view of the woman's face, Alex spun her away.

As she watched, they began kissing and she became aware then of the smell of her own vomit, in the trash can, on her hands, her clothes, her hair. She was embarrassed suddenly, horrified. She turned to try and crawl away, to take the trash can to the far corner, but she was so weak. She began to weep. Softy at first, the tears coming from the pit of her stomach, and then more loudly. Loud enough for them to hear.

LIGHT CAME EVENTUALLY and with it a knocking. Elana stirred. Her head and shoulders seemed to be underneath the bed. The knock came again. She rolled over just as the door was opening. She could have sworn it had been locked. It was not Alex this time, but a young girl.

The girl's face contorted. She started toward Elana and then stopped. She said lot of things Elana could not translate.

Elana tried to sit up, but her muscles weren't listening.

The girl said more things and this time Elana heard *enferma*, sick.

She nodded and repeated, "Sick, yes, sick."

Sick, sick, sick, sick, sick.

The girl went away and the door closed.

SHE SLEPT AND dreamt of water.

She woke and vomited.

She slept and woke and the door was open.

She scrambled and ran her hands down her body to make sure she wasn't naked.

Her trash can was gone. The door was open. Workmen were passing in the hallway outside. She pulled the blanket over herself, though it was too hot.

The girl came back with the woman proprietor. They said many things, but the only word Elana understood was *enferma*. They bent and hoisted her up by her armpits. She tried to help, but her head was too heavy. They steered her out of the room and toward the stairwell.

"Just leave me here," she said in English as they carried her forward.

A man in the hallway looked at the three of them. He set his sack of concrete on the ground and reached for her, then carried her down the stairs and into a room on the first floor with a big blue bed and a private bathroom. He set her, still clothed, inside the tub and left. The women undressed her.

TIME MOVED ERRATICALLY in the room with the big blue bed. There was a coil of fly paper that hung over Elana's head like a clock pendulum. Mostly time seemed to have stopped. When she finally felt good enough to sit up and drink water, the proprietor woman said that four days had passed. Four days in the span of one afternoon. Maybe this is what had happened to Alex too, maybe he'd stepped into a time tunnel like this and gotten trapped. All she remembered of the past few days was the women bathing her. She'd cried and her tears mixed in with the bath and somewhere in the middle of it the two women's faces had been replaced by her mother's and Dulcie's.

On the fifth day the fever was gone and so were Adair and Dulcie. Elana could drink broth and she could stand up, and the hotel proprietor and the girl walked her to the bus station, one on each side, the girl carrying Elana's backpack.

TWENTY-SIX

The SUV moved out of the compound and drove across the rocky plain where the earth was the color of cayenne. After a while it turned and switched toward the mountains and from inside Alex watched as the vague brown shapes came into focus. He sat in the back beside Neto and both were silent as they passed through a stone canyon and up into the flinty ridges, pocked with juniper. He had not seen Mateo since the night of the party, but Neto had come down to his cell every afternoon for the past few days. He would send the guards away, open the gate, and sit with Alex. He rambled on about a trip he and his mother had taken to the cenotes down in the Yucatán and a new restaurant he was financing in the capital. Strangely, though, what he seemed to want most was assurance from Alex.

"You're okay?" he said with something a little like pleading in his eyes. "My men won't touch you now. They all saw what happened to Flaco."

These words warped Alex, turned his stomach and his mind. He knew what Neto was doing, acting as if his near drowning in the Jacuzzi was the fault of his guards, as if Neto himself had not been standing there the whole time. What he could not figure out was why.

Alex had never fully come up from that Jacuzzi, those hands pinning him down and his lungs screaming. The water coated him still, like a dream that had never quite ended. At the back of his brain now something flickered. A creeping thought that Mateo was avoiding him and a feeling that was layering its way in with his love, a certain bitterness. He remembered surfacing from the water, how Mateo and Neto were both watching him and doing nothing. Alex could not wipe the image away. You thought you knew someone. You thought you knew someone just because they made your blood jump. He would not be here at all if Mateo had not put him in this danger. Still, when footsteps sounded on the basement stairs, his body trembled, lifting of its own accord and then crumpling each time when he saw that it was not Mateo.

"Stop," Neto said to the driver. "We'll get out here."

He stepped down and came around to Alex's side, opened the door for him. Alex got out slowly, favoring his right leg. It had been crushed when the men pushed him into the Jacuzzi and it ached now all the time. Neto climbed the embankment at the side of the road and then turned, offering Alex his hand. Alex looked up at him. Neto's face was lit with a wink of a smile, a spark between his lips and his eyes. Alex watched his own hand grasp Neto's, which was small but surprisingly strong. He pulled and steadied Alex with his other arm until he stood firm.

They walked together, across the embankment and into a forest of tall pines. It was dark and quiet beneath the trees, sunlight glancing in long slices between the boughs and wind shifting the needles noiselessly. Alex looked at Neto again, searching for some intention. It didn't seem to make sense for Neto to kill him out here when he could just kill him at the compound, but it was certainly possible.

"This way," Neto said.

They came around a hillside and an opening appeared. A wide, dark mouth with a scatter of boulders at the entrance. Neto walked ahead, his boots slipping on the pine needles. The cave exhaled a cold current of air. Neto looked up as they stepped inside and pointed. Alex could see nothing.

He could hear a kind of constant shifting whir, and as his eyes adjusted, he realized that the black above was not the dark of stone but the dark of bats, tens of thousands of leather-winged bodies. He stumbled.

Neto bent to gather a handful of soil. It spilled through his fingers. "Nitre," he said. "Saltpeter." He let the last of it sift off his palm. "My father's family carried sacks of it out of here, day after day after day. They loaded it onto burros to bring it down the mountain for gunpowder, toothpaste, fertilizer." He wiped his hand on his pants. "My grandfather's back was permanently bent like an old man's by the time he was seventeen. He was dead by the time he was thirty." He looked directly at Alex. "And now he's got a grandson who lives like this."

Alex saw a tremor there in his eyes, a questioning flicker that could tip either way, toward rage or kindness. He had seen it in him the night he shot Flaco. Under the cover of violence Neto had grown bold in his body, sure of his movements around the other men, a proud twist to his lips. But there had been a pleading too, just behind it.

THEY DROVE ON up the mountain and startled a family of turkeys in the dirt track where they chortled and flapped, tizzying off into the ditch among the fallen trees. After a while the road leveled out and then a cliff came into view and the outlines of buildings appeared, huge houses up above on the ridge and adobe huts huddled below on the grassy escarpment. The houses on the cliff edge were like some mirage out of the wilderness, turrets and domed roofs and spiral staircases. The SUV wound past the huts where pigs and dogs shifted slowly out of the road and children's faces appeared in curtained doorframes. As they rose, the road emptied of people and animals and the big houses took on a ghost-chill, looming up above.

They parked in the driveway beside a three-story pale pink mansion, the windows thick with dust. Neto led the way and Alex followed slowly, searching him again for some intention.

"You'd be hard pressed to find an adult man in this town," Neto said as he opened the front door and a rat skittered across the entryway into a side room. "They're all in your USA now. Coming home *someday.*"

The grand staircase was covered in dirt and the front rooms had all been filled with sacks of seed, fertilizer, and hay bales.

"Someday dreams," Neto said. "This is what money from the North feeds. They come home once a year for Saint's Day and throw a huge party, show how much money they've made, and promise they're coming back someday. In the meantime, the men too old to leave, they store their feed here." He waved his hand at a teal Jacuzzi filled with corn kernels. "It's not a real rich man's house without a Jacuzzi, right?"

Alex turned away, he could feel the water in his lungs, the hands forcing him under.

"No one's ever even tried to drill a well up here." He kicked the side of the Jacuzzi. "It's fucking embarrassing," he said. "What the North gives our people, I want to give them that instead. 'So far from God and so close to the United States.' You know who said that?" He turned to look at Alex. "Fucking Porfirio. It doesn't have to be that way, though. You all in the US, you'll snort and shoot up as much as we can give you. We need growers, producers, truckers, runners, you name it, we need people on every level, and we're making more money than the fucking government. We're making more money than anyone. No one should have to go north anymore, begging and scraping and letting someone else take care of them. I want my men living inside their dreams now." He pointed to the ceiling where a chandelier hung, crooked, the wiring half chewed through and insulation sticking out.

"I hate somedays," he said. "That way of living splits us all apart. Everybody making good for their own selves. It's like the opposite of how we evolved. You know, ages and ages ago we domesticated ourselves." He walked toward the far end of the room and a row of empty cupboards with their doors hanging open. "Selfish violence is in us still, of course, we still like to watch men kick the shit out of each other in a ring. But our larger brain helped us coordinate, control each other for the good of the whole. We figured out that it was better for us to live in community instead of each for his own, like in the wild." He turned to face Alex again and walked back, his footprints overlapping on the dusty tiles. "Of course, our larger brain can also help us manipulate and deceive the group for the good of the individual. Think about traveling on an airplane. You fill a plane with apes and they'll all kill each other before it lands, but humans have figured out how to sit there civilized for eight hours and not one fight breaks out. Only you have to go through all that security first, just to be sure that one person didn't plant a bomb to bring the whole thing down."

Alex wasn't quite sure that he was following Neto's argument, but it was interesting to hear him talk. He'd never heard Neto go on at length about much of anything other than his promotion company.

"Sometimes I think we're in the middle of another big change." Neto walked up the staircase. "Like, as a species, we're heading the other way, toward individualism. A generation back, it seemed like your name and the patch of land you were born on meant more. Where you were from really made you who you were. Now we're scattered, cutting ties and striking out. It seems very American, actually. The North for us, the West for you. It's funny when you think about it, how much they have in common, the stories we tell ourselves about the North and the West."

From the second floor the valley was visible through huge panoramic windows, the long grassy slope of the village and the tall pines beyond, falling away into deep arroyos, rifts of blue shade and, far off, the spread of red sand and cloud shadows floating over a lunar landscape.

"It's like something out of *Pedro Páramo*, no?" Neto said. "A fucking ghost town."

Alex raised his eyebrows.

"What?" Neto said. "You think I don't read? Come on, you underestimate me." He winked. "You think we have nothing in common? Is that it?"

They were standing quite close, Alex realized. He could smell Neto's scent: musky soap and cigarettes.

"You never felt for your wife what you feel for Mateo, did you?" Neto said. "Not even in the beginning."

Alex's throat closed. He blinked. "How—"

Neto pointed to his hand. "I know that ring didn't come from Mateo."

Alex balled up his fist.

"It's crazy, isn't it?" Neto said. "When you realize it, just how much you can desire someone. Frightening."

Alex looked away. He could feel something uncoiling, a whisper making its way into a thought, a realization: there was an offer being made here, a sort of test or trade.

"If I could have been with someone when I was your age . . ." Neto leaned toward the glass and Alex could feel his body stirring the air between them. "At least I never got married. Did you know the male ear can go deaf in perfect proportion to the female voice? I know, I know, it sounds like a joke, but really, when my father went deaf, the doctor said the decibels he could no longer hear matched perfectly with his wife's voice." Neto snorted. "Not my mother, it was his third wife that made him go deaf."

Alex kept his eyes on the window.

"If I could have . . ." Neto breathed. "My god, the rotten waste I've made."

Alex looked at Neto's hands, pressed to the glass. He heard his own heart beat dull and loud and his body flushed cold as he brought his hand up and twined it with Neto's. Neto turned and Alex closed his eyes fast. A throb in his neck and his breath went. He opened his eyes, choking.

"I thought you loved him," Neto said. He was almost laughing, his hand around Alex's neck and his eyes huge. Neto kept his gaze locked for a moment before he loosened his grip.

AT THE EDGE of the village Neto's SUV blew a tire. There was a pop and the driver halted and jumped out. Neto had not said a word to Alex since their moment at the window. They sat in silence in the backseat until Neto opened the door and called to the driver. Alex stared out the window to where a spotted pig rousted a mangy dog to take his place under a shade tree. Alex could hear Neto and his driver talking, something about no spare tire or a damaged spare tire. The door opened and Neto's face appeared.

"A little holdup," he said. "You're comfortable in here?"

"Yes," Alex said.

The driver took the tire off and rolled it up the road and Neto paced and smoked. He kept glancing at Alex's side of the vehicle and finally he came around and rapped on the door with his knuckles. Alex opened it.

"You sure you're all right in there?" Neto asked. He tilted his head to the side and his face looked younger suddenly, shy.

"I'll take one of those," Alex said, and nodded toward his smokes.

Faces appeared in windows and then there was movement in the road. The children approached first and the mothers after, calling out halfhearted reprimands. The children stuck their fingers in their noses and stared openly, pointing at Neto's calfskin boots. Neto tousled their hair. He spoke words that Alex could not hear and then he was reaching into his pockets, pulling out money. He offered paper pesos to the mothers who shook their heads, *no, no, I couldn't.* But the children were already leaping, giddy, and Neto tossed it over their heads, looking back to be sure that Alex was watching.

AT THE COMPOUND Neto's men came out to meet the SUV. Alex felt his muscles tense. They were there to escort him and he could smell the basement already. He stepped down, braced, but Neto waved the men away. He clapped a hand on Alex's shoulder.

"Come on upstairs," he said.

The room was on the second floor, fourth door. It was spare and dark, blue curtains, navy-blue bedspread. Alex held his body locked at attention. Neto waved him in and he stepped across the threshold and stood frozen.

"Relax," Neto said. "What do you think?"

Alex nodded as if responding to a command. "This is your room?"

Neto laughed. "No, it's yours." He walked over to the bed and sat down. "Hey, come here," he said, and Alex followed. He sat beside Neto.

"Just relax," Neto said. "You need some rest."

He pressed a hand against Alex's chest and pushed him back until he was lying flat and then he brought his thumb up to Alex's lips. He traced the bow of his mouth. The house was silent, nothing but the sound of his own measured breath and a rock pigeon cooing on the outside window ledge. Nothing but the tremble of that finger on his lip, a vibration he could feel even after Neto left.

TWENTY-SEVEN

Elana watched out the bus window as they wound down from Creel and into the penumbra of desert dusk, the Chihuahua–Ahumada Highway flashing by with lonely huddles of ranch lights and, between them, nothing but darkness. She arrived in Juárez at dawn and crossed over, dragging her weak-sick body through the turnstile to flag down a cab.

The front door of the apartment was plastered with notes. One was big, typewritten and laminated, and read:

Alex,

Call your mother immediately. Daddy is sick in the hospital and this disappearance business of yours is not helping.
In case you've forgotten: 304-445-2859.

The second one, posted below, was smaller and handwritten:

Elana,

Noreen's gone back to WV. If I'm not here, I'm over in Juárez. I've been checking your phone like you asked me to. A girl named

Vivy called you a few times. Oh, and Noreen says to tell you she paid your January rent.

Be back soon,

Simon

Vivi. Elana felt her pulse spike. Vivi *was* involved. She unlocked the door. Her cell phone was sitting there on the edge of the table beside Alex's. A scribbled note, tucked underneath, read: *Vivy 52-55-5598-2491, Morales 52-656-445-2859.*

Vivi answered on the fifth ring.

"Hello, you—" Elana stumbled. "This is Elana, you called me? You know where Alex is?"

"Elana, hey, yes, I was trying to find you. Ana told me you've been—"

"Where he is?"

"Alex? No, I don't—"

"You said yes." Elana could feel tears forming in the backs of her eyes, swelling up in her throat. "You said—"

"I didn't mean yes about Alex, I meant . . . I'm sorry, I'm still half-asleep. Your call woke me. Where are you?"

She couldn't talk now. If she opened her mouth, she would cry.

"Elana?"

She was crying.

"Elana, tell me where you are."

She hung up the phone and went into the bedroom. She wished Meyer would have called while she was gone. She wondered how he was doing, alone in that big house in Hartsville. He'd been there with the ghost of Simon's violence for months, waiting, and now he was alone again. Was he relieved? She thought of her mother and Dulcie's faces from her fever dreams. She needed someone parental, someone comforting, although Meyer wasn't the person for that, really. He had left her several messages after Noreen found out about the situation with Alex and had told him what was happening, but Elana had not called him back and he'd stopped trying. Maybe he thought Simon was there for her and that was enough, but Simon was not there for her, she knew that. No one was there for her, really, when it came down to it. Her mother had left her through death and then Simon had found new interests and split away and then she'd found Alex, but Alex, she saw now, must have been drifting for far longer than she'd allowed herself to admit. And Meyer had always kept her at too far of a distance. Was there a correct distance for your children, though, a not-too-close, not-too-far? This was why people made makeshift chosen families. She thought of the kolektivo kids with their communal meals and sleepovers. How much weight could you trust it to hold, though? The ties that bound people seemed to her so shockingly fragile, it was horrifyingly easy to give up.

She flipped open her phone. How do you call your own father and say, *You should really check on me more, I'm not okay.* She stared at the screen and punched in Dulcie's number instead.

"Hello?" a man's voice answered.

Elana's breath sucked in.

"Hello?" he said again.

It was Coe, of course, she didn't know why she was so surprised. "Hi, is Dulcie there?"

"No, who's this?"

"Elana."

"Oh, hey, Lana, no, Sheila run her on down to the doctor's, they'll be back this afternoon. You want me to tell her to call you?"

"Okay," Elana said, and then as she was lifting the phone away from her face, she called out again, "Coe?"

"Yeah?"

She pictured Coe alone in Dulcie's house, pilfering through her bedroom while she was out. Coe had always been funny when she'd known him; when she'd lived with Dulcie, he could warm the whole room with his laugh. *I loved that man*, Simon had said, *trusted him*.

"Are you sorry about Simon?" she asked, before even fully thinking it.

"What's that?"

She felt fear rush up from her gut. Fear of what exactly, she wasn't sure, that he would deny it, maybe, or that he really did not feel any remorse at all. She hung up the phone quick and lay back on the unmade bed, the dirty sheets musty around her face. She could taste tears in her throat and so she turned over, pulling the covers with her until she was swaddled.

When she woke four hours later, there were three new messages on her phone. Two from Vivi and one from Simon. She called Vivi back more out of anger than anything.

"I said 'You know where Alex is?' and you said yes!" she yelled as soon as Vivi picked up her phone. "You said *yes*."

"I said yes. But—Elana, where are you?"

"El Paso. In my apartment."

"Come over to Juárez."

"Why?"

"Just come over. Meet me at Cafetería Norma on Galeana and Bartolomé de las Casas."

The restaurant was packed and it smelled heavily of cleaning products, refried beans, and enchilada roja sauce. Elana felt her stomach turn. She hadn't eaten anything since the tea and broth in Creel. Strangely, though, she didn't feel proud, she just felt weak and sick. It took her a good few minutes to locate Vivi, and as she stood there, turning her head this way and that, she could sense the prickles of embarrassment she would have once felt—silly lost gringa in a crowded restaurant—only now she was too deeply exhausted to care.

Vivi stood and waved at Elana. Her hair was gathered into a messy bun on top of her head and she wore a threadbare T-shirt, tight black jeans, and combat boots. Nothing like the sleek gallery girl from a few weeks before. She grabbed Elana, kissed her on the cheek, and pulled out a chair for her.

Elana laughed. "What are you doing?"

"You look like you could use some gentlemanliness." She sat down and leaned back in her own chair and her breasts moved under her thin T-shirt, her rounded shoulders rising and falling as she spoke. She was beautiful.

Elana looked away.

"You didn't find anything in Creel?" Vivi said.

Elana glanced back. "I don't—" She studied Vivi's face, the way her cheekbones sloped down to her red mouth. If he wasn't fucking Vivi, then who were the condoms for? "I don't really know you," she said.

"I'm being too familiar."

Elana shrugged.

"I'm sorry. Before she left, Ana told me what was going on with you and I got really worried."

"Ana left?"

"The whole kolektivo, they're all down in DF now, getting ready for Marcos. But Ana told me you were looking for Alex and I mean I know I don't know you and Alex that well, but . . . I called your phone a bunch of times and then your brother called me back and we chatted."

"You want to fuck my brother?"

"What?"

Elana waved at a waitress across the way. "You talked to my brother and you two hit it off?"

"I guess," Vivi said. "But wait, what did you just say?"

The waitress was at the table. "Un café negro," Elana said, and turned back to Vivi. "I didn't find anything in Creel, except a girl in a restaurant who claimed she recognized his picture. I thought he'd run away with you."

"Like an affair?"

"No, not *like* an affair, an affair."

Vivi's eyes were so full of compassion they made Elana want to punch her.

"I haven't heard from him or seen him since the night I met you," Vivi said. On the table her phone vibrated and lit up. She grabbed it. "Be right back," she said.

Elana closed her eyes. She could feel the sharp edge of her hunger rising then, that moment when it changed from faintness to something wilder. She ran her tongue along the back of her teeth. If she focused, she could understand a lot of what was said at the tables around her, but if she relaxed, the Spanish around her became a wave, a texture. *Agua prieta. Agua turbia.*

"Café negro."

Elana opened her eyes.

The waitress set the cup and saucer down.

"Gracias," Elana said, snatching it. Her hands were shaking. She let herself have half a packet of sugar, stirred it in, and lifted the drink to her lips. She was entirely focused on it.

"Sorry," Vivi said, sitting down at their table again. "I just . . ." She turned and looked back over her shoulder. "¿Viste eso?"

"What?" Elana said, looking up from her cup.

Vivi was pointing now and more people were looking. Up at the front of the restaurant, a man and woman were struggling. The man stood and pulled the woman to her feet. He was saying things, but Elana could not catch most of it. "I said come with me," he shouted in Spanish.

The woman was young, early twenties, thin, with long dark hair.

All the tables were watching now.

"I said *come on*." The man reached inside his jacket and pulled out a knife, he fluttered it up above his head as if showing it off and then brought it to the woman's neck. Her shoulders collapsed. He pushed her toward the door and out into the sunlit street. The door clacked shut.

The restaurant was silent, only the clatter of the kitchen went on behind the swinging doors, and then slowly, faltering at first, the noise started up again: a rustle of crossing legs, a cough, the drag of a chair. The couple were not visible through the front windows anymore. Within minutes, the sound level was normal again.

Elana realized she had been gripping her coffee cup hard enough to almost break it. She set it down in its saucer and looked to Vivi, but Vivi was standing now.

"We let him," she said, not to Elana—her back was facing Elana—she said it to the restaurant. "We let him." More loudly this time. "We let him."

Faces were turning to her.

"Why did we let him?"

She walked toward the front of the restaurant, projecting her voice now. "Remember?"

The room was quieting again.

"Remember when she was a baby?"

Elana leaned forward to hear better. She must be mishearing or mistranslating.

"Remember?"

Vivi held her hands out before her as she walked among the tables.

"Remember when she was *our* baby?"

There were whispers now, a snicker.

"We held her up, like this, above our heads, and she trusted us," Vivi said. "She trusted us."

She'd come full circle now and was back beside Elana. She was walking like a zombie with her hands above her head and Elana felt a chill coming over her as she watched. Vivi bent and grabbed a stack of papers from her bag. She turned to Elana first. "Have you seen me?" she said, and placed a paper beside Elana's coffee cup and turned to the next table. "Have you seen me?"

Elana looked down at the flyer. AYÚDANOS A LOCALIZARLA. It was a poster just like all the hundreds of missing women posters tacked to telephone poles across the city, only this poster had Vivi's face on it. Elana gripped the edge of the paper and something swirled inside her, some bubble rising.

"Have you seen me?" Vivi was placing posters on each table.

People were whispering, stirring and turning to look after her as she left.

"Have you seen me?"

Elana felt an anger traveling up inside her. She stood. Vivi had her back to her. "What are you doing?" Elana said in English. "What is this?"

Vivi turned. She smiled at the whole room. She pulled her cell phone out of her pocket and dialed it, let it ring for a moment, and then clapped it closed. Up at the front of the restaurant, the door opened. The knife-man walked back in, followed by the long-haired woman. They walked until they stood beside Vivi and then they bowed.

The room erupted in voices and the clatter of chairs.

"Ladies and gentleman," the knife-man began, but his voice was drowned out before he could continue.

"This isn't a good joke!" a man shouted, holding the missing girl flyer up and waving it around. "You should be ashamed of yourselves, this is nothing to joke about."

"No, no, it's not a joke," the knife-man said.

Elana looked at Vivi and saw something glint in her eyes. She left the table and walked to her. Vivi grabbed her hand and squeezed it. "You did great," Vivi said to her. "Like you were meant to be part of it all along." She winked and turned to the knife-man. "Let's go," she said.

The restaurant was emptying out now, just a few stragglers looking back over their shoulders. The kitchen guys had come to the swinging door and were peering out into the dining room and the waitresses were clumped around the register inspecting one of the missing girl posters. Vivi took a handful of cash from her bag and set it down on the counter and led the way out.

"What the hell was that?" Elana said. "You invited me over here to watch your performance but decided not to tell me it was gonna be a performance?" Elana didn't know why she felt perfectly comfortable yelling at Vivi though she barely knew her, maybe because she'd decided that Alex had run off with her. Now she had an invented anger-intimacy she could not shake.

"I don't think of it as a performance per se," Vivi said. They were walking up the street now, the knife-man and woman following and a few customers from the restaurant still staring after them.

"That was fucked up," Elana said.

"In what sense?"

"Like traumatizing, triggering. You think people around here haven't seen enough missing girl posters, enough violence? I've put up missing person flyers for my husband all over this city. How many other people in that restaurant have done the same thing? You need to throw it in our faces?"

"I wanted to start a conversation."

"Like people aren't already having conversations about it."

"I don't think so, not about how we are all implicated."

"How are we implicated?"

They were walking side by side at a matched fast pace, though Elana had no idea where they were going. She didn't care. She ran her tongue along the inside of her cheek, savoring the remnant tastes of coffee and sugar.

"Well, there's so much implication on the government level, of course, both yours and ours. But it filters down to the individual too. You didn't know that was acting until afterward. You let Raúl walk Paulina out of that restaurant at knife point."

"*I* let him."

"We."

Elana remembered the feel of the coffee cup she'd death-gripped in her hand as they all watched the man march the woman out.

"You saw how quickly everyone went back to eating," Vivi said. "We want people to think about it. The passivity. Their reaction, or lack of reactions."

"Like the banality of evil?"

"In a way, yes. You've read Arendt?"

"Some. But wait a minute, you think it's our fault? What about the cops, the attorney general?"

"That's part of it, but I want people to notice how it has filtered down and we accept it now."

"Accept what?"

"The valuelessness of an individual life."

Elana stopped walking. "I don't think anyone has accepted it," she said. "The violence just keeps coming."

Vivi nodded.

"You don't think people here are doing enough?" Elana said. "You think everyone's too passive so you have to come in from out of town and show everyone?"

"I just want people to think about it," Vivi said.

"Like they're not already thinking?"

Vivi turned and called over her shoulder to the knife-man and woman, who were walking arm in arm. "You've got supplies back at your place? Stuff for drinks?"

"Yeah," the knife-man called.

It bothered Elana to think that they were a couple in real life, though she wasn't entirely sure why.

"Your brother's project is pretty interesting," Vivi said.

"Evangelizing?"

"The radio thing."

"Ugh," Elana said. "He calls it 'mainlining the word of God.'"

Vivi laughed. "It's pretty brilliant."

"You like evangelism?"

"Not particularly, but nobody else is trying to give those kids a second chance or show them there's something else besides the cartel."

"He didn't come up with that radio idea, you know. And he can barely speak Spanish."

THE THEATER-ART SPACE was an old warehouse with loft beds and giant papier-mâché puppets scattered across the floor. Vivi fixed everyone micheladas and raised a toast to collaboration.

"Raúl and Paulina are coming down to DF with me this evening," she said to Elana. "We're gonna work on a new piece. You should come too."

"Come?"

"To DF, you can stay with me. I'll get you a ticket."

Elana shook her head.

"Come on, tomorrow is Christmas, you don't want to be here alone."

Elana felt dizzy. She took another sip of her drink. "Tomorrow's not Christmas, what do you mean?"

"Yeah, today's Christmas Eve, come on, come with us. My dad is like a gold star member or whatever with Aeroméxico. I'm sure we can get you a seat." She linked her arm into Elana's. "Besides, if Alex has run off with someone, I'm gonna guess they'll be in DF soon. Everyone who is anyone is coming there for La Otra Campaña."

Elana pulled away, staring at Vivi. "You know something about where he is."

She shook her head. "I wish I did."

TWENTY-EIGHT

Sometimes the bedroom door was locked. Sometimes it was not. Food was brought to Alex every day but not at regular intervals. Neto had come to him twice. Mateo had not come at all. He felt Mateo's absence like a boot to the chest. A stepped-on, caved-in kind of feeling. His body useless with grief.

Among the comforts of the bedroom, his loneliness was more present than in the basement. A slithering, snake-backed feeling, it rose up in him until he ran to the bathroom and stuffed towels in his mouth to mute his screams. He almost missed the basement guards—the distraction of their banter and the way that their rotating shifts gave a dimension to his days. In the bedroom there was only the heavy door and, in the hallway, a single, silent guard—sometimes there, sometimes gone. The lack of pattern scratched at Alex's nerves. Without the predictable repetition, he could not fence in his fears. He kept expecting something worse.

On the third day Neto came again and took him for a drive to inspect the progress on a stone wall being built on the far side of the compound.

"You know where I found those men?" Neto pointed to the workers steering wheelbarrows of concrete. "You know where they were headed?" Neto rested his hand idly on Alex's shoulder. He had brushed his arm and the back of his neck with a soft grip, but otherwise he had not touched him. "The United States! I took care of their coyotes and offered these guys jobs, told them I'll pay them more than they can make in the States and when they're done, they can go back home with their heads high. No scuttling and hiding and bootlicking, or fucking one another over for their own individual dream."

Neto got out of the SUV and spoke to the men and Alex watched the way their bodies stiffened, heads nodding vigorously. It was the same way his own body cringed before power. He watched the men watch Neto and he pictured their journey: the smugglers shot dead in front of them and then they were rounded up—the sound of gunshots and the dark leak of blood still fresh in their minds—and brought here, told to work. *They can go back home . . . when they're done.*

At first, Alex too had thought the only way to survive here would be to disappear, like these men were doing now: vacating themselves before Neto. It wasn't true, though. The way to survive was to be near. He was reminded again how well he did with expectations. Now that he knew, or was beginning to understand, what Neto wanted from him, he could feel himself stabilizing. Neto wanted him to transform himself from prisoner to guest or, maybe more so, an imprisoned guest. He wanted Alex to enjoy his company. And Alex had always done well when he knew what was wanted of him—with his parents, in church, and in school. He could show them what they liked to see; inside his smallest, youngest self, before he could even think clearly, he had trained himself to be that way. From the Heart Cry donation box onward, he had cleaved himself into a form that pleased.

Neto did not come to Alex's room often. Most days, Alex was alone. Once, he tried the handle and found the door unlocked. He stepped out. The house was dim and quiet. He made his way slowly down the hallway, past closed doors. At the opposite end, away from the stairs, an archway led into a library.

The bookshelves reached floor to ceiling all along the walls, green and blue and burgundy spines with gold lettering. There were ladders with wheels on the bottom rungs to help reach the highest shelves. Francisco Cervantes de Salazar's *Crónica de la Nueva España* and books by Juan de Guevara and José Joaquin Fernández de Lizardi. Alex had never thought much about Neto's education. Neto had mentioned that his brothers both went to school in the United States and he did not, but Alex had never really thought more about it.

There was a desk just inside the library and, above it, a smaller inset bookshelf stuffed with paperbacks. *Adaptation and Natural Selection; The Variation of Animals and Plants under Domestication; Aggression: Its Causes, Consequences, and Control; The Selfish Gene; Chimpanzee Politics: Power and Sex among the Apes; Demonic Males: Apes and the Origins of Human Violence.*

Alex picked up *The Selfish Gene*. It was heavily highlighted and annotated. He turned to a page where the sentence "The gene is the basic unit of selfishness" was underlined. "Genetically speaking, individuals and groups are like clouds in the sky or dust-storms in the desert. They are temporary aggregations or federations [. . .] in a large and complex system of rivalries."

He closed it, put it back, and pulled out *Demonic Males*. The handwritten notes crawled up the edges of each page: *Two types of aggression: reactive (impulsive reaction to an immediate threat, e.g., rudo wrestlers) and proactive (calculated, planned, e.g., tecnicos) → Humans: low on reactive, very high on proactive—this is part of domestication. Chimpanzees—high on reactive, but also use proactive.*

The word "pedomorphic" was highlighted and underlined with a note: *If part of the domestication syndrome is the retention of juvenile traits in adult life, an extension of childhood, then if domestication goes in the opposite direction, we should see a truncating of childhood. And we do: school shootings and children immigrating alone.*

In the next chapter he had underlined a paragraph that read, "In a cycle that had been going on for at least four years, each of the top three male chimpanzees had already been the alpha at least once, and each had been deposed after the other two ganged up against him. Individual bravado was important, and so was the support of females. But nothing mattered so much as the alliances among the top three males." Beside this paragraph was an arrow and a note: *Constant shifting cycle of alliances—survival and reinvention of the individual self at the expense of stable family, community. Americans trust the individual too much, but think about it: Dawkins, pp. 34–35: "Individuals are not stable things, they are fleeting."*

The slam of a door echoed up from the first floor. Alex froze. There came no other sound, but he put the book down and hurried back to his room.

WHEN THE BEDROOM door was locked, Alex sat on the bed and watched the sun move across the walls. He tried to picture Mateo's face full of love, but all he could see was Mateo beside the Jacuzzi. He choked himself on the memory, glutted himself full of it in order to be sure he was ready. Up until now, he had been something that was important to Mateo who was in turn important to Neto. But now he was ready to move up, ready to increase his value.

No one was coming for him. If Elana were going to be able to help him, it would have happened already. If Neto were concerned about the danger of keeping a kidnapped American citizen, he would have released him by now. When Alex moved to the border, he had wanted to join himself, that's how he had thought of it. Now there wasn't enough of his old self left for anyone to even remember, for anyone to save. He had nothing left to even prove who he was: no ID, the driver's license he'd been carrying was long gone. There was nothing besides his accent to prove he'd come from the United States. And there was really nothing to show that his disappearance was not voluntary—that is, unless you followed the trail to Mateo and Mateo to the Juárez Cartel. But Americans preferred to believe in individual decisions. He was sure that the police would see it that way. And the border formed a sort of seal. He went down there, he *decided* to do that. Neto was right, Americans trusted the individual too much.

It was always a personal, individual decision that led to death, as far as the Americans were concerned. Even as the tide of murders lapped at El

Paso, they said the men who die, they made bad decisions. A man must live with his decisions. Or die. Only the women, the beautiful dismembered women, could not be lumped in with the men who made death wish decisions. And so the Americans could cry for the women, oh the poor strangled women, so far from God and so close to the United States. That would never happen in the United States, no, only in Mexico where the men were too hot blooded, no good at making strong, individual decisions. And on second thought, those poor beautiful women had made decisions, hadn't they? They had decided to work, to take their money and go clubbing, to buy lipstick and miniskirts. Poor decisions. Not like the strong decisions that the corporations made to move their factories from the US to Mexico to China to Bangladesh. Not like the smart decisions of the cartel men who kept their money in US banks. And speaking of individual decisions, it must be an individual who was killing all the women. One depraved, rotten, no-good individual. It could not be the system that was killing them because the United States did not believe in systemic corruption so close to home, so tied in with NAFTA; it went against the bootstrap way.

But Mexicans were not blinded by the cult of the individual. Corruption was a tide that swept over everything, sometimes high, sometimes low, but it never went away. You learned to ride with it. On the television they claimed that the corruption was shocking. It was not shocking, it was more stable than anything. The PRI Party had ruled the country for seventy-one years; it had "won" twelve "democratic" elections. Just as the wrestling referee was "neutral" no matter how many times he took the side of the rudo. When Alex had first learned that cheating was a built-in part of the referee's role, something expected by the audience, when he first learned this was a tradition in the sport, he felt the volume turn up. Wrestling was, he'd come to realize, more than a sport, more than a spectacle, it was a national conversation about power and corruption. It was a chance for people to scream out loud when they saw wrongdoing happening before their eyes, a chance to hope out loud that the good guy might vanquish, or a chance to test the delicious taste of corrupt power.

And maybe the oddest thing about the discrepancies between US and Mexican mentalities was how much the immigrants traveling to the US now paralleled the frontiersman that the Americans loved so much. Neto was right, it was a very American model that they fit into: an individual on his own or with his nuclear family, striking out to forge a new life and reinvent himself, struggling against bad guys and hostile terrain. It was the exact same mold—give them Conestoga wagons and you wouldn't hardly be able to tell them apart—except that when your skin was brown and you traveled north instead of west, you suddenly weren't a frontiersman anymore but an illegal alien.

If he had paper now, Alex thought, he could write a better thesis than anything he had scribbled in his classes. Or maybe it only made more sense now because he could not write it down.

TWO DAYS LATER Neto appeared in Alex's room and woke him, asking if he needed anything.

"You have a library?" Alex said, speaking almost before thinking, still groggy with sleep.

Neto was standing beside the window and he turned and looked at Alex with something in his eyes that seemed almost vulnerable.

"You want something to read?" he asked.

Alex nodded. "Can I borrow *The Selfish Gene*?"

Neto's face shifted again and for a moment Alex thought he might snap into anger, but instead he laughed. "You saw my books."

"What are you working on?" Alex asked, wondering if they were going to sidestep his admission that he'd left his room without Neto. He had never been told not to leave, but it seemed like an obvious transgression.

"I've just been reading," Neto said. "It's interesting, the parallels, you know. We think of humans as so special, like God created us separate from everything else, but *Homo sapiens* are just another primate." He was pacing beside Alex's bed, silhouetted in the morning light. "Maybe that's why I always liked lucha libre. You see men give in to their basest instincts. That's honesty, finally. You know, chimps fight each other for sport too, egg each other on, encourage ruthlessness."

"You think lucha is about giving in to base instincts?" Alex asked.

"Yes."

"You don't think it's about overcoming your rival, rising?"

Neto laughed again. "That's the American in you, talking about pulling yourself up." He shook his head. "Lucha did come from the US first, so maybe you're right." He looked out the window again. "It was always my dream to wrestle, from the time I was a little kid. It's where I thought I belonged." He shrugged and turned back to Alex. "Now I get to own wrestlers instead."

TWENTY-NINE

After his party Neto had sent Mateo out on the circuit again, along with a man named Enrique to monitor him. Mateo fought in Guadalajara, Puebla, Culiacán, Hermosillo, Torreón, Toluca, Durango, Matamoros, Veracruz, and Villahermosa. Each night was one of two variations: the crowd had a lot of energy and threw their aggression at the rudos, like El Vengador, in fits of disdain, or the crowd was lackluster and the whole arena felt hollow, the whole show like a silly charade. He fought Fancy Dragon, he fought Señor Divino, he fought Electrico. He won, he lost, he won. The reporters stopped asking him why he'd left CMLL and joined Estelar. A rivalry story line was sketched out with Señor Divino over whose North was the true North, Tijuana or Juárez. He didn't care about any of it at all.

In the beginning, back with Babe Sharon in the very beginning, it had meant so much it was transcendent. Not just his fights but the lights, the music, the crowd: everybody's family, coworkers, the girl from around the corner, grandma, uncles, cousins; the energy ecstatic and everyone piling into the metal folding chairs around the ring. Your opponent's baby daughter, right there in the front row, bawling her eyes out for Daddy. It meant everything: when your song came on and you trounced in and leapt to the third rope, the adrenaline was not only yours, it was communal. *We* will win! Nothing else matters—not our fucked-up lives or shitty jobs for shitty pay—none of it matters, because tonight we will *win*! He loved it so much he'd never realized that that feeling would go away as he moved up. Now it was just anonymous ring girls bouncing their tits and some jackass announcer making bad jokes at his expense.

His knee had never properly healed after the injury in Acapulco. He took Oxy every day for the ache. The Oxy made him lethargic, so he took a few Dexedrine in the dressing room, a few lines of coke just before entering the ring, and then a few more Oxy afterward to ease the pain for sleep.

After the fight in Hermosillo, he asked Enrique when they would return to the compound. More than a week had passed since Neto's party. Mateo pictured Alex in the corral with Neto. Neto bending, whispering to him. Mateo felt the throb of jealousy, but it was muted now and that terrified him too. He picked at the jealousy until it sparked and pulsed strong again.

"You need a break?" Enrique asked.

"I didn't say that."

"Well, you—"

"I need to see Neto."

"Whatever you might need, I can speak to him for you."

"I need to meet with him. About Alex."

"We're due in Torreón tomorrow and Toluca after that."

They were watching him even more closely now. Once he realized just how monitored he was, he couldn't unsee it, how they escorted him everywhere: to the dressing room, to the ring, to the hotels, which were getting shittier and shittier each week. At night he was in the room alone, but there was a man at the door. He needed to reach out, to ask for help. They were watching his mother and his wife, Neto had made that much clear already. He thought of his ex-manager, Arturo. Obviously, Arturo was tied to Neto, but maybe when he'd made the deal with Neto, he hadn't known it would be this bad. Maybe he would feel guilty once he heard.

The phones in the hotel rooms could be tapped. He needed a pay phone, but he was never alone. In Torreón, though, his room was on the ground floor, with an outside window. He lay on top of the covers for three hours, waiting. Every once in a while he could hear the man outside his door shuffle or pull a lighter from his pocket. Someone in the next room over was watching *Rebelde*, the pop theme song weaving in and out.

Mateo went to the window, frosted glass with a metal handle to tilt the pane. He propped it open. The parking lot was dark and motionless. He had seen a pay phone at the end of the building, maybe a hundred feet away. He lifted one leg out the window into the shrubbery and paused, half in, half out, listening. A dog barked a few streets down. Cars passed on the freeway. He bent and slid all the way out. He gripped his arms tightly across his chest and bent over as if to hold himself in. Run, his mind jumped, just get the hell out of here and don't look back. But as soon as he thought it, he pictured Alex. In the morning the man at the door would come inside to wake Mateo and would see that he was gone and then Neto would know moments later and he would take it out on Alex.

Mateo moved toward the pay phone, keeping his body behind the shrubbery, in the shadow of the building. When he reached the end, he poked his head around: nothing but the yellow-green glow of a streetlight. He went for the phone.

It rang only twice before he picked up.

"Arturo?"

"Who is this?" Arturo asked.

It was him, his voice! Mateo felt a blinding ray of hope surge within him.

"Arturo!" He was speaking quietly, but his excitement could not be contained. He was giddy, his body shaking again. "It's Mateo, listen I need help—"

"Who?"

"Mateo. So listen, things with Neto are pretty fucked up, I don't know if—"

"You have the wrong number. There's no Arturo here."

The line went dead.

Mateo walked back to the open window.

Inside, he didn't even make it to the bed. He lay on the carpet and felt his adrenaline drain down into the floor. He thought of Alex in his basement cell. Neto's men must have been watching Mateo since before September, when he and Alex had met, and they must have watched the relationship grow—that first time in the hourly motel, their meetings at the apartment on Callejon Camomila. He felt a rising pitch as he looked back over the whole thing but from the outside now, an aerial view. Of course, Neto's men wouldn't have actually been watching them from up above, but still, he couldn't shake it: the vision of himself and Alex moving along below—small and unknowing as ants.

NETO CALLED HIS hotel room in Toluca the next night.

"How's Alex?" Mateo paced. The room was small with a dirty cement floor.

"That's all you wanted to ask me?"

"Neto, you can trust me now. We've built trust."

"I'm not sure how much trust it shows, your *telling* me I can trust you. Shouldn't I feel certain of that myself if it is true?"

"When does it end? Alex in the basement?"

"You're right that it has to do with trust."

"So how do I—"

"Shh. All in good time. You have to calm down a little bit. Arturo told me something funny this morning. Something about a wrong number that someone called last night."

Mateo's breath stopped.

"I think you should focus on your fights, on what happens in the ring," Neto was saying. "Stop getting so distracted. Don't think about me."

He hung up and Mateo stood at the window, staring out across Toluca. On the skyline brilliant clusters of fireworks bloomed and dripped, someone celebrating something in purples and blues and reds. It wasn't until he had lain down on the bed and the explosions kept on that he realized it was only a few hours until Christmas.

THIRTY

"Bring his notebooks too," Vivi said.

They were standing in Elana's apartment, shoving clothes and books into bags. Elana had allowed Vivi to convince her to come to DF, but she hadn't been able to move past saying yes and so Vivi had taken over, crossing back to El Paso to help her get ready.

"His school notebooks?"

"Yeah, his thesis research notes, are they here, do you think?"

Elana had not touched Alex's bookshelf, afraid, after the condoms, that there would be something awful there. Besides, his books and notepads had seemed just like school stuff.

Vivi went to a cluttered shelf in the corner of the bedroom and began to rifle through it. She made a stack of yellow legal pads and black notebooks and slid them into a duffel bag. "We'll look at these later."

On the plane Elana panicked. As soon as the doors closed, she was entirely sure she was making a mistake. If she left Juárez now, she would never find him. *Never.* The word glowed hot like a radiant stove-burner coil. She was sweating. The air she pulled into her lungs was something poisonous. She just needed to retrace her steps and go back to the place she'd last seen him. She had to go back, he'd be there. She should have waited for him right there. She unclipped her seatbelt.

"You need to go to the bathroom?" Vivi asked.

Elana could not speak. She had taped a note with Vivi's number on the apartment door for Alex and she had called Simon but had not been able to reach him. She'd left a message at Morales's shelter, but it seemed unlikely that Simon would receive it, everything seemed so chaotic there. She should have just waited.

Vivi unclipped her own belt and stood up to let Elana through, but Elana seized up suddenly, unable to move. She could see the flight attendant fussing with the drink cart. The plane was not moving yet, but she would surely not let Elana out. The door was closed, sealed. Elana bent over her seat and curled, arms into stomach, head tucked. It took all her energy just to draw in a breath.

"Elana," Vivi said. "Elana, are you okay?"

Elana curled tighter. When she blinked, black spots appeared.

"Hey, are you sick?"

Her heart beat in her ears and behind her eyelids everything was suddenly red.

"Elana?"

A hand on her back.

"What's going on?"

There was a jump and a jolt. The plane was rolling backward.

"No," Elana said, "no, no, no, no, no."

"Miss," a voice said, "please stay seated until the seatbelt light is turned off."

"Yes, yes," Vivi's voice said. "Elana, what is going on?"

A hand took hold of her shoulders and pushed. Vivi was reaching and pulling down her legs, buckling her belt.

"Talk to me, Elana," she said.

"No," Elana said.

"Please."

Elana wiped her face with the back of her hand. Out the window, the desert was blurring. "I shouldn't have left. Alex won't know where I am. Simon won't know where I am. What if my note blows off the door and then—" Her throat was full of mucus and her tongue felt swollen.

"That's what's freaking you out? Elana, your brother has my number, he knows you're most likely with me."

Elana glanced at Vivi again. The plane was tipping up now, revving and charging. She closed her eyes. "What do you mean?"

"It was his idea."

She opened her eyes. "What?"

"For you to go to DF. He said you're having a really hard time and you're starving yourself and you need a change of scenery."

"He—" She couldn't even form any more words. "You—"

"I didn't want to tell you because I thought you wouldn't like it, but—"

"You . . . I . . . I'm here because my brother convinced you to feel sorry for me."

"No."

"Fuck you."

"Elana."

"Fuck you both. He said I was *starving* myself?"

"He said you're anorexic."

"No." She turned fast toward the window and pressed her face against it—clouds and sky and desert below—she pressed her face harder until her nose hurt, she covered her ears with her hands. "No, no, no, no, no, no, no."

When the wheels hit the tarmac, Elana awoke with her head on Vivi's shoulder. She jerked away. Vivi smiled at her.

"You passed out and slept through the whole thing like a little baby. I have to pee, but I didn't want to disturb you." She unbuckled and walked up the aisle.

Like a little baby. But it wasn't like that at all, Elana thought. She really had passed out. She brought her finger to her wrist to check her pulse, but she didn't know what number of beats she should be checking for. On her seat Vivi had left a half-eaten package of pretzels. Elana emptied it into her palm and then pressed them one by one onto her tongue.

Out front at Arrivals there was a black SUV with tinted windows waiting for them. Vivi and Elana got into the back along with Raúl and Paulina. The front passenger's seat was occupied by a man in a dark suit.

"I want to go to the Iglesia San Juan Felipe de Jesús," Vivi said to the driver, and then to Elana. "We have to catch the Christmas Eve service."

"Catholic mass?"

Vivi nodded. "You've never been in Mexico for Christmas, have you?"

Elana watched the lights of the city gliding by out the window. They wound in on the freeway through slick-glass neighborhoods and then deeper into crowded streets that turned to brick and then finally closed themselves off to traffic entirely.

The driver pulled up to the sidewalk and put his four-way flashers on, and the man in the passenger's seat got out. He had a pistol clipped to his belt and he followed close after Vivi as she led the way down a narrow pedestrian-only street that squeezed between ancient brick-and-tile buildings strung with tinsel and lights. Raúl and Paulina were laughing with Vivi and talking in Spanish too rapid for Elana to understand. She looked up at the corniced corners of the buildings, the lace-curtained windows and neon restaurant signs. The passageway was full of families, couples, balloon vendors, coffee vendors, tamale vendors, and organ grinders. She paused to adjust her backpack, and when she glanced up again, Vivi, Paulina, and Raúl were gone. She froze. The city noise rose around her: car horns and voices and motors and music. Where was she? What was she doing here? Someone brushed by her and she stumbled. There were so many people. So many people and none of them knew her, none of them cared if she fell down here in the street and never got up. So, so, so many people and none of them were Alex.

"Elana!"

She jerked.

"Hey, over here!" Vivi's face emerged from the crowd. "This way." She grabbed Elana's arm and the dark-suited man shadowed close behind her. Elana wondered how she had managed to move so freely up in Juárez, without drivers or bodyguards. Maybe it was only here in the capital that she was unsafe, or maybe her family hadn't known she'd gone to Juárez, maybe they just thought she was in Texas.

The church stood in a courtyard. Its carved stone doors were flush with the street, but the temple itself was recessed, down a flight of stairs troughed out by hundreds of years of feet. The haughty and intricately decorated face of the cathedral was spotlighted and arrayed with banners of Jesus and Mary and fluttering red, white, and green ribbons.

The sound inside was so sonorous Elana could feel the vibrations in her skin. She took a seat beside Paulina and tipped her head back. The ceiling vaulted into shining saints and angels and all-seeing eyes, and in the front a priest stood, dwarfed by candelabras the size of two men and golden pillars and golden chandeliers and altars upon altars upon altars on high.

Adoro te devote, latens deitas
Quae sub his figuris vere latitas.

The chant swirled around the pews and bounced back.

Tibi se cor meum totum subiicit,
Quia te contemplans, totum deficit.

There was a long silence and then, from one of the invisible wings in the front of the church, a child's voice cracked and echoed. Giddily high and yet solemn. A looping song that was not words but pure emotion.

Elana felt her body perk up and then relax. The song went on, a single threading voice, almost out of tune but beautiful. Her body was trembling, her face gone wet, but it felt good.

* * *

VIVI'S PARENTS' HOUSE was set on a small rise with a guarded gate, fenced gardens, and German shepherds weaving among the shrubbery. The front steps were bathed in buttery light and guests were wandering up and down. Vivi grabbed her own bag and led the way. They had dropped Paulina and Raúl off at the apartment of a friend and now it was just the two of them.

The entryway glittered and huge paintings hung all along the walls. Vivi dropped her bag beside a marble table with a statue of a small angel on it, but Elana kept her backpack on.

"This way," Vivi said.

Elana kept expecting her to acknowledge the opulence, to ask if Elana was surprised or to act embarrassed, or something.

"Viviana!" a woman's voice called from inside the doors of the dining room.

There were tables laid with meat and fruit and cakes. Elana felt her stomach lift.

"Mamá." Vivi pulled the woman to her. She was slightly chubby and heavily made up, wearing a blue silk jumpsuit. "Mamá, I want to introduce you to my friend, Elana."

Elana could smell the chalky scent of her face powder as Vivi's mother kissed her cheek.

"Elana lives in El Paso," Vivi said. "But she's looking for her husband."

Elana slipped her bag off her shoulder and bent to unzip it and retrieve her Alex flyers, but Vivi's mother was already walking away. "Grab yourselves some plates, girls," she said. "There's so much food. Steak, mole, chicken."

"I want to show her around the house first." Vivi grabbed Elana's elbow and steered her out of the room. "It's a lot, I know, you're exhausted?"

"A little," Elana said, though really, since the church, she'd begun feeling better.

"I want you to meet a couple of people and then we can relax, okay?"

ON THE SECOND floor they entered a long hallway and Vivi knocked on the fourth door. "My brother," she said, and knocked again.

The door opened and a skinny young man blinked at them. He was wearing a white T-shirt and black boxer shorts.

"Were you sleeping?" Vivi said.

"No."

"You were watching those videos again?"

He nodded.

"Diego, you have to stop, you'll rot your soul out." She turned to Elana. "He found these sites where the cartels post death videos, beheadings, and—"

"In this one they crucified a man alive." He looked at Elana, but his eyes said nothing.

"Diego, Diego, you know you're just upping their click numbers," Vivi said.

"Right, and if you don't watch them, then it's not really happening?"

Vivi clenched her hands into fists. "Hey, this is my friend Elana, she's going to stay here for a bit."

"I'm looking for my husband." Elana opened her backpack, pulled out a flyer, and handed it to Diego.

"You think he's here, in the city?" He looked down at the photo.

"I have no idea."

When Diego went back into his room, Vivi said, "A few months ago someone tried to kidnap him on his drive to the university. His bodyguard shot the guy, but now he stays in the house and obsesses over the cartels. Our dad works for the PRI and he's got connections in the US embassy; he could easily send Diego to school somewhere else, but Diego refuses. He says he's not going to run away."

Vivi led the way up two more flights of stairs and pushed open a door that led out onto a rooftop patio. At the far end was a structure, a kind of simple hut with a billowing cloth curtain for a door and light spilling out between the cracks in the wood.

"Camila!" Vivi called. "Are you here?"

The curtain opened and a face appeared. A woman with green eyes and brown hair. She and Vivi kissed each other on the cheek.

"I wanted you to meet my friend Elana."

Camila stepped forward with her hand out. She was wearing a long cotton dress and behind her, inside the little hut, Elana could see makeshift bookshelves overflowing with paperbacks and a mattress on the ground.

Elana took another flyer out of her bag. "I'm looking for my husband," she said. The more she repeated it the more ridiculous it sounded—she had no leads at all and was planning to look for him in a city of nineteen million.

Camila took the flyer and studied it.

"Camila is our semi-permanent cuarto de azotea resident," Vivi said. "She's from Madrid, but she's here . . . What did you want me to call you, Camila, other than obsessed?"

Camila shot her a look and then turned to Elana. "You know Arturo Belano, the poet?"

Elana shook her head.

Camila turned back to Vivi. "Have you taken her to Café Habana?"

"We only got here an hour ago. You can take her tomorrow," Vivi said. "Camila is obsessed with Belano. She's convinced that he didn't actually die in Spain but rather faked his death and returned to Mexico again."

"Who else would send a postcard to Anagrama saying 'Home is a world away'?" Camila said.

Elana turned and walked to the edge of the roof. There was a low wall around the perimeter. The wind was blowing, and though it was chilly, it felt nice. She could see the blink of airplanes passing up in the dark and the leafy outlines of trees in the gardens out front and then, off in the distance, a bursting fury of fireworks too far away to be heard.

THIRTY-ONE

Alex was sleeping when the bells began to ring. He had never heard bells at Neto's house before and they meshed into his dream: a church on the hill above the road where a willow tipped its branches toward a gravelly stream . . . he bent, the lacy leaves brushing his head as he scooped water . . . he reached to brace himself and a sound woke him. A sound that came with a flash of light. He reared up, clutching the sheets. Neto stood at the foot of his bed.

The bells were still ringing. The overhead light was on.

"Get up," Neto said.

Alex gripped the sheet and fear licked up over him. He had been afraid so often lately that now he could separate, lift up and watch his body's autonomics: pulse, sweat, stomach, throat. He hovered above it, knowing it would crest and ebb.

"Merry Christmas," Neto said, sitting down on the bed. He reached over and ran a finger softly across Alex's clenched knuckles until they relaxed.

"My mother is here," he said. "I want you to meet her." He went to the closet, opened it, and stood, flipping through the dress shirts he had hung there for Alex. He picked out a maroon one with black buttons.

Alex watched his own body move, slide to the edge of the mattress, and stand up. He wore nothing but boxers and the air was chilly, prickling his skin. Neto watched as he dressed and then he walked around him in a circle afterward, straightening his collar, brushing a speck of dirt off his sleeve. He ran a finger lightly across Alex's cheek and then kissed him full on the lips.

Downstairs, Neto's mother stood in the dining room. She was small and strikingly fragile, dark and sparkly. Black eyes, black hair, black dress, pale skin.

"Mamá," Neto said. "I wanted you to meet Alex. He's a foreign exchange student from the United States. From the state of Virginia, right, Alex?"

"West Virginia," Alex said.

"Ah, so I see you speak Spanish already," Neto's mother said, holding out her hand. "Carlota."

"Nice to meet you."

She withdrew her hand and pulled a silver case from her purse.

Neto bent down and lit her cigarette. "I wanted you to meet Carlota," he said, looking to Alex, "because she's the smartest person I know."

"Don't be ridiculous." Carlota exhaled. "Youngest sons always think too much of their mothers. That's why they're always so soft." She turned to Neto. "And sweet." She winked and then set her eyes on Alex. "If you already speak Spanish, then what are you studying here with my son? You're not a part of this whole wrestling bit he's been on about?" Her mouth crimped.

"No, I . . ." Alex drew in his breath. "I'm studying my patrimony, señora. I was born in Juárez, adopted to the United States."

"Oh, very good," Carlota said. "We always like to hear of a son come home. And in Virginia . . . What is Virginia known for?"

"*West* Virginia," Alex said. "Mountains."

"Then you already feel familiar here."

"Not like these mountains," Alex said. "In West Virginia the mountains are, well, more green, more . . ."

"Like Chiapas?" Neto asked.

"I think so," Alex said. "Yes."

"And do you have Indians in your mountains also?" Carlota asked.

"No, not really."

"Oh, that's right," Carlota said. "You did away with your Indians."

"There was a lot of genocide, yes."

Carlota shook her head and her earrings shuddered, ripples of dark glass. "It makes no sense, you kill your Indians only to turn around and import Africans, when the Indians work just as hard, wouldn't you say, Neto?"

Neto raised his eyebrows. "Not too different from importing French wine instead of drinking tequila," he said.

"Oh," Carlota said, turning to Alex. "My son is *very* patriotic, in case you haven't noticed. Also, *very* sensitive."

Neto was smoking, and as Alex watched his lips tense around the cigarette, he felt again the brush of the kiss, felt his own mouth pulse just a bit.

"I do prefer his obsession to my older sons', though," Carlota said. "They adore anything American. That's why I never sent Neto to Harvard. My older boys can't shut up about it. Those stupid songs they teach them to sing."

"Look at this." She took Alex's arm and steered him toward the banquet table where servants were laying out dishes of food. "Maybe it's to impress you." She looked Alex up and down, smiling a little. "Certainly, it's not for me. I haven't eaten this kind of thing in . . . well, I never really ate much." She waved her hand at the table laden with earthenware dishes. "Christmas salad, tamales, turkey, hominy soup, buñuelos, Christmas punch! The whole bit!" She gripped Alex's arm tighter. "My son is a good person to study your patrimony with. Although this is a little, how do you say? Exaggerated."

Carlota glanced back at Neto. Alex followed her gaze and for a moment, before Neto composed his face, Alex saw in his eyes a look of naked pain. The kind of wound only a parent can inflict.

Christmas morning the wind picked up, throwing sand against the window glass. Alex lay in bed, listening. The house was dead quiet. Months ago, he had imagined this Christmas, his first away from his parents. It had made him feel grown up to think about a holiday without them and he had pictured a lazy morning in the apartment with Elana—he had not yet bought her any gifts, but he was thinking he'd get her *The Selected Writings of Sor Juana Inés de la Cruz*—and after gifts and a late breakfast, sometime in the afternoon, he would slip away and cross into Juárez. He had not bought Mateo any gifts yet either, but he had been eyeing a turquoise belt buckle in the window of an El Paso Avenue pawnshop.

There was no clock in the bedroom, but Alex could tell time roughly from the sun. Sometime after it peaked, he heard rustling in the hallway—voices and feet—and then Neto opened the door.

"You're rested?"

Alex nodded.

"Come," Neto said. "My brothers are here. We're going to eat."

Up on the rooftop, servants were preparing the grill and Carlota and her two older sons were seated by the rose garden.

"Here he is," Carlota said, raising her glass.

One of the brothers stood. He had pointy cowboy boots and a round belly, round shoulders, round head.

"The student!" he said. "Mamá's been telling us about you. You're studying, uh, mexicanidad, right?" He winked. "With our brother?" He was grinning. "Very good, very good. Nice to meet you. I'm Elías."

The other brother stood. "Sergio," he said, and shook Alex's hand.

"Have something to drink, have a seat," Carlota said, and motioned to the table. A large crock sat steaming full of cider with stewed fruits floating in it and slices of raw sugarcane.

Alex filled a cup and walked to the edge of the roof. The sun was strong, but there was a chill to the air and the wind was still whipping the sand up in great gusts. He turned and watched Neto standing between his brothers, shoulders up and neck stiff. He had that same flicker look in his eyes that Alex had seen before, the almost-rage, almost-love face. Alex watched the way Neto held his body, so careful and utterly aware of every movement, and he could see a lifetime of caution in it. The strain of keeping the secret that began long before you even knew what it was, before you could even say what made you different. No wonder Neto loved wrestling, the relief of choreographed masculinity. He remembered again how Neto had moved when he shot Flaco. Neto's men all watching his control, and how Neto's body had relaxed in that moment, arms spread, feet planted firm and easy, the confidence it had unleashed in him, the obliteration of the awkward hedging self. He would do it again, Alex realized, something to top that, something huge and electrically violent. He would do it again, and who knew who would be in the way next time.

Alex had crossed paths with Neto's dreams and now he was in them. He thought of Neto's desires pulling him forward like a dark cord and Mateo's dreams leading him up from Creel to Juárez and then crossing his life with Neto's and then Alex's own days spilling into Mateo's. You could look at your life like a stack of dominoes tipping one into the other, but you were never really isolated like that. You were always at the mercy of someone else's dream. He guessed he'd known that all along, ever since he stopped believing. When he was thirteen, the realization had come rushing in and replaced his faith. That year, when he had been preaching the most, was when he had believed the least. In front of the church audience he'd cried real tears to show the power of God, but God was gone and their lives were as simple and complicated as balls of yarn, lines of string pulled by desire, intersecting violently. I'm rushing this way and you're rushing that. Call it wrong place, wrong time, call it fate, call it God. That was all that religion and philosophy were trying to get at: a way to contain the unmerciful intersections of everybody's dreams.

"An inability to face today," Sergio said.

Alex glanced up. Neto had left his brothers and was busy talking to the servants at the far end of the roof. His brothers moved toward Alex and after a minute Neto disappeared back downstairs.

"It shows a weakness," Sergio said to Elías. "And I'm not just talking about Neto, I mean in general, the ideas people have, their obsessions with the rose-tinted past. Those fucking fake peons he's got out there."

Elías laughed loudly.

"No, I'm not joking, come here."

The brothers approached the edge of the roof near Alex, and Sergio pointed to the wall the migrants were building, a low stone wall that trailed out into the desert, separating nothing from nothing. The wall began on one side of the horse stables and on the other end the migrants huddled around their own asado, the grilling meat sending up smoke trails toward the afternoon sun.

"Ah, a Christmas asado for the hardworking men," Elías said. "What a kind master!"

"Were it up to him, we'd go back to before the Revolution," Sergio said. "All this paternalism bullshit. And Mamá paying good money for him to play master."

"Shut up," Carlota's voice shot up behind their backs. "I've spent money on worse for you. You who were going to put *me* on a stipend. You ungrateful bastard."

"What's that?"

Sergio, Elías, and Alex turned to see Neto standing at the top of the stairs.

"Nothing," Carlota said. "I was telling your brothers that they should sing us one of those delightful Harvard songs!"

THIRTY-TWO

Elana woke to the sound of bare feet on a tile floor and opened her eyes to see Vivi setting a plate of fruit on a bedside table. Sunlight through the open doorway, white sheets, bare walls. She blinked and remembered finally where she was, though not how she had gotten to bed last night.

"I didn't mean to wake you," Vivi said.

Elana pushed herself up, clutching the sheet. She was wearing only a T-shirt and panties. She could not remember undressing. "You're trying to force-feed me."

Vivi shook her head.

"Simon put you up to this," Elana said.

Vivi was almost smiling. "I like your essay," she said.

"What?"

"Your notes for your essay on miraculous fasting."

Elana tried to focus. Her throat was incredibly dry and her head throbbed. She wondered if she'd gotten drunk the night before, or if she was drunk now. Everything felt fuzzy. "You read my . . . Wait, what are you doing with my stuff?"

"I didn't know it was yours at first." Vivi leaned against the doorframe, silhouetted against the sunlight, the outline of her body visible through her cotton shift. "I was looking for Alex's notes and I thought it was his. It's good, could make a great essay. Though I kept thinking . . ." She shifted so that one leg was tucked into the other. "I saw you have Anne Carson's book in your bag. Don't you think that the female fasting you're writing about is sort of just a way of inverting, or maybe even extending, the Greek model of self-control that Carson talks about as a closed mouth?"

"How do you mean?" Elana said. Somehow she had woken up into the middle of an academic question-and-answer session. Maybe she was actually still dreaming.

"Well, Carson writes about the Greek ideal of a woman with a closed mouth, like a woman who lets nothing out, she is silent and chaste," Vivi went on. "And you're talking about letting nothing in, which is a different kind of closed mouth, but you're still submitting to the patriarchal idea of the importance of self-control and aligning self-control with intellect and intelligence."

Elana looked at the plate of fruit. It was obscenely bright and beautiful: glowing red strawberries and juicy pineapple.

"Carson says that 'closing women's mouths was the object.' Both mouths," Vivi said, smiling. "Right?"

"Oh," Elana said. "Yeah, I'm not sure. You're a lot more awake than I am right now."

Vivi laughed. "I see in your notes that you are going for an argument of fasting as self-control and self-control as self-definition. But what if really it's just a honing of self toward what patriarchal society defines as right and good in a woman: a closed mouth?"

Elana rubbed her eyes. Vivi was not going to let this go until Elana said something substantive. She needed a drink of water, but she couldn't get out of bed without walking past Vivi in nothing but her panties and T-shirt.

"Well," she began, "okay, but it's also the patriarchy who's telling us that we have to care for our 'precious' bodies in a certain way."

"Like how?"

"Like we should be skinny but not *too* skinny. We shouldn't eat too much, but we also definitely shouldn't eat too little. We have to love our bodies, we have to *love* being girls, or else we're not good feminists."

"So you're saying that not always loving your body, not being a happy girl, should be viewed as a radical act?"

"Yes," Elana said. "I think, in a way." Her brain still felt sleepy, but the more she talked the more she felt that maybe she was crystalizing out loud what had been a tangled mess on the page. "Like it's not a passive personal failure but a real active choice to refuse to pretend like everything is okay in a world where everything isn't."

"But what if the active choices include self-harm?"

"Well," Elana said, "okay, so you go out into the world and put on your protest plays to express yourself, but that's not the only kind of activism. When Emily Brontë said, 'I'll walk where my own nature would be leading: It vexes me to choose another guide,' it doesn't mean she was a stubborn girl who died because she made stupid choices and failed to thrive in the real world. She was making a radical choice."

"Did Emily Brontë commit suicide?"

"No, but people say she 'chose death' because she had consumption and she refused to treat her body the way that other people told her to. She refused to lie in bed like a good little sick girl and let doctors poke and prod her."

"I see," Vivi said. "Interesting. This theory, though, it still seems like a little bit . . . oh, I don't know, dangerously close to promoting self-harm in girls?"

Elana looked away. Vivi was not just talking about Elana's writing, she was talking about her body. Elana looked at the plate of fruit and then back at Vivi. "Did you find Alex's notes?"

"Yes, nothing too helpful there yet. Nothing too original either."

"What do you mean?"

"A theory he's calling 'perpetual west,' this idea that, for those Americans who are still caught up in some form of the frontier thesis and manifest destiny, Mexico is the final and perpetual frontier, a place of eternal contrast that America can always compare itself favorably to. Mexico as the ultimate crucible for the formation of individual identity, a great plow to break yourself against and find out who you really are. 'To be a gringo in Mexico—ah, that is euthanasia.'"

Elana nodded. "Ambrose Bierce."

"You've read him?"

"Some. Before the fasting essay, I was working on an essay on Anglos writing about Mexico and Mexicans."

"What happened to that one?"

"I don't know, it was probably a stupid idea. Simon said I was just another Anglo writing about Anglos writing about Mexicans." Elana focused on the sunlight on the wall, the boxy outline of the doorway broadcast against the flat white. After a while she said, "So Alex didn't write anything about lucha libre in his notebooks?"

"Oh, I don't think he'd gotten to that yet in the one I was looking at." Vivi was standing outside the doorway now. "You want to go for a swim?" she said.

THE POOL WAS on the roof, not the same roof where Camila's room was but a different one over a different wing of the house. Camila was there, though, laid out on a lawn chair with a book over her face. A middle-aged woman in a maid's uniform was using a net to clean the water. Beyond her, the city was visible, leafy esplanades spoking in toward the clutter of skyscrapers and a pale brown smog that crept up from every direction.

Vivi lifted her nightgown over her head and dove into the pool.

Elana took a seat on a lounge chair. She wished she had brought her notebook up with her. She wanted to write down what she had said to Vivi and what Vivi had said. Radical. Active. That was the crux of it, what she was wanting to say, to refute the veil of pathetic passivity that everyone hung on figures like Emily, or her Catherine Earnshaw, or Ophelia. Vivi surfaced. "You're not coming in?"

"In a minute," Elana said.

Camila took her book off her face and sat up, squinting.

"Hi," Elana said.

Camila nodded and stood up. She glanced over at Vivi and then turned and walked away.

Vivi dove and rose again. "Don't worry about Camila," she said. "She gets moody."

"She's in school here?" Elana asked.

Vivi pulled her hair back and wrang the water out. "No, I met her in Madrid and she came over . . . Well, we were working on a translation of *Reverse Thunder*. Do you know that play?"

"No."

"It's a Diane Ackerman play about Sor Juana Inés de la Cruz, you've heard of her?"

Elana shook her head.

"In the seventeenth century she lived here, in the city. She was a nun, but she was also sort of a proto-feminist and a poet and scholar. Anyway, Camila and I were going to translate Ackerman's play into Spanish and put on a production of it, but Camila got furious about the romance Ackerman made up between Juana and this Italian ambassador. I guess she would have rather that Juana fell in love with one of the other sisters or something." Vivi laughed. "And I got bored with the literalness of the play, or bored with literal plays in general, I guess. Like if you're going to try and depict a life super realistically and intricately, why not make a movie? The act of *live* theater can be used for so much more. Anyhow, that was more than a year ago, but Camila stayed."

"Oh, uh-huh." Elana stood up. "I'll be right back," she said.

Catholic nuns, that was it! The choices of nuns like Saint Catherine of Siena: she starved herself, she cut off all her hair, and that was accepted as radically active, not a pathetic inability to thrive, as long as it was under a religious guise.

Elana made her way quickly across the roof and down to her room where she spread her notebook out on the bed and tried to slow the words enough to get them on the page.

IN THE LATE afternoon Vivi came to see if Elana wanted to go out. The city was intensely quiet. Until they left the house, Elana had forgotten it was Christmas Day and for a moment the empty streets and sidewalks seemed apocalyptic. The silence of a suddenly still city was so much heavier than the silence of a forest; the forest was breathing, but the city was holding it all in, the thousands of people who had filled the downtown last night—gone, wiped away. A paper bag blew ahead of them up the street. They rode in the darkened SUV with the driver and the bodyguard and neither one of them spoke. On the street corners Virgin shrines bristled with tinsel.

"You said Ana is down here?" Elana said. "And Chucho and Luis and María and all them?"

Vivi nodded. "I think they're staying in a collective house way out in Iztapalapa."

"And when does Marcos arrive?"

"Who knows exactly, but probably not for a few weeks at least. He starts the campaign from La Garrucha on January 1 and then there are stops all along the way. I think Ana said she and the guys are maybe going down to the Yucatán for an event next week and then traveling up with the caravan."

The performance/practice space for Vivi's new play was on the first floor of an old apartment building converted into artist studios in the bohemian neighborhood of Roma Norte. It was on a street full of cafes, bookstores, hipsters, leather jackets, and small pampered dogs. The sidewalks were not empty here. Raúl and Paulina were smoking and drinking paper cups of coffee out front of the building. Vivi spoke fast Spanish with them and

Elana watched the sky turning from pale brown to soiled white. She accepted a cigarette, though she wasn't sure she wanted one. She felt a bite of guilt for not focusing immediately on searching for Alex, but it was Christmas Day, she told herself, there was nothing much she could do on Christmas Day.

"Today we have Elana." Vivi had switched to English. "She can be the stand-in audience. She doesn't know anything."

The theater was a bare room with a red floor and black walls. Chairs were arranged in a square, ten against each wall. Elana felt awkward as soon as she stepped into it. Where to sit? Or was she even supposed to sit? She looked to Vivi, but Vivi was on her phone. She looked to Raúl and Paulina, but they were kissing. She walked away and pretended that the wall was very interesting.

"Okay, so we'll run through it from the top," Vivi said.

Elana turned. They were all sitting, each one on a different side of the square. Elana sat down in the empty row. They were quiet. Paulina was looking at her phone. Raúl reached down and tied his shoe.

"Will you help me?" Vivi said in Spanish.

Elana looked at her. She was running her hands over each other again and again, as if wiping something from one palm with the fingertips of the opposite hand.

"Will you help me do this?"

Elana raised her own hands from her lap, tentatively. "Is this a part of the show?"

Vivi did not respond but just kept moving her hands. Elana mimicked and in a moment Paulina joined too and then Raúl. There was nothing but the slight papery sound of hands brushing.

"Thank you," Vivi said, and she froze with her hands clasped. "Now imagine a well."

"We've known this well our whole lives," Paulina said.

"And for the lives of our mothers," Raúl spoke too, "and grandmothers and great-grandmothers."

"Will you join me?" Vivi said, and she got up and walked to the center of the square and put her hands out flat in front of her.

Paulina stood up and walked to her.

"Like this," Vivi said, looking down at her hands and then up at Elana. "Will you join me?"

When they were all in the middle, Vivi turned her right hand over so that it formed a scoop. She held it high and then turned her left palm to receive. She switched them. She switched them again. Paulina began to mimic.

"You brought your laundry today," Vivi said, looking over at Elana. "And you brought a pitcher to fill for drinking," she said to Paulina. "You brought your baby girl to bathe," she said to Raúl.

Their hands were all scooping and pouring.

"Remember when you were small and your mother would lift you and bathe you like this," Vivi said, her hands still moving. "And she knew your body and everything it needed and she loved it."

Vivi began to move in a circle, still scooping but walking now too and Raúl followed and then Paulina and Elana. "Your body was perfect and you loved it." They walked slowly, circling.

"When did it finish?" Vivi said. "When did it end?"

She dropped her hands to her sides suddenly, turned, and walked to her seat.

They all stopped moving and one by one sat down.

It was silent. A motor passed in the street.

"You wake in the night," Paulina said. "You cannot sleep so you go to the well."

Vivi stood up and walked to the center and held her hands out.

"But the well is empty," Raúl said.

"You feel afraid."

"The well has never been empty."

"You cover your face."

Vivi covered her face with her hands.

"But you are not alone. Someone else could not sleep."

Paulina stood up and walked slowly into the center of the room.

"And someone else," Raúl said, and stood up himself. "And someone else."

Elana stood and walked in.

Vivi lifted her hands from her face. "Will you help me?" she said, and put her hands back over her eyes. "Like this. Will you hide me?"

Paulina covered her face and then Raúl too and so Elana cupped her eyes also.

"Will you catch me?" Vivi said, and then there was a crash.

Elana pulled her hands off her eyes and Vivi was crumpled on the floor. "Is this . . . ?" Elana said, and looked at Paulina and Raúl, but their hands were still covering their faces. She bent over Vivi.

"Will you hold me?" Vivi said.

Elana sat down and awkwardly began to try to gather her into her arms.

"Will you leave me?" Vivi said.

Elana froze.

"Will you leave me?"

Elana stood up and walked back to her seat.

"Will you join me?" Vivi said, and this time Paulina took her hands off her eyes and moved toward her. "Will you hold me? Will you leave me?"

When Paulina left, there was only Raúl still standing.

"Will you join me?" Vivi asked.

Raúl took his hands off his eyes and turned to Elana. "Will you lift her?"

"Will you hold me?"

Raúl walked toward Elana. "Will you lift her?"

"Will you leave me?"

"Will you lift her?"

Their voices rose together.

"Will you leave-lift-me-her?"

Raúl was standing directly in front of Elana. She stood up. He stepped away. She walked toward Vivi and then Raúl turned to Paulina. "Will you lift her?"

"Will you leave me?"

Elana knelt beside Vivi and Vivi sat up. "Break," she said. "Okay, great. In the performance we'll have enough people here to actually lift me. That was great. Everybody feel okay?"

Elana turned quickly so Vivi could not see her face. She felt a lot of things, none of them okay.

WHEN VIVI AND ELANA entered Vivi's parents' house, it was all hushed. The hallway was dim and the eyes in the paintings followed them. They were returning from a bar in Roma Norte. For the past four days Elana had been working on her essay and Vivi on her play. They would meet up in the evenings for tacos and mescal at a little place down the road from the theatre. Elana felt guilty that she had not made any progress in finding Alex, but the mescal helped with that. She'd hung up all the flyers she had, but the city was so enormous her effort felt pathetic, an action taken solely so she could feel like she had not done nothing. If she hadn't been able to find him in Creel, a town of five thousand people, a town where she had proof that he had been, then how in the world could she find him here? And the truth was that her essay was going really well and she did not want to stop. Here, the essay was not something she was working on instead of her homework, it was not something she needed to hide from Alex or Meyer or try to fit into their academic paradigm, it was just her work. And the more she focused on the essay, the less she obsessed over eating or not eating. She would write until her brain fizzed out and then she would go up to the roof for a swim and a snack and after a while come back and work again. Meanwhile Vivi was practicing her play and Camila was doing whatever she was doing, untangling her poet mystery. Here, Elana's writing made sense.

She followed Vivi up the stairs and they came out onto the roof where Camila's room stood.

"Camila," Vivi called.

The night air was chilly and clear. A car alarm sounded in the street below. No response came from the room, though there was light within. Elana hung back as Vivi approached.

"Camila." Vivi pushed back the curtain and stepped in. "Come swimming with us!"

"You're drunk," Camila said.

"No, I'm not, come on."

"It's late," Camila said. "Go, I don't mind."

Vivi brushed the curtain aside and walked out. Elana could not see her face in the dark. She followed her down the stairs and up onto the pool-roof.

"Hey," Vivi said. "So I was thinking about your essay. Are you writing about your mother at all in it?"

Elana stopped walking. "My mother?"

"Yeah, I—"

"Simon told you about her?"

Vivi nodded.

"I don't know."

"I was just thinking about how so much of what you're writing about is women's bodies and choices and then here you have your own mother who made such a big choice about her body and—"

"She might have died anyway. I mean even if she'd aborted Simon. The cancer would probably have still killed her."

"Well, okay, but the interesting thing is that she went against medical advice, right? Made her own choice."

Elana looked away across the rooftop. She knew Adair was all tangled up in her writing, of course she couldn't write about women and body choices without thinking of her. But she didn't want to bring her into it because she'd always felt slightly ashamed of her mother's decision. It didn't feel radical, even though, in many ways, it fit the mold of what she was claiming, in her own writing, was radical. Adair's choice had always reeked of the maternal, domestic, patriarchal, rural, religious. Maybe because Adair's family had all supported her decision so much. It had felt to Elana like a sacrifice, not a radical choice.

"Motherhood, right?" Vivi had kept walking ahead and talking.

"What?"

"How does motherhood fit into your theory?"

Elana shrugged.

"Your mom was from West Virginia, right?" Viva looked back. "So how do you identify?"

"What do you mean?"

"You're Jewish, sort of, right?"

"What do you mean 'sort of'?"

"Simon was telling me how you're Jewish from your dad's side, but he never took you to temple and you grew up in Appalachia, but that's not where your dad's from."

"Yeah."

"Do you identify as Appalachian? Jewish?" Vivi took her jacket and T-shirt off and dropped them onto the tiles.

Elana shrugged again and watched as Vivi wriggled out of her jeans, leapt and split the surface of the water, her shadow trailing after. What she didn't want to say to Vivi was that she'd grafted her identity onto Alex, she'd let him become where she belonged, her home, her identity.

"Come on in," Vivi called from the deep end. "It's heated."

Elana slipped her jeans off and eased into the water in her T-shirt and underwear, trying not to look down at her own body. She looked instead at Vivi's body, breasts floating in the blue water-light and ass jiggling as she turned and swam toward the far end. She wondered if Vivi would have sex with her. It seemed like Vivi and Camila had maybe dated at some point or at least fucked. She wondered if she wanted to have sex with Vivi. Probably, yes, but at the same time she felt too exhausted for the complications that would come with it. As soon as the thought rose, though, she felt both guilty and sorry for herself. What a depressing thing to think. She was twenty-one years old. Now was when she was supposed to be having thoughtless sex, not feeling too tired to deal with the drama of it.

There was the sound of footsteps on the patio and Elana looked back, fully expecting Camila, but it was Diego.

"Vivi!" he said, but Vivi was still underwater. He stood frozen, his face full of panic.

"Hey, are you okay?" Elana said.

"Viviana," he said again, and this time she rose.

"Diego! What's up?" She wiped her face with the back of her hand. "What's wrong?" She swam quickly to the edge of the pool and hoisted herself out.

"I need to show you something," Diego said, and then looked at Elana. "You too," he said.

Elana clutched her clothes to her chest and Vivi went to grab towels from her bathroom.

"Diego, wait a minute," Vivi said, but he kept on toward his own room.

"I need to show you right now," he said. "It could disappear."

His room was dark, lit only by a single lamp and the large desktop computer screen. He sat down and moved the mouse. There was a paused video. He picked up a piece of paper from beside the keyboard and held it up next to the screen. The paper said: SE BUSCA ALEX WALKER.

Elana felt suddenly dizzy. She grabbed the back of his chair.

Her Alex flyer beside the screen.

"Look at this face here," Diego said and with two clicks he zoomed in.

The video was pixelated and shadowy. There was a group of men leaned up against a fence around an animal pen. Inside the pen stood two men and a horse. Click. Diego zoomed the picture again and lifted the flyer up beside the screen.

"Is that your husband?"

In the fuzzed video on this stranger's computer screen was what appeared to be Alex's face.

"What?" Elana leaned in. Alex's nose, his eyes, his full lips. Elana felt a cold rush run over her. Diego unpaused the video. There were voices, some background static and shifting of feet. Alex's face did not move, but his eyelashes beat one, two, three. Diego zoomed out. There was the young horse. And now Alex was holding its reins.

Diego paused it again and spun his chair to face Elana. "What is your husband doing there?"

"How did you do that?" she said.

"Do what?"

"Put him in your video like that?" She was shaking now, her legs gone weak.

"I didn't *put* him in that video. That's not *my* video. Jesus Christ. I was looking at the video and I thought one of the faces looked like the face from your little poster."

Elana reached out to steady herself on something and Vivi grabbed her hand. "Here, come here." She led Elana over to Diego's bed. "Where's that video from?"

"I have no idea, they don't tag them with locations." Diego laughed. "It's a new one, though, just up today. The lower-rank cartel guys will shoot videos like this on their phones and post them, but usually somebody higher up gets a sniff and it disappears pretty quick."

Elana balled her hands into fists and pressed them into her legs. Waves of nausea rolled up and over her. "How . . . I don't understand, where did you get that video?"

"You search the darker corners of the web long enough, you find sites like this." Diego said. "Like snuff videos or whatever, bestiality porn, you know, it's all out there. I've been studying the faces in these videos, the audience. I've been looking at these faces thinking I might recognize someone sometime, I was thinking it would be someone from one of Dad's parties, not my sister's friend's husband."

Elana felt the blood rush to her head and for a moment she could not see. She pressed her hand against her eyes and then lifted them away. "What happens in the rest of the video?"

"Nothing really," Diego said. "The horse gets loose and runs around."

"Let me see it again." Elana stood up and walked toward the screen.

It was Alex. It was definitely Alex.

"They kidnapped him," Elana said.

"You think?" Vivi said.

"No, I mean, that's the only way. He's not there on his own. We don't know anybody in the cartel, he's not . . ." Even though she was speaking English, she still felt like she needed a translator.

Diego spun in his chair. "The cartel doesn't kidnap Americans. Not worth the trouble. And besides, you haven't gotten a call for hostage money, right?"

"We have to call the police," Elana said.

"Whoa, whoa, no," Diego said.

Vivi led Elana back to the bed. "You do not want to call the police," she said. "That is not a good idea, it's too difficult to tell who is and who isn't mixed up with the cartel."

"Well, who do I call?"

"He didn't look like he was being held against his will," Diego said.

It was true. Elana looked up at Diego, her pulse jumping. "Alex is not there because he wants to be there."

Vivi sat down beside her. "My dad can talk to someone at the embassy, they might be able to help."

"The cartels don't bother with Americans," Diego said, and spun back to his screen.

"Let's go talk to your dad," Elana said.

"In the morning." Vivi led her toward the door.

"We could trace the video, well, not us, but someone could, right?"

"Not likely," Diego said.

Alex's face flickered, half-shadow, half-light. Elana opened her eyes, she was in her room at Vivi's house. She closed them again. Alex's eyelashes beat, one, two, three.

"Here, take these so at least maybe you can sleep."

Vivi pressed two pills into her palm and handed her a glass of water. "Let's watch a movie," she said, scooting onto the bed with her laptop.

Elana leaned back against the pillows and tried not to close her eyes. Vivi clicked on a few things and finally put on *Breathless*, which Elana had never seen before. Vivi was explaining something about the inventiveness of the use of the handheld camera, how revolutionary the documentary style was at the time. Elana nodded.

Michel was flirting with Patricia on the Champs-Élysées.

"Will you sleep with me again?" Michel said.

Elana focused on her breath, on not closing her eyes. She let her fingers find her hips under the waistband of her shorts, but the bones were buried, barely decipherable, it was all those tacos she'd been eating, all the time she'd been spending thinking about her essay and not worrying about what she was eating, not worrying about Alex. She pressed her fingers into her hips until they pulsed. She should call someone and tell them about the video right now . . . Simon? Her father? The El Paso police?

On the screen Patricia was musing, "I don't know if I'm unhappy because I'm not free or if I'm not free because I'm unhappy."

The words looped momentarily in Elana's mind and she felt the brush of a memory: Alex, that last night before she left, on their walk to Vivi's art opening. *I think you're scared*, he'd said, *I think you're scared of what would actually make you happy.*

VIVI'S FATHER, EDUARDO, had long, delicate fingers and kind eyes.

"Can I get you a drink?" he asked.

They were in his office on the first floor of the house. He was standing beside a bar cart under a tall, frosted window. It was 10:00 a.m. Elana shook her head.

"So Vivi told me about your husband," he said.

Elana nodded. "She said you went to the embassy? You told them?"

"Yes, they'll keep their ears open."

"What's that supposed to mean?"

Eduardo looked up. "Please, have a seat." He motioned toward the leather chair in front of his desk.

Elana did not move. "What's the next step?"

Eduardo laced his fingers together. "To be truthful, Elana, we don't have a lot to go on. The website is gone."

"The website . . . what do you mean?"

"The video, I mean, not the website. The video is no longer there."

Elana felt her brain lurch. "Ask Diego," she said. "Diego can find it."

"I already did. He says they get taken down all the time. I talked to some people at the embassy, though. They will put out the word to the intelligence groups and if anyone hears of anything—"

"You told the *American* embassy and they're not going to look for him?"

"Look where?"

"Fuck." Elana felt the blood rising to her head.

"You're sure I can't fix you a drink?"

She looked at Eduardo, his soft eyes. "Fine, mescal," she said, and sat down in the leather seat.

He placed the glass in front of her and motioned to the telephone. "You can make whatever calls you need. To the US also, it's fine." He placed his hand momentarily on her shoulder and then left the room.

Elana took a sip of mescal and went back to her room for her notebook with the phone number for Morales's shelter.

A woman's voice answered. "Simon?" she said. "Wait, just a minute."

Elana could hear a whirr of background noise, footsteps, muffled voices. She took another sip of mescal. The phone grew quiet.

"Hello?" she said.

The line was dead.

She placed the phone back in the cradle, then picked it up directly and dialed the shelter again. Busy.

She drank the rest of the mescal and paged through her notebook until she found Toño's number. It rang and rang and finally he answered as she was about to hang up. He sounded sleepy or sad or something. Elana told him about the video.

"So then your friend's father goes to the embassy?" he said.

"Yeah and all he says to me is, 'They'll keep their ears open.'"

"Uh-huh."

"What do you mean 'uh-huh'? He's a missing American citizen. Isn't there a legal obligation to search for him?"

There was a long silence.

"Hello?" Elana said.

"Hey, listen," Toño said. "Just because you're American doesn't mean everything turns out all right in the end. This isn't a movie, okay? In the movie version the retired detective falls in love with the damsel in distress and swings into action for her and uncovers a sinister connection between the Americans and the cartel. Also in the movie version the detective and the damsel make it out alive but just by the skin of their teeth. This is not the movies."

Elana stood up and walked over to the bar cart.

"The scope of the cartels, you don't just take them down with a call to your embassy."

Elana refilled her glass of mescal.

"We don't know who all is involved. Even the wrestlers that your husband was working with could . . . Look, if, and I'm saying *if* your man walked himself into this thing freely, then maybe he can walk himself back out. The more authorities that get involved, though, the more dangerous we'll make it for him. You should know enough about Mexico to know that your friend's father's conversation at the embassy this morning has more than likely already reached the group who made that video, right?"

Elana took a big gulp from her glass and sat back down again. "You're saying just forget about the kidnapping of an American citizen?"

"I'm saying I value my life."

DIEGO CAME TO his door after Elana knocked five times. He was wearing nothing but boxers, rubbing sleep from his eyes. He turned away but left the door open. Elana stepped in and he pulled a T-shirt out of his hamper and slipped it on.

"The video's gone?" she said. She was feeling the mescal now and the intense darkness of the room was making it hard to orient herself.

"They usually go down pretty quick."

Diego's white T-shirt and gray boxers were the only light spot in the room.

"Some techie person could have traced where it came from," Elana said.

Diego pushed his hair back from his forehead and squinted at her. "Probably not. I mean possibly you could get the IP address, but even then, you're not going to physically locate him like that. What was he doing in Mexico anyhow?"

"What do you mean? He's a student, a sociology student."

"Studying the cartels?"

"No, lucha libre."

"You sure about that?"

"No." Elana was still holding her glass. She tipped it up to her lips, though it only held a few drops.

"You want something stronger than that?"

She looked up at Diego. "Like what?"

"Valium," he said. "They gave me a prescription after the attack."

SHE SET A deck chair up on the corner of the pool-roof under a potted palm that clapped its fronds loudly in the dry wind. The maids had taken the poinsettias away after Christmas Day, but one remained, half-hidden and drooping behind the palm. Elana cupped her hands and carried palmfuls of pool water over to it before realizing that the chlorine would almost surely kill the plant.

She lay down and closed her eyes. The Valium was making her a little dizzy but in a warm, fuzzy way. She could hear a dove cooing somewhere on the roof up above and traffic moving out on the big avenue. No horns, just traffic moving smoothly, like lapping waves.

Studying the cartels? Maybe he had been. But why would he say . . . Maybe lucha libre had led to the cartels? Or maybe he'd been lying to her the whole time. You thought you knew someone, but then—her mind flashed to Simon with the knife, Meyer cowering in the car. She laid her hand across her eyes to block out the sun.

The other waitresses at Susie's had always been talking about online dating sites and Facebook and Elana had never understood how you could feel comfortable going on a date with someone from the internet. As if you could really know someone from that. You checked the right boxes and said that *Natural Born Killers* and *Pulp Fiction* were your favorite movies and bingo: a prefab identity. She'd judged the other girls at work, but what the fuck did she know? She'd thought she'd understood who Alex was because of . . . what? The classes he took at university? The books he read and the bands he liked and the clothes he wore? That's why she'd started hanging out with him. And then the closer you get to someone, the fewer questions you ask because you think you already know them. You think you already know what they are capable of.

FOR THREE DAYS Elana baked on the pool-roof with mescal and Valium. She cast her mind wide and let her thoughts swerve and blow, and when they circled inevitably back to Alex and she started to cry, she would get up and dive. Underwater her face was not a sticky mess. Underwater she could not even be sure if she was still crying. Underwater she felt sharp and lithe.

Sometimes her mind went to her mother too. She thought of what Vivi had said that night in the pool. Motherhood and bodies and choices. She picked at the place in her brain where the shame for her mother's choice lay. If she theorized that Emily Brontë going against medical advice was radical, she couldn't let her mother's choice stay there in her mind unexamined. But it was all tied in with her memories of Dulcie's *I knew you'd leave me.* Passivity and complacency. Of course, Adair's was not a passive choice, but somehow it stank of that, of giving in. Perhaps Dulcie wasn't so utterly passive either, though. Perhaps Elana had just assumed apathy and overlooked the agency in staying. You could say you were left, or you could say you stayed.

On the third afternoon Elana woke cramped and sunburnt on the deck chair while the maid swept studiously around her and her almost empty bottle of mescal. Vivi was gone, working on her play, and the house was silent. Elana listened to the city all around her, traffic and muffled car horns, and she thought of Ana and the others, on the far side of town, excitedly preparing for their subcomandante. It was now what? January 2? Marcos would have begun his tour and the kolektivo kids would be ready to greet him, ready to change the world. Meanwhile, Alex was apparently hanging out with the cartel. It split her wide open to think about it directly and so she got up and dressed and let herself out of the house. She was standing on the sidewalk, lightheaded and fluttery, before she could think of a destination. She took a right, past a shoeshine stand. The street was quiet, the smell of bread and chocolate from a cafe made her stomach punch. She kept walking. A dog yapped and lunged from behind barbed wire and shrubbery. She moved on.

Fifteen minutes later she was outside of an enormous grocery store, El Super. The doors swished open and she stepped into the air-conditioning. It was so American, more American than the grocery store in El Paso had even been, nothing like the little corner tiendas and market stalls in Juárez. She rode the escalator up to the second floor. Everything gleamed. And the aisles, the aisles were enormous, something like the corridors of a basilica, shining wide and long and dripping with goods. Elana felt her shoulders relax. She didn't even have any money with her, but that was not the point. She could walk this store for hours and no one would notice or ask. Anonymous, that's what it was, that's why it felt so American. It was communion between you and the stuff, direct Protestant worship with no saintly intermediaries.

Elana ran her fingers down the rows of crackers, cookies, chocolate, avellana, vainilla, crujiente, más crujiente. What are you, a crunchy-cookie kind of girl? Or soft baked, homemade, grandma's way? You can be anyone. You can do anything. Make yourself. Change yourself. Born this way.

She rode the escalator up another floor.

Whenever anyone else entered an aisle, she bent close to examine the packages, to disappear into them, and when she was alone again, she floated up into the swirl of it: fresh, new, hearty, traditional, new look–same product. We're here for you, always, forever, everything you know and trust. Depend on us.

THIRTY-THREE

Mateo watched the glimmer lights of Hermosillo drop away out the plane window as they flew northeast into the great dark night of Campo Verde. Enrique, his minder, was asleep in the seat beside him and a silence like a sea fog spread through the cabin, lifting Mateo and holding him up above his present moment, above his choices and life explosions. And Alex was there, in the in-between place, waiting.

When the plane hit the runway at Neto's compound, Mateo woke with his body seizing. He stood up and staggered, a net of sleep-dreams and Oxy smearing everything. It was 2:00 a.m., but he insisted on seeing Alex.

He turned to the basement as soon as they had stepped inside, but Enrique called his name and nodded toward the upper stairs.

Alex, Mateo mouthed.

"This way," Enrique said, and pointed to the staircase that led up to the bedrooms and where, on the topmost step, Alex stood.

Mateo felt his blood stop, change directions, and speed up.

Alex stood completely still, in an indigo shirt and black slacks, hair combed back.

Alex, Mateo mouthed again as he walked to the stairs. There was something growing in him, something rising up, hot and muddled. When he had seen Alex down in that basement cell, he'd felt such a drum of emotions, but this was worse. That had been a clean, terrific pain, but this was stained. Repulsion pulsing under every stair. He reached the top step and Alex grabbed him, pulled him in. Mateo felt the slick shirt, warm arms. He smelled of Neto.

Mateo pulled back, looked over Alex's shoulder. "Where is he?"

Something fluttered across Alex's face. "Neto?"

"Who else?"

"He's sleeping. I wanted to stay up for you. He told me you were coming back tonight."

Mateo stepped to the side so that no part of their bodies was touching. "Now you'll go back?"

"Back?"

"Now you see that I'm safely here, you'll go back to his room to sleep?"

"My room," he said, and motioned with his hand. "I'll sleep in *my* room."

"Your room?"

"I have a room, a few doors down from yours. I've never seen Neto's room. You have?"

Silence bloomed up, taut as the skin of a bubble, until they both spoke over each other.

"No."

"You wish—"

"What?"

"You wish I was back in the basement."

"No, no." Mateo stepped toward Alex. "God, no."

"God, no?"

Mateo shook his head. "I'm so tired." He looked Alex in the eyes. "You're okay?"

"Okay?"

"You hate me?" Mateo said.

Alex's lips stretched into a forced smile. "No, no," he echoed. "God, no."

Mateo studied Alex's face, his dark eyes, perfectly still, letting nothing in or out.

"It's late," a voice behind them said.

Mateo turned to see Enrique coming up the stairs. They were being sent to their rooms, like boys. Mateo felt a glut of fury lodge in his chest as he opened his door. In the dark he lay on top of the blankets. Alex's room was not the one directly beside his, but it was only a few doors down. How long had he been up here? Why was he up here? What had he done? Mateo gripped his arms across his chest, dug his nails into his skin to focus the pain. What had he done? Jesus, he'd done nothing. How could Mateo even ask that? He'd done nothing, ever, unless . . . *You're right that it has to do with trust,* Neto had said. Neto had been watching them for so long, had been watching Alex. This had been his plan all along, all of it, every move. It was like being inside a chess match, the individual pieces unable to see the game in its entirety.

IN THE MORNING the house was silent, and he did not see Neto or Alex. Enrique escorted him back to the plane immediately. From the window he watched the compound grow small below them. The sun was slicing across the sand hills and there was nothing at all to show that this day was any different than the one endless day he had been living over and over for so long.

After a while Enrique came to him with a glass of mescal. "Cheers," he said.

"Cheers?"

"Alex is fine, you don't need to worry." Enrique refilled his glass.

That night they were in Mazatlán and then on to Puerto Vallarta and Ciudad Guzmán.

The days cycled endlessly. Each night was a new place, but all of it looked the same. He won, he lost, he won. A loop like a carnival ride he could not stop. All day, while traveling, he swallowed Oxy to blunt out the pain and the scratching-rodent terror in his brain and then later, in the dressing room, Dex and coke to sharpen up. He would surface suddenly, the walls coming alive with color again, the music notching loud. He tore through the soft gauze of the Oxy and pounced into the ring. In the audience he saw Alex and his son, Martín, sitting side by side. He saw them over and over again, in Monclova, Saltillo, Ciudad Victoria, but when he approached, they looked away and disappeared.

Mateo did not sleep. He did not eat. He could not remember the last time he took a shit. He felt Neto's men watching him constantly. He would not eat the food they brought him because it seemed infected somehow, like if he swallowed it they would be able to watch him inside his body as well as out. He pushed the Styrofoam plate of tacos al pastor to the end of the dressing table and refilled his glass of mescal. Enrique appeared to be watching the TV, but as soon as Mateo glanced away, he could feel Enrique's eyes on him. He needed to get out from under their view, it was sickening him. It was like a smog over everything. If he could just get out from under the cloud for a moment, then he could start thinking clearly.

In Morelia he wrestled a tecnico called Flying Star, his costume all slick blue-and-silver sequins. The man was fast on his feet and slippery. Mateo struggled to control his own body. Each time he moved, he felt a vague surprise that his actions should go on so far ahead of his consciousness of them. Midway through the second round, Flying Star pinned him to the mat and Mateo looked up past the tecnico's shiny mask and saw the crowd all around him in the bleachers and up above them, painted across the whole sky, Neto's face. All of them pressing down on him. He'd been pinned for so long now and he'd done nothing, nothing at all to stop it. He bucked up, surged with a thrill of adrenaline, and threw Flying Star off. He struggled to his feet, the crowd loud now, his blood jumping. He turned with a sweep and caught sight of Flying Star just as he vaulted from the top rope, soaring straight at El Vengador's chest, feet first.

When Mateo opened his eyes, everything was smeared. The lights, the air, all of it shimmered as if underwater. He tensed and his breath came fast—the world around him gone slack and unfamiliar. He tried to focus. He was on his back, but he was not in the ring. Hands and voices moved over him. He squinted and saw Alex in the corner, and Martín. Alex was bending over Martín and handing him a McDonald's bag.

Mateo's body was pushed up and wheeled out of the room. He tried to look back. Time kept buckling. He was pretty sure he was on a plane. His ears rang and rang. He just needed to focus and slow it all down, but the effort was like clenching a fist that no longer belonged to him; his whole body a leaden burden he could not lift.

It was Alex who snapped the dream away. His face appeared again but this time sharper, coronated in sunlight, a curl of tawny hair across his forehead.

"You're awake," he said.

Mateo reached for him and he was there, the warm skin of his arm, firm and real.

"I'm awake," Mateo said.

Alex brought him a glass of water. Mateo set his lips at the rim, and when he went to swallow, he found that his body followed his instructions. The water moved cool across his tongue and down his throat and his hand held the glass without spilling and it felt like magic. He drank until the cup was empty.

When the water was gone, reality rushed back in, a weight in the center of his brain. He was in his room in Neto's compound, he realized, and there was a guard with a gun visible just outside the open door. The coolness of the water left his mouth immediately and it was dry again, his tongue too swollen to move.

"Are you hungry?" Alex asked.

Mateo looked up at his face. He could not read it, but he felt a bolt of something run through him, a feeling that was not anger but was not love. Alex was turning, he thought, Alex was becoming one of them. He wanted to feed Mateo their food and ease him in too. Mateo reached up and ran a finger across Alex's cheek to wipe away the oily miasma of their gaze. He needed to get the two of them out. He remembered the adrenaline he'd felt in the ring with Flying Star, the jolt of the realization that he had do something—act, move fast. He felt the resolve strengthening in him again now, although even the simple action of raising his arm brought on waves of nausea.

When he woke, Alex was not there and Neto was in the room. The sun was gone from the window. Neto stepped toward the bed and Mateo's muscles jerked. He pushed himself up on his elbows, his brain sloshing as he moved.

Neto put his hand out, palm first, as if to push Mateo back. "Relax," he said. "I just wanted to see how you're doing."

"Good." Mateo met his eyes and held them. He tensed his arms and legs, released and tensed them again.

"Relax," Neto said again. "I'm just glad to see you're doing better." He stood over Mateo. "You need anything right now?"

Neto's eyes looked warm and this disturbed Mateo. He shook his head.

"Just rest then, okay?" Neto said. "We'll talk later."

Mateo lay back slowly onto the mattress and pulled the blankets to his chin.

"Rest," Neto said.

Mateo flicked his head in agreement. Was Neto going to stand there, verifying his restfulness? Mateo closed his eyes. He heard footsteps and then the door. He opened his eyes. Even alone, he felt watched now. He felt cold and panicked—filled with a need to move, to feel the outside air against his skin. He thought of Alex—here, alone, never leaving, for weeks now. Though he wasn't in the basement anymore, that thought flashed up in Mateo's mind. Alex seemed to have freedom of movement, he realized, he had come and gone from Mateo's room, alone, without guards following him.

Something had flipped. Alex was free to move about while Mateo was guarded, in bed, confined to this room. *Just rest. Relax. Rest, okay?* His chest tightened. He needed to get his body back together. He needed to go and fight. Though nothing like this had ever been mentioned, he felt somehow that if he fought enough matches, then Neto would . . . what? Let him go? Lose interest in him?

Alex came back into the room after a while. Mateo felt his heart lurch. He watched Alex carefully. Where had he been when he was not in the room? Did he roam Neto's house freely now? He brought Mateo another glass of water and then sat in the chair at the end of the bed and picked up a *Box y Lucha* magazine. Mateo wanted to say something, but his throat was seized up with jealousy, great swaths of it running through him. He slid his legs off the bed and stood carefully.

"Alex," he said.

Alex looked up and their eyes met. "Mateo," he said. "Jesus, you're trembling. You need to eat. You haven't eaten anything yet?" He broke eye contact and turned toward the door. "I'll get the guard to send something up for you."

And with that, he left.

Though the food was certainly poisoned, Mateo had no choice, really, he needed his body back. He ate and then lay in bed, tensing and releasing his muscles, regaining control over them. He fell asleep, and when he awoke, he sat up, this time much more easily. He scooted himself to the edge and stepped down. He could stand now without shaking. He walked to the window and pulled back the curtain. The sky was immaculate: stars upon stars upon stars. And down below, the endless expanse of rock and scrubby sand. There had been a wind all afternoon, and though he had not noticed it then, he noticed its absence now. He left the window and walked a lap around the room. He paused and then walked the perimeter again, and again and again, feeling his body move, *his* body, it was his—his to use and move. He just needed to get out from under their gaze.

The next morning after breakfast, he sat on the floor and tried a few sit-ups. He rested and then attempted a few more, off and on like that all afternoon. He was gaining strength. At night he lay awake and traced the possible ways that things could have gone—the paths that led him here and the paths that would not have. Half the time the paths felt fated, like there hadn't been anything he could have done, he was trapped from the beginning. And half the time he felt he could have stopped this whole thing if he had just said no when he was first approached about sponsorship.

After two days he added push-ups to the sit-ups and then, the next day, modified burpees. That evening Alex came upon him in the middle of a rep.

"What are you doing?" Alex stood in the doorway.

Mateo was sweating, his heart beating fast but good. He wiped his forehead and bent over, stretched to his toes.

"You should get back in bed. You need to be resting," Alex said.

Mateo snapped his head up. "You know that you sound exactly like Neto?" he said. "You know that, right?"

A shadow of emotion crossed Alex's face before he turned and pulled the door closed behind him. Mateo lowered himself to the floor. They were corrupting Alex, rotting him.

After that Alex did not come to his room for one whole day and Mateo agonized through the hours, repeating his exercises over and over until he could not breathe. He pinched his skin, slapped himself, stood, and started the burpees again.

When Alex opened the door the next afternoon, Mateo felt his whole being leap. This was it, he thought, they had to go now. Now or never. He might never see him again. He felt giddy and tried to hide it.

Alex held a tray of tacos which he set on the table by the bed.

"Thank you, thank you so much!" Mateo said.

Alex looked at him quizzically. "You're okay?"

Mateo nodded. He ate slowly, and when Alex's head was turned, he rolled two tacos tightly and stuffed them in the pocket of his sweatpants.

"Hey," he said. "I know you think I should rest, but I'm getting stronger and I want you to come to the gym with me, so I don't overdo it."

"The gym?" Alex said.

"Neto built a training gym here for me, out past the stables." Mateo reached for his sneakers. "Tell the guard to take us there. Neto built it for me, he shouldn't mind me going."

THE AIR OUTSIDE felt hallucinatory—chilly, despite the full sun, but smooth, filling up his lungs with each step. The compound seemed rather deserted as they rounded the horse barns and headed to the concrete bunker of a gym. The guard walked a few feet behind, his boots loud on the gravel.

Mateo had used the gym rarely and there was a fine layer of dust across all the equipment.

"I'm gonna run a little," he said to Alex as he headed to the treadmill, watching the guard leaned against the far wall. When running, he had always felt a childish rush of confidence. He let it roll over him now, even as he kept his eyes focused on Alex, where he sat on the stationary bike, and the guard against the wall. Sweat rose to his skin and he felt in control again, in rhythm, counting toward an unknown number. One hundred, two hundred. He just had to sweat them out, get them off his skin. Three hundred, four hundred. He was seeing things clearly now for the first time in a long while. He'd made it all so laughably complicated in his head. It was like a riddle; the answer was right in front of him the whole time. He just had to *do* something about it.

Mateo reached six hundred and leapt off the belt midsprint and headed to the free weights. He was breathing deeply, cleanly now. With each lift, he scooted himself half an inch closer to the guard who was watching dust motes dance in the middistance. Mateo squatted and glanced at Alex, still on the bike. He lifted and scooted again. He squatted and focused, lifted, and swinging in one smooth arc, brought the fifty-pound weight up to meet the guard's head.

A sound like a wet cry left the body. It fell. The noise of the bike stopped. Mateo let go of the weight and it dropped. He turned, arms out, and ran at Alex.

"What the fuck?" Alex said, his eyes huge with confusion.

"Go." Mateo clutched at him, pulling him from the bike. "Let's go."

They'd nearly reached the door when he dropped his grip on Alex and grabbed two bottles of water. "Go, go, go."

The air outside was bright and full of wind. He pressed one water into Alex's hand and grabbed his arm again.

"Where the hell are we going?" Alex said, pulling away.

West, Mateo thought, though he wasn't entirely sure of the direction. "The mountains," he said, and gestured with his chin.

Alex stood there, glancing over his shoulder at Neto's house and then back to Mateo. "I . . ." he said. "I don't know . . ."

Mateo lunged to grab his hand and Alex recoiled, a look of indisputable fear on his face. Mateo froze. Sadness spread up through him. *No, no, no, no, they can't have you.*

"Let's go," he said, and gripped Alex's arm.

He half-dragged him past the back paddock. It was empty now, no sign of the yearling. Mateo did not look back, he lurched forward, past the last fence, into the scrub and sand and mountains.

When they reached the first dip in the ground, he slowed and glanced over his shoulder. No one was following them. How long until the guard woke and alerted everyone? Or if he was . . . no, he couldn't be dead. Mateo remembered the smack, how little resistance the man's head had given. He'd seen no blood, but . . . He moved his hand from Alex's arm to Alex's hand, linked fingers, and picked up their pace again.

"What's on the other side of the mountains?" Alex said. His face was red and his voice shaky.

Mateo felt the wind snatching at their clothes and for a brief moment he realized the ridiculousness of their situation, out there in nothing but sweats and sneakers running into a blank wall of wilderness. He felt the pull of memory: a childhood friend, José, he'd known all through primary school. After lunch they would cut class and run, hands twined and pumping, down the road and into the tall grass, out across the high pasture to where the piñons fell back and the rock had worn away to the bones of the land, a sheer open view out across the Valle de las Ranas and on down below, the tremendous tilt of the earth herself nearly visible there. They would stand at the edge of the escarpment, wind cupping their faces, lashing their cheeks with tears as they drank it in, measured it out: the size of the world.

Alex slowed, let go of Mateo's hand, and opened his water bottle and Mateo stopped beside him. The sun raked across the sand, striking in long sideways glances. It was later in the day than he had anticipated, but from the bedroom there had been no way to tell. There were no clocks anywhere in the house that he had seen. Alex put his water bottle in his pocket and glanced back and Mateo looked with him. The house reared up, still horrifyingly close. He jerked Alex's hand and they ran toward the mountains again.

They were breathing hard and before too long they weren't running but rather shuffle-jogging. Still, no one was following and soon Mateo's fears shifted from the house to the mountains, the long shadows crawling up over the ridge and settling across the sand. The sun gashed its way down, spewing riotous oranges and pinks. Mateo slowed their pace and watched as the last light disappeared behind the ridges spread like the great sloping backbone of some creature long extinct.

The temperature dropped immediately, a chill that rose up from the ground and enveloped them. Mateo felt all the angles of his bones, the exposed skin of his fingers, neck, and face. They were not wearing nearly enough clothes.

"Stop for a minute," he said, pulling from his pocket the two tacos. He pressed one into Alex's palm.

"What's this?"

"Eat," he said.

Above them in the bluing air, bats juttered and quipped, all staccato motion. There was nothing but the sound of those wings and their own mouths chewing as they ate their pork and tortilla. The stars came into focus, a tide of them, rushing in. Mateo tilted his head back and his breath came out in a glistening cloud.

The mountains were still outlined, ever so faintly, against the sky and Mateo balled Alex's cold fingers into his own and led him on. They stumbled over rocks and scrubby bushes. When the sun had still been out, it had seemed as if there were nothing between them and the mountain, nothing at all but sand. Now, though, there were sticks and thorns and stones. They moved slowly, dragging their feet more than lifting them, afraid to twist something, to break.

"Fuck," Alex said, his voice wet with emotion. "I don't want to fucking die."

Mateo could barely make out the contours of his face in the dark, but even that was too much. He had to turn away.

"I was always looking for something more, Mateo. Like every moment was only a step toward something bigger. I've never lived for myself, only for what Jesus wanted from me and then through books, patterns, theories. I was so afraid."

Mateo stopped moving. He held his breath. He could feel them cupped there in the dark, held in between one moment and the next.

"And now I just want to live," Alex said. "I came here to know myself." He let out a cracked laugh. "What a stupid, pointless idea. Impossible, and why would you want to know yourself, or anyone else?"

Mateo grabbed Alex's hand. He had to stop the words or they would never find their way out of here. They had to have hope.

"We know each other," he said. "That's enough?"

He hadn't meant it as a question, but it came out that way.

"Mateo, I was never here." Alex squeezed his hand. "From the moment we met, I was off somewhere seeing how the steps fit in. I couldn't even let myself love you without making you part of my theories."

The words hung between them and Mateo wanted to erase them with his own, but Alex was talking again.

"I was going to start living," he said. "Once I knew myself, once I knew everything. I thought I'd meet myself, walking along the street, I'd find the real me." He tilted his head back. "Youth is such a luxury and I never even tasted mine. I stepped over it and tried to run ahead."

Mateo pulled Alex to him. He wrapped his arms all the way around Alex until their bodies crumpled into one another and they fell slowly together to the ground. The cold was great and their bodies were shuddering. He looked out over Alex's head and saw Neto's compound down among the wash of dark, the lights of it seeming now quite far away, like the lights of a star only twice as big.

Alex's whole body was jerking and Mateo tucked him in against his chest. Alex struggled and pushed, but Mateo held him tight. He lifted his head and watched his breath climb. The stars were jagged and gorgeous, the whole ripped-open space of them, the torn universe.

"I loved you before I even knew I could love you," Mateo said, his hands burying themselves in Alex's curls. "I had the love for you in me and I hated it because I carried it everywhere, but I didn't know what for. I thought it would always be just mine to carry. Ever since I was a kid. Lalo and I had something for a minute, but he didn't want it to mean anything and he gave the weight back to me. I thought I would carry it forever. And then I met you."

He could feel tears sliding down his cheeks. He waited for Alex to say something, but the only sound he heard was the wind. He tugged at Alex, tipped them both over so their bodies lay curled in the dirt, he could feel Alex's chest against his own—filling and emptying, filling and emptying—and he could feel the cold pressing in on them in waves.

THOUGH MATEO WAS sure he had not slept, he must have, because he woke when the sky was pinkening. He watched Alex's breath clouding from his mouth, watched the sunlight lick up the raw face of the umber rock and flanks of ocher sand: the world made new in the climbing sun, unspeakably beautiful. All night they had rocked on the scrabbly ground, bodies tight and convulsing in the cold, shrinking into one another, blood gone slow. Mateo had always thought of death as a lifting, but in the night he had seen that it was a settling, a dropped-down curdling escape.

He untangled his stiff arms from Alex's waist and sat up, training his eyes in the direction of Neto's place. It took him a moment to find it, and when he did, it seemed ungodly close—a dot, yes, but not a small-enough dot—and in the wrong direction, as if they had turned and backtracked somehow in the night.

"Alex." His words billowed out in white. "Hey, Alex."

Alex jerked and bolted up, eyes wide. He stood, swerving, unsteady. He took three steps and opened his pants to piss and started laughing.

Mateo sat with his arms hugged around his knees and watched him, arc of urine steaming hot and bright into the rising sun.

"You see what we did?" Alex said.

Mateo pushed himself up to his feet, willing his blood to move.

Alex was gesturing at the mad trample of footprints all around. "We walked in circles last night, backtracked!"

THEY FOUGHT LIKELIHOODS of death in the rising sun.

"There's no going back, he'll kill us," Mateo said.

"If he wanted to kill us, he'd have come for us already. How hard could we be to find in this nothingness?"

"If we can just make it up over that ridge."

"You think he doesn't know where we are?"

"What? Like a game? Like he's letting us wander until he wants to come for us?" Mateo pictured Adam and Eve in their garden, two tiny, silly creatures watched from on high but too busy with their own new self-awareness to know, God letting them cover themselves uselessly in fig leaves, timing his entrance precisely.

"Well, what else? You think he's really going to let us walk away?"

"I think you got too close," Mateo said.

Alex made a sound in his throat, a sort of cough-laugh. "Me?" he said, and his lip quivered up into a smile or a snarl.

They walked more slowly than they had the first day, not even a jog but a stumble-walk with a good distance between them. By midday it was much warmer, but blood had still not returned to Mateo's fingers and toes. His water bottle was nearly empty and they had eaten nothing all day. The distance to the mountains rippled and concaved; each time they had nearly reached them, the land gave way for more space. Mateo had stared at their outline so long he could see it etched against his inner eyelids, the nothing-nothing-nothing and then the rise.

It was evening again when they heard the plane. Mateo's heart slammed up to his throat and he crouched, glancing over at Alex who had stopped and looked up and waved his hand.

"What the fuck are you doing?" Mateo lurched and grabbed his arm, pulling him down to the ground. Alex was laughing, or shaking at least. Mateo tried to see his face, but Alex wrestled free, stood up and turned away, staring out to where a long plume of dust rose behind the black dot of an SUV.

The plane circled above them, humming.

Mateo watched the SUV. It seemed suspended, moving but somehow not yet approaching. The distance to it equaled the time he had left here with Alex. He could see it, hanging there, about to decrease, and he knew there were words he should say, but he had already blubbered about love last night. He should just touch Alex again, right now, while he still could. He pushed himself up to his feet, but Alex was facing the approaching SUV now, moving toward it, out of reach.

THIRTY-FOUR

Elana woke blinking, no idea where she was. Her throat was so dry she couldn't swallow. White curtains, white blankets, blue tiles. She was in the guest room at Vivi's house. On the desk her books and notepads. And on the chair: a pile of Alex's notebooks. Four black pleather notebooks with lined pages and marking ribbons, $11.99 each at Walmart. When he bought them, they'd fought about the price, about why couldn't he just use regular spiral-bound ones? Elana got up and went to the bathroom.

She filled a glass with water, drank, and filled it again. At the bottom of the mirror was a white smear where a sticker had been torn from the glass and for a moment her eyes saw Alex's looping script from his mirror notes: *Elana, I love you, hope you have a good day!*

"Hey."

She looked up. Vivi stood behind her, reflected. She wore a red cotton dress, hair piled on top of her head.

"Want to go to UNAM," she said, "with me and Camila?"

* * *

The university was in the south of the city, big enough to fill its own entire neighborhood. Vivi's driver brought them to the main campus and parked in the shade of the social sciences building. Vivi told her bodyguard to stay in the SUV while they set out with stacks of flyers for the play. *¡Brota!*, it was called, and there was an image of flowing water behind the text.

Neither Camila nor Vivi spoke as they trooped across the quad from building to building. There were endless departments, floor after floor, and countless corkboards. It was hot. Elana's head pounded. She followed behind Vivi and Camila, holding the extra flyers and feeling like a little tagalong child.

When they reached the Facultad de Filosofía y Letras, Camila turned to Vivi. "I'll see you in half an hour," she said, handing over her flyers and moving quickly, practically running to the stairwell. Elana looked at Vivi and raised her eyebrow.

"Alcira Soust," Vivi said. "She's going to pay vigil to Alcira Soust."

"To who?"

"The army invaded the campus here in 1968 and there was a woman, a poet, who helped student activists escape and then hid herself in the women's bathroom on the third floor of the Filosofía y Letras. She stayed there for fifteen days." Vivi turned and walked down the hall, looking for corkboards. "Camila's beloved Belano wrote about Soust and now Camila comes out here and lights a candle in the bathroom and prays or something, I don't know."

"She stayed in the bathroom for fifteen days?"

"Yeah, she tucked her feet up so when the army swept the building, they didn't know she was there. They claimed they emptied the campus, but she was here the whole time, reading, writing poetry on toilet paper squares, eating the toilet paper eventually. Some people say she was trapped out of fear. She was an immigrant and didn't have all her paperwork in order. They claim she was just frightened and got stuck here, but others say it was an act of protest."

"And Camila does a vigil in that bathroom?"

"Yeah, want to see?"

They wound up the concrete stairs to the third floor. The classrooms were empty, silent, the winter break not quite over yet. Vivi led Elana to the bathroom at the end of the floor where Camila was seated, a candle burning above her on the ledge of the sink while she stared out the window across the grassy expanse dotted with ash trees and pines and tiny people strolling toward the reflecting pool and library.

"I'll be back in a minute," Vivi whispered, and turned to leave.

"Hey, wait a second," Elana said. "Do you have a pen I can borrow?"

She flipped over one of the flyers and scribbled fast: tanks and troops and screaming students, the pastel bathroom, echoing footsteps, and a woman, tucked up with her feet on the toilet, her steely protest mistaken for feminine fear.

THE PLAY OPENED at eight o'clock and the theater was full, every seat in the rectangle of chairs occupied. Elana sat across from Vivi and waited for her cues. All of them, Vivi and Raúl and Paulina, blended with the audience and no one could know, until they initiated the story, that they were anything more than spectators too. Elana was to blend thoroughly and step up only if no one else readily joined.

"Will you help me?" Vivi turned to the man beside her and the room went quiet. She was running her hands over each other as if wiping something from one palm with the fingertips of the opposite hand. "Will you help me do this?"

The man watched her hands. "Is it part of the show?" he said.

"Will you help me?" Vivi repeated.

The man glanced at the woman on the other side of him and laughed a little nervously. "I'll do it if it's a part of the show," he said.

"Will you help me do this?" Vivi repeated.

Finally, the man on the other side of her began to imitate her movements and then the first man joined eventually and the woman beside him and it rippled around the room until everyone was moving.

“Thank you,” Vivi said, and she froze with her hands clasped. “Now imagine a well.”

“We’ve known this well our whole lives,” Paulina said, and everyone looked over at her.

“And for the lives of our mothers,” Raúl spoke too, and the attention shifted to him. “For the lives of our grandmothers and great-grandmothers.”

Vivi got up and walked to the center of the square and put her hands out flat in front of her. “Will you join me?”

No one moved.

“Will you join me?” she said again. There was a rustle of crossing and uncrossing legs, but still no one stood.

She looked over at Elana and Elana walked to the center of the room.

“Like this,” Vivi said, and Elana held her hands out flat. Vivi looked beautiful and shimmery under the stage lights. “Will you join me?” she asked again, and this time an audience woman stood and came forward.

When there were five of them the middle, Vivi turned her right hand over so that it formed a scoop. She held it high and then turned her left palm to receive. She switched them. She switched them again. Elana began to mimic and soon the man beside her did too.

“You brought your laundry today,” Vivi said to Elana. “And you brought a pitcher to fill for drinking,” she said to man beside her. “You brought your baby girl to bathe.”

They had made it to the point in the story where the well is empty when the alarm went off.

“The well has never been empty,” Raúl said. “You cover your face.”

From somewhere outside a *wa-wa-wo-wa-wa-wo* began blaring.

Vivi stood in the center of the room with her hands over her eyes. She lifted her hands.

Elana looked from Vivi to Raúl. She thought the alarm was part of the play until she saw Raúl’s face, eyes huge. The sound kept on and then suddenly, all at once, everyone was moving. Everyone was surging. Vivi lunged toward Elana and grabbed her arm.

"What?" Elana could feel the terror in the air, but she still did not understand.

"Earthquake," Vivi said, gripping her hand.

The crowd was all pushing in the same direction, but they seemed to be blocking one another, somehow no one was moving. The alarm continued to sound. The room felt suddenly hot. All the lights were turned up now and the bodies were squeezing, bottlenecking.

"Thirty seconds," Vivi breathed as she pulled Elana with her. "There's thirty seconds after the alarm begins. We gotta get out of this building."

They pushed into the lobby, Vivi jerking Elana behind her, and once they were out the front door, they broke free from the crowd, running. People spilled from doorways all up and down the street, feet pounding down stairwells, dogs barking, babies crying, but hardly any adult voices. The adults were all silent, deadly calm. *¡Alerta sismica! ¡Alerta sismica!* the alarm repeated, and then it stopped.

Everyone froze. Nothing moved. Up above, the stars were visible and the clouds were shifting with the wind, but below, the streets were full and frozen. Hands held, hearts stilled. One minute passed, then two. The alarm stayed silent and nothing moved and finally a cheer went up. "Deep," someone yelled, "and weak!" Applause rippled up the street. Too deep, this seismic shift, to even be felt. Too weak and low and deep.

EPILOGUE

In the highest cleft of the San Juan Mountains, the faintest shiver begins. To the west lies the Pacific; to the east, the Atlantic; and below, the never-ending ice sheet is seeping. A stroke of sun hits the rocky field and the frozen membrane fissures, a bubble erupts, and a teardrop drips, burrows through the shiny green Parnassus grass. The rivulet reaches across the summer-softened tundra, slipping through the treeless flats, raked millennia ago by the receding hands of dying glaciers. At the timber line it gathers speed. Under the pendulant paper cones of the blue spruce, it rushes, down, down, and gurgling audibly, it joins another stream and doubles its size. Strong enough now to crest over instead of wriggling around the lichen-clad boulders strewn about by the clash and shove of lava and ice. It joins another and another, full throated now as it tumbles down the aspen-studded slope; jostling with brown trout, it catches the eye of a black bear moving through the deep shade; delirious, it moves on into human territory, abandoned silver mines: Holy Moses, Last Chance, Stringtown, Creede, and Amethyst.

Past Creede, it hits the Farmer's Union Dam and backs up, spreading out into a reservoir before squeezing through, persistent and plummeting.

Narrow again, frothing and furious for having been held back, it tears on down, down until gravity all but leaves, and it bells wide into the alluvial plain of the San Luis Valley.

At the end of the valley the croplands disappear, replaced by gentle volcanic hills, sagebrush strewn. The river begins to dig down, slides under the wooden planks of the Lobatos Bridge and on into New Mexico. Here, it remembers adrenaline. First there is a tip, a tilt, and then, gravity-drunk, it slices through the grama grass to the basalt below, gashing a canyon with house-sized boulders and a roar that shakes the sagebrush above. The plateau is flat-flat, scrubby chamisa and nothing more until it reaches the serrated lip and shears down, one thousand feet from rim to river. And there it is at the bottom, slamming, gouging, screaming plumes of shock water against the blank walls until it is sated and the floodplains make way and it is joined by the Red River and later the Chama.

Albuquerque is its first real city. Blocked by a bluff and a levee, converted and contorted by ditches and drains, the river nonetheless squirms its way through the heart and on south to the riparian towns of Isleta, Los Lunas, Chloe, and Belen. It is blocked here, stopped there, but continues, eyed by hawks and fishermen, paralleled on the east by the Dead Man's March desert and atomic testing site, until it reaches Truth or Consequences, where it is cut. All those miles and miles of current, from the tundra on down, empty into the bathtub bowl of maroon-ringed rocks and slurp up against that fortress: the tall teeth of the army corps dam.

It is here that the river forgets itself. The bit of water that slips through is met with another dam just before Hillsboro and it is halved and halved again. Sucked up and snarled amid the tangles of tamarisk roots, it cannot remember why they call it the Great River, the Fierce River. It has been called by other names too, Mets'ichi Chena, P'Osoge, Paslápaane, Río Caudaloso, Río de la Nuestra Señora, Río Turbio, Río Guadalquivir, Río de la Concepción, Río de la Buena Ventura del Norte, Tiguex, River of May, Río del Norte y Nuevo México. Its adjectives are big, strong, fierce, angry, turbulent, and grand, but now it is nothing much more than a salt cedar stream, dribbling past the spot where Alvar Nuñez Cabeza de Vaca once stumbled through the switchgrass to reach the water's edge, sick on dog meat and unaware that after almost a decade he had finally found his fabled Río de las Palmas, some twelve hundred miles from where he had sought its mouth.

The river wanders on, braiding through marsh tangles and uprooted tamarisks, piled for burning. It is here that it killed a horse belonging to the Basque, Don Juan de Oñate, and earned its adjective *bravo.* It cannot kill a horse now. It can hardly keep enough of itself together to spill over into the Mother Ditch and wind down between the raw brown hills into the Paso del Norte, the thorny tail end of the stark unwooded San Andreas Mountains. It passes the empty smokestacks of the dead ASARCO smelter, hits the 32nd parallel north, Boundary Monument No. 1, and it is transformed, if not in body, then in significance. It holds back, on both banks, whole nations now. Sheet metal shacks, charred rubber, and deadly desperation. Arsenic-laced middle-class lawns, brand names, and strange delusions. It rolls east past Chamizal, the swath of land it gave to the United States when it decided to dig its way south. It rolls past border guards and fishermen, whispering under the high-armed gates of narco mansions, two blocks from the pastel walls of the Heart Cry Holiness Mission House of Juárez and five miles from the El Paso International Airport, where a plane has just landed.

Among the trail of exiting passengers, Elana stands out in her cobalt-blue dress. She carries only a small handbag. She hails a cab to the border, then walks across on the same bridge where she once sat and watched groceries spill across a cracked windshield. But she does not think of this now, she is tired from the flight and filled with a heavy almost-panic energy. On the avenida she grabs another cab that takes her south. At the Municipio Libre roundabout the traffic is backed up and the cab stops beside a wall of wheatpasted posters: LUCHA LIBRE—ARENA COLISEO—EL VENGADOR DEL NORTE VS. PAGANO, ESTE SABADO, 08 DE AGOSTO. Elana's mind wanders and then loops back and snags. El Vengador. She focuses on the posters pasted one after another after another. The wrestler on the right wears a mask with a joker's smile and the other is unmasked, his face marked by a thick scar. The traffic moves on but the scratch of a half memory stays with Elana as they drive out past the factories.

The sun has barely crested the horizon and already it is over eighty degrees, but Simon and Morales are too busy to pay much attention to the temperature. Simon meets Elana at the gate. She tells her cabdriver to wait. He points to the running meter and nods. She turns back to Simon, takes off her sunglasses, and looks at him—his rumpled dress shirt untucked and crusted with who knows what, his hair grown lank against his neck. She pulls him in, kisses the side of his head.

"How are you?" Elana looks over Simon's shoulder.

"Sorry about the mess, we've been swamped," Simon says. "He's back this way."

The courtyard is filled with mattresses and scraps of blankets, bodies curled in sleep like husks of leaves.

"How's your book coming along?" Simon asks.

"It's just a chapbook."

"Okay, but when's it coming out?" Simon looks back over his shoulder at her.

Elana shakes her head. "I don't know, it's such a small press and they run on a shoestring budget."

"What about your thesis?"

"I meet with my advisor on Monday," Elana says. "How about your radio evangelizing, how's that going?"

"No, not mine," Simon says. "This is all Morales's brilliance. I just help as much as I can."

Elana nods.

"See Pablito over there." Simon points at a boy carrying an urn of coffee through an open door. "He was a hawk, heard Morales's message on his radio, and showed up here. It's getting more dangerous, though. There's something shifting with the cartels."

They duck through an arch and down a whitewashed corridor.

"Before we go in"—he meets her eyes, then looks away—"I didn't know how to say . . . On the phone I didn't tell you everything. You'll see, but, well, he's doing much better, but he's still recovering, I think . . . I told you how I found him at a mission in Chihuahua City? Went down there to help with a new building project and Alex was there. I saw him when they gave us a tour of the whole place, he was working in the infirmary. I couldn't believe it. The pastor who runs the mission told me he'd been seeing him around Chihuahua for a while, wandering in the market or on the side of the road, but he would always disappear. Then, back in June, he showed up in the zócalo and never left, started sleeping on a bench beside the cathedral until they invited him to the mission. He still hasn't told any of us about his time away."

Simon turns and walks on. The voices of children rise and quiver in the clear air. He leads Elana into another courtyard with open doorways on all sides. In the center a group of children ring round and round, hands clasped, their bright outfits fluttering in the sun. And just beyond them, a young man is sweeping. A man of unmistakable beauty: full mouth, dark eyes, and dirty-blond hair.

"Alex!" Elana's voice leaps.

He looks up, face focusing and then opening as she moves toward him.

He holds the broom still, lips curving into an almost smile. "You came back," he says.

She stops, three feet from him, her body suddenly unable to move. "I never left you."

He tilts his head. "What do you mean?"

"You left *me*."

His forehead tightens in concentration, his eyes searching her face.

In the corner behind Alex, a group of women sit folding laundry, their fingers moving expertly, flattening each crease. Elana focuses on their efficiency. She had not known what she would feel when she saw Alex, which emotion would win out, frustration or tenderness or grief. But what she feels is simply distance, like a long release.

"You ready?" She brings her eyes back to his face.

"Ready?" he says.

"To go."

His eyes are soft, but there is a tension in his lips.

"Not yet," he says. "No."

Elana looks away. Out beyond the compound, the craggy ridge of the Juárez Mountains rises, layers of brown and sand and tan and, at the far end, the white horse running—the paint faded but still moving, striding west. And from the far side of the wall the burble of the cabdriver's radio rises, a steady norteño rhythm spreading out into the heat of the day. She wonders how long he will wait.

ACKNOWLEDGMENTS

Thank you, Matt, for everything you do for me always and for loving this book.

Thank you, Bill, I am so grateful.

Thank you, Pagano.

A huge thank you to everyone at Kasa de Kultura para Tod@s—Tubi, Selene, Nain—and to Alia for bringing me there.

Thank you, Kathy, Fernando, Adam, Elle, Kim, and Kate.

Thank you to everyone at La Mujer Obrera, especially Eleazar, Ana, Guillermo, Blanca, and Lorena.

Thank you, Mama and Papa and Asha and David.

Thank you to the 600 Highwaymen for *The Fever* and to Todd for telling me I had to go see it.

Thank you, Juárez. Thank you, Miss Kath. Thank you, Teatro Telón de Arena.

Thank you to the WV Humanities Council and the UNC–Chapel Hill Kenan Fellowship.

Thank you to the Writing is Thinking group.

And thank you to David Wojnarowicz, Roland Barthes, Sylvia Wynter, Frantz Fanon, Octavio Paz, Sergio González Rodríguez, Gloria Anzaldúa, Audrey Wollen, Alejandro González Iñárritu, Guillermo Arriaga, Roberto Bolaño, Elvia Liliana Chaparro Vielma, Anne Carson, Paolo Freire, Robert Stone, Susana Chávez Castillo, Leonard Gardner, Sam Baker, James Salter, Charles Bowden, Heather Levi, Carmen Boullosa, and Anabel Hernández.